Dead Whisper

Lauren McLaren

PublishAmerica
Baltimore

First printing

ISBN: 1-4137-5606-9
PUBLISHED BY PUBLISHAMERICA, LLLP
www.publishamerica.com
Baltimore

Printed in the United States of America

Dead Whisper is dedicated to all those out there who believe that even the most improbable things can happen. And often do for good reason.

Acknowledgments

First, I would like to thank The Bone for providing me with a steady diet of love and laughter that made this whole project seem like something I could really do. I would also like to thank all my folks: Evy, Jack, Margo, and Linval for their constant support and patience with my "interesting" choices in life. To all the people who were far more confident than I that I could finish this: Lisa G, Margaret Y, Lights, Kupcake, Lee Ann Austin, Downski, Mr. & Mrs. P., KTM, my varied and sundry house mates over the years, and all the kids at Bed Restaurant — thanks for believing. Finally, I would like to thank JLove and Red & Black Creative Consortium for making all this possible.

Chapter 1

It was a Tuesday in September, early morning, maybe about 5:30, when I awoke to find a hand across my chest. It was a nice hand as hands go. Long, slender fingers with nails that didn't appear to have raking violence in mind. Fortunately, the hand was attached to an equally nice arm which was attached to a similarly nice body. Not really a bad way to wake up. Until I realized exactly what was going on, where I was, and who was beside me. I was naked. The body next to me was naked. There was a guilty looking bottle of vodka on the dresser. It's nakedness matched my own. *Why, why, why do I drink?* My brain went into seizures of the grand mal variety, flip-flopping around like the distilled contents of my stomach. Then, I did the most logical thing any man can do in this situation—a drunken one-night stand with a girl who has learned more about his psyche than is respectable—I calmly decided that panic was appropriate and exiting as soon as possible was the most important thing I could ever do for myself.

I stood in the center of the room, turning circles as though I could bore a hole in the floor and neatly drill myself into oblivion; all the while, questions and memories of the night's events went rushing through my head sending me into deeper and deeper panic. *What did I do with my glasses? Where are my clothes? Living room. No, hallway. I remember. It's all coming back to me now. Oh God, I stripped in someone's hallway, like I'm a character in a romance novel. Why, why, why? What was in my pea brain to do this? Just because she has...Right, back to the job at hand. Now is not the time to beat yourself up. You can do that once you are*

7

safely housed within the protective metal of your car, choking back dry heaves and rummaging through the glove box for Tylenol. Right, except my car is still at Dodger's. That's just great. How wonderful. Okay, Mac, stay focused. Find the watch. Of course, by the bed. Why does it have to be by the bed...

I got dressed with almost as much stealth as haste, mostly hiding in the bathroom, while playing the desperation prayer card. Basically, I was making promises that I didn't intend to keep to a god I don't believe in. Not logical, but whatever works, works. *I swear if I get out of this apartment without waking her up, I will apologize to Gail and be nicer to her. I'll never drink again, and I'll be more patient with Joe at work. Please don't let her wake up, please don't let her wake up. I promise I'll never do anything like this again.*

The hand stirred just as I was getting my shoes on. I didn't bother to look back to see if the hand had disturbed any other part of the package. Said hand is the property of Rachel Strong, a name I didn't even know three months ago, a person I'd never spoken to until two weeks ago, someone I'd never seen until last night. Someone I wasn't sure I ever want to see again.

Walking out into the street, I lit a cigarette and exhaled, my breath mingling with the smoke in the early morning chill. The previous night's rain left ice on the September streets. I looked up and down the street. It was narrow and lined with trees. I had no idea where I was. No idea at all which way to go, so I picked a direction, stuffed my hands in my pockets, and started walking. I could still hear my own drunken voice echoing in between the pulses of the headache beginning to form over my left eye. "I just wanted him to be alive so badly."

I'm not sure what I hoped to accomplish with a confession like that, but really, I didn't seem to be sure of much of anything.

When I finally got to an intersection, I headed in the direction of what looked like a coffee shop. Ducking inside, I ordered the largest, strongest, and blackest coffee they had from a balding man in a yellowing apron that drifted past his knees and clung to his shins with the all the enthusiasm of winter static cling. His fifty-some years rested in the lines carved around his eyes and mouth, which jumped around as he poured the steaming black liquid into a cup the size of a beer tankard. I took it gratefully and brought the cup quickly to my lips taking a few hurried sips. Drinking it gave me time to put things back in perspective, but when I thought about the muddled events of the night, I could only conclude that I really had gone off the deep end this time. I found a hard bench in the back corner of this tired, dated little all night diner and sat down heavily; the weight of my thoughts working as gravity's ally, pulling my shoulders forward in an exhausted hunch. My hands began to shake. They quivered so recklessly I dropped my cigarette three times before I got it lit. Taking a long breath, inhaling the smoke so deeply it hurt, I tried to piece together what happened to me in the last 12 hours. For that matter, the last three months could use some clearing up. My history was getting muddier and sloppier with each breath I took. I half expected to feel my lungs filling with the muck I was sure would drown me sooner or later.

I looked up at the guy working the counter. He was polishing forks, getting ready for his morning rush of customers on their way to work. We made eye contact for a minute, so I held up my cup to him. He nodded and picked up the steaming pot next to him, then began his slow amble towards me. I watched his steady hand pour the coffee, and I thought that it would be nice to just pour coffee and serve toast to a few lonely people. His eyes were bright and clear, and I was so filled with green jealousy of this man's simple little life that I wanted to cry.

"You all right, fella? You look a bit sickly." The concern in his eye belied his light hearted tone.

I gave him a weak grimace that I hoped passed for some kind of smile. "Yeah, I'm fine. It was a pretty rough night."

"Oh, yeah? Good for you. Young people should get out and enjoy themselves instead of worrying all the time. It doesn't do any good, anyway. Things are going to be a mess whether we worry about it or not. That's a lesson age'll teach you." He switched the pot to his other hand and looked intently at my face. "So, you new to the neighborhood? I haven't seen you here before."

"No, I live on the other side of town. I was just in the neighborhood with a friend who lives nearby."

"Oh, yeah. Who's that? I might know him. Pretty much everyone around here comes in sooner or later. Best basted eggs south of the river."

"It's a her actually, and..." I realized that I was still in her neighborhood. I never considered that she might walk in any second, and wouldn't that be a great conversation to have in the middle of buddy's coffee shop and egg stand? "Wow, it that the right time? I've got to take off. How much do I owe you for the coffee?

"Uh, three bucks."

I pulled a five out of my jeans and handed it to him. "Could you call me a taxi, too?"

"Sure, you're a taxi." He winked at me and chuckled as he walked back behind the counter. He was still laughing to himself when he picked up the phone.

I got my jean jacket back on and headed for the door. My man behind the counter was holding out my two dollars change. I looked at him and saw his bright blue eyes, his shiny white head fringes with a silver halo of hair, and I felt that jealous pang again. I headed for the door, mumbling, "Keep it."

It wasn't long before the taxi pulled to a stop in front of the curb. I felt relief when I saw the bright yellow car turn the corner and head towards me. As soon as I was inside, we pulled away and my relief started to turn into regret. I didn't know any more this morning than I did yesterday. I felt like a hole had opened up in my stomach, and I teetered on the precipice, tempted to jump into the bottomless well that housed my anxiety. It was all too much. *Air, I must have air.* I rolled the window down and gulped it in. It was so cold I thought my lungs would turn into porous ice crystals. When I absolutely could not take another breath, right before my lungs shattered, I rolled up the window, and the driver sped onto the freeway, carrying me back to my sorry apartment and my sorrier life.

I always thought that as we grew up, life became easier to understand. That is a horrifying untruth, created by a parent, I'm quite sure, in order to pawn off the responsibility of explaining the more difficult aspects of life's weirdness. Like when you were six and found Trini the goldfish floating belly up in the tank, and you asked his mom "What's wrong with Trini?"

Your mom said, "Trini's gone, Honey."

"What do you mean? She's right there."

"No, sweetie, she's dead."

"What's dead, Mom?"

"Oh, darling, you'll understand when you're older."

I'm older now, and the only thing I understand is that I have less of a clue now than I did when I was six. If I could find a way to go back to what I thought I knew when I was a child, I'd jump at it and live in blissful ignorance the rest of my days, whiling away time trying to figure out how they got all those people inside the television set.

When the taxi pulled up in front of my building, I looked at it for a minute before getting out.

"Hey buddy, you at the right place or not?" Taxi drivers everywhere are known for their patience and understanding.

"Yeah, this is the right place."

"Then get out. I got other fares to make. Eight fifty for the meter."

I handed him ten and climbed out of the taxi. The cab pulled away, but I was having trouble getting past my hesitation. Finally, my exhaustion got the better of me, and I pulled my keys out, heading for the door. I lived in the basement apartment of a three story walk-up. It was small and not very nice, but it was cheap.

When I opened the door, I noticed a slip of paper on the floor. A note from my landlord about my late rent. I'm usually very good about that kind of thing, but lately I've been a little preoccupied.

Taking off my jean jacket, I threw it on my old hand-me-down brown sofa and walked through to the kitchen. There was nothing in the fridge, but I scrounged enough grounds to make a small pot of coffee. The perky bubbling of the pot was soothing.

I stood listening for a moment before I decided it was time to shower off some of last night. I got the water running hot and stripped. Cold as my apartment was, I didn't waste any time getting into the stream. I could feel the water, so hot it almost scalded my scalp and back. The tension I'd been carrying in my stomach for the last hour or so finally started to let go, and I let my mind wander, asking myself for the millionth time how I ended up here. Well, I suppose I can guess how it happened. The truth is I can't believe I ended up here. I never thought that this is how my life would turn out. I guess no one never really know until it's too late.

Out of the shower and dry, I wiped the steam away from the mirror to have a look at myself. If only I could have wiped away the cloudiness in my life like that—start fresh. *Tabula rasa*. Not exactly. It might have been a bit late for that.

11

Chapter 2

My name is Macbeth Shaw Williams. It's not a name I'm proud of. I really think I would have been happier as a Michael or a Rob or even a Zachary. I'm not really sure why I'm so fixed on the name thing, except that I can't help but think that names are defining in some way. Maybe if I had some toothpicks behind the whole handle it would be more acceptable, in a completely bourgeois way, which, frankly, would be fine with me. However, I'm the son of an ex-hippie interior designer, who, while doing well for herself, has no connection with and only disdain for the society page. The academy would like to send special thanks to my mother Gail Williams for her strange and unusual naming ritual.

While pregnant with me, she was studying English lit at the community college. In her ever-continuing effort to become a better human being, she regularly enrolled in various courses that would broaden her mind. Important, interesting, and let's not forget practical subjects like The Mayan Language–Pictogram or Ideogram and The Literature of Great Britain through the Ages. Her thirst for knowledge was really an admirable quality, except for her accompanying obsessions with thematic continuity and meaning in all aspects of her life. You know the type. Every room in the house was decorated in a specific color scheme with great attention to the current theories on room psychology and color field. This made her a great interior designer, but her quirky self just got carried away when it came to naming her sons.

The culmination of her studies in English lit was a deeper understanding of the mastery of Shakespeare as a dramatist, an appreciation for the subtleties of late nineteenth century colonial literature, and a son she named to "symbolize the twin peaks of British literary history." Her explanation as delivered to me at age eight. WHAT? As an adult, I have only a moderately better appreciation for her attention to detail. As an eight-year-old, I had only shame and embarrassment at my ridiculous name. Imagine what it was like on the first day of school. I hated that first morning when the teacher would take attendance. And to make it worse, I had to wait until W to get the whole ordeal over with. For ten years, I tried to miss the first day of school. One year, I think I was in third or fourth grade, I actually colored little red dots all over my body in a vain attempt to convince my mother I had the measles.

"Macbeth Shaw Williams, you get out of bed immediately and wash those ridiculous marks off your body."

I really hated it when she used my full name. It just made the whole experience more mortifying.

"Just be happy I wasn't doing a children's lit course. Your name could have been Hans Grimm Williams."

She had a point. Leave it to my mother to find a hypothetical situation that made mine look slightly less horrifying. She's just the type of person who would offer to slap your face to keep you from feeling the agony of a stubbed toe. But, at least she had an appreciation for the humor of it all.

I was somewhat less than convinced, mostly because my name was still Macbeth, and I still had to go to school and wait in anticipation of the Ws when every eye in the room focused on my bright red face. Up until grade five, I sat in the back of the room, hoping to escape notice. I'll admit that I can be a bit dense. It took me a few years to figure out that if I sat at the front of the room, I didn't have to witness every member of the class turning in my direction when they heard my timid "here." By the time everyone had turned to look at me my face would have gone from its usual sickly pale hue to a bright feverish crimson extending from my hairline all the way to my collar. Even my arms turned red with the snickers and whispers. It was at times like these that I formulated some of my more drastic suicide fantasies. My favorite involved a really sharp pencil and my

13

jugular vein. Unfortunately, I'm fundamentally opposed to pain and death—always have been. Cowardice and suicide generally don't work too well together. So, I suffered with my red face, all the while imagining hurling myself out the window moments before my name was called, sending shards of glass flying up at my classmates like little projectile missiles. Blood would be dripping from Mrs. Nublicki's face as she tried to calm the other kids while they screamed and writhed on the floor in agony. Can't you just hear the television report?

"He was such a quiet boy. Very shy. I just don't know what could have come over him to do such a thing. I have heard though that there was trouble at home." Mrs. Nublicki would be dragging out a few tears to really make the most of the tragedy. And, of course, there would be the requisite clutching of a blood soaked handkerchief to her face to emphasize the drama. You can always count on the teacher for a regular dose of melodrama. It's the "if you don't pass math, it will go down on your permanent record" ones who are convinced you can't contribute anything to society unless you have a working knowledge of Pythagoras and iscosoles triangles; those are the ones who work up the best sympathy play.

Later that day, my mom would appear in front of our house, her eyes bloodshot and swollen, looking like a prize fighter who's gone ten rounds before delivering the final crushing blow. "It's my fault. I drove him to this. I should have named him John. I'm sorry. I'm so sorry." At this point, she would faint with guilt, and I would have my final revenge. Except I'd be dead! What's the point of vengeance and vindication if you're a big puddle of goo on the ground? The whole idea loses most of its charm when you consider the fact that you can't even say "I told you so!" Generally, at about this point, I would remember that I'm not nearly brave enough to hurl myself through a screen door, let alone a plate glass window. I would squeak out that I liked to be called Mac and that would be the end of that ordeal, at least until recess.

Once we hit the playground, I would have to endure the whoops of laughter generated by my thoughtful and sensitive playmates.

"How come you got a girl's name, Beth? You a big sissy or what?" Rocks were thrown, fists were thrown. I went home with many a scraped knee incurred while trying to run from the neighborhood

14

bullies—all with names like Tommy and Ricky, I might add. Fortunately, this only lasted for a week or two until the trials of school work took over or a new kid moved in to replace me as the object of scorn and ridicule in the class. But every year, I suffered the embarrassment of my name on that first day and every day we had a substitute teacher.

Later on, when I got to know the character I was named for, my resentment multiplied tenfold. Not only did I have to carry around this archaic moniker, I come to find that I am named for a greedy, but essentially weak, traitor who's life begins with honor and accolades but ends in ruin and disgrace in part thanks to the outrageous ambition of his wife. Wow, nice work, Gail. I admit that, as an adult, I realize my name does not define me, but the experience of growing up with it certainly has. I am indeed meek, and I have an unnatural desire for anonymity. And it has not only been my name that has troubled me through the years. It seems that so many of the events of my existence have conspired to make me oddly afraid of both life and death.

We all fear death to some degree I suppose, but I'll be the first to admit that it petrifies me. Not just because of the pain I habitually associate with the experience either. It's the whole muddled, confused unknown of death that really does me in. And what I do know of it is not an enticing picture. I'm not talking fire and brimstone here, I'm talking pure, unadulterated boredom. Like being forced to read the same edition of the *National Enquirer* over and over again into the pale blue abyss of eternity. Nothing to look at but the unflattering photo of Michelle Pfeiffer and read the same headline about Elvis' return from the grave to be sighted by a middle aged housewife named Gloria who swears he pulled up to her house to ask directions to Des Moines. This is the kind of thing that would drive someone to suicide if they were alive. Life is a raw blast of irony to give you that happy sentence upon death.

The reality of death, as I've come to understand it, is that it is eternity presented for you on a dry, endless prairie road. As far as you look, there is nothing to see, and whatever marks you make on that road are irrelevant because there's no one else to see them. Death is a great isolation booth for both the dead and the living. You are nothing but alone in death, which is why I try to remain alone in life. I'm not a hermit or anything. I'm just a bit closed off. Really, it's the obvious choice for pragmatists like myself. I can't avoid death outright, so I'm just trying to make the transition a little bit smoother than it was for my brother Newton, as in Sir Isaac. He was born during Introductory Physics.

Being dead, Newt has been instrumental in my formation of a philosophy on life. He doesn't really agree with it, but he's already dead, so what difference does it make? What he needs is a death philosophy, and, after talking to him posthumously for the better part of the last decade, I'd say he's not having much success forming one. It still sounds odd to me, even after all these years, but let's face it, you don't expect to be having conversations with a dead guy and still be in your right mind, do you? But I am in my right mind. Really.

Death is following me. It took a position just two steps behind me when I was six, and it dogs me day and night. Death carries its baggage with it, trotting it in front like a show dog for everyone to acknowledge. I've tried to ignore it, but it is persistent, tenacious, untiring.

Chapter 3

This thing with Newt has been strange. Well, strange is not really an adequate description of my special situation. Actually, I don't think words have been coined to describe with any accuracy the kind of bizarre ride I've been on for the better part of a decade. I'm pretty sure that Newt is the main reason I'm in conscious limbo. It's my own private type of hell. It would be slightly less hellish if I could talk to anyone about my dead brother without spending several months in a special facility for people who hear voices. I tried that once. I won't be doing it again.

My brother Newt. My big brother. My dead brother. I really wish I could say he's a successful, charming corporate gelding who's walking a fine line of ethics while paying off his BMW and living on his extended credit. Or that he's just finished dragging his exhausted body through med school. Or that he's a waiter in a fried egg diner on Jackson Street. But I can't say any of those things because he was killed at the tender age of 16. Barely out of childhood, and we're sharing memories of him while scattering his ashes on the lake.

It was sad. It was horrifying and tragic and messy and, generally speaking, awful for everyone. Especially Newt, although I didn't find that out until later. What makes the whole thing even worse is that he died because he suffered from an invincibility complex demonstrated only by the young male of the species, usually in the teen years. Well, and because he was stupid.

Hey, I resent that. The whole thing was just a mistake. I wasn't trying to get killed. How was I supposed to know the shock would fry me?

"Shut up, Newt! I can't believe that you are still defending yourself on this. There was a sign like one foot away from your body. You remember—the big red and white one that had the word DANGER in eight inch letters? Just admit it. You were stupid."

I don't want to talk about this anymore.

"Fine. I'd like a little peace."

As you can see, death has not made him any smarter. It did pretty much cure the whole Superman attitude of invincibility though.

Here's what happened. It was a Thursday in the beginning of May. Spring had sprung, and with the longer days and warmer air, the seeds of restlessness had sprouted in teenagers everywhere. Newt and two of his friends were out driving around. They didn't have anywhere to go, but they did have a car and a driver's license between them. So, there they were, Newt and Dave and Roger, cruising around for action, really for anything they could find that might be remotely entertaining. Well, as can be expected, there's not that much to do on a Thursday night when you live in suburbia. It being a school night, they couldn't very well drive into the city, so they settled for a quick cruise of the 7-11 to look for girls who wanted nothing to do with them, a couple of burgers, and a drive out to the power plant.

About five miles out of town was this major horror of horrors: a nuclear facility. It had a great look about it at night: the grounds all lit up in amber, the red lights on the roof dotting the sky as they warned away air traffic. It became a popular getaway for the children of early suburbia who had to live in the absence of sprawling shopping malls where they could idle away their evenings bonding with the other vacant youths in video arcades and record stores. As vacant youths ourselves, we bonded, but without the glamour of fluorescent lighting and shiny reflective glass everywhere. Instead, we forged our friendships in the orange glow of the plant lights after dark. The plant was our mall, except that instead of buying cheese dogs and looking for Judas Priest records, we were humming with the thrill of fusion. It was just a little dangerous being so close to all that radioactivity, but when you're a teenager, danger is your middle name.

The power plant was a well-guarded affair with a ten-foot chain-link electrified fence surrounding it. There were security cameras all over the plant to make sure no one was inside the fence messing around. The only way in was through the front door. To get in, you had to go through security at the main gate, sign in, check in, get a pass, with no eating, no running, no spitting, and so on like that. My seventh grade class went on a tour once.

Three sides of the plant were open to view from the road. The south side sat right on Highway 2 with access to the main gate. The east and west sides were flanked by open fields. The owners of the plant had bought up all that surrounding land in the interest of safety. They did their best to make the whole place say, "We're not at all dangerous here. We're just like any other factory, but maybe you should just GO AWAY!"

The north side of the plant offered wonderful cover for the curious teen though, and this is usually where we went to smoke or play cards or drink or whatever kids do when they are out from under the watchful eyes of parents. This side was nothing but bush. Most of the land had been cleared before the plant was built, but this section was left untouched. It was like a tiny forest filled with birch and poplar trees. Squirrels lived there. I'm pretty sure that this was just a marketing thing. In the era of no nukes, the plant management used to get a lot of grief from the tree huggers. Personally, I think they left the trees to make it seem like a safer, nicer kind of nuclear thing—a happy bunnies and butterflies kind of place. Radioactivity and nuclear holocaust were hot topics in the chill of the '80s.

Of course, we used to discuss the possibility of becoming mutants from our repeated exposure to the plant. At that age, any kind of weird mutation was preferable to being normal. I was at a serious advantage here because I had the weird name. Anyway, we were constantly checking each other for the appearance of big ugly moles, festering wounds that wouldn't heal, extra eyes—anything remotely similar to a character in Mad Max. As it turned out, eyes were the problem in the end. If Newt had used his, he might not have died. If he had lived, I could at least ignore him.

What is with your attitude today? You're acting like you wish I wasn't around.

"Newt, you're not around. You're dead! You're a chatty, meddling, bossy dead guy!"

I don't think it's fair that you keep insulting me.

"Yeah, well, life's not fair."

As you are so fond of reminding me, I'm not alive. "Life" does not apply to me.

"Right, well, sorry man."

Don't you think this is painful for me? Hearing my death retold is not exactly a fun tale from the crypt. I'm dead! This is me you're going on about! This happened to me!

"Okay, I get it. Sorry." Brothers—who knew they were so sensitive?

Right, so there they are, the three of them. Hanging out in the bush just north of the plant. They're doing guy things. They're smoking. They're swatting a tennis ball back and forth with sticks they've found in the bush. They're talking about girls: lying about the ones they've already had, bragging about the girls they're planning on getting in the near future, and dreaming about the girls they'd really like to score. It's basically a game of sexual one-upmanship. We all play it. We have to. We're guys. It's what we do.

This naturally progressed to the physical one-upmanship that is the core of existence for all males in the animal kingdom. Why are we like this? Not a clue. I didn't make the rules. I just follow 'em. I have stuck my tongue to metal fences in the dead of winter; I have jumped off garages; I have shot at living things with a BB gun. All for the sake of impressing the guys. Sometimes, I think it's a sickness. It only ends up with blood or guilt or both or worse.

In Newt's case, the results were slightly worse. He ended up dead, and Dave and Roger ended up with a powerful fear of electricity. Newt says he didn't think that touching the fence for just a second would do anything. He was expecting the kind of shock you get when you drag your feet on the carpet and then touch a doorknob. He figured he would be able to let go of the fence. He obviously hadn't been paying attention in science. He didn't expect to be paralyzed by the current running through his poor 16-year-old body. He didn't know that the voltage would blow the ends of his toes off. He had no idea that his heart would stop almost immediately when his system tried to process the abundance of electricity that came flying out of the fence through the two fingers that he rested so gently on the wire. I talked to Dave about it a couple of years after the accident. He said that Newt's body actually smoked, like he was on fire. He was, I guess. On the inside.

By the time Dave and Roger got him into the car, Newt was already dead. Dave drove to the hospital anyway. Roger was in the back seat, trying to remember how CPR worked. He was fully hysterical by the time they got to City General. The ER staff thought he was the patient at first. At least until they saw the smoldering remains of my brother stretched out on the back seat, looking like a heap of clothing just pulled out of a campfire.

It became readily apparent that they could do more to help Roger than my brother. He was given a pleasant IV drip of friendly tranquilizers for about three days worth of doctor-induced coma. When he woke up, his best friend was nothing more than a pile of ashes being nibbled on by lake trout and jackfish. Roger was never the same after. He moved out of town as soon as he graduated from high school. The last I heard he was living out on Vancouver Island raising chickens. I'd be willing to bet he has a special little mushroom plantation as well. He was forever trying to recapture the calm of his three days in medical never-never land. I guess some pharmaceuticals can give you a taste for that sort of thing.

Dave's a computer salesman now. Not a glamorous living, but at least he didn't turn into a freakish, doping recluse like Roger. Dave is a very careful man, but he seems to have come out of the whole ordeal with his mind pretty well in tact. He's married to a nice girl he knew in high school—Mary or Marie or Maureen—something like that. They have a couple of kids, I think. He has a pretty regular life. Lucky him.

As for us, things got pretty strange right away. We got the call from the police at about 1:30 in the morning. My mother, Gail, woke me up, blathering about her baby. I didn't really get it at first. I was the baby, after all. I thought she was talking about me. I figured she was having some kind of deranged nightmare. She was deranged, and it was a nightmare. Too bad we were never able to wake up from it.

Gail really flipped out at the hospital. She started screaming at the nurses almost immediately. "Where is my baby? What have you done with him? I want to see him right now!"

I remember looking at the nurse as if she was going to make everything okay again. She was wearing green scrubs, and she looked like she hadn't slept much in the last seven years. "Mrs. Williams, we really need you to calm down so we can explain the situation. Newton has been in a serious accident. There are things you should know before..."

"Fuck the explanations. I want to see my son." Gail's voice was lined with anger and fear like I'd never heard before.

I flinched visibly and stared at Gail with surprise. I had only ever heard my mother swear once before. It was directed at an insurance lackey who was holding up the claim on my father's policy after he died. She regularly voiced her opinion that the use of profanity demonstrated a sorry lack of imagination and an inadequate vocabulary, so I knew when she started cursing like a trucker at the nurse that this was a situation that had robbed her of her senses. I think this scared me more than what was to come.

"Mrs. Williams, I don't think you understand." Even I could hear the strained patience in the nurse's tone.

"What I understand is that if I don't see my kid in the next thirty seconds, I'm going to..."

About here, a doctor stepped in.

"What exactly are you going to do, Mrs. Williams? You have to realize that it's not going to make any difference to Newton if you see him now or ten minutes from now or three hours from now. He's dead. I'm sorry, but he just is."

About here, Gail collapsed. I stood there at her side, trying hard not to cry, while the doctor passed smelling salts under her nose. Some doctor had just said my big brother was dead—no build up or easy lead in—he was just dead. Two seconds ago, I was under the impression that he was my living brother, and now, he was dead. At 14, I really wanted a parent to envelop me and do whatever it is that parents do to make things right. Instead, I held Gail's hand and waited while she sobbed into my shoulder these great heaving sobs that scared me and attacked my heart with the depth of pain they carried.

For a long time, I hated that doctor for being such so callous, for blurting out that horrible truth like he did. I was under the impression that he didn't care about my mother's grief, about her pain, or about mine for that matter. Newt had his own ideas about the doctor's technique. He offered it up to me about six months after he started talking to me.

Don't you get it, Mac? Gail was hysterical. He needed to get her attention. It was cruel to shock her like that, but it would have been nastier to let her rave and rage on like she was going to. At least, this way, the shock pushed her past the freak out stage and into the unconscious stage. All things considered, everyone just did the best they could.

"When did you get to be so forgiving? When you were alive you were still holding grudges about stuff that happened when you were six."

I'm dead. What's the point of staying angry? It's not like I can change anything now. I can't go rattle chains in Joey Upson's closet because he stole my favorite marble in grade one. It's easier to just let it go.

Back at the hospital on that hot May night, I felt numbness set in as I waited patiently for my turn to break down. I waited through those long perilous minutes for the maternal comfort I expected as soon as the hysterics passed. Gail's sobs eventually dwindled to sniffles and then to a dry eyed and icy calm. I was still waiting when she rose from her chair and started toward the last room my brother would ever occupy. I followed her like a forgotten puppy. She didn't even hold my hand when we walked into the treatment room. She was hardened cement. Her mouth set in a grim line that cut her face apart in a way I didn't recognize. She looked at the body, shed one single tear, and then just turned and walked out of the room. I don't think she even noticed that I stayed there in that brightly lit room with what was left of Newt. I sat there with his scorched body for an hour. After a while, the lights started to hurt my eyes, so I shut them off and just sat there in the dark, staring at the form on the bed that used to be Newt. I didn't wail or cry or anything. I just sat there staring. It was completely unreal to me that my brother was dead. My mind just rejected the idea. I think I was waiting for him to open his eyes or sit up. Anything that would prove this was a dream or some kind of awful mistake. I couldn't believe he was dead.

I've always wondered if the fact that I wouldn't let go has something to do with the fact that Newt talks to me now. Maybe if I had left right away, one of the nurses would have been saddled with this weird burden.

How many times have I got to tell you that it wouldn't have made any difference if a three-toed sloth had been sitting next to me in the hospital? You were the one I was going to be stuck with. You're my punishment for whatever stupid thing I did that deserved this kind of reward in the afterlife.

"What the hell is that supposed to mean? You think this isn't punishment for me? You think this is fun? At least you don't have to face the consequences of the situation in this world."

All I know is that when I die, I'd better not have to sit in limbo for ten years after putting up with Newt for all this time. My penance must be paid in full by now. Penance for what, I'm not sure. I haven't really done anything except harbor the secret of my dead brother.

Maybe that's the problem, Mac. Maybe you ought to try doing something to get me out of here. Anything would be an improvement over the big zilch you've done so far.

"Do you have any idea how much I want to get rid of you? Do you know what kind of celebration I'm going to have when you finally shut up permanently? If you want to hurry things along, maybe you could give me a hint as to what it is I'm supposed to do instead of just hauling out the 'poor me' act again. It's gotten pretty old."

You think if I knew I wouldn't tell you in a heartbeat? You think I wouldn't do everything it took to say good bye to you forever? Well, let me straighten you out here. If I thought it would help, I'd tell you to buy a Ouija board, have a séance and get guidance from the rest of the dead out there. I don't know what to do. That's the puzzle, Mac. If we can't figure it out, no one will.

The cynic in me snorted with disillusioned contempt. A likely story. For all I know, Newt made the whole thing up just to torture me for the better part of a decade. He says not, but I don't think he has any more idea what's going on than I do. How ironic that now all I want is for my brother to disappear forever, when on that night in the hospital all I wished was for him to reappear, be resurrected by some divine force that realized he was too young and innocent to die.

I sat in that room with my brother for a lifetime. I watched my life with him dribble past me, stopping so suddenly with the acrid smell of burnt hair and flesh. And when I looked around at the dark room lit only by the antiseptic light coming from the hallway, I realized that I was alone now. I was there, and Newt wasn't. Just like my father wasn't there, but I was. Dan, who died without knowing that he was important to me, leaving me with the first drops of blood on my life.

The clean slate I was looking for? No. Definitely not.

Chapter 4

It was just Gail and me left to carry on with our little lives as best as we could. At least, that's what I believed until I realized that Gail was there in body, but she had left me just as surely as if she had gotten in her Toyota and driven to the other side of the world. Something inside her just broke. She held herself together with incredible dignity and calm through the funeral, through the "I'm so sorry" and the "it's such a tragedy" and all the rest of the condolences that do so little to console. She was stoic and taciturn and utterly devoid of emotion. After we had scattered his ashes, she went into her room and didn't come out for a week.

We came home from Newt's funeral to a house filled with an emptiness that smelled of chrysanthemums. I watched Gail mount the stairs heading to her bedroom, the black dress she wore hanging on her like a shroud covering the relic finger of a long-dead martyr. She didn't speak to me; she just disappeared with the silence of anguish following her. I lay on the couch, wondering at the fact that I would always be an only child now. I'd wished for it often enough in Newt's lifetime, when he tormented me for being a bookworm, when he teased me about my utter and complete lack of physical coordination, when he set fire to my comic collection. But I never thought my wish would be granted in such a vile way. I swallowed the bile of guilt that crept into my throat, threatening to choke me where I lay.

I kept expecting Gail to come out of her room and check on me, bring me a cup of hot chocolate and a Kleenex to soothe the feelings of loss and remorse that were fighting for supremacy in my heart. But she didn't come. She let me lay there, watching the shadows in the living room grow long as the sun gave up its power position at the top of the sky. Trees grew up on the walls, their leaves rippling with light like the water on the lake where Newt's ashes now served as tasty morsels for patrons of that great aquatic restaurant. Eventually, I fell asleep. Not to be found and covered by my caring and concerned parent, but to come awake in near darkness, shivering with the cold of disorientation. Out of habit or instinct or maybe both, I called for Newt. He didn't answer, and I knew then that this was all realer than life was meant to be for a 14-year-old. I called for Gail next. She, too, failed to answer, so I managed my grief on my own. That was my first real lesson in independence. It was a lesson that quickly grew into a full class on how to play role reversal with a parent who had lost the plot.

At that moment, I stepped into an unwanted, if necessary, role as caretaker. I stopped going to school because I couldn't just leave Gail to fend for herself when she was so obviously incapable. I concentrated on food, as if nourishment could wipe away all the pain. I subsisted primarily on grilled cheese sandwiches. Tomato soup and crackers rounded out the menu. It wasn't gourmet, but it was as many food groups as I could put together. Inside a week, I had gone from 14-year-old care needer to 40-year-old care giver with no training or benefits.

Resentment? Not at first, but I got there.

Gail was inconsolable at first. She spent hours in her bedroom, moving around the space like a wraith. The cheerful flowers of her wallpaper seemed to fade visibly as her despair washed over the walls of her prison. Her day was divided up between staring into space, staring at pictures of Newt and staring at pictures of Dan, my father. She didn't speak to me or even look at me when I skulked into the room like a guilty servant disturbing the mistress of the house carrying my tray of small offerings. I was just a shadow from a past where she had two sons and a husband. All she knew about the present was pain and loss.

I wanted to be angry, but it seemed pretty futile. What was the point? My anger would have gone unnoticed anyway. The truth, and it was obvious to me even at 14, was that complete withdrawal was the only way Gail had to deal with the reality that eight years after she buried her husband, she had to scatter the ashes of her first born. And in those first days after we said our goodbyes to Newt, Gail felt all the pain she could allow. She looked at the photos of Christmases gone, knowing she would never have another as happy as the ones she had left behind. I got the feeling when I stared into her vacant eyes that she was living all of the miserable birthdays and holidays to come; all the moments she would never again share with her family, she dispensed with now, saving herself from the renewal of her overwhelming grief on each of those days that were lurking just ahead of her.

And when she finally started to emerge from her state, like a butterfly breaking free of its cocoon, she was a complete unknown to me. It was a stranger transmutation than anything my friends, and I could have imagined happening as a result of radioactive exposure. She looked the same, but she was not. Under her skin, in her mind, where once freedom and passion had flowed unchecked, there was now only the conventional shell of motherhood. I no longer recognized her; my Gail was gone. She had been replaced by a capable maternal figure that I had little desire to know and less desire to be related to. The change was too stark to ignore and too sudden to deal with. For 14 years, the mother I had was very different than anyone else's. And now, I didn't even have that familiarity to find comfort in.

She's had a hard time, my Gail. There can be no arguing that point. But up until the time we lost Newt, she had held things together with an independence and determination that would have made anyone envious. After Dan died, she went through a period of mourning that I've successfully blocked from memory. I was only six then, so the few memories I have of him and his death were easy enough to set aside in some small corner of my mind where they would gradually be covered with dust and cobwebs. I remember riding on Dan's shoulders feeling taller than Dr. J. And I remember his laugh. It was big and deep, and it tumbled out of him like stones falling down a mountain side. Besides that, all I can bring back are a few vague images of family: mother, father and two boys camping in the mountains, father and sons riding bicycles in the park.

The only other memory I can dredge up is the one I don't want: the police car parked outside the house on a cold night in late November. It's red and blue lights turned circles around the neighborhood, bathing it in the light of disaster. I crouched on the floor of the front room, hiding from the tall man at the door speaking in low tones to my mother. I can still see his boots glistening with the moisture of melting snow, shining in the light of the porch. It was this man's sorry task to tell Gail how Dan had lost control of his sedan on the ice of the Fourth Street Bridge. He had to say the words out loud, describing how the car had skidded and slid, picking up speed on the dangerous slope only to come to a crashing and fatal halt when the driver's side of the car finally made contact with the steel and concrete of the meridian. The car flipped over the concrete that divided the bridge sending it, squealing metal against pavement, headlong into the Kenworth truck that would mutilate the car beyond recognition and wipe away the life of my father in just seconds.

I have often wished I had more than just scattered hazy pictures. There have been times when I think I have remembered something significant, but it can be difficult to be sure if these faint recollections are the stuff of imagination or actual memories. At times like that, I would look to Gail to fill in some of the blanks for me, but she has never been much help on this issue. All she would ever say about Dan was that he was the love of her life; a kind and generous man who loved books. I can see her now, pointing at the three six-foot bookshelves that lined the walls of our den.

She would say, in a small voice tinted by both the pain and the joy of remembering, "That's where our library came from, Mac. It was his collection. He used to read to you when you were small." A faint smile would play about her mouth before she went on. "You loved it when he read to you. You would stare at him, wide-eyed, waiting for the next words." And then, as if she were a well suddenly run dry, she would get very quiet and withdraw.

It's a small stockpile of memories that make up my father. It doesn't really matter that much to me though. You can't really miss what you've never really had. Can you?

28

"Hey, Newt."

Yeah?

"You really can't talk to Dan, can you?"

No, Mac. I've told you before. I can't talk to anybody else. It's just you.

"I know. Sorry."

Chapter 5

I think Newt is a bit depressed lately. I mean, it's been eight years, and the only person he's had to talk to is me. Not that I'm anything but a fabulous conversationalist, but it has to be fairly tedious talking to the same person day in and day out. I know that I'd be wondering what the hell was going on if I were him. Actually, I am wondering what the hell is going on. And how much longer it's going to continue going on. And why it happened in the first place. And if this happens to everyone, or are Newt and I just especially charmed individuals. I have a lot of questions. None of which can be answered to my satisfaction. I've had to learn to live with disappointment.

This seems to be a common thread among the surviving members of my family. Gail lives with the disappointment of a dead husband, a dead son, and a living son who just can't seem to get it together. Yep, that's me. She's so proud. Honestly, I think she's amazed that I made it this far without being permanently committed to a mental institution. She's probably even more amazed that I have a job. Not a good job, but a job nonetheless. I know she hoped I'd be more, hoped I'd have a happy life. So did I. It just doesn't seem to be in the cards. The deck was stacked against me before Gail stepped out of her bedroom. Afterwards, I knew happiness was going to be an unlikely outcome.

After the seclusion ordeal, what emerged from Gail's room was a very close physical replica of my mother who bore no resemblance whatsoever to the woman I had known for the last 14 years. This clever imposter came out of that bedroom wearing a dress with flowers on it. This, on a woman who gave new meaning to the words flowing natural fibers. I didn't think she owned anything other than tie-dye t-shirts and bell-bottom jeans. I had seen her wearing a tent kind of dress thing once, but it was entirely earthy and not at all like the outfit that rolled down the stairs that morning. She floated in. I think that's the right way to describe it: she floated like Donna Reed toward the stove.

I was in the kitchen eating cereal. I nearly choked on my raisin bran I was laughing so hard.

"Good morning, Mac. Would you like some eggs instead of cereal? You really should have a hot breakfast. It's so much heartier."

"Uh, sure. Why not? You okay, Gail?" I was anxious suddenly. The last time Gail worried about breakfast was, well, I couldn't actually think of any time that she'd been concerned about it.

"Mac, I am your mother. I am not one of your tarty little friends. I'll thank you to address me properly."

This was alarming. I'd been calling her Gail for ten years. And I couldn't imagine who she might be referring to as one of my "tarty" little friends. She was scaring me, but she'd been through a lot in the last weeks. A little latitude was easily granted for the time being, "Uh, okay. Whatever you say, Mom."

"That's better. Thank you."

Then she made eggs. She scrambled them up, toasted some bread, and I had my first post-Newt hot breakfast. Gail sat there and watched me eat the food. She just sat there, staring at me the whole time. It was creepy. I tried to talk to her, but all I got were these short non-answers.

"Really, Gail, I mean, Mom, are you, you know, okay?"

"I'm fine, Mac. No need to worry about me. Aren't you late for school?"

"Yeah, but it's no big deal. I haven't been there in a week. Are you sure you're okay?"

"I'm sure. Thanks for asking, sweetheart." She gazed at me with a sickly expression on her face, like a lovesick puppy locked in a wire cage at the local animal shelter.

I raised my eyebrows and returned Gail's look with one of my own, questioning and slightly dumbfounded. Grossly mushy terms of endearment were never Gail's style. And I was certain the other shoe would drop once she'd digested what I'd said about missing school. I waited, holding my breath for the lecture that I expected, even looked forward to, as some example of a reality that wasn't warped beyond all identification. It never came. When I finished eating, she took my plate from the table and went about the business of cleaning up, as though that's what she always did, what she always had done. I was the only one in the room who thought anything out of the ordinary was going on. The only explanation I could come up with was that she was suffering some kind of post-traumatic shock syndrome disorder thing. I left it at that, hoping that in a few hours, or a few days at most, my Gail would return to envelop me in patchouli-scented arms and let me cry away the death of my brother. It's been nearly ten years; I'm still waiting.

That morning, so unlike any other I'd experienced, was the first in a long line of events that began the slow process of parental alienation in my life. Until Newt died, my relationship with Gail was good. Better than good really. I'm of the opinion that if you've got the right one, having a single mother can be a good thing. I'm willing to concede the point that it's not an ideal situation, but Gail really pulled it off well. She was better than anyone else out there, as far as I could see. When other mothers were sewing Halloween costumes, Gail was planting an indoor herb garden. When I needed a Halloween costume, she cut a ping pong ball in half, glued each half to my forehead, and colored black dots on them. I was a four-eyed circus freak. It wasn't glamorous or particularly scary. And it certainly didn't hold a candle to Mark Duskie's Spiderman costume. But it did have the advantage of getting me the pity vote. I always got way more candy than any of my friends. I didn't know it was pity candy. Don't think I would have cared, anyway. When you're eight, all that matters is how full your pillowcase is at the end of the night. And unlike other parents, Gail believed whole heartedly in the goodness of our neighbors' intentions. Never once did she sort through my candy, throwing out all the best goods under the suspicious assumption that someone in our area might want to poison a perfectly innocent child.

Gail used to do yoga. She chanted and stood on her head. She meditated, for God's sake. She was rubbing lavender on our cuts before anyone knew that smell counted. She laughed all the time. We ate bean curd and rice. I knew how to use chopsticks before I was very good with a fork.

She was relentless about the pursuit of knowledge. Dan inspired that in her, I think. It was his love of learning that made school a non-negotiable issue for Gail. She went. We went. We paid attention. We did our homework. Coming to a class unprepared was just not an option. Cutting class was grounds for execution. Newt did it once. Gail went to class with him for three days. She tagged along like she was a visiting cousin or something. She even participated. Newt never cut class again. The week I skipped was the first time I'd missed more than an afternoon in my nine-year career.

So, it was her apparent disinterest in my absence from school that I found most disturbing. Something was very, very wrong with my mother. I didn't expect her to pitch a full blown fit. I had just suffered a substantial loss after all. But I did expect a small reprimand, at the very least. What did I get? Nada, no yelling, no scornful gaze over the supper table, not even a comment about making up for lost time.

My patience was expansive, though. Like me, Gail had been suffering, steeling herself for a new kind of life that included not two sons, but just one. There had to be room for some oddities in behavior, and I really believed that the dime-a-dozen mom she appeared to have become would fade away once she recovered from the shock of it all. I was sadly mistaken. After two months of the new Gail, I flipped out.

It was after school. I'd just walked in the door, and there she was, decked out in yet another piece of Harriet Nelson's wardrobe. She was holding a plate of cookies. They were still hot. I nearly puked.

She smiled at me brightly, her breath Colgate fresh and her skirt smartly pressed. "Cookie, Mac? There fresh from the oven."

Now, there is nothing wrong with a mother baking cookies for her child. It's a sweet, maternal thing to do. But I was looking for even the smallest sign that Gail was still somewhere inside this thing occupying her body, and what do I get? A steaming plate of chocolate chip cookies for an afternoon snack. What can I say? I lost it.

"Is this some kind of joke? Are you seriously standing there offering me cookies?" My contempt rolled out to meet Gail, stopping her short.

"Don't you want any? I baked them just for you." She was taken aback at my harshness. I, in turn, was appalled by her Stepford Wifeliness.

"No shit, Gail. There's no one else here. What happened to you? Is this some kind of demonic possession? I know things have been hard for you, but what about me? Newt wasn't just yours, you know. He was mine, too. I lost him, too. You can't just turn into a totally different person and pretend nothing happened."

"Mac, how dare you speak to me like that? What's the matter with you?"

I started shouting. I couldn't believe that this was all I had left after losing my brother. "What's wrong with me? I can't believe you're asking what's wrong with me. Go look in the mirror, 'Mom.' I think there's something wrong with you. What is with this insane politeness? Not to mention the clothes. And let's not forget the 'I'm so wholesome' attitude that has taken over. I don't even recognize you."

With that, I knocked the plate out of her hand, pushed past her, and locked myself in my room. Not one of my more charming moments as a human, but I was 14 and completely freaked out. I'll never forget the picture of Gail standing there, shocked, hand out as if she were begging for spare change. A pile of broken plate and broken cookies all mixed together at her feet. It's a pathetic image. I wish I could forget it, but it's there still in my mind's eye, fresh as if it had just happened an hour ago. And right beside that picture is the memory of what she was like before.

The years passed, and I've gotten used to the new Gail, in a way. I don't really like her all that much, but we have a relationship of tolerance anyway. Newt has really helped a lot in this area. He seems to understand what's happened to her.

God, Mac, you can be such a dork! Don't you get it? Gail has lost two of the three most important things in her life. Of course she's different now. She's changed so much because she figures it's her fault. Somehow, in her brain, it's the new age wife-mother that she was that caused all this. The only way she can break the pattern is to change who she is. I'm not saying it's true, but she believes it. As long as she believes it, you're stuck with Mrs. Cleaver. Sorry, buddy.

"Well, aren't you just Mr. Insight. Are you going to analyze me next?"

Shut up. I didn't figure that out. Someone explained it to me.

"What do you mean? I thought you were alone."

I am alone. There's no one else here.

"Being dead has really messed up your brain, Newt. You just said someone explained it to you. I thought you were all by your lonesome."

I know what I said. But it's not like there's anyone else here. It's like I get a thought in my brain that comes from someone else. I didn't think of it, but the thought is still there.

"Newt, that makes no sense."

Really, and the fact that you can hear me makes sense does it?

"Right, good point. So, you're by yourself, but you're not really alone?"

Yeah, pretty much.

"Kind of like me."

Yeah, pretty much.

I've accepted that Gail is the same person. She's just broken. She's protective and domineering. She wants to be involved in my life. I imagine that she wants to make sure I'm not going anywhere because I'm all she has left. She's paraded a series of men by me as if searching for a suitable candidate as a replacement father figure, and the best thing I have to say about that is that at least she had the good taste not to make me call any of them "uncle." When I look at it from outside myself, it's almost funny that in her staggering efforts to be close to me, all she's really done is push me further and further away.

I miss the old Gail more than I can admit even to myself. She seems to have completely forgotten about herself and the person she was. It kills me that the old Gail is probably the only one who would have really understood my situation with Newt. The new one certainly couldn't get her head around it when she was given the opportunity to try. Instead, she bundled me off to the nearest head shrinker and started praying that she wasn't losing another one.

Chapter 6

I turned 25 this year. This was to be the year when it all happened, the year when I would finally start to make sense of my life, the year of my long awaited success.

This is the year when I would muddle through another job I didn't want because I was desperate and didn't really believe I could make myself even more miserable and depressed than I already was. Wrong again.

In my twenty-fourth year, I entered the exciting field of criminal rehabilitation. You might think I grew up to be a psychiatrist or a criminologist, but I don't seem to be destined for anything that glamorous. In fact, I don't seem to have grown up to be anything other than a guy who takes one job he doesn't want after another because he has to pay the rent on his dingy basement apartment somehow.

The current non-job of choice is censoring mail at the Eastglen Medium Security Prison. I'm really so proud. You always think you're going to have this amazing life, that you're going to do something big, change the world somehow, that you're destined for greatness. Disappointment is a bitter pill, and I'm choking on it every time I remember that I'm the penal porno postman. Of the many unsatisfying, unfulfilling, un-jobs I've had, and the list is long and infamous, this one is the clear winner in the categories of depressing and degrading.

I've been at Eastglen for almost a year now. The warden is suitably impressed with the duration of my employment. Apparently, most suckers don't last longer than six months. I might even get a raise soon. Wow! I think the only reason I've lasted so long is that, while gross, depraved, and certainly deviant, nothing I've seen or read has been nearly as disturbing as the fact that I'm living in a perpetual séance. I thought I would be more, well, shocked by everything. It mostly just slides off me though. Don't get me wrong, there are some sick people out there, and not all of them are in the prison.

When I took the job, I thought that the photos would be the worst. That's what the warden warned me about. He sat behind his mahogany desk in his pinstriped Armani knock-off, looked me right in the eye and said, "Mr. Williams, you will be confronted with a number of graphic photos, some of them quite distasteful."

All I could think was, *Really, in a prison, how unusual*, but what I said was quite different. "I'm quite certain I can deal with the nature of the photographs, sir."

I really needed a job. Any job. Even this one. I'd been out of work for three months and Gail was practicing her tough love routine. Despite the fact that she was living in relative luxury after winning a substantial settlement from the Norco Power Plant, she regularly lectured me on the value of hard work and goal setting. She withheld all but a pittance of an allowance in favor of the good lesson that work was going to teach me. I think she kept hoping that I was going to straighten out one day, become the son who would be something other than a burger flipper, gas station attendant, night clerk at the 24-hour convenience store or, in my current situation, a mail censor. She had issues with the idea of censorship at the best of times, and I think my role as Big Brother in the prisoners' lives made her far more uncomfortable than she could admit even to herself. Whatever the reasons she needed to help her sleep at night, we certainly weren't looking at the world through the same set of rose-colored glasses. Mine were cracked, and the job at the prison looked like the tape that would hold the frames together for a while longer, at least.

The warden, who looks suspiciously like a chubby Chuck Norris gone to seed, loved my energy and enthusiasm. I can really act up a storm when I have to. It's the one benefit of all those years spent hiding the fact that you regularly talk to a dead guy. Ironically, the warden seemed almost as desperate for somebody to do this stupid job as I was to have it. We both pretended, and I got the job.

My desk is by the window—seniority has its privileges—looking out onto the exercise yard. Not really the greatest view, but at least I don't have to stare at the mint-green cinder block walls that remind me so much of my painful elementary school years. At this desk, armed only with my black magic marker and my list of forbidden material, I peruse the filth of the prison world. Warden Chuck was right about the crap that comes in here. It's all there: animals, children, fruit. It's like the Marquis de Sade's wish list. I know I'm troubled, but these people are seriously warped. I've seen photos that would make even the hardest of the hardcore porn guys cringe. I've developed an immunity of sorts to them, so they don't bug me so much anymore. Now, I look at them as though I'm sorting laundry—animals and fruit in one pile, tits and ass in another. Pretty mundane, really.

Now, the letters are a whole different kind of screwed up. Once you recover from the thrill of reading some one else's mail, which takes about fifteen minutes, it gets really, really depressing. I mean ultra-pathetic depressing in a regular human kind of way. There are all the "Dear John" letters that range from the irate to the hysterical to the apologetic. Then, we have a healthy number of "I'll Get You" revenge letters that find exciting new ways to use the fork. And then, there are the sad family letters from parents and wives and children. It's horrifying to see the drawing little Suzie made of the Christmas tree—all green and red and slightly lopsided—knowing that she's not going to see her dad until well after she's lost her virginity in an alcoholic stupor in the back seat of a Camaro to a guy named Doug because her old man is serving a ten-year sentence for robbing a bank with a 12-gauge shotgun. What a pleasant prospect.

You are not an up person, Mac.

"Hello, Newt."

You are one of the most depressing people I've ever known.

"Oh yeah, and you really know a lot of people, being deceased and all."

This is what I'm talking about. Why are you so sarcastic all the time? If cynicism were a sport, you'd be an Olympic hero.

"Yeah, well, it's not, I'm not, and I have every right to be depressed. Look at my life."

Is this going to turn into another one of those pity me speeches, because if it is, I'll just pass, thanks.

"It absolutely is going to turn into one of those. It might even be a full scale rant. Are you quite sure you don't want to stick around to hear it?"

Fine. I get the message.

"Good." I don't think I'll ever get used to the interjections of my dead brother. It's no wonder I'm always losing my train of thought. I was talking about the letters, wasn't I? Well, let me just say, the worst of the lot, the hands down winners in the category of absolutely insane are the ones from the women. There are women, hundreds of them, writing love letters to the most depraved and degenerate men in a thousand mile radius. And not all of them are nearly as gross as you might think. They send photos—of course. Many of them look pretty much as you might expect. Biker chicks with tattoos wearing lots of leather who look like they've spent too much time inside a bottle, and quite a few specimens who appear to have a serious inferiority complex about their hair. But there are some who appear to be quite normal. No noticeable birth defects, features all there, right number of eyes and ears. The letters from these ones just kill me. Some of them even propose marriage. Why? So they can set up conjugal visits—what else? I just don't get it. At all.

While we're on the subject, Mac, did you write the letter yet?

"No, Newt I did not write the letter. I won't be writing the letter. Stop asking about the letter. There is no letter. There will never be a letter."

Mac, did you always have this problem with overstatement? I don't remember you being this repetitive as a kid.

"Quit bugging me and drop dead already."

Good one, Mac. That's really funny. I'm serious though, why haven't you written the letter?

Newt has it in his dead and rotted brain that I should write a response to one particular letter. I think this is possibly the worst of his many bad ideas. It's not quite as bad as the one about touching the electric fence, but it's a close second.

Are you ever going to stop throwing that into my face?

"Are you ever going to stop bugging me?"

I'll stop bugging you and go away forever if you just do this one thing.

"That's a good one. I'm not falling for that again. The last time I went for that deal, I ended up committed. You remember those three months I spent in the straight jacket, don't you?"

There you go with that sarcasm thing again. You were only in the straight jacket for like a day. Stop being so melodramatic.

"What did you say? Melodramatic? Is that the word you used? You are a piece of work, Newt. I was committed to a mental hospital because of you. They gave me electro-shock therapy, you asshole! You know, I realize that you're dead and all. I realize that you are all by yourself on the other side. I'm sure that it's a real drag being dead at 16. But you have to remember that I'm here with the living, trying to have a normal life of some kind. The fact that we're having a conversation at all makes that damn near impossible. Stop making it harder. Just for once, be a good brother and try to understand that listening to you has gotten me nowhere. Nothing you can say, no deal you offer me is going to make me write this letter. "

If you're not thinking about writing the letter, why do you still have it?

"Newt, I swear to God, if you were still alive I'd gladly spend the rest of my days as an inmate at Eastglen just to have the pleasure of killing you."

Fine. Good realistic threat, Mac. But seriously, just think about it. Writing this letter might be the greatest thing you ever did.

"It might also be the stupidest thing I ever did. I could lose my job, Newt."

Ooh, that'd be a hardship. I mean to lose all this glamour, the view of the exercise yard, the scintillating photos, and the seven bucks an hour. How awful. You're absolutely right, Mac. Forget I said anything. This is clearly your destiny.

Okay, he has a point here. I'm not in the slightest prepared to admit it to him, but he does have a point.

"Newt, just butt out. It's my life, you know." My God, did I really just say that? I've turned into a 12 year old again. Next, I'll be giving him the "I know you are but what am I" routine.

"Newt, can I just be alone for a while?"

Yeah, sure. It's your life, right?

"Right."

40

I have a little secret. I really have thought about writing the letter Newt is talking about. I just don't want him to know. The truth is I'm scared. That's all it boils down to really; nothing more than plain old pit-of-the-stomach loose-bowel fear. I'm scared to contact this woman. I'm terrified at what I might say, or what she might say. Most people think it's an awful thing to live with fear, hedging your bets at every turn because of what might happen, but sometimes it's just better to be safe. I think.

Chapter 1

About two months ago, I was wading through the assorted piles of filth, looking for something that might be a good start the day sort of letter. It was one of those bright blue mornings that just make you feel like getting in the car and driving at heart stopping speeds until you get to the mountains where you realize that you've never really breathed air before the moment you stepped out of the car. It's not often that I feel like this, so I like to roll around in the feeling for a while before I wipe it out with the first of the disgust-o-grams. I'd smoked three cigarettes and had two cups of coffee while I stared out the window looking past the wanderings of the scum in the yard, at the hills in the distance.

My moment of peace ended abruptly with a resounding thump. Ah, the day's mail. How I hated the sound of that mailbag landing on the table that presided over the center of our workspace. Its metallic top rang through the room with a cold, clinical echo. It always made me think of the sound of the oven doors closing around Newt's casket. It's a short sound, over before it starts almost, but its resonance hangs in the air taunting you with unspoken feelings and lost chances.

I lit another cigarette and went to the table where Joe, my eager co-worker, was already digging through the contents of the bag.

He pulled out a yellow 8 ½ x 11 envelope and grinned at me. "Hey, Mac, check it out. I bet these are glossies."

I grunted in response and continued to pull out the letters. Joe is a nice enough guy, but he's a little too enthusiastic for me. He likes this job because he doesn't have to deal with real people, but he still gets to be intimately connected with the basest aspects of reality. It also feeds his need for sordid truths. He's one of those people who are obsessively interested in serial killers. He actually has the Zippo lighter with Manson's face on it. He's even been to the farm in California. I've seen the photos. Some people go to Graceland, Joe visits the sites of bizarre crimes. He likes to watch shows like *Investigative Reports* and *America's Most Wanted* when he's doing his vacation planning. His next big trip is to Waco, Texas. I think he's sort of crazy, but who am I to judge?

"Hey, Mackie, look at this." Joe couldn't hide the excited tremor in his voice. He was holding up a letter-sized envelope, waving it with anticipation

Joe is the only one besides my brother who has ever called me Mackie. I tried to discourage him, but he has remained deaf to all my protests. After the first few months together, I realized that like so many other things about Joe, this was something I would have to learn to live with. I sigh audibly every time he uses that diminutive form of my name, thinking that he'll get the point eventually, but he hasn't seemed to notice yet. Now, I do it more from habit than anything else. In truth, I'm grateful to have Joe working next to me. His demented fascination with death—the gorier and more gruesome the better—makes me feel slightly more normal than a housewife earning some extra money now that the kids have gone off to school would. With this in mind, I looked up from the photo of a 165 pound woman in a black latex dominatrix outfit and stubbed out my cigarette on the corner of the table, "What you got, Joe?"

He came over to my side of the table and handed me a letter. I turned the envelope over in my hands. It looked like any other letter to me. It was addressed to Milton Pasker, a relatively new guest at the Hotel Scumbag. He was convicted of raping and murdering two college students last January. He's not a permanent resident here, but we're holding him in solitary until a suitable box can be found for him in one of the maximum security penitentiaries—all currently suffering from bulging cages. He won't be getting out of prison ever, I think, but this is the kind of guy who makes arguing against capital punishment a really hard thing to do.

Joe was thrilled when Milton was brought to Eastglen. He followed the trial with that same rubberneck instinct that makes people slow down and gawk at car wrecks as they drive by. Joe told me that at his trial, Pasker hardly moved. It was like he was catatonic or something. Joe figures Milton just didn't care what happened. I figured it was just a last ditch effort to make an insanity plea believable. The jury might have bought it until the cops described the crime scene which Joe felt obliged to relay to me. Who knows, though, maybe he is nuts. I don't think anyone who pops out the eyeballs of his victims is anywhere near normal. Joe reveled in all the gory details. I tried to stop him from relaying them to me, but Joe goes deaf when he starts talking true crime stories. Gruesome is close to right, but it doesn't quite capture the essence of this act.

Milton Pasker, unlike me, is not the kind of guy who matches his name. With a name like Milton, you expect him to turn out as a plumber or a computer programmer. It's a name that just reeks of pocket protectors and mechanical pencils. Mr. Pasker did his best to get out from under his name, though. When I think about it, it strikes me as creepy how many of the really weird crimes are committed by guys with names like Milton or Bert or Julius. It's lucky I just work for the prison.

Pasker should probably change his name to Josef Mengele after the performance that landed him here for an extended stay. He didn't just rape these two girls, he butchered them. He tortured them for hours with knives of various shapes and sizes. He cut holes in their bodies. He taped their eyes open, so they would have to watch the whole thing happen. Joe mentioned pop bottles, but I tuned out for that part. Then, he shot them. I wonder if it's not a good thing that he killed them after it was all over. How much therapy do you think it would take to recover from that kind of thing?

I wasn't that surprised to see Joe fawning over this inmate's first letter. "What's the big deal, Joe? Milton's first letter? You want to frame it or something?"

Joe gave me a scathing look. "No, stupid. Look at the name in the return address."

I glanced at the letter's top left corner. "Rachel Strong? So what? Is this a name I'm supposed to recognize?"

Joe was quick to give me another reproving look. "Don't you watch the news, man?"

"As little as possible, brother, as little as possible."

A big sigh from Joe. "Rachel Strong is Melanie Strong's sister."

I felt like we were playing twenty questions, and I wasn't getting any closer to the right answer. "And I should know that name because..."

Joe started tsk, tsking me for my indefensible lack of interest. "God, it's like you never hear a word I say, Mackie. Melanie Strong was one of the chicks Pasker did. Don't you remember me telling you about how the sister flipped out at the trial?"

I vaguely remembered the story. "Oh, right. The one who started screaming at Pasker during the sentencing hearing?"

"Yeah, right after she tried to attack him."

"Is this the one they chucked in jail?"

"Yep. That's her."

"Why'd they lock her up? I mean, buddy killed her sister. You'd think they'd show a little compassion."

Again, I was met with Joe's patronizing expression. His lips pursed in silent rebuke. "Because the judge thought she was going to really try something. She was only in overnight. They let her go once she cooled down."

The conversation seemed to have no foreseeable end or purpose. I certainly didn't want to spend the entire morning rehashing the incarceration of Milton Pasker. "All fascinating stuff, Joe, but tell me again why I care that she wrote to the scum who killed her sister?"

"I don't know, Mac. She was pretty freaked out. It might be good reading." Joe shrugged and looked at me with a hopeful grin on his face.

"Well, be my guest, Joe. I'm sure she'll provide you with yet another intricate and overdeveloped plot for revenge."

Joe is still interested in the human drama of the letters. He really enjoys the meat of them, especially the revenge letters. I'm pretty much immune to most of that now. Now, it's just a search for the stuff to cross out with my black marker. I had just gotten into some homemade *Swank*, when Joe reappeared at my desk holding the letter.

"Problem, Joe? Not sure whether 'stab you a zillion times with a screwdriver' is acceptable? It's not." I returned to the graphic photos in front of me. Joe didn't move. He stood there holding the letter, looking first at me, then back to the sheet of lined yellow paper on which I could see the neatly curled handwriting of Melanie Strong's sister.

"No. It's just that..." His voice trailed off like a train whistle receding into the distance. I waited for him to go on, but he just stood there, staring at the letter.

"Just what? We've got a bag of filth to go through here." My patience was starting to wear thin. I'd been through this with Joe before.

"I dunno, Mackie. The letter's just creepy."

"Really, well, we hardly get any of those. What will we do? Come on Joe, sink it or send it."

Joe shook his head and thrust the letter toward me. "No, Mac, I mean it's really creepy. It's like she knows stuff she shouldn't know."

"What do you mean she knows stuff? What's the problem?"

He was practically waving the letter in my face by this point. "Here, you read it."

I snatched the letter away from him and lit a cigarette off the butt still smoking in my hand. Joe can be really aggravating about this kind of thing. Once or twice a week, I'll have to read over a letter because he's not sure what to do with it. I've told him that it doesn't really matter, but he just can't get past it. He can't decide what to do with the letter, and he can't move on until it's taken care of. I can't imagine what his life outside work looks like if he's paralyzed by this stupidity.

I've learned over the last few months that it's just easier to take the whole thing out of his hands than it is to get him to deal with it. He starts to sweat and shake, fumbling with his marker, not sure if he dare cross out everything or only a word or two. I've seen him start to pace around our small office, letter in hand, reading it over and over as though he's an actor running lines. It's really awful. Having so much less attachment to the people behind the words, it's considerably easier for me to deal with these troubling items. If I left it in Joe's hands, he'd get through about a letter a week, so I handed him the home made photo album and read the letter.

It was a tidy affair that followed the usual form of a business letter. It looked like the kind of thing you'd expect to see addressed to the phone company inquiring about an errant long distance charge, not the crazed ramblings of a grief-stricken sister writing to the man who caused her so much pain.

Dear Mr. Pasker,

This will be the only letter I write to you. After it's done, I'm going to attempt to live my life as though you had never dragged your evil, deranged mind into it. But I can't begin to do that until I tell you what you've done.

You remember me, I'm sure. I'm the one who was screaming at you right before you were sentenced. I might have gotten through that day if it wasn't for the look on your face when they brought you in. You had a sort of half grin on your face, as though it didn't matter what happened because you'd already had your fun. And I'm quite sure that it was fun for you. Melanie told me you giggled the whole time — the high pitched laugh of a child at a funhouse. And that you wore that same smirk you plastered on your face at the trial.

I'd never known hate until you crawled into my life. I would have been quite happy to go through my life never knowing what it felt like to really hate someone, but you've taken away any chance of that. I hope that you rot in that prison. Rot from your soul outward. I hope the memory of my sister spitting in your face haunts you at night. I hope that you see her poor, bloodstained body and remember how she begged you not to hurt her. I hope her words ring in your head. Can you hear them now? "Please don't, please. I won't tell anyone, I promise. I can keep a secret. I'm real good at secrets." Do you remember how she screamed when you cut out the tattoo on her thigh? Yes, I know all about you carving your initials on her body. Did you think death would keep her quiet? You were wrong. I hope you still hear it, a clear, loud song in your head. I hope every minute of your life from now on is torture, and I hope that your only friend is misery.

I wanted to tell you about my sister, all the good things about her, but she tells me you'll be deaf to that sort of thing, that a monster like you couldn't understand or feel guilt about what you are.

I know you're not crazy. I know you just went out and did this horrible thing because violence is what drives you and makes you feel whole. I just want you to know that you can never be whole. You are barely a fragment of a man. The evil you have done to me, to my family, you have only brought to yourself. You will never have peace.

It was unsigned, that last sentence dangling on the edge of the page. It rang through my ears and went straight to my guts. I could feel the color draining from my face. I tasted acid at the back of my throat.

"Mackie, you okay?" Joe was standing over me, watching me read the letter than troubled him so much.

"Yeah, fine. Too much coffee." I felt my heart pounding in my chest, my blood racing through veins that suddenly seemed much too small to bear the pressure.

"Are you sure? You're whitewashed, man."

"It's nothing. Maybe too many smokes."

"All right. What do you think about the letter? Isn't it weird the way she keeps talking about what her sister is saying. I mean, this girl must be ready for the nut house."

"Not now, Joe. We'll talk about it later, all right? I'm not feeling so good right now."

"Sure, Mac, whatever." Disappointed that I wasn't interested in dissecting the letter, Joe reluctantly wandered back to his desk while I struggled to keep my coffee in my stomach. I noticed my hands shaking when I reached for another cigarette. I used both hands to steady the lighter and reread the letter.

This time my guts wrenched so badly I ran for the bathroom. I sat there sweating until my heart slowed down. I still had the letter in my hand. It was so clear, I couldn't believe it. This girl knew something. She'd been talking to someone. Someone who knew exactly what had gone on that night, and I was pretty sure it wasn't Milton Pasker. I folded up the letter and pocketed it.

When I got back to my desk, I was still shaking. My mouth was filled with sand, and my tongue felt swollen. I started to pack up my stuff, knowing that I couldn't take another second of the clamminess of the office.

"Mackie? What's going on?" Joe was up in an instant and hovering around as I did a quick check of my desk.

"I'm going home, Joe, what does it look like?"

"Yeah, but…"

"But what, Joe? I'm sick. You want me to perform my duties from the john?"

"Well, no. It's just that…What'd you think of the letter? Weird, huh?"

"Yeah, weird." I was trying not to think about just how weird the letter was, but Joe just couldn't leave it alone.

"All that stuff about last words, it's like she was there or something. And the tattoo on the thigh. I don't remember hearing about that at all. Not even at the trial."

"Yeah, I guess so. Look, I've got to get out of here. See you tomorrow."

As calmly as I could, I got my coat on, punched out and headed for the door. All I wanted to do was run outside and hyperventilate until I puked. After that I could face the drive home. But I work in a prison. You can never just run outside. The whole fucking place is built to keep people in. I had to sign out with John at the Special Services desk, then I had to wait for him to buzz me into the outer office where I had to get the morning guard to open the outer office door after which I had to casually stroll across the yard walkway to the main gate where Al let me off the goddamn property, but not before a casual search of my knapsack. The whole time, I made stupid inane conversation with every person I encountered; all the while thinking that I could feel the letter through the material of my shirt, stabbing at my chest just like Pasker had stabbed at those girls.

I was clawing at the paper by the time I reached my car. I had to read it again to make sure I wasn't crazy. Who was I kidding? If Joe could figure it out, it should have been obvious to anyone. Rachel Strong had been talking to her sister.

My hands were shaking so badly it took three attempts to get the key in the door. I got into my car and sat there. I wanted to get in the back seat and lay down, but I didn't want anyone coming over to see if I was okay. My car was parked in plain view of the gate, and Al was just the kind of do gooder who would amble over and check to see if I needed help. I rested my head against the steering wheel until I felt like I could drive home, all the while rethinking my conclusion. Maybe she was privy to details that weren't public because she was family to the victim. Maybe she just thought she knew what her sister had said. Maybe they were really close. Like me and Newt. That did it. I cranked the engine and got the hell out of there.

Chapter 8

When I got home, I went immediately to the kitchen and poured myself a large vodka. It was only 11:30, but I was pretty sure the morning's events warranted a shot or two. I have to justify the drinks I have now. It's the only way I can keep from feeling creepy about drinking alone. Creepy or not, I had one and then another vodka until I could feel my insides growing calm and my brain clearing. The whole time, I sat at the kitchen table, staring straight ahead, examining first the letter and then my emotions.

I was experiencing a sensation I didn't recognize. Something like excitement, but it had been so long since I'd felt anything but fear or anger or disgust that I couldn't be sure. I was holding a letter written by a person who—maybe—was having the same kind of experience as me. It was almost too good to be true. I mean, I didn't want to wish this sort of thing on anyone, but I'd rather have company on the astral plane express than ride by myself. Or maybe I was reading too much into the letter. What had Joe said about the tattoo? He never heard anything about it. That almost cinched it. If Joe didn't know about it, it never happened. Or it was never released to the public.

But what was I going to do with this hunch? What if I was wrong? Should I contact her? How much or how little should I say? Maybe I should just forget the whole thing. This Rachel woman was probably just rambling out of grief and none of my imaginings were even close to the mark. I should just send this letter on to Milton Pasker and move on with my life, such as it is. After all I've learned my lesson about talking. You know, loose lips sink ships, or in my case, loose lips land you in a nut house where you are treated for a series of doctor specific dementia for a period of several months. That decision made, I tried to put the letter out of my head, but I couldn't get away from the feeling that there was more going on here. I felt like my protective coating was being sanded away, exposing me to the elements of life. I reached for the bottle, and Newt showed up.

Hey, little brother. Hitting it kind of hard today, aren't you?

"Hey, Newt." I slumped forward in my chair, my head resting on the table. I didn't want to talk to Newt. I didn't want to do anything but get numb so I wouldn't have to think about Rachel Strong anymore.

Tell me about the letter, Mac.

"Not now, Newt, not now."

Why not now? All you're going to do is drink yourself into a stupor by three this afternoon, pass out, and wake up around seven feeling like shit. Let's just skip the booze and get right to the feeling like shit part.

"Don't be so condescending. You're the reason I'm like this."

Look, Mac, don't blame me because you drink. I don't have any control over this. You know that as well as I do. Things are the way they are for a reason. I don't know what it is, but I know that there is one. Stop feeling sorry for yourself and put away the bottle. If I was alive, I'd pop you one to knock some sense into you.

"If you were alive, I probably wouldn't drink so much."

Just tell me about the letter.

"The suspense is killing you, isn't it, Newt? You are absolutely wound up over the fact that you don't know what's in the letter. I think that's very funny. What's the big deal, Newt? It's just a letter from some nutty broad to some nuttier dirt bag at the prison. Why so curious?"

Mac, you don't run out of work shaking and reeling because of an ordinary crackpot letter. I've seen you read hundreds of letters. You've never reacted like this before. What's going on?

"I'm tired, Newt. Tired and weary and worn out." I took a large mouthful of vodka and swirled it around my mouth savoring its clinical taste. "Do you remember the first time you talked to me?"

I could hear Newt sigh. He knew he was too late. The only advantage I have over Newt is the fact that he can't see and hear everything. He sees and knows a lot about my life, but he can't get at it all. It's a good thing, too, because without some measure of privacy, I really would have gone off the deep end a long time ago.

Of course. I thought you were going to wreck your bedroom, looking for the tape recorder. God, it took me forever to convince you that I was real, that it wasn't some sick joke. I finally had to bring up that time we found Gail's stash of pot. Remember how we laughed thinking about Gail smoking up?

I started to laugh then at the memory of it. I laughed until I was weeping at all that I had lost over the years. The memory of a brother long absent from my tangible life, the absence of a memory of my father, the memory of a Gail who would smoke up. I lurched out of my chair and went to the phone to call Gail.

Mac, don't call Gail right now. This is a bad idea.

"Fugg off, Newton. I'll do whatever I want. Stupid brothers."

I poured another drink while I waited for her to answer. After all, she called me every day. I was just beating her to the punch.

"Hello?" Her voice was clear and sunny. I imagined she was having a second cup of coffee on her plant lined porch, reading the newspaper.

"Hiya, Ma. Whas goin on?" I didn't bother to try to hide my slurring.

"Mac?"

"Yep, iss me. How are ya, Ma?"

"I'm fine." Hesitation, pregnant with disapproval, passed through the phone and lingered in the air for a moment before she continued. "Mac, have you been drinking?"

"Thas real nice, Ma. I call you up to say hi, and you jus think I'm drunk. Thanks a lot. Thas jus great. My own Ma thinks I'm a drunk. I bet you're pretty disappointed in me. Wonderin' why it wasn't me instead of Newt, aren't ya? Well, it goes both ways, Ma. Both ways. Maybe you shoulda paid more attention. Maybe you shouldna been so selfish."

I could almost see Gail's lips pursing as she recoiled from my drunken attack. "Mac, I'm hanging up now. I'm not going to let you be abusive to me because you're drunk. I will call you tomorrow when you're more yourself."

Even through the vodka haze that was washing over me, I knew I'd gone too far. "I'm sorry, Ma. I din mean it. Iss not me. I don know what I'm sayin. I'm sorry."

"I know, Mac, so am I. Good bye." It was a curt brush off, but somewhere deep inside, I felt like I probably deserved it. I dropped the phone to the floor and sat there filled with longing and disgust.

Good one, Mac. Nice gesture.

"Fugg off, Newt."

I slumped down onto the table and fell into the blissfully blank sleep of the drunk where it didn't matter if my life was completely screwed, where I'd never heard of Rachel or Melanie Strong, where Newt couldn't talk to me.

Chapter 9

When I woke up, a dim, dusty light filled the kitchen. The blinds covering the one window in the room left the gentle light of twilight outside. It was all but dark in the apartment. It took me a few moments to realize that my head was pounding in time with the ringing of the phone. I groped for it in the darkness unwilling to subject my throbbing head to the flood of light that would come if I flipped the switch. I finally kicked it with my foot on the fourth ring. "Yeah?"

"Mackie? It's Joe."

"Hi, Joe."

I looked around for my cigarettes as my eyes became accustomed to the dimness of early evening. Fumbling for my lighter, I brushed my hand across the letter still lying on the table. I pulled back like it had burned my hand. I felt the bile back up my throat into my mouth. I sucked deeply on the cigarette fighting back the urge to throw up.

"What do you want, Joe?"

"I just called to see if you were okay. You took off in a hurry. I had to tell everyone you got sick and had to leave. Is that okay?"

I wanted to hang up on him and return to the sleep of escape, but his need for approval, his eagerness to please made me temper the shortness of my remarks. "Well, that's what happened, isn't it, Joe?"

"Well, yeah. I guess so. I just wanted to make sure."

"Relax, Joe. It's fine."

"So are you okay? It was really boring without you there. Are you coming back tomorrow?"

"Yeah, probably. I think it was just a 24-hour kind of thing. I'll be fine."

"Cool, so you want to go get some pizza? We could talk about the letter. Hey, that reminds me, did you take it home?"

For all his simplicity, Joe was sharper than I gave him credit for. I didn't think he would have noticed that the letter was gone, but I should have guessed that he would want to read it again. I played dumb, my ruse as a flu sufferer serving me well. "Take what home?"

"The letter, stupid. I was looking all over for it after you left."

"Oh, yeah, I must have put it in my pocket when I got sick."

"Mac, you know we're not supposed to take stuff out of the prison. It's like mail tampering. You could get fired."

I was starting to lose my patience and my cool. "I could if anyone said anything about it. But no one is going to say a word about my accidental removal of this item from the prison. I was sick. I wasn't thinking of some stupid letter. Besides, I'll bring it back tomorrow." I had no intention of bringing it back to the prison yet, but Joe really didn't have to know that.

"Yeah, I guess so." Joe seemed unconvinced but willing to let it go in the name of friendship. "So you wanna?"

"Wanna what?" I felt like this phone call would never end. My mouth was beginning to water for another shot of vodka.

"Get some pizza, loser."

"Uh, I don't think so, Joe. Not tonight. I should really stay home and make sure I'm over this flu. Maybe next week, okay?"

"Yeah, whatever."

"Hey, Joe, remember what you said about the tattoo on that girl, that it was the first you heard of it?"

"Yeah, weird, huh?" 'Weird' was Joe's mantra.

"Yeah, really weird. So do you suppose this woman's crazy, or do you think it really happened?"

"I don't know, man. Maybe they told the family but no one else. I mean it's pretty gross, don't you think?"

"Do you think we can find out for sure?"

"Maybe. I know this guy down at the court clerk's office. He might be able to find out. Why so curious, Mackie? I thought this kind of stuff wasn't your bag."

"It's not. I just want to know, that's all. Can you find out?"

"Sure, man. Why don't I come over, and we'll go see my buddy together."

"God, could you do it without me? I'm still feeling pretty sick. I'd hate to give you whatever I've got."

Joe didn't hide the disappointment in his voice, but I was too agitated to care. He agreed to talk to his friend and get back to me the next day. Feeling like I'd done something to get some answers, I hung up the phone and picked up the letter. I couldn't read it in the semi-darkness of the room, but I didn't really have to see it anyway. The words were ringing in my head, "I won't tell anyone. I promise…I'm real good at secrets." This girl knew her sister's last words, knew them as if she had been told what they were.

But what if I was wrong?

Chapter 10

You know when people talk to God or Christ, it's perfectly acceptable. The pious and not so pious regularly offer up their Hail Marys and their Heavenly Fathers without anyone ever batting an eye. Churches and synagogues and mosques are full of millions of people yapping incessantly to the Virgin or to Mohammed or to St. Whatchmo of Whatever. There, they sit or kneel or prostrate themselves appealing to whatever big power they're affiliated with for help with their family or with their taxes or with converting the heathens. There are some big questions out there, real life and death questions that are important. And is anyone coming out of church saying, "Well, God told me to get an accountant to help me with the taxes, to get Jenny into counseling for her drinking, and He says not to worry about the increase in immoral television—it's just a phase." I don't think so. If anyone out there is getting this kind of hard advice, they're sure not talking about it. As I see it, the message here is that we're supposed to talk to someone who is never supposed to answer us.

Yeah, right, that makes sense.

They used to be called prophets—the people who claimed that they were in communication with God. Christ was a prophet and look what happened to him. He announces that he God's son or hears the word of God—depending on whether you want the Christian or Hebrew interpretation—and bam! His ass is nailed to a cross faster than Moses can part the Red Sea. I realize the motivation for his crucifixion was largely political, but even 2,000 years ago, the line between politics and religion was barely more than a muddy stream being forded at every turn. It seems to me that we might as well accept the unholy union for what it is—a tool for engendering fear and control.

And even predating Christ, we can look to poor Moses for a lesson in how to be persecuted for having a personal relationship with God. He has a couple of innocent chats with a burning bush and promptly goes from prince to slave to outcast, wandering in the desert with a bunch of bloodthirsty Egyptians chasing him. These are not inspiring role models for someone who's thinking about fessing up to the fact that they're communing with the Almighty.

And think about it, that was centuries ago. You'd think that after all this time we would have found a civilized way to deal with this or at least explain it. Is it that unreasonable to think that with so many people praying, one of the millions might just get a direct response? I have to say that it seems way crazier to continue praying when you never get an answer and aren't really supposed to expect one. I've apparently got this faith thing backwards though, and, let's face it, things haven't really changed that much. If Christ lived now, a committee of doctors would diagnose him as a schizophrenic, administer a vile assortment of drugs, destroy his short-term memory with electric shock treatments, and lock him away from the rest of the community in a place where he'd wander around looking at the other zombies wondering why he ever confessed to anyone that he was chatting with the Creator of the universe.

"Oops, my mistake. Sorry, I just meant that I pray to God. Yeah, that's it. He never answers me. That would be crazy. Only nut cases think that Gods talks back. It's a one way conversation, really. I was just confused. Okay, I admit it, I'd been smoking pot—yeah, that's it. It must have been some kind of drug inspired hallucination."

Then the committee of doctors would send him to rehab so that he could get over his addiction to marijuana and then to counseling so that he could begin to lead a normal productive life.

And all the while, Christ would be saying to himself, "Okay, won't be making that mistake again. I don't think I really need to share my special conversations with any of these pill-pushing, shock-happy lunatics."

Unless, of course, Christ was a wealthy business tycoon, in which case he'd be called eccentric and left to continue doling out thousands of dollars to ensure that his surroundings were germ free while he contemplated the monstrous length to which his fingernails had grown.

It becomes more and more apparent to me that sanity and insanity are based more on economics than anything else. Really, it's all a question of solvency, isn't it? If you've got enough zeros behind your name, you can tell people you're Teddy Roosevelt and run around whacking things with your big stick all day long.

As for the rest of us, I've learned that we're better off just keeping this sort of thing under wraps.

Newt started talking to me when I was 16. In the two years since he'd died, I had grown used to being an only child, although orphan is probably closer to the reality of my situation. Gail had dropped out of the picture, replaced by the "mom" who didn't seem to remember that we had lost half the members of our family. I spent most of my time alone; immersing myself in books that would spare me from the world I lived in and transport me to one where things made more sense. I never realized just how much I had depended on Newt as a source of fun and companionship when he was alive. Alone, I just missed him and wondered at the strange way my life was shaping up. I had no idea just how strange things could actually get.

It was November, a Tuesday night not long after I'd marked the anniversary of Dan's death off the calendar. We'd just had a huge dump of snow, and the temperature had dropped until the air was almost visible. It was still snowing lightly, that silent fall of snow that only comes at night. The world always seems to grow mute when it snows in the late hours. It's as though all sound is muffled by the big white flakes, and all we're left with is this black and white and amber scene from a silent movie colored in sepia. I was in my usual spot, sitting in my room, watching the snow fall through the street lights as it drifted, sparkling and shining in and out of visibility directed by wind and gravity in a gentle dance that seemed to have no foreseeable end. I didn't find it hard to imagine that it could snow forever, the flakes slowly becoming drifts that would eventually overtake the cars, the trees, the houses of my neighborhood encompassing everything in a blanket of ultimate security.

In the years since Newt died, I had taken to secluding myself in my room to escape from Gail the Inquisitive. I'd stare out the window and smoke furtive experimental cigarettes, blowing the smoke out into the cold night. I spent many a night wrapped up in blankets crouched near the sill, searching for something I couldn't name and hiding from the mother I didn't know anymore. We were as estranged as we could be living in the same house.

Silence had become like a plague in my house. Gail and I hardly spoke anymore. That's not quite right, actually. Gail spoke a lot. She talked about the way my grades had fallen. She talked about bringing friends home, or more precisely, my failure to bring friends home. She talked about prospective girlfriends. She asked about my summer job. She asked about college. But she never really said anything. It was all superficial nonsense. I kept waiting for her to talk to me about Newt, or about how I felt about things, but she never did. After a while I just stopped talking back to her. I started to close down. By the time I turned 16, we had a grunting relationship. She would chatter away about something, I would grunt a one syllable response and then lock myself in my room. She would usually attempt one conversation through the door before uttering a consumptive sigh and walking away. I always imagined that she was walking away from my closed door, head bowed, tears running down her face onto the carpet. I wanted to open up the door and run into her maternal hug, but I just couldn't. I didn't know her, didn't trust her—didn't want to. Instead, I just got used to being alone. I got used to burying my fear and anger deep down where no one could find it.

Except Newt.

I was attempting to master the finer points of French grammar, when I first heard him speak.

Your pronunciation sucks, Mac.

That was Newt's first sentence to me. In perfect Newtonian style, he chose an insult to open conversation. That's how he always did it when he was alive, so I guess it shouldn't have been a surprise that he chose the same for his first dead conversation.

His words were faint at first, as though he wasn't sure he'd be heard, or wasn't sure he wanted to be heard. I wasn't sure I'd heard anything. It was like a loud whisper in my head, familiar but indistinguishable. After all, it was the first time I'd heard his voice in two years. It was my imagination. It was wishful thinking. It was nothing. I went back to the French, but Newt had seen me look up. The whisper got louder after that.

Mac, can you hear me?

I looked around the room, more and more certain that I had heard something. I called out to Gail, thinking that the closed door was muffling her voice. "Mom, did you say something?"

No answer.

I went back to conjugating verbs, with the sensation that I wasn't alone anymore. I took a final hit off the cigarette in my hand, staring at the smoke as my breath pushed it through the open window.

When did you start smoking, Mac? Gail's going to go ballistic when she finds out.

Louder this time, the voice made me flinch. I threw the cigarette into the snow and went to the door. I threw it open and jumped out into the hall, looking for the owner of this voice. Nothing. No one. I went back to my post at the window and lit another cigarette, thinking that I must be exhausted or sick or something. But once the whisper started, it just wouldn't stop. The voice was a lot louder now. Not at all like the whisper had it begun as. It was a loud clear voice. And now I could assign an owner to it—there could be no mistaking Newt's voice.

Mackie, tell me you can hear me. Come on, little brother, say something to me.

Nobody called me Mackie anymore. Not since Newt died. It was the name he gave me when I was eight, and he was employing my services as indentured servant—Mackie the Lackey, he used to call me.

"What kind of sick joke is this? John, I swear to God if this is you, I'm going to rip your tongue right out of your mouth." I was growing nervous and angry at this intrusion into my sorrow. What kind of person would play me for a fool in this heartless way?

Mac! It's not John. It's me, Newt. This isn't a joke. Boy, I'm glad you can finally hear me.

"So you think you're funny, do you? You guys are the sickest jerks I know. I hope you're getting a good laugh out of this. I hope it was worth it. Now, joke's over. Take your fucking mike and your fucking speaker and shove them up your ass!" I had begun to tear apart the room, searching for evidence of my hilarious friends. I was just about to flip the mattress when Newt brought up Gail's stash.

Really, Mac, it's me. I can prove it. You remember about a month before I died, we were searching through the basement for those pictures of our camping trip to Yosemite. Remember what we found in the box with the 8 millimeter films? In one of the film boxes, we found a whole bunch of pot. Gail's stash. We laughed about it for days, just picturing Gail getting high.

In spite of myself, I laughed at the memory. Then, I remembered what was going on right now in my present.

"That doesn't prove anything. Newt might have told dozens of people about that."

In a month? What am I going to do, tell a bunch of your 14-year-old friends that we found pot in our mother's possession? And then they'll wait two years to use the information to play a really awful practical joke on you involving your dead brother? Don't be such an idiot. Look, Mac, this is your brother talking. Whether you believe it or not, it's me. Remember how we took a little of the pot and got high out in the back yard by the garbage cans? You were so paranoid about your eyes being red that you made me sneak inside to get the Visine.

"Newt? It's really you?" I hesitated, staring out the window trying to catch Newt's reflection in the glass, hoping I could see him as well as hear him; hoping that the last two years had been an awful dream. I was having trouble making the world stop spinning. The wind had shifted, and the snow was driving toward my window making me feel as though I were rushing through space, hurtling forward into unknown terrors.

Newt seemed ecstatic. His voice was filled with the same tremor of excitement that used to betray his cool façade when we were kids about to embark on some new adventure. *Yes! Finally. I've been talking for months now. I thought you were never going to hear me.*

"Newt, you're dead. How can you be talking to me? What am I saying? Newt is dead, and he can't be talking to me. I'm hearing things. I've fallen asleep, and I'm having some kind of nightmare. Okay, deep breaths. This is just a dream. It's only a dream. It's only a..."

Macbeth Shaw Williams! This is not a dream. You are not crazy, and I am talking to you!

My head was spinning with the thought that it might be true, that I really was hearing the voice of my dead brother. It was impossible, yet his voice was so clear in my mind. It was as though he was standing at my shoulder, just out of my line of vision, whispering, first in this ear, then in the other one. I could feel the tears welling up in my eyes, and my throat was beginning to close, constricting with the fear that I really was losing my mind. It was the only explanation that made sense.

I was choking on my own cries to Gail for help, thinking that I didn't deserve this on top of everything else. I knew that being a teenager was meant to be hard, a trial of sorts, but why was this happening to me? Hadn't I been through enough trials?

Okay, Mackie, let's try this one more time. This is your dead brother, Newt. I'm not a figment of your imagination. This is real. I can talk to you, and you can hear me. I understand that you are having a hard time believing it, but it is real.

"Newt? This is insane. How is this possible? You can't possibly be talking to me. You're dead, you know."

Yes, Mac, I know I'm dead. I was there for the whole thing.

"Well, you were pretty much outta there by the time I got to see you."

Yeah, I know. Sorry about that. Thanks for sitting with me that whole time in the hospital, though. That was nice.

"You were there? You saw that? Cool. Were you up in the corner of the room? How come I didn't know you were there? What's going on, Newt? What are you doing here? Have you talked to Gail yet?"

Slow down, Mac. I don't really know what's going on. I've been trying to talk to Gail forever. She won't hear me. Or can't. I don't know.

His voice sounded far away and sad. It had a tinny echo to it, like he was calling long distance from Jupiter, lost and trying hard to find a way home. I don't know if I should have stopped feeling so scared then, but I did.

"Newt, are you a ghost?"

Well, kind of. I guess. More like a spirit, really. I'm not sure.

"Cool. So do you look really gross? Are you going to go and haunt Roger and Dave? You know, you really shouldn't bother Roger. He's kind of freaky now. He never really got over what happened to you. Are you going to tell Gail? You know, I'd really appreciate it if you would talk to her. It's like she…"

Mac.

"Yeah, Newt?"

Could we stop with the chatter? I've got some stuff to say.

"Yeah, sorry. I didn't know there were rules about how to converse with dead guys."

There aren't, but I just want you to know as much as I do about this.

"Okay, what's to know? Is this like heaven and hell stuff?"

Not exactly. I don't think those places exist. At least, I'm not in either one.

"Well, where are you?"

Good question. I don't really know. I'm just sort of here.

"Newt, you're not here. I can't see you or anything. Am I supposed to be able to see you? Can you make stuff move around? We could pull off some great tricks, you know. Maybe you could come to school, and we could flip desks and freak out the guidance counselor who's been…"

Mac, this isn't a game. It's not about pulling pranks. I'm dead, remember?

"Right. So, you're not in heaven or hell. You can't haunt people. I can't see you, but I can hear you like you were right next to me. What's going on, Newt?"

If you'd shut up for more than three seconds I'd tell you.

"Geez, sorry. Excuse me for being curious. It's not like this is a regular thing for me. Dead people aren't banging down my door to talk to me, you know."

I know. I'm sorry. It's just that I've been trying to talk to you for months, and now that you can finally hear me, you won't shut up long enough for me to talk.

"Okay, consider me a mute. Speak, oh ghastly, ghostly brother."

It had been two years since Newt died, and he'd been trying for six months to get me to hear him. He babbled on for a couple of hours, trying to explain what had happened and what he thought was happening. As a 16-year-old, I can't pretend I understood much about what he said. Even now, after all these years, I'm not sure I understand any of it.

He remembered dying. *I remember the smell mostly. It was foul, like the campfire at the lake when we burned all the garbage.*

"Did it hurt, Newt? Did dying hurt?"

Not really. Not in a physical pain sense anyway. The first few seconds hurt like hell, but after that, it was like I was numb. You know how it feels when your arm falls asleep.

"You mean all pins and needles?"

No, I mean when it really falls asleep, like it's not yours. You touch it and poke it, pinch it and move it around, but you can't feel anything. It could be anybody's, but it's not yours. You could light the thing on fire, and you wouldn't know, except for the smell of burning hair. That's how it felt. I remember trying to let go of the fence, trying to move around, but I couldn't feel it at all. I had no control.

"I'm glad you didn't feel it, Newt. I mean, you looked really bad, all burnt up like that. It was pretty gross."

Yeah, I'm glad, too.

"Did you see anything?"

You mean like the white light at the end of the tunnel thing? Not really. I mean, I didn't walk through a tunnel to get to the light. There was light, and I was in it, but I didn't meander down any tunnel trying to decide whether or not to go on. I was at the end before I knew if there even was a tunnel. I think it's because the shock killed me almost instantly. I was just there. One second, I'm grabbing at the fence, the next I'm in this space, like I'd been transported or something.

"Cool. So who else is there? Have you met any cool people?"

Mac, this isn't a vacation. And can you please stop saying cool. It's driving me nuts.

"Yeah, whatever. You didn't answer my question. Is Dan there?"

No, Dan's not here. No one's here. It's just me.

"Well, that's stupid. There are jillions of dead people out there. There's got to be someone else. Maybe you just haven't seen them yet."

It's been two years, Mac. I'm pretty sure I'd have seen someone by now.

"Maybe not, eternity's a pretty long time, you know. Wasn't there an orientation or something? A 'Welcome to Being Dead' meeting for first timers?" I thought I was being clever, but Newt didn't appreciate the humor.

No, there was no orientation. God, you're aggravating. It's not like joining AA. There's no big circle of dead people saying, "Hi, my name is Bob. I had a heart attack, and I'm dead." I don't know where everyone is, but I do know that this isn't like Sunday school. There aren't any angels flying around. There's no pearly gate. It's just me.

"Wow. You must be bored stiff."

Very funny. I could hear the irritation in Newt's voice as though he was alive, and we were arguing about whose turn it was to do the dishes. It all seemed so familiar and vaguely normal that I actually welcomed the thought that my dead brother was talking to me.

"Well, at least I can see the humor here. So what have you been doing all this time?"

I'm not sure. Time doesn't really affect me the same way it does when you're alive. It's almost like slipping in and out of a really deep sleep to find that weeks had passed without any sense of time at all. And sometimes, I have the feeling that I've been somewhere else, but I can't quite remember it.

"You mean like a dream that you can't quite get a hold of after you wake up?"

Yeah, a lot like that.

The conversation carried on like that for quite a while. I had to turn on the stereo after the third time Gail asked me who I was talking to. It was then that I realized I was just as alone in this thing as Newt. "Do you mean to tell me that I'm the only one who can hear you? You can't go talk to Gail or anyone else?"

Nope. You're it.

"Why me?"

I'm not sure. All I know is that you are the one I get to talk to. I think that I'm supposed to help you do something. And I can't get out of here, wherever here is, until it's done.

"Well, what am I supposed to do? I'll just get it done, and you can move on to where ever you're supposed to go." It seemed like a reasonable enough suggestion to me, but my plan was met with an immediate obstacle that has continued, over the years, to stand in my way.

I have no idea.

This really wasn't the answer I was expecting. "Okay, let me get this straight. You're dead, but you can still talk to me. You can see and hear stuff going on around me, but not around anyone else."

Well, I can't see you that well. You're kind of hazy around the edges, and most other people are almost completely blurry. I can only recognize Gail because I can hear her voice a little. Most other voices sound like mumbling nonsense. It's really just you that's clear.

"And you think you're on some kind of mission to help me do something, but you don't have any clue what that something is. Have I got the situation right?"

As near as I can figure, yes.

"Well, that's just great. If you don't know what I'm supposed to do, how am I supposed to do it?"

I don't know, brother, but maybe this is what's supposed to happen. I've never been dead before.

"Come again?"

I think that I have to do dead what I didn't get done alive.

"I don't get it."

Listen, Mac, do you believe in fate? Or destiny? Or reincarnation?

"I don't know, Newt. I remember Gail talking about recycling souls when we were kids, but that always seemed so hokey. And after you died, you were just gone. I guess I never wanted to think about what might have happened to you afterward."

Well, think about it now. What did you think happened to me when I died? Did you think I went to heaven and became an angel? Did you think I just stopped existing when my body died, that a few ashes were all that was left of me?

"I guess I thought you went to heaven. I'm not really sure."

Well, Mac, give it some thought, Goddamnit! This is eternity we're talking about. My spirit! My peace!

"Well, I guess you didn't go to hell for taking the Lord's name in vain like Grandpa Dixon said you would."

I think that you never lose the knack of driving your family crazy, no matter how long it's been since you've seen them, no matter what their metaphysical state because Newt really lost it then.

You know, I think I would rather spend the rest of eternity looking into the great nothing that's all around me than help you so much as wipe your stupid nose. You don't deserve any help. You're there studying goddamn French, smoking and feeling and just being fucking alive. And you sit there and tell me you never even thought of what happened to me. That I must not be in hell. Maybe I am in hell, and this is what it is for me, stuck with only a physically and mentally underdeveloped companion—a selfish, scrawny little jerk like you.

I wasn't sure, but I thought I heard sniffling. My guilt was overwhelming. I tried to explain. "God, I'm sorry, Newt. It's just been so weird since you died. Gail's this other person now. She's started dating again, and she won't get off my back about how I should try to fit in better. The kids at school look at me funny, like I've got a big burn scar covering my face or something. I can't seem to get along with anyone. It's all just so hard. And then you show up and start talking, and I'm supposed to just say, 'Okay, let's just pretend this is normal and figure out what I'm supposed to do.' Like everyone talks to dead people, and it's no big deal. I don't know what's going on. How should I?"

I was crying now, thinking how I'd like to crawl under the bed, or just call for Gail and confess everything that had happened in the last hours. And then, as if on cue, Gail knocked on the door.

"Mac, are you sure you're okay? I keep hearing you talking."

When I heard her voice, I knew that I wouldn't tell her anything. I couldn't get past the feeling that she'd abandoned me when I needed her most. My peevish tone broke out as I hid the distress in my voice. "I told you already. I'm fine. Just leave me alone."

I heard the sigh and then the sound of her footsteps receding down the hall. There was a sharp click as she closed her bedroom door.

Always the first born son, Newt was quick to come to Gail's defense. *Jeez, Mac, give the woman a break. She's doing the best she can.*

"Hah! Yeah, right." I grabbed the blanket off my bed and went to sit by the window, wrapped up in my homemade cocoon. I lit a cigarette and stared at the reflection of the street lights on the snow. Newt was talking, but I wasn't really listening anymore. He kept bringing up Gail and how hard she was trying. How hard it must be for her. After a while, I got sick of listening.

"Look, Newt, I'm tired of hearing how hard this is for Gail. I took care of her. I know what she was like after you died. I also know that nobody seems to care about how hard it is for me. I don't give a shit how hard things are for Gail. She can rot in her pathetic little world of cloth swatches and paint samples and dorky, middle-aged jerks pretending to like me so they can get in her pants. I don't think I care much anymore how hard it's been for Gail. Now, this has been a very weird night for me, and I'm tired. I'm going to bed. If this isn't a hallucination, I'll talk to you tomorrow."

Sleep didn't come quickly to me. Newt carried on for a while, but my stubbornness outlasted his, and his voice eventually tapered off into a dry whisper like leaves rustling in an alley. I tried to clear my mind, but Newt's words kept creeping into my thoughts. Eventually, I fell into a desperate sleep, filled with exhausting dreams of lightening and skeletons.

I woke up the next morning groggy, with little pebbles in my eyes and the dry scratchy sting of too much nicotine rummaging at the back of my throat. The first minutes I was awake were the last peaceful ones I would have for a while. Then, it all came back to me. In a nightmare of flashback, I remembered the previous night's conversation with the dead and shook my head until it started to pound. In the bright white light of day, the impossibility of what had happened in the night was a black smudge of contrast. Just as my mind was clearing enough to form an explanation for what I had experienced—the imagination was a powerful thing after all, and I had been freaked out by the stress of my relationship with Gail, and school was turning into a big headache—

Morning, little brother. Time for school.

"I guess this means one of two things—either I'm crazy and desperately need help, or I'm not and things are much different all of a sudden."

You're not crazy, Mac.

"How do you know? You're dead."

You're just going to have to trust me. You are not crazy.

And because he was the only reliable source I had, I believed him.

Chapter 11

So began my other world relationship with my brother. In the beginning, he was always hanging around, mouthing off. I couldn't get any privacy. Every time I turned around, there was Newt—figuratively speaking, of course—with his running commentary on the happenings of my life. He talked about Gail and me. He talked about whatever prospective papa Gail was currently parading before me. He talked about school. He talked about the future. He talked about girls. He never shut up. It was like he was the color guy on the sports broadcast of my life. He made suggestions about what I should wear. He made suggestions about what girls I should ask out. He suggested teams and clubs for me to join. It didn't take a rocket scientist to figure he was trying to recapture his glory days before the big fry.

On top of listening to his constant blathering, I had the unenviable task of trying to hide the fact that I was talking to my dead brother. The first few months were really rough. I kept forgetting that no one else could hear him. We'd discovered that I didn't need to vocalize my responses to him. I could pretty much think something in his general direction, and he would get it. But telepathic conversation is a hard skill to get used to. Talking is habit forming, and rewiring my brain to have a silent conversation didn't come easily or naturally to me. At first, I would just respond to him out loud wherever I was. Just picture the school cafeteria at lunch: me, in line, waiting for my ritual sustenance of fries and jello; Newt, in my ear, big brothering me about all the crappy food I ate. Well, it had been a strange and difficult couple of months having this voice whispering in my ear all the time. Who could blame me for flipping out?

"Could you just shut up, and let me eat in peace, just once! Christ, it's like having Gail whispering in my ear all fucking day long. I didn't ask you to come along and serve as my personal nutritionist. I don't need or want your advice, opinions or input. Now fuck off!"

The sniveling behind me distracted me from my tirade. I looked back to see one of the cheerleaders—decked out in pom poms and pigtails—the giant G on her sweater heaving with barely contained sobs. The room was a crypt, and apparently, I was the deceased because everyone had their eyes on me. I could feel my face coloring to that most hated shade of red as I stuttered out an apology.

"I wasn't…I didn't mean…I mean…I wasn't talking to you. I was talking to myself. It didn't…I didn't mean to say that out loud. It's…sorry."

I stumbled out of the cafeteria trying not to meet anyone's eye, and in my ears, I could hear the sound of my name being scratched down on the counselor's list of things to do. At least I could hear that until the sound of Newt's laughter drowned it out.

"Newt, do you have to be in my face every second of the day? How am I supposed to explain that one? Are you trying to screw my life up on purpose? Is this all part of your mission to help me?"

Mackie, don't blame me for this. You just have to pay closer attention.

Remember what I said about the timeless ability to thoroughly annoy your family members? Newt hadn't lost his touch either. "Pay closer attention? How about this—you have to get lost, Newt!"

C'mon, Mac, it's not my fault things are the way they are. It's not like this is that much fun for me, either.

"Yeah, well that was obvious from the roaring laughter coming out of your dead mouth. Just leave me alone. I'm not interested in your little mission. Find your own way out of limbo, brother." With that, I stalked out of the school to the parking lot. Unfortunately, you can't outrun the dead. Newt kept badgering me about destiny and eternity.

Look, Mac, as much as you may hate it, you can't walk away from this. I can't just sail away. Don't you think I would if I could? Do you have any idea how boring it is in eternity? There's nothing here. There's no one here. It's bad enough that I'm dead. I got screwed out of a perfectly good life. It's gone—all gone. You don't have a goddamn clue what this is like. So keep your self pity and your righteousness. At least you're alive.

So, there I was standing in the parking lot of my high school. I'd just humiliated myself in front of most of the school population, and my dead brother was bitching at me about how boring death is. I felt like I was being swallowed by an enormous snake, and the digestion process was just beginning. There's nothing like the sensation of being completely trapped to make you freak out.

I started shouting at Newt. Really shouting—out loud with absolutely no reservations. Like in the cafeteria, but with way more volume. I think the clinical term for it is hysteria. "I didn't ask for this, Newt. You're the one who deep fried yourself. You're the stupid one here, not me. You got yourself into this, and you can just fester and rot for all I care. I wouldn't care if vultures were ripping out your eyes right now. I want you to get as far away from me as possible. This whole thing is too weird for me. It's just too much! Now, piss off."

I unlocked the door of my car, got in, and started the engine. While it was warming up, there was a tap on my window. I lifted my head off the steering wheel to see the face of Mr. Green staring at me with an expression of great consternation on his liberal, social welfare state face.

"Thanks a pile, Newt. I really wanted some more conflict in my day. How do you propose I explain this?"

Hurt and retaliatory, Newt was curt with his answer. *I thought you didn't want my help, Mac.*

"You're right. I don't need you. I can handle this myself."

I stared back at Green, attempting my best innocent smile. *Okay, he's either going to bust me for cutting school, or he's going to want to know why I've been standing in the middle of the parking lot, shouting at nobody.* Did you ever feel like your life had become a Salvador Dali painting? I fully expected the snow to turn into liquid mercury as Mr. Green's face started to warp into the face of a melting grandfather clock.

As calmly as I could, I rolled down my window, resisting the urge to put the car into gear and speed away into the city for a reality break. "Hi, Mr. Green. Something wrong? You don't look so good."

"I might say the same of you, Mac. Not planning to attend the afternoon classes today?"

"Well, actually I'm not feeling all that great, so I thought I'd just go home and…" I let the sentence trail off. It was a lame excuse, and I was too tired to think of a better one.

"Maybe you ought to come back inside for a few minutes. I'd like to have a word with you in my office."

Super. This was exactly the kind of thing I was looking for. I kept looking around for a ref to call interference and send Green to the penalty box. As surreal as the whole day was turning out though, that was just too much to hope for.

I reluctantly got out of the car and followed the caring and concerned lope of Guidance Green back into the cinder block haven of Griffith High School. Walking into his office, I had the distinct impression that I was not going to enjoy this next magical interlude in my day.

"Have a seat, Mac. I'll be right with you."

He shut the door and left me to wait, surrounded by pictures of baby animals and posters about drug abuse. On the bookshelf to my right were volumes on child psychology, addiction recovery, career planning. It was a self help nirvana. I looked at the titles—"Teens in Trouble: How to See Them Through" and "Effective Parenting and The New Freud"—while canvassing my weary brain for ideas and excuses to explain my outbursts. I was just forming a clever one about a play I was writing in my spare time when Green walked into the office carrying what I presumed to be my file.

"Mac, I've just been looking at your file."

Why is it that whenever teachers talk about your file, they appear to be discussing the FBI dossier compiled on your subversive activities? I took a peek at mine once. It was full of grades and aptitude tests. It's not like it revealed some evil plan to fire bomb the school, but whenever they bring up the file, you know they're convinced you're some kind of counter intelligence terrorist.

Green stared at me as though waiting for some kind of response. I didn't have one to give him, so I just sat there staring back at him.

Finally, after several pregnant minutes, Green broke the heavy silence that surrounded us. "I want you to know, first of all, that you're not in any kind of trouble here."

I was quick to jump to my feet. "Perfect, then I can go?" I was halfway to the door before he shot down that idea in a barrage of counselor-speak.

74

"Not just yet. Sit down, Mac. I want to discuss some of the behaviors I've been hearing about the last few weeks. I'll be frank, Mac. I'm concerned about you. Your tests indicate that you're highly motivated and quite creative. You've scored well on all your aptitude tests, and yet over the past few weeks, we've seen a substantial decline in attendance. I've had complaints from your teachers that you are not turning in your assignments, that you've stopped responding in class, and that you've cut yourself off from most of the other students. Then, there is the issue of the display in the cafeteria today, not to mention the outburst I saw in the parking lot a few minutes ago. I wonder if you have anything to say that would explain the way you've been acting."

I looked hard at Green, trying to imagine what he would say if I told him the truth. I couldn't imagine him embracing the idea that I had been talking to my dead brother. I decided at that moment that I wasn't going to give him the opportunity to start practicing his therapy on me. The best offense was a good defense, or something like that, so I countered his question with some standard teen stuff. "Um, not really. I'm just going through a stage, I guess."

"I see. A stage." He looked over his glasses at me, nodding. He was writing notes in my file as he was talking to me. The whole thing just reeked of psychotherapy. I kept expecting him to ask me if I was dreaming about sailing ships and Greek tragedies.

"Well, Mac, I think that you're not being entirely truthful about your situation. Are you having trouble at home?"

I let out an audible sigh and shook my head, knowing full well that this was going to be a difficult situation to talk myself out of. "No more than anyone else, I guess. You know how it is, Mr. Green. Parents can be a real drag sometimes."

If I was lucky, Green would be satisfied when I blamed the whole thing on Gail, and at worst, I'd have to spend a few hours with a family therapist. Green wasn't that easily fooled, though.

"That's so, Mac, but the fact is that your mother has been in contact with us, wanting to know how you're doing here. It seems she's concerned about you, too. She says that you've started talking to yourself, having animated conversations, laughing out loud at nothing. Mac, this is very serious. I know you've had a hard time since you lost your brother. Grieving can be a long and difficult process, but we must know when it's time to ask for help. Now, I need you to be completely honest with me. Are you using drugs?"

I burst out laughing right there. It didn't do much for my case. He looked up from my file and raised an eyebrow in my direction. "Something funny, Mac?"

"No, sir. I just didn't expect that question, that's all."

"So, you're not involved in drugs." He was scribbling furiously.

"Nope. I mean I've tried pot and stuff, but the only drug I'm using is nicotine. I know I shouldn't, but it's better than being a crack head."

"So, you're not a regular drug user?"

"Nope."

"Mac, who were you talking to in the cafeteria?" Out of nowhere, as if to catch me off guard and trick me into honesty. I was on to him though, watching my step as though I was surrounded by quicksand.

"Myself. I was just talking to myself."

"Really, and in the parking lot?" He seemed decidedly unconvinced, but I didn't have anything else to offer up in the way of an excuse. Besides, it was almost true.

"Same thing. I've just got a lot on my mind right now. Sometimes I need to say stuff out loud to get it straight in my head. I know it seems weird, but..."

"Can you tell me what's going on, Mac? I'd like to help." His sincerity was overwhelming, and, for a moment, I thought I might tell all, get all my cards on the table and see if Mr. Green could make more than a dead man's hand out of what I held. And then, just before I answered, I saw the corners of his mouth turn up in the faintest hint of a victory smile, as though he was pulling one over on me, and I knew in that moment that he wasn't to be trusted.

"Uh, well, it's kind of personal, Mr. Green." I knew he wasn't going to go for this non-answer, but I was determined to keep my secret. Green wasn't buying any of my bullshit, and I was running out of ways to stall him. I could feel the blade slide closer to my neck every second I sat there.

"Everything that's said in this office stays here, Mac. It's all strictly confidential."

"I'm sure it is, but I'd still rather not talk about it."

"Mac, why are you being so uncooperative?"

"I'm not trying to be. I just don't have anything to say."

"Okay, I can see we're not getting anywhere here." Whew. Safe at last. "What I'm going to do is have a long chat with your mother about this. And then the three of us can sit down and discuss this situation together. Maybe we can work out a solution. You don't have to feel helpless here, Mac. There are people here who care about you and want to help you."

Not for the first time in my short life, I wished I was dead. I sat there listening to Green go on about my well being and how it was important to share feelings and emotions, especially when I was troubled, and I thought that it would be nice to sink into some eternally blissful sleep where parents and teachers weren't breathing down my neck, where I could do what I liked and not be hassled by anyone. And then I remembered what Newt had said. I wasn't talking about being dead, I was talking about being free, and, according to Newt, death wasn't freedom, it was boredom. So, there I was again—trapped. And you know how a trapped animal acts. Believe me, being human doesn't exempt us from the laws of nature.

After years of looking back at the next part of this conversation, I realize now that shutting up would have been the best thing for me to do. If I had only just kept my mouth shut, things would have turned out much better. Unfortunately, I wasn't that smart, and I'd had more than enough lecturing, caring, and concern from everyone. I told Green he could talk to Gail all he wanted, but I certainly wasn't going to be a part of that conversation. Then I told him that I wasn't interested in his help. I think the words I used were "Mind your own goddamn business, you meddling faggot." We had our suspicions about the sexuality of the skeletons hiding in Mr. Green's closet. After telling him that, I got up and stalked out of his office. I slammed the door so hard I heard the picture frames rattling. I left him sitting in his chair, his mouth slightly open and shoulders slumped forward, shaking his head with hurt surprise and the bitter disappointment that failure leaves.

I sprinted out of the school. I was at a dead run three steps out of Green's office, and I didn't stop until I got to the car. The scene was playing out well in my head. Misunderstood teenager storms out of school, jumps in his Mustang, and hauls ass out of the parking lot racing toward destiny at incredible speed. The next time he's seen in this piece of shit town is after he's gone on to fame and glory as a

Nobel Prize winning chemist or football star or some other glorious thing. Reality was not quite so generous with me, though. I drove a '78 Dodge Valiant. It was winter, so I had to let the car warm up for ten minutes before the oil started to liquefy in the crank case. And I really had no desire to rush into a destiny I didn't have a clue about. All I wanted to do was get far, far away from where I was. I'd stunned Mr. Green thoroughly enough to keep him out of the parking lot while I made my getaway. He was just walking out the door as I was pulling away. As stupid as I was, I actually believed that I had gotten out scot free. I laughed out loud at my own cleverness.

"What do you think of that, Newt? I managed to handle that situation, didn't I?"

Oh yeah, you handled it, all right. I'm not really related to you, am I? I know you weren't adopted, but maybe I was. That would explain it. I can't possibly be a blood relative of someone this stupid. This must be a mistake.

"Come on, Newt. That was great. Did you see the expression on Green's face when I called him a fag? Pure comedy. He was so stunned, he probably forgot what we were talking about in the first place. I'm home free."

You really are stupid. Don't you think your little outburst is going to give Green more ammunition? I'll bet you ten bucks he's on the phone with Gail right now. When you get home, you are going to be in it my friend. You've really screwed yourself now.

You see, I never really considered that Green would actually call Gail. Newt was right; I was stupid. That left me driving around wondering what I was going to do next. I certainly wasn't going to go home right away. I couldn't. I wasn't going to set myself up for yet another meaningless confrontation with Gail, but I didn't know what to do next. I just kept thinking that Newt was right. I'd really messed up. Gail was going to go into hyper flip after she talked to Green. I drove around and around, trying to come up with an explanation. A plan. Anything. I pulled into a gas station to top up the vapors I'd been driving on, and that's when I really lost it. The gas guy came to the window, and I just sat there staring at him. I couldn't move. After a couple of seconds, he rapped on the window. I could hear him talking, all muffled like he was speaking through layers and layers of cloth. I couldn't answer him. I couldn't roll down the window. I was frozen by the thought that if I talked to this guy, I wouldn't be able to stop. Everything was going to spill out. I dug in my pocket for some cash to make him go away. Five dollars. All I needed to do was give him five dollars. Then, I'd get my gas, and he'd stop looking at me like he knew I was crazy. Just as I got the window down, Newt started.

Mac, you need to get a hold of yourself.

I started screaming. Pounding the steering wheel. Bill or Bob or whatever miscellaneous name was sewn onto buddy's coveralls got the full brunt of my rage. Somehow, in the confusion of the moment, I got it in my head that he was my brother. I looked at his pimply face and saw my own brother smiling, telling me to calm down and suddenly, I wanted to kill him. I wanted to send him back to a place where I couldn't hear him anymore. I smashed him with the door of my car, grinding the handle into his thigh, and then took off at full speed. I was swinging the car around to take a run at this poor guy when I lost control of the car. I began to slide on the ice unable and unwilling to slow down or stop. Suddenly, I saw the light of police cars in my mind. The shiny boots of the cop who had come to tell my mother that my father was dead flashed in my eyes before I saw the wall of concrete hurtling toward me. The impact of metal against cement brought me to a sudden and rather uncomfortable stop. I lurched forward against the steering wheel and felt the wind go out of my body. Then everything was black. The last thing I remember thinking was that I would finally have some peace and quiet. I was due for a nice break from everything that was going on.

The next few hours are hazy in my memory. They gel and dissipate whenever I try to pin down what happened next. I know what the cops say, and I know what my car looked like, but I can't get a picture in my head that doesn't jump around in and out of focus. I remember waking up in a darkened room to find a tube in my arm, telling a nurse that I was going to straighten everything out. I just needed to talk to Newt for a minute. Then, I was unconscious again.

Ah, the blissful sleep of the unconscious. Personally, I think unconsciousness is a completely underrated state of mind. What's so bad about sleeping and having someone attend to all of your basic needs? You're not troubled with the tedium of conversation, you don't have to work, and you certainly don't have to find a way to convince everyone around you that you're not insane. I'm pretty sure that the 34 hours I spent without the full use of my brain were the happiest I'd had since Newt died. The problem is that the rest of the world thinks that this is a most unfortunate circumstance for a human being, so they work non stop to try to bring you back to consciousness, whether you're ready for it or not.

Chapter 12

So, I was brought back. And then the real fun began. Gail, advised by the psych ward at the hospital, invited Dr. Makken, a self-proclaimed healer of the mind, to enter the picture. And then the two of them, telling me that everything would be fine. Gail held my hand and looked matronly. She was wearing a blue shirt that day with little embroidered flowers on the pockets. She sat beside me in Dr. Makken's office at the Lynwood Centre for Mental Health, nodding in agreement with everything that the doctor said. I just needed some time and some help to get over Newt's death. And for a while, I believed them. I saw all those degrees and awards all over his office, and I sank back into his puffy sofa, relaxing for the first time in many months. I wasn't alone anymore.

I believed that I really was crazy. I was relieved, actually. It was so nice to have everything out in the open, to stop hiding the fact that I was nuts. I practically ran into the psych ward. And then I saw what it was all about. The bars on the windows, the leather straps over my wrists and ankles at night, fastened tight to the bed so that I couldn't attempt another suicide—what they thought I was doing that day at the gas station. They thought I was trying to kill myself. I should have left them with that misconception. When they discovered that I was trying to kill my brother, I started visiting that dark room where they zapped me time and again to wipe out the memory of Newt's voice ringing in my head. Traumas with electricity seem to run in my family. Believe me, the irony hasn't escaped me. Neither has the memory of what it was like to have that plastic bit shoved in my mouth to keep me from severing my own tongue when they flipped the switch. I can still taste it, sour like the dreams of so many destroyed minds.

And the smell—stale urine and disinfectant mingled with the scent of fear that oozed out of every pore of every inmate in the place. I get wafts of that smell in the prison some days. It slides under the door of our office and slithers toward my olfactory system, undermining all the work I've done to forget what it was like to have no control over anything in my life. Even now, years later, when I walk into a bathroom that's just been cleaned, I have to work hard to swallow the gag that begins automatically in the back of my throat when the odors from that time come flooding off the porcelain surfaces. The smell of Lynwood got into my hair and clothes and hung onto me like a child clutching a blanket. I washed my hands so often that I had to spend an entire session with Dr. Makken attempting to convince him that I was not an obsessive–compulsive.

I spent five months at Lynwood, and as dark as I thought my life had become hearing the voice of my dead brother, I was surprised at how much further into darkness I could go.

The first couple of months were only totally horrible, providing you didn't consider the pharmaceuticals that helped to block out everything that was real as well as everything that wasn't. Oh, and let's not forget my fellow patients, my comrades in arms, who would rock for six solid hours, clutching themselves in an embrace that would strangle most mammals; or emit high-pitched buzzes, mimicking the white noise if a TV; or scream at regular intervals throughout the day and night, long anguished wails brought on by the pain inflicted on them by their tortured minds.

I eased my own plight considerably by accepting the fact that I was delusional without too much hesitation. That really should have tipped them off. I would have been a much more believable loon if I was in denial all the time. Isn't that what Catch 22 is all about? You say you're crazy, so you're clearly sane. You say you're sane, so you must be crazy. The shrinks at Lynwood had obviously never read Heller. I just kept agreeing with them, and they kept patting themselves on the back for a job well done.

An average day at Lynwood would begin with the line for meds. The twenty or so inmates of my ward would line up outside the drug cage waiting for their little paper cups of dope that calmed them down or perked them up or whatever state it was that the doctors thought they should induce. Then, it was off to the cafeteria for a hearty meal of oat-flavored gruel. No sugar allowed though because it interfered with the drugs. If you were a good little inmate, you would then get to go to the library or watch TV or sit in the common room with the other good weirdoes until it was time for daily therapy. If you were a naughty inmate who didn't eat all your gruel, say, or wouldn't swallow your meds, you got to spend the day with one of the electrical technicians or in a special room all by yourself with an attractive, graying jacket that tied up behind your back. I spent most of my first two weeks by myself without privileges because I was hoarding my medication. After seeing what I had to contend with in terms of my fellow sufferers, I thought it was wiser to be clear headed than in the near comatose state the drugs brought on.

I soon discovered that misuse of meds was a great and terrible sin, and amassing a stock of them even worse in the bad behavior category. The nurses naturally saw this as potentially dangerous. I tried to make it clear with rational talk and logical explanations that I just didn't need to take all those pills every day, but the staff didn't see it that way. I was left with the choice of being treated as a malcontent with no hope of ever getting back the use of my arms again or swallowing what was given like an obedient little maniac. The decision wasn't that difficult. Besides, when you're surrounded by people trying to pluck out their eyelashes because they are convinced that caterpillars are growing over their eyes, a little pharmaceutical high really takes the edge off.

It also didn't take me long to decide that therapy treatments were considerably easier than shock treatments. Dr. Makken was pleased when I started showing so much enthusiasm for the sessions. An average one would go something like this:

"Mac, do you think you have a problem?"

"Absolutely. Normal people don't have dead people talking to them, do they?"

"No, they don't. But it's important that you really understand what has happened to you. I notice how you phrased your response. It implies that you really believe that the dead can speak from the grave. Is that what you think?"

Do you see the kind of thing I was putting up with? Psychiatrists are very sneaky characters. Some people prefer the term perceptive, but I think sneaky is far more accurate. They're always messing about with context. Like the right-wing Bible-toting politicians who want to ban *Of Mice and Men* after having read two paragraphs that appear somewhere in the middle of the book. None of them are willing to admit that more often than not a train entering a tunnel is just where the tracks go.

"No, that's not what I meant. Are you trying to trick me?" Makken would always back down when I started to show suspicion. Trust was so important. Whenever I felt like I needed a little boost, I would narrow my eyes and accuse him of trying to manipulate me. It worked like a charm.

"Of course I'm not trying to trick you, Mac. I just want you to be completely honest with me. Now, I'll ask you again. Do you think you understand what's happened here?"

"I understand it all right. I flipped out."

"Well, I don't know if I would use that term, but I understand what you mean. Do you still believe that your brother was communicating with you from the grave?"

"Nope." He was always frustrated when I chose one word answers. I had very few weapons at my disposal but passive aggression was a good one.

"Would you care to expand on that at all?"

"Not really. That sums it up, doesn't it? I believe what you said about displaced guilt and grieving and all that. It makes sense. A lot more sense than believing that Newt was really talking to me."

He hesitated before answering. "Right, well, just as long as you really understand it." Dr. Makken tried hard to hide his skepticism from me, but it always hovered around the surface of our dialogues, as though he was never quite sure if I was serious or not.

"Yep, perfectly. I'm quite relieved to know I'm crazy, actually. It's much easier to accept than the possibility that Newt's voice was real."

And so on.

Then came the sessions getting into the nitty gritty of it all.

"So, Mac, how are you feeling today?"

"Pretty good, Dr. Makken. You?" The truth was that I'd felt awful since I'd been committed to Lynwood. I was lonely and lost and hurt beyond belief that Gail would allow her only living son to be ripped apart in this way. I felt so isolated, and nothing anyone had said to me made me feel they were worthy of my trust. So, I played the therapy game as best I could, trying not to let my cynicism get the better of my responses as I erected the walls I needed to protect myself from the probing questions of my doctor.

"I'm fine, Mac." He smiled his oily smile, watching me closely with his deep set eyes, trying to assess my sincerity. "Have you heard anything from Newt since we last talked?"

"Yeah," I was about to go on but was interrupted.

"And what did Newt's voice tell you?" I could see the excitement on his face and was sorely tempted to tell him that Newt had told me to start wearing a hat made of tinfoil and pipe cleaners, but I knew the sanity minded doctor would take this much too seriously. I didn't think I'd be able to convince him that it was a joke, so I gave him a more moderate and near truthful answer instead.

"He said the usual stuff about being real and about how I shouldn't let myself be convinced that I was crazy."

I thought Dr. Makken was going to start rubbing his hands together and shout out "hot diggity," but he stayed pretty calm. "And how did you respond to hearing your brother's voice?"

"I did what you said. I told myself that this is just a way of dealing with the loss of my brother and that it wasn't really his voice I was hearing. It's a projection of my memory…" Blah, blah, blah…this kind of therapeutic drivel revolted me as much then as it does now. I'm sure it's very effective for lots of people, but personally, it leaves me cold.

"And how did that feel?"

"Okay."

"Did you continue to hear his voice after that?" His pen scratched words onto the legal pad that rested on his knee while we talked.

"Nope, it pretty much went away."

"Can you quantify pretty much?" His eyes remained trained on the paper as he spoke as if he was barely interested in my answer.

"His voice sort of trailed off into a whisper, and then stopped."

The good doctor looked up at me suddenly. "Mac, are you being completely honest with me?"

"Of course, Dr. Makken. What would be the point of lying? I don't want to be crazy forever. I'd like to get out of here and get on with my life."

"Well, you see, Mac, that's really part of the problem. I know how smart you are. Did you know the school sent over your file?"

"No." The first chance I got, I was going to burn that file.

"It's really quite interesting. Your tests indicate that you're very bright. From our conversations, I'd have to say I agree. I think I know what you're capable of, Mac. I want you to realize that you can't just admit that you have a problem and walk out of here. I want to make sure that you know you can trust me. Truth is the most important part of your therapy."

"I am telling the truth, Dr. Makken. Do you think I would admit to hearing his voice at all if I was just trying to get out of here? I'm telling you his voice just faded away and then disappeared."

And the funny thing was that Newt really did stop talking to me. Things were progressing nicely; I was a good boy, so they let me sleep without being strapped down. The shock treatments were over. I towed the party line, mostly because I really believed it. I'd even celebrated a very bizarre birthday in the big house, which, at least in Dr. Makken's eyes, was a kind of tangible day of reckoning. Even for me, it was something like an epiphany.

Actually, the whole thing was like one of those three dimensional pictures that you have to stare at in a certain way to see the image—otherwise it's just a bunch of blue and red squiggles that make your head hurt after a while. I mean there was a kind of subtext to the whole thing. Normal birthday things transpired. All the nurses came and sang to me. Gail baked a cake. Presents were given. But in the background were all these strange images. The lith-heads and the attempted suicides, the MPDs and the compulsives; they were all walking around on the periphery of my world, part of it, but a step removed. Who couldn't notice the emptiness of my birthday in the midst of their vacant eyes? That was my three dimensional picture: the wasteland that life is for so many people. It made me happy that I wasn't like them. That even at my worst, I was never as bad as that. It made me happy that I could use the past tense. I had been crazy, but now I was well.

And then Newt started talking again.

Mac? Can you still hear me? Please answer me. I really need you.

His whisper, faint and raspy, reached for me at night, before the meds kicked in. I could hear it coming at me through the TV in the mornings. I ignored it. I pretended it was the wind, or the sound of the nurse's rubber soled shoes on the linoleum outside my room. I did everything I could to block out the sound of my only brother's voice telling me again and again how he needed me.

Chapter 13

Loneliness does strange things to people. It's like a wart on your index finger that you try to hide. At first, you're just embarrassed at its existence. You keep your hands in your pockets, and you wear gloves. You use your middle finger, flipping the bird every time you point at something. Then, you become obsessed with trying to get rid of it. You rub creams on it. And it comes back. You try to slice it off with razor blades. And it comes back. And no matter what you do, it's there, everyday, reminding you that you're deformed. Sooner or later, you bring it out to be examined, often only to be told that it's nothing to worry about; it will just go away on its own. Only it doesn't really go away. Even when it disappears from the surface, it's still there, buried just under the skin, burned into you. Loneliness is just the same. It burns a deep scar into you that won't ever fade entirely from sight. I'd known loneliness before I went to Lynwood. I'd felt it each day that Newt was not alive, and Gail was not there to turn to. And I felt it in all its stark depths during the long nights I spent in Lynwood. It was the blanket on my bed, wrapping me in a cocoon so tight, my chest ached.

I was only 17, after all, and I had virtually no friends. I mean I didn't have very many before I was checked into Casa Crazy, but I could count on one hand the number of people who stuck around after my admission. And even those guys were barely more than smoking buddies at school. I'd alienated pretty much everyone after Newt started flapping his jaws, so no one was stampeding to Lynnwood in droves to see me. In fact, the only person I ever spoke to other than Gail and Dr. Makken—my apology to Mr. Green doesn't really count because I was guilted into the whole conversation; I won't go into details; he blubbered like he had just won the Nobel Prize for counseling—was another patient.

Her name was Audrey Jackson. She was 23, amazingly brilliant, but fairly neurotic. At least, neurotic enough to attempt suicide by running herself through with a car antenna. This was a textbook example of the ever popular suicide attempt as cry for help. Even she admitted it was ridiculous. I mean—a car antenna? At least she cut the little ball off the end of it so it would puncture the skin. But really, who runs themselves through anymore? It was a Shakespearean attempt at tragedy, but it came out more like Mel Brooks absurdity. As I got to know her though, I realized that Audrey was a lot less crazy than everyone thought.

The best thing about Audrey, besides her sense of humor, was that she was perfectly willing to show anyone her scars. She'd chosen a couple of great spots to pick up any radio signals she might receive after she drove home the antenna, so she generated some serious interest. The first hole was on the left side of her chest—where you might try to stab yourself in the heart if you thought you could get through the breast bone. This was actually the more superficial of the wounds she gave herself. It was a glancing blow, at best. The second was in the belly, just below the navel, and this is the one that did most of the damage. It wasn't a life-threatening stab wound, but she made sure to drive her weapon in deep enough to tear up her intestines a little. She had some trouble with digestion, but other than that, her attempts at permanent fatal damage failed outright.

Audrey Jackson's were the first live breasts that I ever saw. I'd been at Lynwood for about five weeks. I'd finished with the twice weekly shock therapy, and had fully mastered my short-term memory again. Now, it was just the meds and the daily sessions with Dr. Makken. The gruesome boredom that set in became a kind of routine for me. Most mornings, after breakfast, I would sit in the day room watching TV, waiting for my call to be escorted through the cage out of the residential wing into the treatment wing to recline on the sofa in Dr. Makken's office where I would drive him crazy by dropping cigarette ashes all over his carpet. He kept an ashtray in there, but for the sake of exerting some bit of control over my life, I chose not to use it.

Thursday was visiting day when all the parents and loved ones of the inmates would come to spend a couple of hours, proving to themselves that they had done the right thing by committing their children to a state facility. Gail was no exception. She came promptly every Thursday at 2:00. She would meet with the great Dr. Makken for twenty minutes or so to discuss my progress and then spend an hour or two with her only remaining family member. Every time I saw her forced cheerfulness and pasted on smile, I wanted to cry. I realized how far from being a family we had gotten. I didn't trust her, and I didn't trust the doctor enough to tell him that things were totally wrong here. My mother would never have let this happen. She would have believed me and tried to help me. She would have held me close crying while I cried, consoling me as I finally got to let go of my brother. Instead, she appeared each Thursday with a magazine or a book as her offering of peace. She would chat mindlessly about the news of the day or about the latest recipe she'd tried out on the date du jour. She could have been visiting her Alzheimer stricken grandmother for all the real conversation we had. And each moment of each of those visits were like the bricks that made up the top most layers of my walls. She opened her mouth and slathered on mortar and masonry until the barricade between us was so high, we couldn't even see each other any more.

Thursdays were the worst.

Most other afternoons, I spent in the library. I used to go right back to the TV when I was done pouring out my guts in therapy, but I learned in my first week at Lynwood that afternoons were spent watching a series of soap operas with Big Bill, a six-foot-three-inch fire plug who was sent to Lynwood because he stopped speaking after his mother's car was struck broadside by a drunk driver, killing the poor woman instantly and leaving behind a son who was already a little behind to begin with. Big Bill was very committed to his "stories." He would sit about two feet in front of the television, cross-legged on the floor, and watch with rapturous eyes the trials and tribulations of these magical people who were all so beautiful, lived in huge and fantastic homes, but who never seemed to work. Big Bill would cry great tears of agony when one of his special characters was betrayed or fell prey to some evil scheme. He rode the highs and lows of those people like they were his own flesh and blood. And God help the sorry soul who tried to change the channel while one of the stories was playing. In my second week at Lynwood, I saw Bill hurl a couch across the common room after a recovering anorexic girl tried to turn off *The Young and the Restless*. He didn't hurt her, but she never tried to change the channel again—none of us did. After I grew bored with the ups and downs of daytime drama—which took until the first commercial break—I started spending my afternoons in the library.

One Tuesday or Monday—they all looked the same after a while— I was sitting in a reading carrel, leafing through travel guides imagining myself in rugged Australia or riding an elephant in India when I heard a voice on the other side of the wood partition. "Did you know that most of the aboriginal tribes in Australia have consciously chosen to let their people die off? They are no longer reproducing."

"What?" I looked up, surprised. I didn't think anyone else even knew where the library was, let alone used it.

This face appeared over the dividing wall of the carrel. It was round, almost a perfect circle. A strand of carrot-colored hair had escaped from the rest which was pulled back into a tight ponytail. It hung down in the center of her forehead, resting on the left side of her nose, dividing her face like the bright red line of a felt marker. She kept blowing at it to keep it from blocking her vision. Every few seconds, she would extend her lower jaw a bit and blow out a quick puff, sending the hair up and out of her line of vision. It would fall back to its place between her eyes and sit for a few moments before she repeated the gesture. Again and again, I watched her blow that strand of hair out of her face. I was hypnotized by the lightness of her hair, the way it floated up and then came to rest, over and over. I put my glasses on to get a better look at this person.

"They don't have sex anymore because they want their people to die out. They can't stand to watch western society continue to rape and destroy the earth that gave them their life. Isn't that wild? You know you kind of remind me of a character from *Doonesbury* with your glasses on."

The next thing I knew, we were in a bathroom, and she was unbuttoning her shirt to show me her scars. Right there, in broad daylight, with no shame about it whatsoever. I ran my finger over the scar on her stomach and told her it reminded me of the pock marks on Newt's hands where the electricity had tried to find it's way out of his body. Audrey and I became friends in that moment. And from then on, we would meet in the library every day, making friends of the books and trying to find reasons why we shouldn't all stop reproducing, for as cynical and untrusting as I had become in the last months, Audrey was four or five years ahead of me in development.

Audrey was better therapy for me than all the well-intentioned Dr. Makkens of the world. In that strange clinical environment, we shared our darkest feelings and greatest fears. I told her all about Newt. She told me what it was like to be an only child. I complained about the random men Gail dated.

She told me all about her father's unbending determination to find fault with her. "You can't imagine the pressure of being a smart girl in a family headed by a misogynist drop out."

I had to look up the meaning of misogynist, but I didn't need a dictionary to understand what it was like to feel unworthy and ignored. "You can't imagine what it's like to be a puppet in the civil suit Gail has filed under the advice of Perry Mason, her current social obligation. Her 'special friend,' as she likes to call him, has convinced her that all this," I gestured to our surroundings, "will definitely increase the pain and suffering portion of the settlement."

We griped and consoled, and days passed as Audrey became my haven from the mundane and the frightening. We turned to each other for our real therapy sessions. We grew closer and closer until one day we stepped over the line of friendship to throw ourselves into each other as if with love, or sex, or whatever it was that we shared, we could feel whole again, untouched by the stigma of disease that we were immersed in.

The first time was in the reading room in between the two parallel lines of reading carrels. Most of the patients had lost their book privileges, and anyway, nut cases aren't generally big readers, so we had the stacks to ourselves, as we would for most of the days we spent together. Audrey had her shirt open, and I was running my fingers over her scars. She was watching me; I was watching my fingers. And then, to my unending delight, she was pushing my hand down into her pants. She was wearing loose surgical pants, the kind that have zero sex appeal, but the bonus of easy access drawstring. Actually, we were both wearing those pants. They were hospital issue.

When she kissed me that first time it was like getting another, but infinitely more pleasant, kind of shock treatment. She slid her tongue in my mouth, and I forgot where I was, who I was. I didn't exist except in that moment, knowing that this was it. I was approaching the gates of paradise, and I was prepared to slam them open with the battering ram that had conveniently developed in my own set of drawstring pants. I fumbled the knot trying to set a new record for speediest strip, but Audrey had my pants off before I could start cursing myself for screwing up the opportunity. The sex was quick, my fault, and panicked, also my fault, but Audrey was perfect that day. And every day after that.

She wasn't pretty really, but she had something about her that made you stop and wonder. Maybe it was her compulsion to exhibit her body at every opportunity, maybe it was just that she was the closest thing to sane around, comparatively speaking, of course. We spent a lot of time in bathrooms and closets; sometimes just enjoying the chance to speak freely, but often concluding in a sweaty daze of satisfaction. I was 17 — at the peak of my sexual prime — and Audrey, well, she was just primed sexually.

She had hot, sweet breath that you could taste when she exhaled. Always with the faint metallic scent that comes from taking anti-depressants and tranquilizers. I remember thinking the first time I tasted Audrey's tongue, how much it drew me back to my childhood; how it reminded me of fresh raspberries just picked off the bush and soaked in milk and sugar. I think I could have lived on just that taste forever. She was all the sustenance I had there. My only friend, and my only lover. And she was the only one who believed that Newt really was talking to me.

Chapter 14

Like I said, Audrey was brilliant. She had moved through conventional schooling at light speed, and while the trip was educational, it didn't do much for her on an emotional level. But she even understood that.

"Let me tell you something, Mac. While the human brain may be perfectly equipped to experience multiple g-force learning, the spirit is not. A lot of the time, I feel like there is too much more for me to learn, and how will I ever find the time to do it? The thought that I might miss something is too terrifying to face. That's the real reason I'm here. It doesn't have anything to do with killing myself. I just needed an excuse to get away from the world for a while. I needed time to breathe, to rest and let the other side of me catch up a bit. Besides, this is a good way to get free sedation, and, man, sometimes I just need to turn my brain off."

I held my own share of disappointment in the performance of my parental unit, felt the rabid injustice of having my father prematurely eliminated from my life, but I felt less and less hard done by as Audrey revealed the failings of her own parents. She was the product of a blue-collar bread-winning father and a meek, domestically inclined mother. They had somehow managed to combine their simple genetic codes into the unlikely product of Audrey, who knew more about genetic codes than most biologists. Her father had dropped out of his unfulfilling school experience at 16 in order to get on with the business of life. Two short years later, he was married to the woman carrying his child in her womb and little between her ears. That suited Mr. Jackson just fine. According to Audrey, her father gave new depth to the traditional father role. He didn't hold with modern thinking about ideas like equality of the sexes. He frowned on her aspirations at education, forbidding her to read anything other than what was in her curriculum. He hung up on the teachers calling to report Audrey's natural ability and heightened intelligence.

She took to smuggling books into her room, reading them by the street light that shone through her bedroom window after Mr. Jackson found her flashlight and confiscated it, saying girls had no business being bookish. "It makes them harder to marry off."

Audrey managed to snatch her education from her teachers, despite everything her father did to undermine her and keep her in a nineteenth century gender prison. She was built of pretty tough stuff. Or so they all thought. She was inspiring to watch. She knew everything. She had read everything. Philosophy and history and physics, literature and art. She was like a walking encyclopedia. Everyone kept telling me how smart my file indicated I was, but I felt barely literate next to Audrey. Before she managed to land herself in Lynwood, she was doing grad work in classics. I didn't even know what that was at the time, but she told me. She knew everything there was to know about Greek mythology. She used to read to me from the *Odyssey*, taking me to places where it wasn't so strange to speak to the dead. I can see now that this was just a warm up. Her way of preparing me for the possibility that Newt was talking to me.

She asked me questions all the time. "What was it like to grow up with one parent?"

"How did you feel when Newt died?"

"How often did you want to kill your mother for naming you Macbeth?"

"Did you ever go out to the plant? To the spot where it all happened?"

"What's your favorite book?"

"Why do you suppose we're here?"

And so on. I always got the feeling that she was never satisfied with the answers I gave her, like she was expecting more. Sometimes she would start glaring at me, throwing her arms up in frustration, particularly when we discussed Newt.

95

"What do you mean you never considered what happened to him after he died? My God, Mac, are you really this stupid? This is the single most important thing there is to contemplate. Why are we here? What is our purpose? Where do we go after this? It's THE issue. Everything else is just filler."

"You know, Newt said the same thing to me when he first started talking to me. Of course, he was a little more insulted that I hadn't considered it. You can't really blame him, I suppose. After all, it was him that I wasn't thinking about. I mean, if he was talking to me. If it wasn't all just a figment of my imagination."

"Listen to yourself, Mac. You're not really buying into all that crap that Makken's been on about, are you?"

"Well, why not, Audrey? I mean it's ridiculous. I'm supposed to believe that I've been singled out to receive messages from my dead brother?"

"Why not you, Mac? Who is a more likely choice than his only brother? Who else was he going to talk to?"

"That's not what I meant."

"Well, what did you mean?"

"It's ridiculous that any dead person would be talking to any live person? It's not possible. The world just doesn't work that way? If it did, I certainly wouldn't be in here, would I?" I thought I'd gotten her here. I really thought I'd worked my way around her brain. Instead she just exploded into fresh ammo.

"It's not possible? The world just doesn't work that way? What makes you so certain that you have any idea whatsoever how the world works? You people make me crazy The way you try to order nature even though it's inherently chaotic. My God, look at the calendar! It's completely arbitrary. It doesn't follow the patterns that nature set out. Nature is the ultimate guidebook, and it is arrogantly and unceremoniously ignored because we can't explain it in a way that fits into a neat compartment in our tiny little brains. This isn't like understanding the principles of a steam engine, Mac. Why do you think we have a leap year every four years? Because, my ignorant friend, no one could conceive of a day with 23 and a quarter hours. Haven't you ever noticed the moon? How it changes every few weeks from full to new and back to full again? How the sun rises and sets? That's what time is about. Not the numbers on the clock or the months in a calendar. Do you know why we have twelve months in a year? It's because a couple of megalomaniac Roman emperors had to put their two cents in so they'd be remembered and revered. Surely even you've heard of Julius and Augustus Caesar. Believe me, if Germany had won World War Two, not only would the world be Jewless, there'd be a Hitlember on your calendar today. You can't honestly believe that anyone making the rules has any idea what's going on? The whole idea of trying to control and quantify nature is much more ridiculous than me poking holes in myself or in your brother talking to you from the great beyond. We don't have any idea what the universe is about, so I ask you, why can't Newt be talking to you?"

"But Audrey, if this kind of thing happened, wouldn't we have heard about it before? Don't you think that with all the people who've died over the centuries, there would be examples it?"

"Mac, you really are stupid. Look around. Read a book every now and then. The hundreds and hundreds of stories about hauntings can't all be hoaxes. Do you know how many people have reported seeing and hearing the ghost of Catherine Howard? What do you think that's all about? It's basically the same situation. The only difference is that you've been singled out by your brother for some reason."

"Who's Catherine Howard?"

"She was one of the wives of Henry VIII. He had her beheaded because he wanted to marry someone else. Look, the point is that people, lots of sane and rational people, have heard her screaming in agony and seen her strolling around since she was killed. Maybe there are certain kinds of people who are more receptive to this kind of thing, something about the energy they carry, I don't know. But I do know that not all of these people could possibly be lying. There has to be some truth in it. I don't think we can just call it mass hysteria and close the book on it."

"Right, so this whole experience is some kind of Amityville Horror show designed specifically for my pleasure? Please, give me a break."

"Don't be dense. I'm not suggesting that you should run right out and join Paranormals Are Us. What I'm saying is that we don't have any right to discount this as being unreal. I don't know if this is really happening to you or not. Only you can answer that question. But consider this in your deliberations: you can't count out the improbable, only the impossible, and while this might be totally improbable, no one, not Makken or your mom or me or even you can say for sure that this is impossible. And anyone who tells you different is getting a paycheck for doing it."

"Man, Audrey, you should be a lawyer."

She swatted me with the worn copy of Virgil she was carrying. "Shut up, Mac."

It was right about that time that Newt got going again. I felt a little like the two of them were ganging up on me to try to bring me around to their way of thinking. I even eyed Audrey suspiciously for a couple of days, wondering if maybe she wasn't hearing Newt herself.

Mac? Can you still hear me? Please answer me. I really need you.

I had been hearing his whisper but not really listening to it. I called it the trees brushing against the window cages. I convinced myself that it was the nurses at their station talking in lowered voices. But it was getting harder and harder to ignore. I didn't want to carry this secret around with me, but somewhere in the pit of my stomach, I knew his voice was real. So when I heard the sound of his voice pleading with me from whatever dark and lonely place he was in, I decided that I had to answer him.

"Yeah, Newt, I can still hear you."

I think he was grateful that I'd answered him because he didn't really say much. He stopped talking to me when I was in public, something I'm still grateful for. And, more importantly, he started thinking about getting me out of Lynwood. Between him and Audrey, I had the joint figured. We worked up a steady ruse of sanity that had Makken and Gail jumping for joy.

I cried; I yelled; I purged my feelings; I wallowed in self-pity. I even did a little muck-raking with Gail to relieve her of some guilt. I felt like I was the monkey in a two-bit organ grinder's street show, but it worked. Inside two months, I had the paper signed and was preparing to go merrily on my way with a clean bill of mental health. Truly a great triumph for the deceivers of the world. But I never could have done it without Audrey.

Audrey remained a paradox for me. I would have stayed in Lynnwood for Audrey, but instead, I left because of her. She saw the need for me to be out in the world. She saw something in me, something I've never really seen, but, in my few moments of optimism, something I suspect might still be there. It's funny, in a bad joke of fate kind of way, that she could see that something in me, but never could find it in herself.

I am a champion of guilt. Seven long years have passed, and I still carry the guilt of leaving Audrey in that place, the guilt of being smart enough to fool everyone, the guilt of Audrey's blood on my hands. I didn't think twice about leaving her there. I didn't even say goodbye to her, a fact I regretted almost pathologically after she succeeded at finding a way to end the swelling conflict between her father's ideas about her life and her own, when it was too late to say thank you or I love you or anything that would have told her how much she meant to me. After the Jackson clan had receded, after Audrey's grave had been covered with fresh earth and all that remained was the contradiction of cheerful flowers resting on her headstone, I carved my initials into the stone in rough child like letters with my pen knife. I left my mark there so she would know, if she ever cared to look, that I was out there still, trying to dodge whatever bullet fate had loaded in its chamber for me.

Gail watched me with a careful eye for weeks after Audrey's death, sure I might lose it again. She and Dr. Makken had a little tête-à-tête, thinking that I could do with a little more therapy. I'm sure they wanted to lock me up in case Audrey joined the ranks of dead people I imagined were talking to me. Dr. Makken called it a post-traumatic psychological relapse episode prevention measure. I love head doctors. They really know how to string together some 50-cent words to completely intimidate the herd. Personally, I was too busy packing to consider it.

Now, Audrey comes to me only in dreams—always the same passionate girl that she was, but my memory is kind. It wipes out the scars on her body; it erases the blood that soaked her green bathrobe after she managed to get the job done to her satisfaction. Some hospital. They let out one still hearing voices, and they keep one until she saws through her flesh and bleeds to death.

The librarian found her in the bathroom adjacent to the reading room. She had broken one of the mirrors, smashing it with her hand to get a good sized piece of glass for the task at hand. She slashed her wrists and plunged them into a sink of steaming water to encourage her blood to run more enthusiastically. Once she became too weak to stand, she slipped down onto the floor and that's where the librarian found her a few hours later. She had slumped down over herself, a copy of Ovid's *Metamorphosis* resting in her lap, soaked with blood.

I poured through that book for months looking for an answer, trying to find out what she was trying to say, but I've never been able to guess what was in her mind when she sat there on that cold tile, waiting for the last of her blood to drain out. I wonder if she couldn't bear the thought of seeing the abject disdain in her father's eyes when she accepted her next scholarship, knowing full well that he believed stoutly that she had no place in a world of real, legitimate academics. It's either that or perhaps, and me and my conscience fervently hope it's the former, our long discussions about Newt and the nature of death showed her that her curiosity about this world was superceded by what she might learn in the next. I have since bought so many copies of this last book of hers that it's almost a compulsion. Maybe it's some kind of invitation to her spirit. I wonder who Audrey's talking to.

Chapter 15

So here I am, seven long years, one failed attempt at higher learning, fifteen or so bad jobs, dozens and dozens of bottles of vodka, and thousands of cigarettes later. And where have I gotten? I managed to graduate from high school and even made a play at college. I managed to move out from under Gail's watchful eye. Between you and me, I don't think she ever really bought the whole get-out-of-the-crazy-house-free scenario. For all her faults, Gail's a pretty smart cookie. I had to move away to really beat the rap with her.

That was easy enough. Enroll in university, get some free dough from the government, find a room in student residence, and, hocus pocus, no more Gail. This plan was like the icing on the cake. Gail couldn't possibly be angry at me for wanting to continue my education. It was all she talked about for the 18 years that I'd been alive. She didn't really want to, but she had to agree that university was a good idea. And I really couldn't live at home; it's was too far to commute. Student housing it had to be.

I really did want to go to school. It was a bonus that I got to do it away from every one who had watched me go off the deep end in high school. This was the perfect opportunity to reinvent myself. I thought that I could do anything I wanted. I didn't know exactly what that was, of course, but that's what learning is all about. So, I did what pretty much every lost teenager does when they decide to climb into the ivory tower without a clue about which room they want—I entered the arts. This is a lot like test driving every car on the lot before deciding which one to go in debt for.

Of course, I didn't have to go into debt for it. Gail could easily have funded my academic venture given the hefty settlement she was awarded by the power company that owned the plant where Newt died. I didn't think she had a hope in hell of extracting a penny from the corporate nukes, but the mouthpiece she dated while I was in Lynnwood managed to squeeze them for a goodly sum. They settled out of court for a couple hundred thousand after a few threatening letters from the boyfriend's firm that used phrases like "lax security procedures" and "inadequate warning notices." He even got the award increased by using my breakdown as leverage. It feels really great to be a pawn in some legal battle that benefits everyone but you. By the time I was ready for university, the lawyer's firm had been paid handsomely, the lawyer himself had been replaced by an accountant, and the cash was all tied up in T bills and trust funds.

So, I was on my own. I got a pat on the back from the accountant and a lecture from Gail about how much more worthy I would be of my education if I took some responsibility and paid for it myself. I'm not sure where Gail got the idea that I was so irresponsible. I thought that besides the time I tried to drive my car over that gas station attendant, I had always been a pretty reliable kid. She didn't share this opinion, citing my lax attitude toward school and the irrational behavior that led to my mental health crisis. That's what we called it now: The Mental Health Crisis. I felt like a public service announcement every time she used the phrase, but I couldn't dissuade her from the reference. I suppose she got the term from Dr. Makken. It sounded a lot like him. It's either that or she got it from the social worker that came between the lawyer and the accountant. Between Gail's interpretation of my psyche and the varied and sundry men she dragged home to fill in as strong male influences in my life, I was termed irresponsible, and it was deemed that I should try to make my own way. It was going to teach me a lesson. After so many years, I'm not sure what that lesson was, but I did my best to live up to Gail's opinion that I couldn't really be trusted to straighten up and fly right.

I didn't do it intentionally. I enrolled in my courses with the excitement of a child crawling inside a refrigerator box for the first time. I was venturing into something more important than my little world and all its strange problems. Newt babbled on about higher learning and all that it held. He was a little disappointed that I hadn't gone for something more manly like business or science, but he still gets confused about whose life I'm really living. He forgets that we are not the same person. Or, more accurately, that I'm not him.

I approached the prospect of school as my salvation. It was the vehicle in which I would flee from Gail's watchful eye six days of the week. She continued to reserve Thursdays for herself, scheduling a weekly dinner together during which we could share all that was happening in our lives—read, my life. After just a few weeks, I was able to negotiate a monthly dinner calling on the heavy work load of a first year student as my hole card. She couldn't protest, and I took one step further away from her. And I enjoyed school. I really did. It was like having the chance to make myself over in surroundings that were anonymous.

The only problem with school was that everything about it made me think of Audrey. I made it through until March of that first year. I was getting good grades. I tried to let myself be helped by the memory of Audrey and her formidable intelligence, imagining what she might think about a certain book or political theorem. The practice served me well for many months. Then we started what I'd been dreading since the semester's beginning—halfway through the reading list, there it was: *Metamorphosis*. I had 12 copies of the book by then, and I certainly didn't need to read it again. There were passages I knew by heart having poured over them in my endless search for Audrey's suicide note.

The first day the professor held the book out for our initial consideration, I could almost see Audrey standing there, the small volume resting in her open hand as she offered it to me the first time. I quietly excused myself from the classroom, walked off campus, and never went back. I couldn't face it. It was too tangled up in my pain and personal suffering. I was sorry I couldn't go back. It was hard to stack that much fuel on Gail's fire, but I could better deal with her disappointment than I could deal with my guilt about Audrey.

Dropping out further estranged me from Gail. She still insisted on the monthly dinners, and she was the only person who called me with any regularity. But other than those small filial requirements, I have remained pretty much on my own. Well, except for Newt.

In all this time, I have not managed to get out from under my brother. Maybe I haven't really faced the fact that he's here for a reason, or whatever mystical jargon you'd like to apply to the situation. Newt would say he's here to help me get somewhere. Where that is, he doesn't seem to be able to pin down. How typically non-helpful. Whatever the reason, most of the time, it all sounds like so much crap that I can't bring myself to seriously contemplate the problem. I've resigned myself to having this other-worldly sidekick. I don't like it a lot of the time, but consistency is important. Besides, it has given me a tremendous edge on what to expect in the not so grand future that is death. And really, who needs a lot of people hanging around anyway?

I've cultivated solitude like Virginians cultivated tobacco. It's an art form to be alone, and it's one I've specialized in. I never intended to let anyone back inside, and I certainly didn't intend to let Rachel Strong find her way through the labyrinth of my psyche. It's mine, and she's really not invited in. No matter what I may have thought about her and her sister, the whole thing was just bad judgment on my part. A good roll in the hay but not for repetition.

I know this is my fault. I was the one who called her up out of the blue. I was the one who convinced her that I wasn't a nut job. And I was the one who arranged the meeting. It all seemed like such a good idea at the time, but I realize now that it was just bad, bad, and bad.

Chapter 16

I picked a bar downtown for my first meeting with Rachel Strong, a drab little place on 42nd street called Dodger's that I like to frequent in moments of depraved insecurity and fear; generally, two or three times a week. I like it because it's cheap, and I can always count on a smoke-filled room to provide maximum comfort for me. The owner, Steve Riles, opened the place in 1978. Steve is from Seattle originally, but he transferred his country of residence in 1971 to avoid getting bits of his body blown off by groups of disgruntled Vietnamese in the jungle. While I'm sure this would have been an exciting adventure vacation for some, Steve didn't have quite the same take on it. I'm with Steve on this one. I'm with Steve on a lot of things, actually. He's the closest thing I've had to a father for the last six years.

I stumbled into his place just after I'd dropped out of college. I was on a four-day binge and had been kicked out of most of the nicer places in town. I was rambling drunk by the time I rolled into Dodger's. I mean stammering, slobbering, puking on my t-shirt drunk. Apparently, I picked a fight with the bartender, who was not interested in my demands for vodka. They tell me I lunged over the bar at him. I think it's more likely that I was making a grab for the bottle, but since I'd blacked out by that time, I have to take Steve's word for it. Anyway, in my effort to get a drink, I slipped and slammed my head against the bar. For some unexplained, but I'm sure perfectly good reason, I wasn't wearing shoes, so this added some extra slip to the whole transaction. I ended up sitting in Steve's office bleeding and puking, puking and bleeding.

I spent the rest of the night with an icepack on my head, lying on a cot Steve had installed in his storeroom for those nights when he had swum in too much good Canadian Rye Whiskey to make his way home. Steve went back to tending his bar, periodically checking on me to make sure I hadn't asphyxiated on my own vomit. While not dead, I was barely coherent, my blood alcohol level hovering around a near-lethal level, I'm sure. When closing time rolled around, he rooted through my wallet for some scrap of personal information and then bundled me into his half ton pick up and dumped me on the doorstep of my apartment building. Lucky for me, I had changed the address on my drivers' license, or I'd have ended up on Gail's doorstep instead of my own. A meeting between those minds wasn't one that I saw as being particularly positive. Probably the only thing Gail would like about Steve was that he had rejected the military industrial complex's plans for him, but I couldn't see her really warming up to him. No one else has.

I'm still not sure why Steve was so good to me that day. He's not a nice person. Ask anyone; they'll tell you he's a real dink. For him to take me in the back and clean me up instead of chucking me out in the street or calling the cops was totally out of character. He's an asshole to everyone, including me, most of the time. Every time I ask him why he helped me that day, he tells me to pay my bill and fuck off. He's almost civil if I don't bring it up. My guess is that Steve must see a lot of himself in me.

I've spent a lot of time holding up the bar at Dodger's. I didn't really plan to become a barfly, but it happened anyway. It's a comfort to know that there is at least one place I can go where no one will bother me, where I don't have to think about what it is that I'm supposed to be doing with my life that I'm obviously not doing if my brother's continued presence is an accurate indication. Steve's place is my haven. And Steve has become a good friend to me, although I think he'd deny it, given the opportunity.

We've shared some good times, and he doesn't mind so much when I want to pontificate on the nature of life and death. I think he gets a kick out of seeing me spill my drink down the front of my shirt while I go on about what it must feel like to be cast down into hell. After I finished reading Dante's *Inferno,* I went on for a full five days in a row about what the nature of hell must be for each person that entered the bar. I would casually wonder up to some other poor sucker with no where better to go than the dive we were all in and hit them with my question, "What does your personal hell look like?"

As though I was doing a survey, I would earnestly note each answer on the back of a bar napkin and dutifully pour over them trying to read my increasingly unintelligible script. Most of the answers were standard biblical ideas, fire and brimstone and Satan torturing, raping, and pillaging souls into the long night of eternity. One or two people didn't ascribe to the hell theory at all and wouldn't play.

Steve's answer was probably the most surprising, although it was like pulling teeth to get it out of him, "Mac, why do you want to rake over all this muck all the time? Why don't you go get yourself laid so you can see what heaven looks like instead of worrying about hell all the time?"

"Come on, Steve, play along for once." He smirked at me while he poured my next drink. "And quit being such a light weight over my glass. I could use a real drink once in a while."

Steve stared at me as he poured a heavy shot of vodka into my short tumbler. It was nearly full when he slid it toward me. "I'll tell you what hell is. Hell is assholes like you wanting something for nothing. I'm charging you for the double, Mac."

"You can charge me for a triple if you answer my question."

"You want to know what hell is." Steve slapped the bar with an uncharacteristic display of passion before he continued. "Fine, I'll tell you. Hell is living with the knowledge that most of the guys you knew growing up went on to die terrible deaths. Hell is the knowledge that you were powerless to stop it. Hell is what you put yourself through when you can't seem to get rid of the guilt that eats you alive for saving yourself and no one else. Life is hell. I hope for something a little better than this dump and jerks like you pestering me for another drink when I die."

Steve poured himself a dark amber rye and water and held his glass to me in a toast. "To a little peace and quiet in death."

I touched my glass to his and made my own silent toast to a little peace and quiet in life, too. I hadn't considered what it was like for Steve to leave behind all those people who were going to go off to war and probably not come back. I looked at him through my spotted glasses while he added the double, and the triple I had no doubt, to my bar tab. He was bitter, no question about it, but he had always seemed righteous whenever he talked about saving himself. At least he had until then. Maybe the whole thing was an act, and he evaded the draft for the same reason I avoided life. Maybe it was just fear that drove us to make these decisions. I couldn't ask him that day. Steve was too worked up and would have just kicked me out for the night. I had to bide my time and wait for the right moment to bring it up again.

It was rainy the night I asked Steve why he left America. The weather had put Seattle in his mind and he'd had three or four drinks, so he was about as loose as it was possible for him to get. We'd been talking about the trouble in the Middle East when I sprung the question on him. "Steve, do you think you did the right thing when you moved to Canada?"

"Shut up with this stuff, Mac. I'm not in the mood." A scowl grew on his face as he pulled a Player's filter out of the pack to light. "It's none of your Goddamn business anyway."

"Okay, fine. I was just curious. Sorry I brought it up." I had to play it cool if I wanted to get anywhere with him. It was the tried and true reverse psychology method that won me my answer. Steve wasn't used to me giving up so easily, and I saw him eye me warily over the red tip of his cigarette. He had grown an ash an inch long before he spoke again. The words came out softly, as though he wasn't sure if he really wanted me to hear them.

"Look, kid. That was a long time ago. You want to know if I did the right thing. How can I know that? I did the only thing I could do. I sure as hell wasn't going to go to some country I'd never even heard of to fight for a cause I didn't believe in or even understand." He shook his head and stared out at the rain driving down from an angry sky. "I got a lot of trouble over leaving. My family stopped talking to me. People who said they were my friends didn't want anything to do with me. The girl I was going to marry called me a coward. Right to my face, then she broke off our engagement. Can you believe that? What a bitch. I'd like to see how she would have reacted if the draft notice had her name on it instead of mine."

"Do you think she was right? Do you think you did it because you were scared?"

"Of course I was scared. Don't be an idiot. Who wouldn't be scared in that situation? But I don't think I was a coward. I just didn't want to die a meaningless death. I sacrificed a lot and maybe for nothing. Who's to say I won't get hit by a drunk tomorrow and die anyway? I don't know if it was worth it or not. I lost a lot when I came here, but I did okay for myself, too. It's a hard lesson when you learn that you are not the person everyone expects you to be. What I think now is that you have to be the person you are, and everyone else can go to hell."

I mused quietly over Steve's words. They put me in mind of something Audrey had said once. I could picture her in my mind so clearly she might have been sitting at the bar with me. Her bright red hair was pulled away from her round open face as she leaned over the cheap laminate table in the reading room so she could whisper in my ear. "Mac, no one—not your mother, not Newt, not all the head doctors in the world—can tell you what kind of person you are. They can't tell you what to believe, and they can't control who you become unless you let them. The power for self determination is in your hands alone. It's a big responsibility. Don't fuck it up."

Sometimes it scared me to realize how alike Audrey and Steve were. I suppose that is why I gravitated toward him in the first place. He and Audrey shared a sense of individuality that I envied. Their inclination toward truth, as bitter and ugly as it could be, was sustenance for someone like me who lived in a world built on a foundation of deceit. The fact that Steve happened to sell liquor was just a bonus. After all, a man living in a world made up of misdirection and carefully lined with solitude needs someone who isn't afraid of authenticity to make the world seem real. I hadn't gotten any legitimate sincerity from Gail in too long to remember, so I found myself feeling lucky that I had stumbled into Steve's life.

I never really considered that Rachel Strong might not find the bar quite so welcoming, and that Steve might not be the kind of father figure she would sit easily with. But by the time I set up our little rendezvous, I was past caring much about what Rachel might or might not think. I can't say I was that surprised to find that she hated the place immediately. I did the only thing I could think of. Against all my better judgment, I got us both as stinky drunk as possible.

Chapter 17

We'd agreed to meet at 8:30 for a drink and a little conversation. I was grotesquely nervous about the whole thing. I drove around the block until 8:45 just to make sure that she'd be there when I walked in. I didn't want to make her wait there, but I just couldn't stand the thought of sitting in there, glancing at the door every few seconds, looking at my watch for the hundredth time, hoping that she wasn't standing me up—going through that whole process of deciding to leave because she's not coming, but maybe I should give her just another minute in case she got lost or stuck in traffic—the whole thing was unbearable. I realize it's unreasonable to feel this way about someone you have zero emotional attachment to, but I hate being rejected by total strangers. If it's someone I know, I can understand it. It's obvious to every one that I'm a jerk. But total strangers, with whom you maintain your innocence and perfection up to the moment when you utter those first words, when they reject you—that's insulting. So, I made her wait.

Rachel was easy to spot. First of all, she was the only woman under 30 in the place. I watched her from outside the picture window that fronts the place. I was almost hyperventilating because I was so nervous. She was pretty in a sort of staid and quiet way. It was hard to imagine her spending more than a few moments in front of a mirror. Her plain, straight brown hair, not really long or short, framed a face that seemed young until you saw the eyes. They showed the many cares she was burdened with. She looked older than I expected, like she had lived many years in the last one. She wore jeans and a short-sleeve button-down shirt. Her sensible loafer type shoes made her look like she was going to a movie with a friend. She looked particularly troubled, but it was too difficult to distinguish whether she wore this sour expression because of her obvious dislike of the surroundings or if that saddened anxiety bloomed from the seeds planted by Milton Pasker and the violent death of her sister.

I saw my own reflection in the window and shook my head at it. *Way to go, Mac.* It was time to play my hand, and I was holding a pair of treys.

I reflected again on the strange circumstances that found me outside the door of this bar on a September evening. It was awkward, the whole letter thing. I was hoping that she wasn't the type of girl who would flip out, screaming about the invasion of her privacy, and the laws against mail tampering. I mean she looked nice enough, but she could get me fired over what I had done, what I was still doing, and, in all honesty, I had no idea how she was going to react when I told her the truth. That is, if I told her at all.

To get her there on that particular Monday in September, I had fed her quite a line over the phone. But I'd committed myself to the deed and here I was doing it. First, I had to get her number, which was no easy task in itself—she was unlisted, naturally, so I had to go through the prison computer system which is conveniently linked to the police department which, in turn, had an address and phone number from the date of her arrest at Pasker's sentencing hearing; how convenient for me that she's the kind of girl who would try to attack her sister's killer. Anyway, after holding her particulars in my sweaty palms for nearly two months, I decided that a letter was too easily ignored, so I called her.

Newt was smug. *I knew it. I knew you'd listen to me sooner or later, little brother. It's about time you saw the sense in what I've been saying all this time.* "Newt, do not begin to talk to me about sense at this moment. This is the least sensible thing I've done since I smacked that poor guy with my car door. If you say one more word, I will burn this piece of paper and never, I repeat, never entertain the thought of calling this woman again."

Okay, okay. My mouth is shut.

"And another thing, the fact that I'm doing this at all has nothing to do with you. It is entirely my own curiosity that has brought me to the brink of this incredibly stupid decision, so shut up."

Whatever. What are you going to say to her?

"I haven't the slightest idea. I'm going to wing it."

Wing it? Mac, you can't…

"One more word, Newt, that's all it'll take. I'm getting out my lighter right now."

All right, I get the message. Newt was peevish, but he knew I would make good on my threat for no other reason than to prove my point. He left me alone to make the call on my own terms.

With the number laid out in front of me, I took the phone in hand and dialed the number. It rang and rang. Beads of sweat were forming on my upper lip. My stomach was tingling with nausea. What was I doing? This was completely crazy. I can't call this girl up and tell her I think her dead sister is talking to her, and I know because my dead brother has been talking to me since I was sixteen. That's telephone harassment, that's a loony person stalking some poor girl, that's…

"Hello?" The cool detachment in her voice surprised me. I don't know why, but I expected her to be weepy and more childlike.

"Hello. Is that Rachel Strong?"

"Yes." No hesitation at all. And a strange lack of curiosity.

"Hi. My name's Mac Williams." Big pause here while I scrambled for some kind of reasonable excuse to be calling this poor woman. The real one certainly wouldn't do.

"That's nice. How can I help you, Mr. Williams?"

"Um, well, I uh, I've been asked to contact you by a group I belong to."

"What sort of group, Mr. Williams?" She was a little curious now, but watchful, cautious.

I stumbled along. "It's a, well, it's a support group. You know a sort of help, group therapy kind of thing." I was rolling now. What a great inspiration. "It's new, you see, so you may not have heard of us. We don't actually have a name or anything. We're just a group of people who get together in a real sort of informal way to talk about, you know, the things we've been through and how we're dealing with life now, and stuff like that."

"I see." This wasn't looking good for me. Cold was a tropical vacation in the Bahamas compared to the temperature I was receiving from this girl.

I scrambled to find something plausible to say. I decided a half truth might work. "Look, Ms. Strong, I realize this is a bit unusual, but it's not intended to be insulting or condescending or anything. We're just interested in helping people get through trauma and carry on with their lives." At least I was interested in getting through my trauma and carrying on with my life.

"And what exactly makes you think I need your help in dealing with things, Mr. Williams?"

"Well, I'm not sure you do. I'm just guessing really, just a shot in the dark, that maybe your sister's death is harder to get over than you might have thought. Even though the guilty party is in prison, even though justice has been served…"

That stirred her up. Her cool as a cucumber façade vanished. "Justice, Mr. Williams, has not been served. That monster cannot be punished enough for what he did to my sister. Even if he lived an eternity of suffering, it would not be just."

"Right, well, this is the kind of thing I'm talking about. Maybe it would help you to talk about some of these feelings with other people who know what you're going through. It's just a suggestion, but it really might help."

I could hear the catch in her throat. I knew that I was making her cry, but I didn't care. I just wanted to meet this woman. I had to know if I was right.

"I'll think about it, Mr. Williams. Is there a number where I could reach you?"

"A number?"

"Yes, a phone number in case I want to join. You are calling from somewhere, aren't you? You don't run your group sessions out of a phone booth, do you?"

Nice cutting sarcasm in this woman. I was beginning to like her already. "Of course, but this is for evenings only. I can't be reached during the day." Couldn't you just picture her calling me at the prison where here sister's killer is doing time?

"Fine. Whatever you like."

I gave her the number, and she made short work of the good byes. The moment I heard the click of the line disconnecting, I was immediately seized by regret. What was I thinking? Now that I've made up some ridiculous story about a support group—the idea of which was revolting enough—what was I supposed to do? Call up seven or eight of my closest friends to masquerade as recovering victims of heinous violent crime. Now, there's an idea. Supposing I could even find these nonexistent friends, what was I going to say to them?

"Okay, I need you to pretend to have siblings who were killed in violent ways so that I can fake out this girl in order to find out if her dead sister is talking to her."

That was sure to go over well.

Why don't you just tell her the truth, Mac?

"Shut up, Newt! I can't possibly tell her the truth. She'll think I'm some kind of sick freak who stalks survivors. She'll call the police. That's what I'd do if someone like me spit out that kind of story. She's probably on the phone right now to some social services agency to find out if this group I've manufactured even exists. Why do I do things like this? God, I hate dealing with people. They're so fucking unpredictable!"

Maybe you should give the woman a little credit. Who knows what she's going to think? Maybe she'll be happy that someone out there understands what's happening to her.

"Yeah, right. Whatever, Newt. I hate to be the one to remind you of this, but you're dead. That excludes you from making any kind of judgment call about the living. Me or anyone else. So pipe down, death breath."

Well, I wouldn't worry about your meeting, Mac. I mean, you're just so charming and subtle, I'm sure you'll sweep her off her feet and into a haven of trust. She'll confide in you in no time.

"Thanks loads, Newt. You're a real confidence builder."

Well, don't you think you're worrying for nothing anyway? She might not even call, you know. If she thinks you're as big a lunatic as you do, she's already thrown away your number.

"Hey, good point, Newt. I could be sweating over this for nothing. She probably won't even call. Why would she? She's got family to talk to. She's got friends to rely on. What does she need with me or some stupid support group? She's not going to call. There's no way she'll call."

And was that a relief. A narrowly escaped blunder like that is a precious thing. I sighed with relief at my good luck. Everyday she did not call, and every day I felt more and more relieved.

And then, after two weeks, out of nowhere, she called.
"Hello?"
"Hello. I'm looking for Mac Williams. Is he there?"
Just like that. All confident sounding, like there was nothing out of the ordinary going on. This was just another phone call, like the one you make to the garage to see if you're brakes are done. I, after lulling myself into a self designed cocoon of protection, was hardly as calm.
"Yeah, um, yeah, well…"
"Is that you, Mr. Williams?"
"Yeah, it's me." I couldn't lie. I didn't have a quick enough reaction time. She caught me unprepared.
"Are you all right? You sound kind of funny."
"Funny, ha ha or funny, peculiar?" I was stalling now. What cleverness. I was sure to distract her from her purpose with that kind of gifted chicanery.
"What?" She wasn't going for it, and who could blame her really.
"Nothing, nothing. I, uh, what do you want?"
"Well, I, you did say I should call if I was interested."
"Right, sure I did. Does this mean you are? Interested, I mean." I don't know if I've ever had such an awkward conversation. I felt like I was a feral child having his first chat with the civilized folks who adopted him.
"Well, I'm not sure. I sort of think I am, but I don't know. Everything's so difficult, you know?"
"Yeah, I know." Boy did I ever know.
"It's just that, well, there doesn't seem to be anyone to talk to. I would have talked about this kind of thing with Melanie, but…" Her voice trailed off like a kettle running out of steam. I could hear her sniffle, trying to hold back her tears. The emptiness of the pause that hung between us was so hollow that I could hear it echo, bouncing around the room only to land in the pit of my stomach, closing around

me like vice grips. I was silent while I came to grips with the sadness and need in this girl's voice.

"Mr. Williams? Are you there?"

Now was my chance. I could just hang up. Tell her the whole thing was just a big mistake. Apologize and be done with her. But there was something inside me that wouldn't be callous, something that wouldn't let out the stockpile of insensitive insults that have been the foundation of my armor for so many years.

"Yeah, I'm here."

"So, if it's all right, I'd like to come to one of your meetings. Just to see if it would help. I'm not sure this is my kind of thing, but I'd like to give it a try. Is that okay?"

I could have told her we disbanded. I could have said we couldn't find a room to meet in. I could have told her a million things that would have gotten me off the hook, but I didn't.

"Well, listen, we don't really have any sort of regular time or place or anything. And since this is your first time, maybe we should just get together, the two of us, and talk."

"Um, well, is that normal? That you just meet one on one like that? I thought this was a group kind of thing."

"Oh, sure. It is. I just thought you might want to start off kind of slow. One stranger at a time, you know. It could be in a public place, if that would make you feel better."

What was I doing? Now I was back to convincing her that this was a good idea. All those opportunities to bail out wasted and washed away by Rachel Strong's tears. I was almost completely disgusted by the sap I was apparently turning into after hearing this woman cry just a few tears. Not my usual style, but hell, I'd gone this far out on a limb, I might as well see how much weight this branch was going to carry before it crashed to the ground.

"Um, okay." She was tentative, but I could almost hear relief in her voice when she agreed.

"Okay? Really?"

"You sound surprised, Mr. Williams."

"No. Well, a little. I really didn't expect you to call at all. That first step can be a hard one to take." *Thank you, Dr. Makken.* I knew eventually I'd have a place for some of his lines.

"Yeah, I guess you're right. So when should we meet?"

"How about tomorrow night? There's a little place called Dodger's on 42nd Street. It's not that nice, but it's usually pretty quiet."

"A bar? You want to meet in a bar?" Back to skeptical and cautious.

"Well, yeah. Is that a problem?"

"No, I guess not. It just seems a little odd. Talking about life and death in some bar."

"Really? It's funny, but that's pretty much all I ever talk about when I'm in a bar."

That must have convinced her because before I knew it, she'd agreed, hung up, and left me sitting in my dim little apartment, wondering what had just happened to me.

Chapter 18

So there I was, standing outside of Dodger's, looking at this girl who was waiting for me. She was plainly uncomfortable. I could see her looking at the cheap Formica table she was at, trying not to let her skin come into direct contact with any of the three or four layers of scum built up on it. She kept eyeing her surroundings as though she might be attacked or harassed or brushed up against. She didn't know that most of the people who frequent Dodger's are far too caught up in their own personal misery to bother with anyone else. You have to work at engaging someone in conversation. It's an endurance test, actually. You have to be really committed to the idea of discussion, persist in your attempts to have one, and make it clear that you're not going away until someone answers you. Otherwise, the people in here will just wallow in introspection until Steve turns off the Coors Light sign and kicks every one out.

There's no handbook on Dodger's etiquette though, so Rachel sat there alert and on guard. More than anything, I thought, I should put this girl out of her misery. Besides, if I didn't show soon, she was going to bolt. I swallowed hard, smoothed back my hair in a futile attempt to make myself presentable, and opened the door. I could hear Newt going at me. That he would start yakking at that specific moment just proved to me that he didn't have a clue what being alive was like anymore. I considered telling him this, but I chose to ignore him instead. It infuriates him when I do that and has far more effect than any verbal duel I might engage in.

I walked over to the table she was perched at. I'd say sitting at, but she was so close to the edge of the chair that if someone had bumped it with their foot, she'd have been ass down on a carpet that had seen way too much human carnage for the likes of Rachel Strong's jeans. I couldn't decide whether to read this as general uptightness or situation specific uptightness. Attempting my best winning smile, I figured I could find out in a matter of minutes which kind of uptight she was. And either way, a couple of drinks could make all the difference getting over that first awkward hump of communication.

"Rachel? Rachel Strong?" I laid a hand on her shoulder as I spoke.

She jumped a good couple of inches off the chair when she heard her name. It was as if she'd gotten so lost in her discomfort and her preoccupation with the safety of her person that she'd forgotten she was expecting someone. She had a startled deer in the headlights look on her face when she looked at me. I couldn't help myself. I started to laugh. Not hard, not loudly, there was no belly holding or anything, but I was definitely laughing.

Oh, but I do make a great first impression. I hadn't even gotten as far as hello, and I'd already pissed her off. She was quick about it, too. She jumped off her roost and was on her way to the door before I'd even let out my last chuckle. Suddenly I was staring at an empty chair. Steve was behind the bar, looking at his watch and grinning. I had to get her back, if for no other reason than to avoid weeks and months of jeers about the shortest date in history, the small bulge theory, harassment about premature edatulation, and other gems in Steve's collection of jibes.

I turned around to see her pulling on the door. I had to act fast if I expected to get anywhere. "Hey! Rachel!"

I didn't exactly shout, but it was loud enough to get her attention, and the attention of most of the other patrons of the bar. It's so nice to work with a live studio audience. It gives the performance a real edge.

When she turned back to look at me, she had sparks shooting out of her eyes. I'm sure she would have happily emptied a can of mace in my eyes if she had thought of it, but I guess I surprised her by calling out like that. She just stopped at the door, holding it half open, and at first, I was stuck just looking at her. I met her eyes and looked at her for only a few seconds, but I got paralyzed in those small increments of measured time, and the world grew marshy and heavy with the pregnancy of our exchanged gaze.

This was one of those moments in my life when I felt as though I was watching myself on film. It wasn't a happy moment or an angry one. It wasn't romantic or scary. It was just cool. The setting, the girl, the scratchy recording of the *Eagles Greatest Hits* that Steve just can't get rid of, the way we just stared each other down. All of these things that didn't make any sense together just fit in a totally unique way. I had this tremendous urge to shout, "CUT! PRINT!" and then run to the editing room so I could stare at the frame for hours.

And then, it was gone. I walked over to her holding out my hand in a gesture of peace. Rachel let go of the door to shake my hand, her good manners getting the best of whatever was left of her indignation.

"Hi. I'm Mac. Before you say anything, I'm really sorry. Could we just sort of start over?" I delivered the only disarming grin in my repertoire. I had the feeling it came out as a lopsided effort at a smirk, but it was all I had.

She looked me over for a couple of agonizing minutes trying to decide whether or not I was sincere. I felt scrutinized, judged, graded. I really hate it when people give you the whole up and down once over, but I figured she owed me a little payback discomfort. I stood there smiling like an idiot, willing myself to give off an appearance, however false, of safe, clean-cut, honest boy material. I must have succeeded because eventually she started walking back to the table.

The fact that she hadn't said anything yet was really starting to make me nervous. She just strode back to the table and sat down. I followed her, babbling like a moron.

"Yeah, I'm really sorry I was late. There was this car stalled on 9th street, and I got stuck in the jam there for a while. Then, I couldn't find a place to park, so I had to go around the block a few times. Did you have any trouble finding the place? It can be a bit tricky if you don't know the neighborhood. I probably should have given you directions. But I guess you found the place because you're here, aren't you?"

She was staring at me again. It wasn't hard to figure out why. I'd gone from just being late to being a blithering idiot.

"Mr. Williams? Are you going to sit down?"

"Of course. I thought I'd get us a drink first. Name it."

"Is that normal for this kind of thing, Mr. Williams?"

There she was on that normal thing again. The girl seemed a bit wrapped up in the trappings of normality. I was going to have to try to slide over that bump if this game was going to get me anywhere. Fortunately, I was starting to regain a small amount of dignity now that I was back in my element.

"Sure, I'm not too concerned with a whole lot of formality. What do you want?"

"Um, I guess I'll have a gin and tonic."

"Coming up." I dared a friendly wink and headed toward the bar, hands in front of me surrendering to the inevitable. "I'll take a gin and tonic and a vodka soda. Better make mine a double."

"Careful, playboy, don't want you to come down with a bad case of whiskey dick. You just barely kept that girl on the inside of the door. You might never get to date number two if you can't keep it up 'cause you got vodka runnin' through your pipes instead of blood."

Did I mention Steve's compassion and great sense of humor?

"Steve, please. Just help me get through this night, and you can harass me until I cry, if you want. You can tell stories about this all day tomorrow, make up lies at will to amuse everyone in here, I'll even agree with you. I'll fill in details if you want. Whatever makes you happy, just please, not tonight. Not with this girl."

Steve looked at me, stared at me hard. I stood there, enduring it. I'd been stared at more in the last five minutes than I had since my high school graduation. It was really starting to bug me. Then, he poured the drinks and slid them across the bar to me.

"You could make me happy by paying your bar bill." Well, at least he's consistent. He turned and walked to the other end of the bar, leaving me to my own designs.

When I got back to the table, Rachel was looking slightly more relaxed. I set her drink down in front of her and placed myself on her right with my back to the bar. I didn't even want to tempt Steve by giving him a corner of my face to leer at.

I took a large sip of my drink and watched as Rachel did the same. Alcohol is wonderfully reliable. It never fails to spur conversation, chase away shyness.

Before, I'd even set my drink down, Rachel started talking. "Mr. Williams, I'm really curious about why you decided to approach me. Not to mention how you got my phone number."

Just like that, I'm in the shit. "Listen, before we go on, could you stop calling me, Mr. Williams? It's kind of creeping me out. My name's Mac. I'd feel way more comfortable if you'd use that instead."

"Okay. That's no problem. So, why and how did you call me?"

I took another big swallow of my drink, carefully avoiding direct eye contact with any part of her face. Then I reached in my jacket pocket for my cigarettes. I held the pack out to her, but she shook her head. While I fumbled about with my lighter, I could feel her eyes drilling little holes in my skull. What could I do? Was it time for more lies? The truth seemed to be completely out of place at this point, so I stalled her with a diversionary tactic.

"Rachel, I really think we should talk about your sister. I mean, you were bothered enough to call me back, even if you claim to be only curious, so let's just dispense with all the little details for now, and get down to the heart of it all."

She looked at me as though I'd just stuck her with a safety pin, not really hurt, but quite surprised. I thought I might be losing her again, so I plunged in with some grit. "Your sister's story was really well publicized. I remember reading about it in the paper. It must have been awful seeing the story in print like that all the gory details on display for the world. Weren't you angry at them?"

That did it. A bit strong for an opening comment, but very effective. Any curiosity she had about me vanished in the wake of her hatred and sadness.

"Angry? No, I wasn't angry. I was disgusted. The press hounded us. They dug through our garbage looking for information about Melanie. They printed everything they could get their hands on. You know they got into the home where my grandfather lives to pry information out of him. Too bad for them he's not all there anymore. He didn't have any idea what they were talking about. Personally, I think the fifth estate is a pile of shit. They raped Melanie, too. And they raped me and my parents and everyone else who knew her."

"Did you ever tell them that?"

"Oh sure, but they didn't care. The little weasel that covered the story for *The Sun* just looked at me like I was the one screwing him over. All he wanted was a front page story and a promotion. The little smut monger. I hope his laptop blows up in his face."

Once she got going, Rachel was hard to shut up. It was like opening a bottle of soda that had been bouncing around in the back seat for an hour. The cap came off, and the stuff just poured out. She talked and talked. She talked about Melanie's childhood. She talked about the injustice of it all; about how her parents couldn't get past their daughter's death.

"You know, they can't clean out her room. I mean, I know it's hard, but they can't let her go. It's been almost a year since she was killed, and they're still expecting her to walk in the door any second. Her room is like a museum. They're preserving it for her. I went over there for dinner last week, and they had a place set for her at the table. It's creepy. I don't want her to be dead, either, but she is, right? They just can't accept it. They're in total denial."

And while she talked, we drank. And as we drank, she talked more. "Melanie was always the favorite, you know. Mom and Dad really did love her best. They'd deny it if you asked them, but it's true. You can tell, you know. When you grow up, you can see stuff better, clearer. And it's clear she was the favorite. I wonder if they wish it had been me instead."

Boy, did that sound familiar.

"I mean, I know they don't want me to be dead or anything, but if they had to choose, would they have picked me to go instead? Do they wish somewhere deep down that it had been me in that alley instead of Melanie? And if it had been me, would they be taking it this hard?"

"Rachel, you really can't think that way." I didn't know who I was to talk. I'd had that feeling about Newt and Gail more times than I could count.

"Look, I can think any damn way I want to. You haven't been living in my shoes; you don't have any idea what I've been through. You don't know what this is like!"

Rachel's tirade of self pity started to get to me. "Oh really? You're so sure you've got the only sad story out there? You think no one else has ever suffered? You think you're all alone in the grief community? Well, guess what! We all have our sad stories to tell. We all suffer every day in this stupid little petty world. You are not the only one wallowing in self pity, you know. And don't look at me all hurt and surprised. That's exactly what you're doing. Wallowing. It's pathetic. 'Mom liked her better. They wish I was dead. Woe is me.' Get off it."

She was clearly taken aback at my venomous strike, but she didn't cower at my accusations. "Where the hell did that come from? I thought this was supposed to be a free discussion for support. I thought this was supposed to be about me letting out everything that I've been feeling. Isn't that what therapy is all about? And I don't hear you offering up any stories to share. I don't need this kind of shit from you. I don't need your permission to feel sorry for myself."

"Nope, you sure don't, but if all you're going to do is feel sorry for yourself, don't bother to beg me for sympathy. I don't have any left." Oops. Guess I went a bit too far there. I couldn't help it though. She hit a sore spot with me. I knew exactly how she felt. She hadn't only lost her sister; she'd lost her parents as well. They changed or got stuck or something. Just like Gail had. All my guilt, all these years, all the wondering if Gail might have reacted better if it had been me that got fried on that fence. All those awful feelings crawled out of my belly and spat themselves right in Rachel's face.

She sat there, shaking with rage. I admit I was a bit scared. I'd never seen anyone look so angry before. She stared hard at me for a minute or two, and when she made a move, I was certain she was going for the door. Instead, she picked up her drink and plunged three fingers into the glass, scooping ice cubes into her palm as though she were a greedy child with a jar of cookies. She leaned very close to me, breathing gin into my ear and gently whispered. "Screw you."

Suddenly, I had a handful of ice in my shirt. Water dripped down into the waistband of my pants like liquid pellets of sheer cold. Then she reached over, pulled a cigarette out of my pack, lit it, and blew a mouthful of smoke in my face.

I sat there, dripping, thinking of the wet spot that was forming at my waist, thinking vaguely of how this must look, of how I was never going to get this girl, but oh, how I wanted her. She was full of surprises. Any sensible person would have walked out, never looking back. Instead, she sat there smoking.

I opened my mouth to speak three or four times, but I couldn't form any kind of sentence. I mean what could you possibly say in that situation? Newt had a number of suggestions.

Mac, for god's sake, apologize to the girl. Tell her you're drunk. Tell her the truth. Tell her something quick. You're way out of line here. You're going to lose her.

But I didn't do any of those things. I just stared at her.

"I'll have another drink, Mac." Then, she started to laugh. A little giggle that grew into loud yops of laughter. Pretty soon, I was laughing, too. Laughing until tears filled up my eyes and started to roll down my cheeks in a breathless and free way that I hadn't felt in too many years to count. And then, before I'd wiped away the last tear, she was kissing me. It was a slow unhurried kiss, but I could feel the intensity in its laziness. Her tongue had the tangy essence of quinine on it, and I imagined we were in India, worrying about mosquitoes instead of sitting in this sad, dingy little bar, griping about loss and pain.

She pulled away first. She looked embarrassed, like she'd been caught browsing in the porn section of her video store. I wondered if she regretted the move, and I thought I'd better act fast, before she had too much time to think about it. Downplay the event. I coughed a bit and put on my best sheepish grin.

"Let me just get that drink for you. And maybe one for myself."

The rest of the evening was a blur. I remember moving to the bar and introducing Steve to Rachel. I came out of the men's room to find them head to head at the bar. Steve was whispering something in Rachel's ear. My stomach clenched in a spasm of jealously for a minute, seeing her face so close to Steve's, her hair tucked behind her ear.

As I approached the bar, Steve winked at me and patted Rachel's hand. He set up three shots of tequila and went about finding a salt shaker while I took up my position next to Rachel. "What was that all about?"

"Steve was just filling me in on a little background. You know he said he's seen you in here at least twice a week since you left college."

"Yeah, I'm probably in here too much for my own good, but Steve's been real nice to me since I stumbled in here the first time."

"Yes, he told me about that. He also said that you're probably the closest thing he's got to a son, but that I shouldn't let you know that. I guess I shouldn't have told you, but it just seems funny."

"What, that Steve should look at me like a son?"

"No, that this is the first he's heard of your little support group when he seems to know so much about you."

Oops. The bells in my head started tolling. I hadn't thought that she might actually bring up the reason for our meeting with anyone in here. I wondered how much damage was done. I couldn't tell from her face if she was upset or just drunk. I tried to sneak a furtive glance at her while Steve set her up with salt and lime for her shot. She was smiling at Steve. He was fawning over her like cupid's latest victim the way he rubbed lime on the fleshy part of her hand between her thumb and forefinger and then sprinkled salt on for her. He handed her the small glass of tequila. They both looked at me in anticipation, Steve with his foolish lopsided grin and her with an arched eyebrow, more questioning than anything else.

I picked up my glass. "Bottoms up."

We drank one and then another shot. It started raining, and the streets grew to be a hazy field of amber light on wet pavement. I saw the neon sign in the window flash, spelling out Miller High Life in a backwards reflection off the wet glass of the front window. Miller. High. Life. Miller. High. Life. High. Life. High. Life. Life. Life.

I was singing "You Must Have Been a Beautiful Baby" when Rachel announced that it was time to go. I managed to get myself into the back seat of the cab, slumped over and almost slobbering. Rachel got in the front and asked where she could drop me. My answer was a heart rending version of "He Ain't Heavy, He's My Brother." I heard her give the driver an address south of the river, and then lay my head back and watched the rain form little streams and rivers on the window.

At some point during the ride, I remember flashing to another time. I was in the blue room at Lynwood. We called it that because all the furniture, the walls, everything was blue. It was the room they sent you to for shock treatments. I used to love the color blue. Any shade of it was calming and radiant. It always spoke of peaceful and warm days at the park. The quiet of the sky on a still day. Now, it brings the taste of the rubber bit in my mouth, the coarse nylon of the straps across my shoulders and chest, across my wrists and waist, immobilizing my legs. I used to cry when they started strapping me down, shouting that this was all some mistake. But fear makes me truthful, so I told them what I thought was the truth, that my brother really did speak to me, and that I wasn't crazy. How cooperative of me to give them the very evidence they needed to justify their actions.

I'm not sure why my mind sent me back to that place while I was riding in a taxi with Rachel. It certainly sobered me up, though. At least enough to start talking about Newt. I told her about the electrocution and about his smoldering remains in the hospital. How I still have to suppress my instinct to vomit when I catch a whiff of burnt hair. And I told her about Gail. "Remember what you said about your parents not being able to let your sister go? Well, I'd be happier if my mother was like that I think. She acts like Newt never existed.

"There was a time when we were a happy family. Now, I don't even remember what it feels like to have a mother. I just have this shrew who insists on dinner once a month. We're like miserable strangers stitched together by the thread of who we once were. And she won't even mention Newt's name. Every time I bring him up, she looks at me like she's not even sure who I'm talking about. As if she's got amnesia of the soul."

Rachel was staring at me over the front seat of the taxi, sitting next to an anonymous driver who didn't give a damn about either of us. I was reclined on the back seat staring at the rain on the rear window. I met her eyes for a moment when I finished talking. They were glistening with the well of tears they stored. She looked sad and relieved at the same time, but she didn't speak. She just looked at me with big brown eyes, and then, suddenly, she was in the back seat with me. She lay her head on my chest and wrapped her arms awkwardly around me. I put a comforting arm on her shoulder, reached up to feel the softness of her hair, and lost myself in the freedom of the moment.

Chapter 19

I could hear the phone ringing in the other room. It had been ringing, six rings at a time every fifteen minutes for an hour. I knew it must be Joe calling, or Gail, maybe even Rachel, but I didn't want to talk to anyone. I wanted to lie there on my bed until it was time for me to join Newt in his purgatory. An ashtray balanced on my stomach; my cigarettes were in easy reach. I stared at the television on my dresser with the sound turned all the way down. In several days, if I didn't drink any water or eat any food, if I was lucky, I'd be a corpse, and none of this would make any difference. I felt unspeakably tired of everything: tired of Newt talking to me, tired of making a superior jackass of myself every time I opened my mouth. I was tired of doing stupid jobs that left me cold and uncaring. I was just so tired of this life. I'd been looking for a clean slate for more than ten years, but I couldn't seem to find a way to erase all the confusion and misgivings that filled in the empty spaces of my life. It seemed all I had left were my wits, sorely used and ready for retirement, and the near constant buzzing of Newt's voice in my head.

Why don't you answer the phone, Mac? Why don't you tell me what happened with Rachel? You should get out of bed, Mac.

And so on, and so on, forever more. If only I could turn him off. If only I knew how to get rid of him. If only I knew whether or not he was real. I felt like I'd spent half my life wondering if I was sane and the other half protecting myself from the people who would surely believe I was not. The whole world kept saying that this was abnormal, impossible, all in my head. But it all seemed real enough to me.

There are no guarantees about the quality of life we'll have. You take what you get. I didn't know how long I'd been laying there—a couple of days I guess. I'd seen the morning news shows come and go. I'd seen the daytime dramas start, and I wondered whatever became of Big Bill. I wondered if he ever found the words to draw out his pain for everyone to see, words to explain it to all the Dr. Makkens that have come and gone in the last ten years. Maybe he had the right answer all along. Shut up and immerse yourself in someone else's drama. Or maybe Audrey did. I just didn't know, and I was far too unimaginative to figure it out.

The phone kept ringing and ringing. I knew I should answer it, but I was so exhausted by just the thought of all the things people expected me to do that I could barely raise my head off the pillow. I wished that sleep would find me and hold me in an embrace that would last a thousand years.

I was jarred out of my requiem by the sound of someone rapping on glass. I knew that, sooner or later, I would be forced back into the world by one of the few friends or family members I had left. I thought that I shouldn't get up to see who it was, but the compulsion to know who cared enough to see what had become of me seemed to make me a marionette. The whole time that I was getting myself out of bed and walking to the front window, I thought, *Just turn around and go back to bed. Whoever it is will just go away, eventually.*

But I didn't go back to bed. Something made me keep walking all the way to the window. I drew back the curtain to see who might care if I was alive or dead, not really knowing what or who to expect. Because I live in a basement apartment, all I could see when I pulled back the wrinkled drapes were two shiny, polished black boots. I could almost see my reflection in them they were so perfectly cared for. I didn't need to see any more to know whose feet rested inside those well cared for boots. I would have known them anywhere. From the vantage point my low window afforded me, I could see only the boots. The same image was first burned into my mind's eye when I was six. Craning my neck up, just as I did so many years ago, I saw the uniform attached to the boots, all the way up to the straight stiff police cap that rested on the head of the cop who had come to pay me a visit.

I didn't know why I was scared. I hadn't done anything—ever, really—but there is something about a cop at your door makes you feel guilty even if you're Mother Theresa. My hands were shaking as I tapped the glass to get his attention.

He pointed at the door and started walking toward it. I buzzed him into the building and waited for the heavy footfalls those boots would make as they approached my door.

"Newt, you there?"

Yeah, brother, I'm here. I didn't think you were ever going to speak to me again after the other night.

"There's a cop at my door, Newt. Why is there a cop at my door?"

And suddenly, he was there at the door, hat off, a polite if detached expression on his face. "Macbeth Williams?"

Nodding was the best I could do.

"I'm Officer Danning. I have a couple of questions to ask you. Do you mind if I come in?"

"No, not at all." I swung the door open wide in a gesture that, to me, seemed filled with innocent candor. I tried my best to hide the general alarm sounding in my head as I realized I was letting a cop into my apartment. I led him into the kitchen and could feel him scoping out the place, taking note of the stacks of books, the dirty dishes and clothes everywhere. Suddenly I felt very self-conscious. "Sorry about the mess. The maid quit."

I smiled and attempted a weak chuckle, but Officer Danning only looked at me and nodded. I took a seat at the crowded kitchen table and gestured to a chair for my guest. He waved it away and started flipping through a small coil notepad.

"I'll get right to the point Mr. Williams. Do you know Rachel Strong?" Thunder and lightening crashed through my head. I could see myself nailed to a cross, head bowed.

"Well, kind of. I met her a couple of days ago. We really just barely know each other. Why, what's wrong?"

"She's disappeared. Her mother filed a report last night when she couldn't reach her. We're just retracing her steps. It seems she was with you at a bar called Dodger's night before last. Is that right?"

"Uh, yeah, we had a few drinks."

"And this was the first time you'd met?"

"Yeah, but we'd spoken on the phone a couple of times before that."

"So this was kind of a blind date then?"

"Well not really, but..."

"And after the bar, Mr. Williams? Then what did you do?"

"Um, we took a taxi to her place, I guess. It's all pretty hazy, I was pretty drunk."

"And what time did you leave her apartment?"

"Um, it was morning, early, about six I guess."

"And you haven't spoken to her since then?"

"No, I haven't spoken to anyone really."

As if on cue, the phone started ringing again. This time I answered, if for no other reason than to stop the inquisition from Officer Danning.

"Hello?" Trying hard to sound normal even though I wanted to scream at whoever was on the other end to come and rescue me from this uncomfortable line of questioning.

"Finally, I've been calling you for two days, man. I was getting worried. How come you haven't been at work? Are you sick? What's going on?"

"Hi, Joe. I've been a little under the weather that's all. Listen, now's not really a good time for me. Can I call you back?"

"Yeah I guess so. But what do you want me to tell them here? Warden's really put out. It's been a real heavy load down here. You know what fall's like. When are you coming back? He's going to ask you know."

"Look, Joe. I'll call him and tell him I'm sick. If he asks, just tell him you haven't talked to me. I'll sort the whole thing out. I'll call you back Joe. I really have to go." Hanging up the phone, I saw my cop staring at me, making little notes in his pad. I walked back towards him, smiling my best recuperative smile.

"Am I to understand that you haven't been at work, Mr. Williams?"

"Uh, well, yeah. I've got a bit of that bug that's going around, I guess. I've been home resting." I was getting more and more reluctant to say anything to this cop, but I tried to sound confident and trustworthy.

"Anyone been here to check on you?"

"No. Look, are you trying to involve me in something here because all I've done for the last two days is lie in bed? No one has been to see me. I haven't even answered my phone." So much for cool as a cucumber. I didn't mean to sound so defensive. It just came out that way. It's not like I had anything to hide. I guess that wasn't exactly the truth either. I had a lot to hide, but I wasn't guilty of anything but incredibly bad judgment.

I saw a half smile form on Danning's lips, like I'd just confessed to the gruesome murder that was going to make him a lieutenant. "I'm not trying to involve you in anything, Mr. Williams. I'm just doing my job. You know Ms. Strong has some very worried parents right now."

"I'm sure that she's just fine. Maybe she just took a little holiday without telling anyone."

"Maybe." He didn't seem convinced. "It seems she left without packing anything though, and she seems to have left her car, too. Any thoughts on where she might have gone?"

"No, I told you, I barely know her." I don't think I've ever wished so much that I'd just stayed in bed.

"Yes, so you said. Well, thanks for your help, Mr. Williams. I'll be in touch if I need anything else. And here's my card. Give me a call if you think of anything she might have said that would be helpful."

When I took the card out of his hand, our eyes met, and I could see that he didn't really believe anything I said. On his way out he took a last look around the place, as though I might've hidden Rachel's body under the couch or in my front closet. The door finally clicked shut behind him. It was obvious that things had suddenly gotten a lot more complicated.

"Newt. You there?"

Yeah. brother, I'm here. What was that all about?

"It's Rachel. She's missing, and I'm pretty sure the cop that was just here thinks I know where she's at."

Do you?

"No, I don't know where she is. I left her sleeping two mornings ago. I haven't talked to her since. I haven't talked to anyone since. How do I know where she is? I wonder what happened to her. I hope nothing. She's nice, you know."

Yeah, I know. What are you going to do now?

"Do? I'm not going to do anything? That's why we have a police department. It's their job to find her, not mine."

Well if you think this cop suspects you of something, maybe you should try to clear your name.

"Clear my name? Listen to yourself, Newt. We're not on TV here. I haven't done anything to get my name dirty. I'm not involved in this. This cop will find her, or she'll turn up at her parents in a couple of days, and that will be that."

Are you sure? You just said that this guy thinks you know something.

"And that would be a problem if I did know something, but I don't. So let's just forget it."

All right, Mac. Whatever you say.

Chapter 20

I resumed my position on my bed. A group of overweight teenagers were parading themselves across the television screen wearing too little to mention. I tried to focus on one of them as she raised her fist to the audience in a gesture of rebellion and defiance. I saw her mouth form the words "fuck you" before she turned her back to the audience and waddled back to the chair placed on center stage for her. A troubled looking woman in her thirties was dabbing Kleenex to her eyes. She looked nearly paralyzed with embarrassment. Just another happy balanced relationship between mother and child.

I tried not to think about Gail, but I couldn't keep her out of my mind. Maybe we needed Jerry Springer, too, but I couldn't imagine the abject horror of sitting in that studio hanging out my dirty laundry for the world to see while Jerry made a killing off the shameless exploitation of our sad story. I lit my millionth cigarette, drawing deeply to implant the tar and nicotine firmly in my lungs. The sour taste it left in my mouth made me want to gag almost as much as the frivolous bad taste of the five girls on the TV, so I stubbed it out.

Restless now, I couldn't just lay there anymore. First, I was thinking about Gail; next, I was thinking about Rachel. Where could she be? Did she go off the deep end? Did I tell her I talked to Newt and he talked back? What did she say about her sister? My memory of that night's events tapered off after the taxi dropped us off. I knew we'd talked for a while longer. I could only guess that I had revealed everything to her, and that the knowledge that I was nuts drove her into some kind of hiding. But who was I kidding. I had no idea what I'd said or how she reacted. Well, I knew it couldn't have been too bad, considering the condition we were both in when I woke up. I just didn't have enough information to try to piece it all together. I was going to have to talk to her. But first I had to find her.

I got up and walked to the kitchen. The light on my answering machine blinked at me with a seductive wink of promises that will likely never be kept. It wasn't difficult to ignore the urge to listen to the many messages left by Joe and, more than likely Gail. I was having a harder time convincing myself that Rachel wasn't one of those seductive winks, maybe more than one.

I held my finger over the play button for a full minute. Before I made the decision to unleash the machine the phone started to ring again. Now that I knew Rachel was missing, I didn't hesitate to answer. If I had her on the phone, I would have no reason to worry about her, or the cop looking for her.

"Hello?"

"Hi, Mac. You ever coming back to pick up your car?" Steve's voice sounded old and corroded with rust.

"Steve. Hi. Yeah, I'll be down this afternoon to get the car. Sorry I left it there so long. I've been busy."

"Yeah, busy feeding that girl all kinds of stories. Was it worth it? Did you get what you wanted? To hear her tell it, you were quite the Romeo, but I don't think she was too impressed with the way you left." Steve was chuckling for the fun of surprising me with his cache of knowledge.

I, on the other hand, was reeling with an odd mixture of relief, regret and vague jealousy that Steve had spoken to Rachel. Wait a minute, Steve had spoken to Rachel. "You talked to Rachel? When? Did you see her or did she call you? Have you told the police?"

"Whoa, sonny. What police? What are you talking about?" Cops always made Steve nervous and cagey. A holdover from his anti-establishment days, no doubt. I probably shouldn't have jumped right in with that question, but I wasn't thinking about Steve's comfort.

I was going to explain everything to Steve right there on the phone. Tell him all about Rachel and Newt and Milton Pasker and

Melanie Strong. My need to confess was growing at an exponential rate. Oh, how I longed for the quiet calm of absolution. Just as I was about to launch into the long tale of death and the afterlife, Steve cut me off. "Look, Mac, I like you. I really do. But if you're involved in something here, I really can't help you. I'd like to, but I just can't. Maybe you should call your Mom, see if she can help."

I pleaded with him. "Steve, I'm telling you, I'm not involved in anything. At least not anything the cops are interested in. Gail can't help me anyway. I'd call her if I thought she could." A large white lie, but I didn't have time to waste on the truth that I'd never call Gail for help. "Look, I'm coming down there to get my car, and I need to talk to you about Rachel. Please, Steve."

There was a long pause. I could see the scales of Steve's mind and the things he stacked on each side, his comfort and security, his prized lone-wolf persona on one side, and on the other, attempting to achieve as much displacement, my need for one living person in this world to believe me, to help me. I didn't ask for help often and Steve knew it. "You know my hours. Don't come before opening time."

Chapter 21

I had my jacket on and was out the door inside two minutes. I had about forty minutes until twelve, the witching hour for Steve's bar. Walking would take nearly that long, but while a taxi would be quicker, I'd still have twenty five minutes to wait before Steve would let me in. And I knew he'd make me wait. I couldn't stand the thought. Walking, one foot in front of the other, was the best way to pass the time and to give myself a chance to think things through with a marginally clear head.

The air was biting and filled with pale light that washed out all the red and gold of September that the advocates of autumn are so fond of. The sky looked more depressed even than I did, its grey folds of cloud overlapping and tangling themselves into a mess of foul things imminent in the coming days or hours, snow and cold winds just waiting for the right moment to descend. The world looked like I felt, downtrodden and wound tight.

I was only steps into the few miles I had to go before I realized that I hadn't interrogated Newt about the situation. It was just possible that he had some information. I was even willing to concede the point that he might actually be of some help in this mixed up disaster.

"Newt, you there?"

Of course I'm here. Where else do I have to go?

"Don't be testy. Not now. Listen, do you know anything about all this? Do you have any idea where Rachel is? Do you know what happened on Monday night? Did you see anything?"

Oh, now you're interested in my opinion? Now you want my help? I don't know why I should bother. You've grown so adept at ignoring me, and you seem to have your life well under control. You should be able to handle this little hiccup on your own. You don't need me. You've made that more than clear in the last ten years.

His sarcasm was deadly, but I knew I had it coming. Newt was still the 16 year old that got fried on the fence. His juvenile system of reasoning was very much in tact, and he wasn't afraid to use it. Still, he had a point, and I couldn't really blame him for his reaction. I hadn't been very cooperative, hadn't really tried to help him get where he was going. I was too immersed in my own half of his death sentence to accept that this burden was ours to bear, not only mine or his. We were in it together, whatever it was. It was hard to admit to him, but I had no choice.

I took a deep breath and dove into the pool. "Newt, I know I've been an asshole. I know I've been dragging my heels. I see that now. Don't blame me for being stupid. It wasn't malicious. It's just that this situation is so scary and confusing. I don't know what to believe half the time. I'm almost ready to go back to the nut house for good. And now, maybe I've driven some girl crazy. Or maybe she was crazy to begin with. I don't know. I just know that I need your help now. I need it like you need mine. Maybe you were right about this. Maybe somewhere in this jumble of people, dead and alive, we're going to find the answer we need to end this." I wasn't sure I believed the words coming out of my mouth, but there was the possibility of truth, and I knew the thought of finally retiring from this game was something Newt couldn't turn his back on.

I walked for a while in silence. Newt was stewing on my words, searching them for sincerity. Eventually, I heard him sigh with complete resignation. Really, what difference would it make if he was a help or a hindrance. How could things possibly be worse?

Mac, I saw you and the girl get drunk. I heard you go on for a while about me and Gail, but I don't think you told her about us. I can't be sure, though. Sometimes you block me pretty well you know. I don't know why you didn't just listen to your messages. She probably called you the morning after you walked out on her. Maybe all the answers you need are on your machine.

"Right, the machine. Good idea." I grimaced. I hated it when he was right. In my haste to talk to Steve, I'd overlooked the most likely possibility for answers. As soon as I was done with Steve and had my car back, I would deal with the messages. Maybe Newt was right. Maybe all I needed to know was right there.

All that and the brotherly forgiveness would have to wait. All I was concerned with now was what Steve had said to Rachel. I hope he hadn't revealed too much to her. In particular, I was hoping he hadn't mentioned that I was currently employed at Eastglen Prison. I couldn't imagine how crazed Rachel might get if she found out I'd derailed her letter and then used my prison access to contact her. I'd be furious if I was her, and I was a pretty easy going person. I wondered what Rachel would look like furious. I could imagine the hard straight line her mouth would adopt as she struggled to find the words to reproach me with, like railroad tracks, solid iron as unyielding as a drunk spending his last dollars on a mickey of rye.

I didn't notice much about the walk, as involved as I was in my own thoughts. Now and then, I would realize that the world was not mine, and I was not alone in it. People passed me by on their way to lunch. Moms with haggard expressions and sunken eyes loaded children into minivans. Two girls about 16 years old came out of a vintage clothing store, their faces caked heavily in the mask of the gothic rebel, black eyeliner and dark lipstick. They looked like the angels of my demise come to collect on a debt that had been outstanding for many long years. I shivered as they passed. I hoped I'd be able to put them off for a while yet.

My mouth began to water for a drink as I approached the block that was home to Dodger's. My mind was crying out for the peace I would get from a large tumbler of vodka mingling with slowly melting cubes of ice, but I knew that I would need a clear head if I was going to make any sense of what had happened in the last few days. I looked at my watch. Ten minutes until opening time, and I was just about there. I didn't know how much I was going to say to Steve, but I hoped he wouldn't chuck me out in the street. My impulse was to tell him everything, let someone else make the decisions about how to act like a normal person when nothing about my life seemed normal.

I heard a sharp intake of breath from Newt and looked up.

Is that what I think it is, little brother?

Ahead of me, parked right in front of the bar was a blue and white sedan, light bar firmly affixed to the top. I could see the cage separating the back seat from the front, offering some semblance of protection to the cop in the drivers' seat who was none other than my very own Officer Danning. His head was turned down, so he didn't notice me when I ducked into the alley way just half a block before Dodger's.

"Sharp eyes, Newt." I felt panic for a few moments. My heart was pounding while my brain spun around thoughts of police cars and missing persons.

Look at you. Are you really hiding from the cops in an alley? I thought you weren't worried. I thought you were happy to let the police find Rachel. You're innocent. There's nothing to worry about. Isn't that what you said?

As I've said before, there is some enduring quality about the relationships in a family that allows its members to retain the ability to drive each other crazy with barely any effort. If Newt and I are any indication, the ability even outlasts a corporeal existence. I tried to remain calm and not let Newt's sarcasm drive me into a fit of shouting about how unfair all of this seemed to be. "Newt, either help me or shut the hell up. Do you think he's already talked to Steve or is he waiting to talk to him? He must be waiting. I can't see Steve opening his door early to talk to a cop."

Yeah, maybe. But you never know how people will react to a badge. Steve might talk tough, but when he sees that shield and that uniform at his door, it might be open sesame.

I wasn't convinced, but since I had all day, I decided to wait the cop out. After five minutes, Danning looked up and around the neighborhood as if he were trying to imprint the street in his memory. I saw a puff of exhaust rise from the back of the car and then in the next second, Danning had pulled the car into the street and was driving past me. I pushed myself up against the wall, trying my best to be invisible. Newt was laughing again.

Is this how innocent people act? It's funny, but I never pegged you to be the type to hide behind dumpsters and run from the police.

"God, you're annoying. I'm not running from the police. I just don't want the complication of another question and answer period with that particular cop. At least not until I've had a chance to talk to Steve and sort things out." I was trying to sound indignant, but I had, in the depths of my stomach a fear that sprang from some kind of guilt. These were feelings I'd grown accustomed to in the last years, fear tempered by guilt, so I'm no stranger to their faces. They are sour companions. I never thought I would grow so close to those emotions. I tried to remember a time in my adult life when I was not carrying them around my neck, albatrosses both, weighing down my every thought, influencing every action. I was sick to death of feeling this way. Especially now, when I had no reason to fear and no guilt to absolve. At least, not about Rachel's disappearance. Or did I? I just didn't know.

Forging ahead, because I didn't know any better, I slipped out of the alley and quickened my pace for the remaining half block that stood between me and Dodger's front door.

Steve was unlocking the door just as I reached it. I was grateful that I didn't have to wait any longer. Anxious to be off the street, I hurried inside, pushing past Steve toward the bar. I looked behind me, as though sure someone had followed me in, but all I saw was Steve. His eyebrows were knit together, a giant furry caterpillar wrinkling in an expression of anger and disgust. I hoped that he wasn't going to aim his diatribe at me. I didn't know how much I would be able to take before snapping entirely.

Chapter 22

"Do I have some kind of curse? Do I have to deal with all the Goddamn charity cases in the world? Is there a sign outside that I can't see that says I give a damn about you or your girlfriend? What the hell's the matter with you, sending the police here? I should kick you out right now."

Steve didn't handle the visit from Officer Danning with much grace. I wasn't sure if I should even speak. I'd never seen him so incensed. He was behind the bar now, slamming glassware around, showing me the back side of his anger. I watched him in shamed silence, even though I hadn't involved him in this, not really. I heard the discordant music of breaking glass, "God damn it!"

Steve turned around holding a towel to his hand. Blood was seeping through it. "Jesus, Steve, are you all right? Let me get the first aid kit?"

"Shut up and stay where you are. I don't need your help." He thrust his hand under a stream of icy water from the tap. I stood there in silence, scared that the one friend I had left was going to turn his back and throw me out in the street without a backward glance. Minutes passed, seeming like hours, while I waited for Steve to calm down enough to open my mouth again.

The water stopped the blood and cooled Steve's temper. He was muttering to himself as he cleaned up the broken glass. He swept the shards carefully into a dust pan. He avoided my eyes, caught in that position only I ever seemed to put him in. I was dragging him into my world again, and I could see he wasn't interested in going for the ride this time. I wasn't up to begging for help, but I didn't see any alternative. Besides I just wanted some information from him. He couldn't begrudge me that.

When he finally looked at me, I could see that most of his anger had drained away. Still, out of habit, he met my eyes with unflinching distaste. I could see he was on the verge of revoking any positive feelings he'd ever had for me. I felt like having Steve abandon me would send me over the falls. I didn't want to let that happen, but I was afraid that if I opened my mouth before he was ready to listen, he would tell me to shut up, get out, and then I would be on my own again. My patience was a ragged shirt that hung on my body, but I held his stare in silence. I had to wait him out. He stared at me for a few long silent minutes before he spoke, letting the full contempt for what I had done sink in. I let the silent accusation fall on my back. I knew it would have a hard time wedging itself into a spot between all the other burdens I carried and would, most probably, slide off before it needed attention.

It was hard to suppress my impulse to jump right in and begin my defense, but I held on, watching him for my cue. He turned his back to me again, this time to pour two cups of coffee. He slid one of the cups down the bar toward me and came out from behind to join me on a hard wooden bar stool covered with cigarette burns and water stains. He slurped the coffee with the expertise of one who has been a frequent drinker of coffee brewed by doughnut shops and gas stations, taking in lots of air to cool the scalding liquid before it blistered his tongue. I was about ready to explode. I'd been in Dodger's for a full 15 minutes, and I felt like time was working against me, like a plot had been hatched to keep me there until the cops returned to take me in. As tempted as I was to try and hurry Steve along, I sat and drank my coffee in silence, watching him out of the corner of my eye. The bile of anxiety was rising in my throat, so I tuned into Newt, who was saying all the things I wanted to say to Steve but couldn't if I expected to get anywhere.

God damn, what's taking him so long? Who does he think he is with all this? Some kind of fucking drama queen? Mac, just ask him. Say something to him. I can't stand the waiting. He's fucking crazy isn't he? Why doesn't he say something? I don't think he knows anything, Mac. This is all some fucking game to him. The cop probably didn't even come in here. He doesn't know anything. Let's just go, Mac. I'm telling you we don't need this guy.

I hadn't seen Newt so worked up in a while, maybe not since he'd gone over to the other side. He was practically hysterical, and while that wasn't particularly helpful to my situation, it did take my mind off the lingering silent treatment I was getting from Steve. Despite myself, despite the predicament I was in, all tangled up with cops and missing persons, I smiled. It wasn't a big smile, barely an upward turn at the farthest corners of my mouth, but it didn't escape Steve's notice. It seemed to compound his contempt for me, but at least it got him talking.

"Wipe that smirk off your face, you lying little bastard." He spoke quietly, a matter-of-fact tone about his voice that I found alarming and comforting at the same time. I didn't recognize it right away. It had a paternity to it that scared me with its unfamiliarity, but I felt soothed anyway, as if it was proof of some kind that I was worth helping.

I didn't answer, but I wiped the smirk off my face without hesitation. I took another sip of my coffee, looking down into the chipped mug that was embossed with the logo of a much too powerful insurance company. I was gathering my thoughts and my courage to begin the long story of what had been happening to me. Steve muscled his way in before anything took shape, "Look, Mac, I don't know what you've got going on, but I don't want any part of it. I don't like cops. I don't want them hanging around my bar, and if you're bringing them here, I don't want you hanging around either. I don't need any more trouble in my life."

And there it was, the last nail in the coffin. I felt him hammer it in; each word was another blow securing that nail trapping me, burying me alive. Steve was going to kick me out of his bar, out of his life, and I was going to lose the last and best friend I had. I didn't expect this. I didn't deserve this. I slammed my coffee cup down on the bar and turned to look at this man in whose bar I had found some small piece of mind in these last stagnant and drawn out years. I was seething with anger at his selfishness.

"You want me to go? You're sorry, but it has to be this way? Is that what you're saying? Well, that's just great. Just fucking great. I thought you were a friend, Steve. I thought you would understand how it felt to be alone and powerless. I thought you, of all people, would understand what it was like to fight an enemy so much bigger and stronger. I was wrong about you, Steve. You're not a friend. You're nothing. I don't know why I ever imagined you were anything other than a self serving coward who ran away from his responsibilities 25 years ago. You're still running, aren't you? God, I'm embarrassed that I ever looked at you for help. I should have known better than to pick a draft dodger for a friend."

I saw stars the slap was so hard. It knocked me off my bar stool and onto the cold tile of the floor. My head was swimming and a deep pounding was beginning over my left ear. I tried to focus on the figure looming over me, but I could only make out an indistinct form for the first moments. Then the world grew less dark, and Steve's face began to materialize before me in all its angry clarity. Before I could straighten my glasses, Steve held his hand out to help me up. I took it reluctantly, not knowing whether to expect an ice pack for my cheek or an ice pick for my temple. I felt my arm yanked taut and pulled against Steve's strength to regain my feet. I rubbed the stinging flesh of my cheek, feeling the swelling that was beginning already under my fingers. I looked at Steve, who held my eyes for a brief moment before turning sheepishly away to get some ice for my welted and swollen face.

Wow. He really nailed you, Mac. Are you going to put up with that? I'd tell him off if I were you. He's got no right to slap you around like that. Who does he think he is? You're in trouble. You deserve some help not a slap in the face. If I were you, I'd...

I muttered under my breath, "Shut up, Newt. I deserved it, all right."

Steve returned with a small towel filled with ice. He held it out to me wordlessly, and when our eyes met again, I knew how sorry he was. I started to apologize for what I'd said, knowing it was untrue and needing to recognize the fact, but he held his hand up, waving off the sentiment we both understood. We sat in silence listening to the clock tick as if it were a timer on a bomb we were powerless to defuse. Waiting for the inevitable explosion that would dismember us both, even if only psychologically.

I wanted him to ask me what was going on, how he could help, but I knew that he wasn't going to. He would wait me out in silence, wait until I broke down and told him or got up and left with the frustration of second guessing my own judgment. He drank his coffee, got up to pour himself a second cup and lit another cigarette. As he exhaled, he looked at me expectantly, not sure whether I'd talk or bolt, probably hoping I'd choose the latter. The bigger part of me wanted to run. Get right in my car, stop at home for a few things and leave everything behind, driving off into my future to reinvent myself as someone less needy, less lost. But then I heard Newt's voice again, and I knew that I could never be alone, never get away from this unless I silenced him permanently in the only way that seemed possible. I just couldn't do it alone anymore. Someone was going to have to help me. I never would have guessed that it would be Steve, but he was the likeliest candidate I had for hero. I didn't know how much I would have to tell him; as little as possible I hoped, but I was sure I'd have to divulge more than would make me comfortable.

"Steve, I am in trouble, but not the kind you think. You have to believe me that I didn't do anything to Rachel. I didn't kill her or leave her on the side of the road. I left her on Tuesday morning sleeping in her apartment. I might be a jerk who snuck out on her the morning after, but that's all. I swear on your record collection, I didn't do anything wrong—at least not illegal." I looked right at him, showing him I had nothing to hide.

"Let me see your face." He pulled the ice pack off my cheek to examine the damage his weighty blow had caused. "I think that's going to leave a nasty bruise, my boy. Sorry about that."

"Look, Steve, I don't care about the bruise. Please, just tell me you believe me." I heard my voice, but didn't recognize it for all the pleading tones.

"Of course I believe you. I told that cop you didn't have the balls to report a traffic accident. You couldn't possibly have done anything to that girl. You don't have it in you."

I rankled at the insult embedded in Steve's testimonial to my innocence but couldn't really claim he wasn't accurate. I was as cowardly as they came. Anyone else in my position who possessed at least some small amount of intestinal fortitude would have found a nice solid rafter to swing from by now. But not me; I wasn't signing up for a finish like Newt's. I sat there, nursing the stinging imprint of Steve's big hand on my face, swallowing my bruised pride. I even thanked him for his confidence in my character, such as it was. Now that I knew Steve had at least vouched for me with the police, I could listen with a calmer mind to his recount of the conversation he'd had with Rachel.

She'd returned to the scene late Tuesday afternoon to pick up her car. It seemed she was brimming with all kinds of questions about me.

"Was she angry? What did she say? Did she seem normal to you?" I fired questions at Steve as out of an automatic weapon with quick, staccato phrases that left him no time to answer.

"If you'd shut up, I'd tell you what she said. You sound like you're 15, kid. Get a hold of yourself." The bell over the entrance jangled with the arrival of one of the downtrodden, searching for the relief that can be found only at the bottom of any number of bottles. Steve inclined his head to the door and then got up to take his post behind the bar. "Hey, Reggie. The usual?" Steve was pouring the drink before he answered. He placed it on a coaster before Reggie's usual stool at the far end of the bar. A dull nod of thanks and a twenty on the bar was all Reggie could muster before sliding onto the stool that would be his home for the next six hours.

I watched, drumming my fingers on the bar with restless impatience, waiting for Steve to return. I couldn't explain the resentment I felt at the attention he was giving to Reggie when I so sorely needed it. His business transaction complete, Steve returned to face me from the business side of the bar. "Now, what was I saying?"

"You were about to tell me what you and Rachel talked about on Tuesday night. Do you think you could get on with it?"

"Enough with the attitude. I've got a business to run here. You think your tab is paying my rent? Well, it might, if you paid it once in a while."

"Okay, sorry. I'm a little wound up over this. Will you please tell me what happened?" I felt like he was going to make me start performing tricks like a trained seal in order to get what I wanted. I would have happily rolled over or played dead if it meant we could just get on with it.

"Well, your little girlie came in to get her car, but I think she was really looking for you. She asked me if I'd seen you since the night before, and she looked disappointed when I told her you usually took a day or two break between benders. She asked me for your address, but I told her I didn't have it. She's a nice girl, but you never know what kind of mischief a girl will get up to when her date walks out on her the next morning without even a thank you note." Steve looked reprovingly at me, shaming me. I acknowledged his unstated reprimand, nodding for him to continue.

"She asked me all about you. I got the idea that she was quite impressed by you, so I thought where's the harm in sharing a little information. She wanted to know all about your family and what kind of person you were. I told her I'd never met your mom, but that the two of you didn't get along very well. I told her you were a real loner, not many friends and no other family besides your mom. She nodded a lot, like she already knew that. She asked about your brother that died, too. She was real curious about him. I told her I couldn't help her much there; that we didn't talk much about that stuff. She brought up some support group, but I didn't know anything about that. I told her I didn't think you went in for all that psycho babble crap. She seemed a bit surprised by that, so I changed the subject by telling her where you work." He seemed proud of his diversionary tactic. A general keeping the enemy at bay with subterfuge; he didn't realize how badly his master plan was backfiring.

I was looking at my death sentence now. Steve carried on recounting the words they'd exchanged, but I'd stopped listening. She knew I worked at Eastglen. It was only a matter of time before she figured out how I had managed to contact her, if she hadn't already. I interrupted Steve in mid sentence. "What did she say when you told her I worked at Eastglen?"

"Nothing special. She asked me what you did, and how long you'd been there. Are you worried that she was looking for a lawyer or a dentist? Did I blow your cover?" Steve laughed, not sharing the palpitations I was now feeling. He must have missed the look of fear that floated across my face because he continued unconcerned. "She's a cutie, that one. She might be a little wholesome for you, but she sure is nice. She didn't seem like the type to get mixed up with the police. I sure hope nothing bad happened to her."

"Me, too. For my sake, as much as her own. She didn't tell you where she was going? No idea about what might have happened to her?" It seemed like wishful thinking even to me, but I was happy to grasp at anything.

"She didn't say much else. I don't know where in hell she might have gone. I don't know the girl." Steve's irritation was beginning to return. Distracted by my own panic, I wondered if Rachel reminded him of the girl he planned to marry all those years ago before he exorcised her from his life with his principles of self preservation.

The bell over the door rang again, rousing me from my imaginings about Steve's past. We both looked up to see Estelle, a matronly barfly somewhere in her pension years, shuffle in the door toward her table by the cigarette machine. She had Steve's attention now. He busied himself with her regular order and left me to watch her unpack her bag in ritual fashion before she took her seat. First, she withdrew two packages of Rothman's King Size, then out came her lighter which she flicked three or four times, checking its reliability for the hours to come; finally, the cards came out, a worn deck bearing the logo of the Sand's Hotel, Las Vegas, a memento from some long ago weekend of gambling and stolen kisses delivered late at night in a neon lit casino now just a pile of rubble left by the wrecking ball.

Estelle's hand shook as she put her first cigarette to her mouth. She started shuffling her deck, pausing only for the length of time it took to nod her thanks to Steve for the glass of wine he set at her right hand. Steve put a gentle hand on her shoulder and murmured something to her, too quiet for me to hear. She smiled at Steve and shook her head answering no to whatever question Steve had put to her. I watched their exchange with little interest at first. I'd watched this scene, or one like it, play itself out too many times to count. I'd always thought of Estelle as sad in a very humanly pathetic kind of way. She should have been someone's grandmother. She should have been baking oatmeal raisin cookies in a kitchen covered with flowered wallpaper, yellowing with age, marked by the lines drawn on it that showed the growth of first her children and then their children. Instead, she was alone, her graying hair complemented by her yellowing skin, sitting in a room full of bottles and neon signs, smoking and drinking sweet white wine, playing game after game of solitaire, passing the time but reinforcing her solitude with every turn of the cards.

I was choking on my depression when Steve returned. Every blink showed me Estelle, all her loneliness bubbling on the surface of her life; Reggie with his quiet anger raging at the last no good boss who fired him. Soon the others would come, all the rest of the Reggies and Estelles out there looking for ways to fill up the hours between the time they awoke from restless dreams and the time they fell back into the semiconscious state of the drunkard's sleep. Looking at them, I felt short of breath, smothered by their emptiness; knowing that it was myself that I saw when I looked at those people, the self I never wanted to be but seemed to be on the verge of becoming anyway. This glimpse of my future was like a poke in my instinct for survival, jarring it into action. I resisted the urge to jump off my stool and race out the door just long enough to give my thanks to Steve.

Chapter 23

My car whined like a petulant adolescent being shaken awake for school in winter. Newt whined in unison.

What's wrong with you, Mac? Nothing you do makes any sense. You didn't even find out what the police said, or what Steve said to the police. I think you should go back in and ask him about that. What if he told the police you work at the prison? He made that mistake once, he could do it again. Come on, Mac. We've got to figure this thing out.

"Newt, relax. Steve didn't tell the police anything that matters. Couldn't you tell that?"

No, I couldn't tell that. I'm dead, remember? I just think you should get the whole story for once. You're always going off half-cocked. It's no wonder you haven't been able to get anything done. You can't stick around long enough to get all the facts. I'll be lucky if I ever get out of here. Can't you just see one thing through, all the way to the end? It's just like with work. You switch from job to job, never giving any of them a chance, never giving yourself a chance to like it or get ahead. What's the matter with you, anyway?

I laughed out loud. "What's the matter with me is that I have a dead brother who won't stop talking to me for reasons that have remained unclear for several years. Everything else is a direct consequence. Satisfied?" It was hard to keep the scornful cynicism out of my voice. I'd already had more than I could swallow, but I was going to have to take a much bigger bite to get to the end. I needed Newt as an ally. As obtuse as he might get, I still needed him. I sat in the car, engine running, waiting for the silence to break like thin ice on a pond shattering under the weight of my words.

I put the car in gear and pulled away from Dodger's. "I'm going home, Newt."

Right, well, I guess it's time to listen to your messages then.

And there it was—our partnership remained in tact. I don't know if I felt relief or disappointment. My heart had never stopped skipping a beat at each instance that Newt spoke to me, as though his words interrupted the normal workings of my system like the shock treatments I was given to convince myself and everyone else that I didn't hear voices anymore.

I was used to it by now, but for the memory of the electric current I associated with it. That, I would never get used to. For Newt and I, the shock of him speaking was safe, not altogether pleasant, but it presented danger only if I allowed it to. At least I was in control of something. It wasn't the clean slate I'd been dreaming of all these years, but my current dilemma was more promising as an eraser for all these awful wasted years than anything else in my past had been. I felt more and more that Newt had been right. Rachel Strong was the key to my freedom. I felt it as something deep in my stomach, hidden well under the swollen river of bile that flooded most of my days. That's what had kept me in bed for two days. That is why I couldn't answer my phone or go do my ridiculous job. I was held in by the fear that soon I might be on my own again. I was afraid to let myself hope. That thing that I'd looked forward to, dreamed about, and finally gave up on was dancing in front of my eyes, just beyond my focus, just out of my reach.

I used to laugh at the people who walked around categorizing their neuroses, as if naming them would make them less dangerous. I saw that naming them actually gave them strength; it legitimized their existence, binding the sufferer with the cause of their suffering in matrimonial anti-bliss. I had tried so hard to escape from the labels of my problem. The doctors called me a normal child with schizoid tendencies. My counselor called me passive aggressive, docile on the outside and seething within. My mother first called me Macbeth and then chose antisocial. They named me many times, and all the while I struggled against the meanings behind their names for me. I had no doubt that I carried the truth of them within my mind as unconsciously as I carried my drivers' license, but I didn't know until the moment I was driving toward Rachel's voice on my answering machine that I would have to add pipe dreamer to the list.

Because it was crazy. The whole damn thing was crazy. The possibility that this girl whose life I'd made a point of stumbing into held some magical key to unlock the prison Newt and I were held in was laughable. She was a girl who lost her sister in an unspeakable way. That was all. I had no real reason to believe that she heard her sister's voice or that she had any special insight into the metaphysical reality of death. All I really knew was that she was missing, and I was the candidate deemed most likely to have got her that way. I had to accept that truth. Even if I hadn't clubbed her with a tire iron and thrown her in the river, I had insinuated myself into her life with lies and deceit, for no one's good but my own. I wasn't sure how you apologized for that kind of thing. I'd never been very good at remorse, except on my own behalf.

I slammed on the brakes. Rachel was crossing the street beside me. She turned to look in the direction of my squealing tires, and I felt my breath escape. It wasn't her. Just the same chestnut hair, pulled tight into a ponytail, but a different set of features were framed by the hair. This girl was a little rounder in the face, a little taller in the body. Close, but no cigar. I questioned my memory, but I knew that Rachel's was not a face I would forget. No matter how much vodka I drank, no matter how much time passed before I saw it again, her face would stay in my memory solid and secure.

I slowed my car to a crawl as I cautiously eyed the girl I'd mistaken for Rachel. She looked at me warily and picked up her pace. I could see I was making her uncomfortable, but I wanted to recapture that feeling I'd had before I knew I was making a mistake about her identity. That elated feeling, as though I'd been filled with helium and tied with string for a child to play with. An impatient honk behind me popped my balloon. I pushed the accelerator and headed toward home.

It was after three when I pulled into the familiar parking lot behind my apartment. I looked at the grey stone face of the building. The wind picked up countless leaves and hurled them at the windows and walls while it stood there unmoved by the demonstration. The wind continued blowing. It seemed to heave a sigh filled with the exhaustion of years of repetition. I knew how it felt.

I stepped quickly into the entry, searching my pockets for the key that would fit this lock. I heard the door open behind me, felt grateful that some other resident was there to help me gain entry, but when I turned to offer them the door I stopped short. It was no mistake this time. There was Rachel Strong in the flesh standing not two feet away from me. I breathed in and out as normal, but just a little more oxygen reached my brain, my heart pumped blood just a bit more convincingly than it had only a minute before.

I was scared to speak, more scared not to. Aimless babble was all I had, "Rachel, thank God. Where have you been? The police have been questioning people. Your parents must be going crazy. You have to come in and call them." I noticed her eyes for the first time then. They were bloodshot, small lines of red like highways marked on a map, and swollen from sleeplessness and tears, "Rachel, are you all right? Are you hurt? Do you need a doctor?"

She didn't answer. I couldn't tell if she was angry. I didn't know her well enough. If she was staring at me with malice or anger, it was at least calm. I'd found the key and was fitting it into the lock. I held the door for her, but she just shook her head. Okay, if she wanted to talk in a hallway, who was I to deny her the choice.

"Rachel, are you sure you don't want to call your parents? I know they're probably crazy with worry about you."

She shook her head again. "No...they're not. I doubt they've noticed I'm gone."

"Rachel, didn't you hear me? They've got the police looking for you. I know. An officer was here to question me this morning. Now, stop this and come inside." I was talking a lot tougher than I felt, but someone had to take control of this speeding bus.

"My parents didn't call the police. I did." She said it quietly, like a sinner at confession. "I pretended I was my mother and reported myself missing."

"You did what?" Dumbfounded, I couldn't believe it. "Do you have any idea how much trouble this has caused me? I'm the number one suspect in your disappearance. We're going inside right now and calling the cops to straighten this out. Jesus, Rachel. Is this some sort of game for you?"

I was plenty mad at being made into a fool like this. I was madder still that I'd attached some kind of fairy tale hope to this girl. I grabbed her by the elbow and tried to steer her into the building. She wrenched her arm away from me and began flailing, attempting to deliver several blows at once, landing none. "A game? Is that what you called it? Yeah, I'm playing a game, just like you are. I regularly seek out people in misery just to exploit it. Yeah, I use my connections at work to get inside people's homes and stir up trouble. I really get off on it, don't you?" Her breath was coming in short, hot waves of resentment and anger.

"Okay, I know I haven't been completely honest with you. I know I went way over the line, but let's be reasonable. I can explain most of it. Come inside. You can yell and scream at me all you want right after you call the police and tell them that this was a mistake, or that you're found, whatever you like. You can throw things at me if you want." I tried to look harmless and charming. I kept my chin down, not meeting her eyes while I spoke. When I heard her breathing return to a slower steadier circuit, I looked up. She was staring out one of the glass walls that made up the vestibule we stood in. She didn't look upset. She stood dry eyed, staring at the snow that was starting to drift in small anonymous flakes from the sky. "Rachel." I reached for her arm as I spoke her name. She caught the movement from the corner of her eye and flung herself as far from me as the few square feet of vestibule would allow her. Looking in her face, I saw that she was beyond upset and well into hysteria. I expected her to begin clawing at the line of metal post boxes, her eyes looked that wild, that trapped.

I took one step toward her, and she started talking. Low and quiet with just a hint of the frenzy she was burying, but with a determination so fierce it stopped me cold. "Look, whatever it is that you think you can get from me, I've got nothing left. My sister's dead. My family might as well be dead for all the living they're doing. We don't have any money. We're not interested in a movie of the week deal. I don't know what kind of person you are, but anyone who wants to torture someone else by making them relive their most horrifying experience isn't someone I want to know. Did you think it was going to be fun, hearing about Melanie and her death? Is that why you used your prison friends to find me? Or did that creature put you up to it? Did you and he have a laugh about this? Or do you do this every time an inmate with an interesting past checks in? No really, I'm curious. We both are. It doesn't really matter though. You won't be going back to work at the prison now will you. I've seen to that."

I launched into my defense, ready to explain the whole thing, Newt and all, even if I did have to do it in a hallway. And then it struck me: she said "we."

"Rachel, you said 'we' just now. What do you mean by 'we'? Who are you talking about? Is there someone else who knows about this?"

"Of course there is." She stopped talking suddenly looking lost for a moment. Unsure of her surroundings and panicked by their unfamiliarity. I heard her breath deepen and become erratic while she took furtive glances at me, the door, the mail boxes. And then the tears came. I moved toward her only to have her stiffen up and move further into the corner she'd put herself in. She held her arm straight out waving her hand at me to keep me at bay. "Stop it. Just shut up. I don't want to hear it anymore. I can't listen to you anymore. I know it hurts. I know. But please, Melanie, please be quiet." Rachel looked at me again, but this time with recognition and purpose. "It just won't stop. Her voice, over and over, her voice. It's so loud. I don't know what to do. Am I going crazy?"

I knew it. I knew I was right. She is hearing her sister. I told you so. Didn't I tell you so? Now, what you have to do is tell her about me…Go on, tell her about me.

"Rachel, you're not crazy. Will you come inside so we can talk?" I stretched my hand out to her, offering her absolution in the only form I was qualified to give, my assurance of her sanity. I watched her fist uncurl, the knuckles white from the force she'd squeezed them shut with. Slowly, she began to unfold her arm. I was half way there. All I had to do was get her hand, then into the apartment and maybe, just maybe we could find the end of this tunnel. Newt egged me on.

That's it, nice and slow. Get her inside. Don't rush anything, Mac. She looks pretty scared.

Her hand was on the door, and she was outside and running before I could take the two steps it would have taken to stop her. I made to run after her, chased her down the block and around the corner only to find … nothing. She'd vanished much as she had appeared, like one of the gods in the myths Audrey cared so much about. I wondered if the whole thing hadn't been my imagination.

"Newt, what happened here? Was Rachel Strong just here talking to me, or have I slid into the deep end of the pool?" The fact that I was questioning my dead brother certainly seemed to affirm that I'd jumped in without my water wings, but I had no one else to ask.

She was here all right. Too bad she wouldn't come inside. Boy, has she flipped out. I'm glad you didn't react like that when I started talking to you.

"Newt, I did react like that. Worse actually. Remember all the months I spent under sedation. Lucky for you, I'm a good actor."

Well, not good enough for Rachel, it seems. What should we do now?

"Isn't it obvious, Newt? I'm going inside to call the police and report that she's not missing, she's just crazy."

You can't tell them she's crazy, Mac. What if they lock her up? What if they can't find her, and she comes back here and gets in somehow? What if she wants to hurt you? What if she comes back with a knife or something?

"God, Newt, will you shut up, please? The more you talk, the less I want to listen to you. Now, I'm going inside to call the police, and I'll tell them any damn thing I want. For the first time since you died, I'm actually interested in what happens to another human being. It's been a long time since I felt this way, so I'd appreciate it if you'd just be quiet and let me enjoy it."

Officer Danning's card was on the table where I'd thrown it. I dialed the number, waited through two rings, then three, then five. Finally, as I was about to give up, I heard the deep baritone voice that had questioned me this morning.

"This is Officer John Danning." All business, my cop was. No offer of help. Just the facts, ma'am.

"Officer Danning, this is Mac Williams. You came by to see me about Rachel Strong. You said I should call if anything came up."

"And has something come up, Mr. Williams?"

"Well, yes, she did actually. She came to my apartment this afternoon."

"Is she still with you, Mr. Williams? May I speak to her?"

"Um, well, no she kind of ran off. I tried to chase her, but she just disappeared." I hesitated before continuing. I had the feeling I was being set up. I wanted to hang up the phone, imagining Danning and his fellow agents of government doom frantically running around the station trying to put a trace on the call. And then I remembered that Danning knew where I lived. He'd been inside my apartment. I was letting all this cops and robbers stuff get to me. I shook it off and continued. "She was here for a few minutes and then she left. I don't know where she was going, and I don't know where she's been, but she did tell me that she reported herself missing. She told me she pretended to be her mother and phoned in the report. Don't you people check these things out? Didn't you have reason to call her parents back?"

"Mr. Williams." The tone was curt and not altogether friendly now. "I assure you we have spoken to Rachel's parents. I don't know what kind of game you're playing with this phone call, but the girl is missing. Now, if you know where she is, you'd better tell me right now before things get ugly."

"I just told you she's fine. She was here a few minutes ago. And she told me herself that she faked the report. Maybe she gave you a fake number or something. Maybe her folks are out of town, and she's staying there. I don't know, you people are supposed to be the experts at this."

"That's right, Mr. Williams. We're the experts, so you just let us do our job and cooperate, okay?" I couldn't be sure, but I thought I heard a threat somewhere in his tone. I heard the words he'd uttered, but the voice carried a message more like, "I'm pretty sure you're guilty of something here, and when I find out what it is, you're going to be sorry." I tried not to get paranoid. After all, I hadn't done anything, and Rachel wasn't missing. It wasn't my job to convince this cop of that. Let him find out for himself that he'd been made a fool of.

"Okay. I just thought you'd want to know that she'd been spotted. I'll let you get busy finding her."

"I appreciate the call, Mr. Williams. I'll be in touch in the next day or two. Don't go anywhere." Again, that threatening tone that carried so much more weight than the words themselves.

"No, I won't go anywhere." I hung up, thinking that I'd probably done more harm than good, at least where my own situation was concerned. Danning was really starting to wind me up. He presumed my guilt based on my sloppy apartment and lack of alibi. And then he wanted to stand there and be the cool cop who means business. He actually told me not to leave town. I was trapped in a prime time police drama.

I can see by the look on your face that that went well. Now, are you going to listen to me? I told you not to call the cops. I knew it was a bad idea. What did he say when you told him she'd filed the report herself? He didn't believe you, did he? I knew it.

"Well if you know so goddamn much, why do you keep asking me all these questions?" I would have punched him in the face if he'd had any kind of tangible face to punch.

Don't be so touchy. The thing to do here is stay calm. We've got to figure this thing out. Now, if you were Rachel, where would you go?

"How the hell should I know where she would go? I barely know the girl. If you're not going to help with actual suggestions, then just shut up." I pondered for a long minute wondering how she found my place. It couldn't have been that hard. If I was able to track her down using my less than formidable resources, she could probably have looked me up in the phone book. I tried to put myself in her shoes, struggling with my unreliable memory of Monday night. She hadn't mentioned any friends; she didn't seem to trust her folks enough to confide in them. It seemed more and more that she was stuck like me, without a confidante and without a clue what was happening to her. I drew the curtains of my small front window and looked at the snow, thickening now into small piles. I shivered as though it was falling on my bare skin. I hoped Rachel would have a warm place to sleep, wherever she decided to go.

Chapter 24

I'd been standing in my living room for at least an hour, trying to imagine what was going through Rachel's mind. I had a pretty good idea, having been in a similar situation myself, but it seemed like she had a lot more going on than I could guess at. Who reports themselves missing? Was this a cry to the parents she thought wished her dead? Or maybe she was intent on teaching me some kind of lesson. I deserved it without reservations. What I'd let myself be talked into was despicable in a lot of ways.

What do you mean "let yourself be talked into"? I wasn't holding a gun to your head. You were the one who snuck into the police records to get her number. I never told you to do that. Don't blame me because you got yourself into this. You know, Mac, that's one of your biggest faults. You never want to take responsibility for the things you've done. You try to blame me for everything. Maybe now and then you should stand up and say, "This is my fault. I'm responsible for this." That's what adults do, Mac.

Isn't it just like a brother to kick you when you're down? "Thanks so much, Newt. I feel much better now that you've pointed out my biggest fault. Maybe you'd like to come back from the dead to pour some salt in my wounds. Or maybe you'd like to just leave me the hell alone for a while. I can't believe you're offering me advice on how to behave more like an adult. Have you completely lost your mind, or are you just torturing me with your ridiculous suggestions for some afterlife amusement?"

You know, Mac, you talk really tough, and you're pretty smart, I'll give you that. But let me tell you something: I don't think you've got what it takes to get me out of here and on to wherever I'm supposed to go. I don't think you give a damn about me or Rachel or anyone else. How am I supposed to help you if you won't let me? How are we supposed to figure this fucking puzzle out so I can move on if you won't even accept a little constructive criticism?

The phone was ringing, drowning out the rest of Newt's tirade. I practically leapt to answer it. Anything was going to be better than hearing Newt's side of the story. I'd heard it before. I knew he meant most of it, but he'd get over it. He'd have to. I only regretted answering the phone after I'd said hello.

"Mac, darling. It's about time. I was getting very worried. You know I almost drove over there this afternoon to see if you were all right. Why haven't you returned my calls?"

"Mom. Hi. Sorry about the messages. I've had a bit of a hard…" I didn't have to worry about confessing to Gail. She went on talking as she always did. I couldn't remember the last time she let me finish a sentence let alone stopped long enough to listen to a problem I might have. I was sure she was afraid I'd start off on some delusional tangent and then she'd have to bear the upset of sending me back to some institution. I wondered if she didn't hope for that anyway.

"Well, don't worry about it now. Our reservations are for 7:30 at Antonio's. Will you meet me there, or do you want me to pick you up?" I could hear the distaste in her voice. It was a hollow offer to pick me up. She hated coming near my neighborhood. Not sterile enough for her. A little too project housing and not enough whole wheat bread. Gail had gotten accustomed to living with money to spare. I hadn't been given the opportunity to do anything but view the lifestyle at the monthly Thursday dinner torture session. And it was Thursday.

The last thing I wanted to do was have dinner with Gail, but I heard myself telling her I'd meet her at the restaurant. When I hung up the phone, I slumped down into a chair. My posture sagged with the weight of the day and the unpleasant prospect of the dinner I was obliged to attend. I would have been grateful to have the chair swallow me whole like an upholstered boa constrictor. I likely would have slouched there for the rest of the night if Newt hadn't prodded me into action.

Mac, the messages. You still haven't listened to them. Come on, you might find some answers on that tape. Get up. You have to do this. It's not going to just go away. Haven't you figured that out by now? Nothing ever really goes away. You're carrying all this around with you. You can't run from it. You can't sell it or pawn it off on someone else. This is yours to deal with. I'm yours to deal with. Now get up and go over to that machine and hit the play button.

Droning in my mind as if on a feedback loop that wouldn't stop, I heard his voice repeating that message. He was my problem to deal with. It made me want to scream in frustration. What had I done to earn this problem? Was this a karmic payback for my past life as a plundering rapist of natives during the settlement of the west? Had I murdered children and innocents as a drug lord in Central America? I just wanted to know why. More than anything, maybe even more than I wanted to be rid of him, I wanted to know why I'd been singled out to bear the weight of my dead brother's spirit and conscience.

His unending and untiring determination to move me to action was ultimately successful. It was hard to spend any meaningful time in contemplative meditation when my brother's persistent voice drowned out my own thoughts. I moved toward the machine with little hope. A red number 11 flashed like a warning light. I rested my finger on the play button searching for the strength it would take to press it.

The mechanical voice of the machine filled up the silence in the darkening room. "Message one: Tuesday, 9:50 a.m."

Then Joe's voice took over. "Hi, Mac. It's Joe. It's almost ten, and I'm calling to see if you're okay. Are you coming to work? You're late already. Call me when you get this."

"Message two: Tuesday, 11:30 a.m."

"Hi, Mac. It's Joe again. Where are you? I told the warden you called and you're sick. Call me."

"Message three: Tuesday, 1:15 p.m."

"Mac, I'm getting worried..." I hit the skip button. It wouldn't have surprised me to find that all the messages were from Joe. I felt a guilty warmth for him and his concern for me.

"Message four: Tuesday, 3:20 p.m."

"Mac, this is your mother. I haven't heard from you in a couple of days. Is everything all right? Call me as soon as you get this message. Don't forget dinner this week on Thursday. Bye, sweetie." I looked at my watch. I still had an hour and a half before I had to meet Gail. A sour taste filled my mouth as I listened to her overly cheerful voice, contriving to sound like she gave a damn about me. I jabbed at the erase button to silence her.

The messages went on: Another four from Joe, expressing his devotion to our friendship and his concern for my well being. Gail left two more messages of the same kind as her first, all displaying her maternal instinct for the benefit of the male voice I heard in the background. One of the messages, left on Wednesday afternoon was from Eastglen's warden. His voice was apologetic.

"Mac, this is Harold Trippet. I've just had a disturbing phone call from a young lady regarding you and a misuse of your position. Your colleague in the mail room tells me you've been out sick this week, but I'm going to have to sit down and meet with you regarding this. I don't need to tell you about the importance of trust and reliability in this field. You've been a model employee up until this incident, so I'm willing to give you the benefit of the doubt. I'm sure you have a perfectly reasonable explanation, but I believe I may have to suspend you at least for a short period. Please contact me at once so we can straighten this out. Thank you."

At least he was polite about it. I deserved a lot more than a suspension, but it didn't matter anyway. I didn't think I'd be going back to the prison, at least not to work. It wouldn't have surprised me if I ended up there as an inmate, but I wasn't going back to reading the letters of the depraved and the desperate. Not ever again.

And the one message I'd been looking for, the only one I was interested was not promising. It did not hold all the answers. It did not give me any clues about Rachel's disappearance. It did not miraculously solve all my problems. Newt's voice didn't stop suddenly or fade away like a weak radio signal through the mountains. It was just the sound of a girl, troubled and hurt, lashing out at the cause of that hurt – lashing out at me.

Left at 5:14 Wednesday afternoon, probably right before she called the police to report herself missing, she let me have a down payment on all the grief and confusion she was feeling. "Look, I don't know what kind of game you're playing here, but don't think for a minute you're going to get away with it. I know who you are. I know all about you, thanks to your friend. I think you're revolting. Almost as bad as that thing in the prison where you work. Yes, that's right. I know all about that, too. I can't believe I let myself think that there was another decent human being out there who actually wanted to help somebody. I can't believe I trusted you. You disgust me. I won't forget what you've done. I've already called the prison to report you. You'll lose your job. If I have my way, you'll lose a lot more than that before I'm done."

It was definitely a threat. And she'd made good on it, too. It was all starting to make sense now. She called the prison to have me fired. Then, she called the police to set them on me like a pack of rabid dogs. When this scheme was in its hare brained planning stages, I hadn't calculated for vengeance as one of the consequences.

Things didn't look good. I was soon going to be out of a job. I was on the verge of being a man wanted by the police. I didn't have any friends to turn to and the only family member I could rely on was dead. The only thing that could make this a grade one disaster was due to occur in about forty-five minutes. I was surprised by how unruffled I felt. Usually in this circumstance, I would be frantic for a way out, but now, for some reason, I felt no panic. I felt no need for desperate action. It was as though I was on the train already with no control over the destination or course. Everything had been laid out. I just had to ride the rails now.

It wasn't a comforting calm that I felt as I stepped in and out of the shower. I went about readying myself for my dinner appointment with Gail with cool precision, but it didn't have a feeling of serenity to it at all. Only a sense of resignation that all 52 cards were now in the air, waiting for gravity to take its inevitable toll on their flight, scattering them across the floor as the events to come would scatter themselves over my life, over my future and Newt's, too.

When the time came, I pulled a clean shirt on, tied my shoes, and put on my coat. I left my apartment dark but for the light still flashing on my answering machine and drove off toward I didn't know what.

Chapter 25

I pulled into the parking lot of Antonio's Italian Bistro at 7:28. I sat in the car, staring at the colors of Italy alight in the sign over the large picture window at the front of the restaurant. Through the window I could see the clichéd red and white checkered table cloths and the empty, wicker diapered bottles of Chianti that served as candle holders. The place depressed me beyond belief. Not because the food was bad or because the waiters all had moustaches that left you wondering where all that hair might get to, but because it looked so normal. Everything about the place made me feel inadequate. I was never going to be the guy who took his family to this place to feed them spaghetti and meat balls, drinking the cheap wine that made cheeks turn red and laughter come more easily. I didn't have that kind of life. I probably never would. I didn't even know if I would want it had I the chance to grab it, but the opportunity to try might have been nice.

Outside the restaurant, the world was being smothered with white, washing out the colors and shapes, leaving only the uniform sameness of snowfall. The clock read 7:35. I knew Gail had been waiting for at least fifteen minutes. She was at a table near the back of the room, her preference in all restaurants. She'd looked at her watch at least five times to gage my lateness, and after five minutes, had ordered herself a glass of the house red, all the while assuring herself that a glass of wine a day was healthy.

At 7:40, I knew I had put off going inside as long as I could. I shut off the engine and opened the door imagining Gail's fingers

165

drumming on the table as she recalculated the mounting list of gripes against me. Add tardiness to the record. Before getting out of the car, I took a look in the rear view mirror. I looked normal enough. I practiced my "Hello, Mother" smile. Not too toothy or enthusiastic or she might suspect that I'm up to something. Deciding that everything was good enough, I got out of the car and shut the door firmly behind me. I let go the door handle reluctantly, as if giving up my security blanket for the first time, not sure if I'd ever get it or the feeling of security back again.

As soon as I opened the door of the restaurant, Gail looked up and began waving. She wore a familiar thin lipped grin that showed her displeasure at having to wait for me. I wanted to turn my back on her and run for the door. I knew that wasn't a possibility, though. Not unless I was prepared for her to make a scene of biblical proportions, one that she would surely jump into before the door had swung shut behind me. I swallowed hard and kept my feet moving toward my mother's table.

She stood as I approached opening her arms to deliver the embrace that was offered too many years too late. I accepted it grudgingly, trying not to touch her too much. My mother's touch had come to make me exceedingly uncomfortable in the years that passed between us. We had grown so distant that, at least in my opinion, it was like hugging a stranger off the street. I wondered at the fact that Gail, once so perceptive and intuitive, didn't ever notice the fact that I stiffened every time she made to wrap her arms around my shoulders. Maybe she did notice but decided it was easier to ignore than confront the fact. After all she'd become a champion not only at putting the past out of her mind, but at keeping everyone around her from drawing upon it as well. I recalled the last time I'd tried to bring up the subject of Newt at one of our infamous Thursday dinners.

"Mom, why don't you ever talk about Newt?" I didn't meet her eyes when I asked the question. I stared at my plate like a guilty child being told for the first time how disappointed my parental unit was in my behavior. I didn't look up until I heard her sigh. It wasn't a sigh that carried any sadness in it. It was more exasperated than anything else. As though she couldn't believe the immaturity of the question I was asking.

She put her knife and fork down, a bite sized piece of chicken still resting on the tines of the fork. Another sigh of annoyance. "The past is gone, Mac. We can't recapture it, and we certainly can't change it by talking about it. I don't know why you insist on bringing it up all the time when you know it doesn't do any good." She picked her fork up and resumed her dinner, changing the subject to an article she'd read on a new procedure to make hens more fertile. The matter was closed.

Her avoidance was plainly set on her face. There would be no discussion of Newt on that night, and it was unlikely that she would change her mind on any of the Thursday nights to come. Gail moved to topics both happier and more mundane so that she might continue running from the haunting memories of her dead family.

As I joined her at the small table set for two, I remembered that conversation. It mingled with all the thoughts I carried with me, and their mixture made me want to break into hysterics. I wanted to get up and yell, as I had wanted to so many times before. I wanted to draw some attention to the fact that maybe I would benefit from a discussion about Newt. Maybe I needed to be considered worthy of consoling, after ten long years of carrying my grief, the grief I never had the opportunity to share or rid myself of.

I watched Gail as she took her wine glass in hand and raised it to the waiter. I stared, looking for some reason to hope that she might once again be someone I could turn to in my time of need. I had trouble imagining what her reaction might be if I told her about my current predicament. I could see her throwing her hands in the air, resigning herself to the fact that I was the son who couldn't stop fucking up his life.

The waiter returned with a second glass of red. I ordered a double Stoli on the rocks, feeling Gail's disapproving eyes fixed on me. Hard liquor made Gail uncomfortable. Probably that's why I had come to drink it almost exclusively. Gail chose not to remark on my choice of libation, deciding instead to give me a liberal portion of silent criticism while I finished the first drink in three good size gulps. I motioned to the waiter to bring another and opened my menu. For the moment, at least, I could avoid her dark hazel look of disapproval by conforming to the established conventions of dining.

The waiter brought my second drink, and once we'd dispensed with the business of ordering, I waited for Gail to begin the diatribe she felt she owed me as part of our mother-son relationship. She didn't disappoint. I only had to wait until the waiter had moved out of earshot.

She fixed her gaze on my fingers gripping the tumbler that held my drink and launched into tonight's effort at mothering. "Mac, I've wanted to discuss your drinking with you for some time. Now, I know this is a difficult thing for you to talk about, but I really want you to hear what I'm saying. I think that you've got a problem with alcohol, sweetheart."

I rolled my eyes and reached for a breadstick.

"Don't give me that look, Mac. I'm very concerned about you. Look at you. You're haggard. You look like you haven't slept in days. Your skin is yellow, and your eyes are bloodshot. Now, I want you to be honest with me and with yourself. We can handle anything if we do it together."

I almost laughed out loud. The idea that we did or could do anything together was so ridiculous that I wondered if Gail wasn't having a breakdown of some kind. "Mom, I'm fine. I don't have a drinking problem. I have everything under control." A lie of staggering proportions, but it wasn't my drinking that I didn't have any control over; it was the rest of my life. In fact, drinking was one skill and habit I had completely under control. Hadn't I just gone two solid days without touching my lips to liquor? Didn't that prove something? Gail didn't see it my way.

"Every person with a drinking problem says that they have everything under control, Mac. And then before they know what's happened to them, they're living on the street warming their hands over a fire in a steel drum, begging for dimes to buy their next bottle."

"Is that how you see me, Mom? You figure that in no time I'll be brown bagging my vodka in alleys and behind dumpsters?" I was nearly laughing at my mother's high opinion of me. Of course, the fact that I had been hiding in an alley behind a dumpster only this afternoon was fuel for Newt's fire.

Maybe you should let her know that you've found a nice dumpster already. I'm sure she'll be glad to know you've got your retirement home all scouted out.

I wanted to give Newt a little shove in front of a moving subway. Not much point when he's only there in spirit, though. I ignored him and turned my attention back to Gail playing the concerned parent.

"Mac, don't be impudent. I'm trying to help you." Gail's voice dropped into her martyred mother tone as she continued. "I don't know why you're always pushing me away, Mac. I only want to help, but you treat me as though I'm a leper. You never want to hear my opinion or take my advice. Did it ever occur to you that I might just have a little wisdom to share; that maybe I might have more experience than you and I might just know a little more about life than you? No, I can see by the expression on your face that you have never given that idea any thought. Well, I'm not surprised. You've always known best, haven't you?"

We hadn't even had bread yet, and I was already being subjected to the full-force lecture. I could only imagine what the main course would be like. This was the usual pattern of dinner with my mother. We would exchange civilities over cocktails. The conversation would then degrade to nitpicking from Gail and surly sarcasm from me, and by the time dessert was on the table, we would have progressed through several rounds of verbal boxing, striking and feinting at each other until we were both exhausted. By the time the check arrived, we would barely be speaking, and Gail would sign her credit card receipt with a flourish before insisting that we leave together, her arm linked through mine in an improbable vision of a harmonious relationship. Anxious to maintain appearances, she would wait until I'd held the door for her before she put her public face away. Then we would stand in the parking lot until Gail was satisfied that I understood the tough love nature of her disappointment.

This Thursday dinner had all the makings of a traditional night of shrewish nagging on her part and silent rebuttal on mine. We had already determined the topic of my drinking as the core complaint for the evening, and Gail was more than ready to deliver a grand harangue. I, however, was having a harder time than usual concentrating on her ramblings. I had Newt's voice in my ear, and Rachel Strong's face in my mind's eye. And every so often, I could hear the warning carried by the voice of Officer John Danning.

Gail fell silent allowing time for her words to sink in. I relished in the few peaceful moments this allowed me. I hoped for her silent treatment to continue right through the main course, but there was little chance of that. I knew her too well to expect that I would get off with just the one round of punches. Sure enough, by the time my fettuccine arrived, she was ready for round two.

"Mac, I don't know why you want to make everything so hard all the time. I only want to help you. You're my son, and I love you. I worry so much about you. Sometimes I think you hurt yourself to spite me. Is that it? Are you acting out against me? Trying to hurt me by hurting yourself? Well, it's working. You've hurt me. I only want what's best for you, Mac. I don't want you to end up in a ditch somewhere with only a ragged shirt and a half-empty bottle for your protection. Now, if you want to think about cleaning up your life a bit, maybe going back to school, I'll help you do that. You could move home, and we could be a family again. Chuck would love it if you stayed with us. He'd be happy to have a fishing buddy, you know. And if you'd just give him a chance, I know you'd really like him. You two have so much in common."

I looked at my watch. We were only 45 minutes in, and she'd already made the offer. Usually, I had to wait until we were nearly through dessert before she started pressing me to move back in with her. I had to give her credit though, she was consistent. But the thought of moving in with her and the boyfriend was laughable. I really couldn't see me getting up to scrambled eggs and toast with the family anymore, and the thought of sharing fish stories over a couple of brewskis with Chuck made me want to puke.

I'd only met the latest in the line of Gail's men once. I was performing obligatory birthday duty, mine, not hers, which I gladly would have ignored had it not been easier to participate than to bear the guilt Gail would pile on if I neglected her on the day she gave birth to me. She seemed to view it as a day to feel grateful for her efforts in labor rather than a day to celebrate the advancing age of her only living relative.

Chuck, fair haired, quite tall, and sporting a smile worth more than I made in a year, shook my hand once, congratulating me, and then spent the rest of the day playing astonished that a woman who looked as young as Gail did could have a son in his mid-twenties. Chuck was about Gail's age but had never bothered with marriage and family. Gail was just right for him because she'd already had the opportunity to fulfill any maternal cravings she might have had in her past, and she had a substantial bank balance that would allow her to fulfill any consumerist desires she might currently have under her own steam. This meant clear sailing for Chuck, a 40-something dentist who apparently could afford to work only half time. At that point, he'd been in the picture for about three months and was just starting to get comfortable. I tried to tell him that he'd probably be out on his ear before long, but he wasn't much interested in my opinion. He assumed that I was speaking from the heart; that my observation was the veiled warning of an overprotective son. Little did he know that I was just speaking from experience. Gail was in the habit of disposing of her men after they'd outlasted their novelty and usefulness. Typically, her affairs lasted a year or so. After that, the attentive nature that made Gail appear to be such a great prospect would begin to dwindle, and eventually, she would sit down with the current date and let him know that it just wasn't working out. I'd seen men better than Chuck go down time and again. I knew it wouldn't be any different with him.

It had been about six months since I'd had that chat with him, and I could tell that Gail was nearing the point where she would move on. Even though she spoke of him as though he was a permanent fixture in her life, he'd moved from being the hot tub in the bedroom to the gas grill in the garage.

It was really only a matter of time until she sat him down and said in her most loving and sincere voice, "Chuck, I think we've gotten too close too quickly. I need some space. Some time to get my emotions clear. This time with you has just been so overwhelming…" and she would carry on with this line of reasoning until Chuck packed his overnight bag and returned to his apartment uptown. This had been her pattern ever since she began her search for whatever it was she was looking for in a companion. At least now, she didn't use me as an excuse to brush off the men she'd grown bored with. In my teen years, it was always, "I just need to focus on my relationship with my son. He's just a boy, and he needs me. I really like you, but a mother has to put her children first…" And John or Peter or Mark would glare at me for screwing up their chance with a sugar mama like Gail, pack up their shaving kits, and hit the road.

I figured that Chuck had about two more months, at best. After that, single men beware. Gail would be on the prowl again for her next victim. I wouldn't like to be thought of as the kind of son who would describe his mother as a cougar, but if the shoe fits, sometimes one is obliged to slip it on.

That's not fair at all . I can't believe you. Gail's just trying to fill a hole in her life. You know she must get awfully lonely. She's been on her own for a long time, Mac. She's just trying to find someone to share her life with. Is it her fault she hasn't found the right one yet? And you don't help much with your negative attitude about the men she sees. You could try to be a little more understanding of her situation instead of criticizing her all the time. She's doing the best she can.

I'd heard all this before, too. In my haste to ignore my brother's staunch defense of our mother, I tuned back into Gail's voice. She was asking me about work. I could see by the expression on her face that she held little more than polite interest in what I had to say about my blossoming career in mail editing, but it was infinitely better than listening to Newt harp on me for my harsh opinion of Gail. It also held a lot more charm than Gail's opinions on my Drinking Problem and whether or not it would lead to another Mental Health Crisis. I was about to launch into a euphemistic description of the quality product I had the honor of sorting through when I blurted out that I thought I was going to be fired.

Gail stared at me, astonishment on her face. I was equally surprised at my own confession. I had planned to reveal the new policy on gay porn at the prison, but instead I opened my mouth and out popped the revelation that I was walking on thin ice when it came to my future at Eastglen.

An unusual silence sprang up between us. Personal confessions on my part had not been the norm in our relationship for many years. I don't think either Gail or I had any idea what to do with the bombshell I'd just dropped. But Gail, probably as happy as she was surprised, wasted no time in snatching up this legitimate moment of honesty.

"Mac, I'm sorry to hear that." Not exactly sincere, but in the neighborhood. "What happened?"

Mac, maybe you should tell her what happened.

Are you off your rocker? was all I could think in Newt's general direction. If I hadn't been so stunned by my slip into true confessions mode, I would have let him know what I really thought of that idea. As it was, I was scrambling to come up with a reasonable explanation for what had actually happened. I felt weak and disheartened. It seemed that all I ever did was dodge the truth and grapple with the mounting list of lies I was living under. It was exhausting, but it was all I had in the way of survival. Would I ever have more than this heavy weight of truths I couldn't reveal to anyone? Was it worth it? Maybe I would have been happier in a nut house. I just didn't know.

I looked at Gail, who was staring back at me expectantly. Should I tell her everything, right here in this Italian restaurant filled with waiters in tight black pants and shiny red vests? Was this the venue I'd been waiting for to disclose all the secrets I had? Was all that was missing from our relationship the safe and trusting environment provided by a really good Alfredo sauce? I found that hard to swallow.

Go on—tell her, Mac. Tell her everything. She can handle it this time. I know it. I can feel it. Come on. I haven't felt like this in ten years. I haven't felt anything in ten years. It must mean something. It has to. Tell her. Please, Mac, I'm begging you. Please tell her. If I was ever any kind of brother to you, if you ever had any kind of feeling for me at all, you'll do this, you'll confess to her, and let her help us out of this mess. She's our mother, Mac. She's not going to turn her back on you, on us, again. She can't. She just can't.

I weighed my brother's words. They were so heavy with desperation that my chest began to ache. It wasn't like him to beg or to plead with me so ferociously, but I would be taking a big risk telling Gail everything. I tried to estimate her reaction to the details of my current predicament. While I was pretty sure she could stand the thought of me being fired because I tampered with the mail, I wasn't sure how she would hold up to the reasons why. I could hardly keep Newt's part in this out of it. And then there was the issue of Rachel Strong and her contrived disappearance. I looked at Gail. Would she readily side with John Danning, just like she sided with Dr. Makken? Would she call the cops, offering up my surrender for questioning in the matter, urging me to tell the truth, confess my darkest sins?

How long had it been since Gail had stood up for me? The last time I could remember her coming to my defense was far more than ten years ago. Newt was still among the living, and we were still a kind of happy family. Gail was a staunch supporter and my best defender when I was accused of copying a history report. She didn't even bother to ask me if I was guilty or not, so sure was she that I would never do such a thing. She'd taught us better than that. The fact that some petty bureaucrat would have the gall to accuse me was like a slap in Gail's own face. I heard her voice, the outrage in it like a raw cut steeped in stinging acid, as she delivered an incensed tirade to my eighth grade teacher about the perils of falsely persecuting her son. I remember how proud I was to have a parent who would believe me no matter what the adults said.

But a few years after that, the only thing that mattered was what the adults said. Gail came to me when I was still in the hospital, before the decision had been made to cart me off to a mental facility. I was conscious again, but my arm was broken, and I had a concussion. My car was a wreck, but fortunately, I hadn't done much damage to anything or anyone else. It was only dumb luck that I hadn't actually hit the poor bastard working the pumps at the gas station. He escaped with only a bruised hip where I'd nailed him with the weighty steel of my Valiant's door.

I, while not suffering in any kind of significant physical way, was thoroughly exhausted by what I'd been going through in the months before my little run in with the concrete dividing wall at the gas station. I was in no condition to handle my dead brother on my own anymore, so I sat up in my bed and, while Gail held my hand, I told her all about Newt and his disembodied voice haunting me. I remember the look on her face as I unveiled my secret to her. If I hadn't been so preoccupied with my own suffering, I would have realized that the look I assumed was one of shocked but concerned understanding was really one of horrified disbelief.

My next visit with Gail included my introduction to Dr. Makken. I didn't take it so hard at the time. The fact that Gail didn't believe me, I mean. I didn't know what to believe myself. But I was 16 then. I didn't know what to think about anything. It wasn't until later that I came to understand how awful it was that Gail had hung me out to dry with the establishment laundry. When I was in the blue room, feeling the tightness of the coarse nylon straps across my chest digging into my biceps, then I began to realize what a gross betrayal she had committed.

I didn't know if I could stand it again.

Chapter 26

It strikes me as both shocking and bitterly depressing how much value people put in popular belief. Whether or not the belief has any inherent value of its own has grown to be irrelevant in a world suffering from a media blitz that has lasted 50 years and looks to be only gaining strength among the general population. If it's on the news, it must be true. If that many people believe it, it couldn't possibly be anything but fact. And popular culture dictates everything, from style to politics; it gives us all the reasons we need to love, to hate, and, most importantly, to fear. That is the best lesson Audrey taught me. That's the lesson I've been squirming and wrestling with since I managed to free myself from the state sponsored care of the Lynwood mental facility.

It's been a hard lesson, but my experience has proved its veracity. There can be no mistaking the willingness of people to accept the easy over the difficult, the probable over the improbable. Everyone was so sure I was off my rocker because I was hearing Newt's voice. I was the weird one, the abnormal one. No one thought for a second that maybe my story wasn't as strange as Gail's, and that maybe she was the troubled one. Not her all decked out in sensible mother wear, baking cookies and behaving well within the parameters of what the world calls normal. No one ever questioned the fact that Gail never spoke Newt's name or celebrated his birthday, even with a day of crying and remembering. It didn't seem strange to anyone but me. No one else thought it was odd that she packed up everything in Newt's room and gave it away only a few weeks after he died. She even boxed up all the pictures of him and then proceeded to hide that box in the back corner of the basement storage room. Only two pictures of her dead son remained on display in her house, and I took one of them with me when I moved out. She used to keep one by her bed, but for all I know, she's stowed that one in a dark corner somewhere, too. Talk about denial. And for years, I couldn't understand why I was the one singled out as having trouble working through the grieving process. It seemed plain that Gail was having at least as much trouble as I was. Probably more trouble, considering Newt didn't really leave me like he left Gail. Her separation was complete, whereas I had no gaping hole in my heart where my brother once lived. He obligingly filled that hole with talk, cheap and funny sometimes, angry and desperate more often. But he was there. Gail had no remnants of Newt, and she wouldn't have any around her, either. She hid her grief, or lack of it, in the persona she now occupied. And the world has fallen for her act like a teenager falling for a pop star.

I've learned that it is more important to look and behave normally than it is to actually be well adjusted if somewhat odd. I've managed to dress up the act so that it's believable. I remain closed off and don't talk about my feelings; everyone thinks that's normal because I'm a guy, and guys don't talk about emotions. I drink more than I should, and while not picture perfect, it's certainly a character trait more acceptable than believing that the spirits of the dead can talk. As a rule, I try to limit myself to casual sex with women I won't have to see again, and that works in the world's view as well. I've seen enough magazine covers to know that men are afraid of any real kind of bonding in a relationship. I'll happily be described as a typical man who can't commit if it means I won't be committed.

Now, if I trusted Newt's deadened instincts, I faced giving all that protection up. Telling Gail meant taking down layer after layer of bricks. It meant exposing my soft underbelly to the world's sword wielded by no one other than my own mother. Was she going to be the kind of mother who turned the sword on the world or was she the one who would sacrifice her child for a second time in the name of her righteous belief in what the rest of the world thought?

In the dim light of Antonio's, I listened to the steady hum of Newt pleading with me to tell the tale while I searched Gail's eyes for something other than the shallow light of reflected surfaces. I wanted to believe it was there. I wished I had the same confidence as Newt did about her. But my faith was tainted by the past. The memories I carried with me held so little evidence of her loyalty that I quickly resolved that Gail could not be the one to save me. I didn't believe she had the strength in her anymore to stand firm against so many opposing forces in defense of her son.

Before we'd finished dessert that night, I'd fabricated a story about being so disgusted by the work I had to do at the prison that I'd started to take too many sick days for the warden's liking. That was the ostensibly plausible reason I fed to Gail to explain my confessed inkling that I was going to be fired. Gail sympathized with me about my reluctance to continue as a mail censor, she applauded it really, but she had to temper any pride she might have felt with a stern lecture about doing things the right way and not behaving irresponsibly, and, of course, the importance of leaving on good terms to secure a favorable reference.

We then began the discussion about what I would do next. I told her I was considering returning to school, but as this was a standard possibility each time I changed jobs, Gail did little more than raise an eyebrow and tell me that she really felt continuing my education was for the best. I left out the bit about the likelihood of acquiring my degree from the prison library after Rachel Strong, John Danning, and the court system were through with me.

And after what seemed like months, the clock finally crawled towards 10:30, and I found myself escorting Gail out to her car in the final fraudulent gesture of filial obligation. We parted on civil terms. She delivered her usual speech regarding the infrequency of my visits and phone calls to her. I made several hollow promises to call and keep her informed about my situation at work. After a few minutes in the chill of the late September night, Gail climbed into her shiny new champagne-colored sedan and waved four fingers at me through the window as she pulled out of the parking lot and headed back to suburbia, Chuck, and a house filled with countless ignored memories, all clamoring for attention from a woman who was completely blind and deaf to them.

I climbed into my old Chevy and cranked it painfully into a clunky reluctant sputtering start. I sat with my foot on the accelerator, giving it just enough gas to keep it from stalling in the cold. Homebound, I didn't really feel like going home. I didn't feel like going anywhere. It would have been nice to just get on a highway and drive for hours, nothing but empty road ahead and behind; only the sight of snow falling through the bright high beams of the headlights to disorient and distract me. It certainly would have been a welcome change from the distraction of Newt tirelessly berating me for not trusting Gail, for not telling Gail.

How could you? I fucking begged you to tell her, and you just wouldn't, would you. Oh, I know. Don't tell me. You're scared. You don't want to go back to the crazy house. No more shock treatments. You couldn't possibly be expected to risk your own skin, not even to save your brother's. Is this what I'm meant to do, teach you not to be such a chicken? I guess I'll just plan on spending the rest of time in this fucking empty hole of an existence because there's no way a coward like you could ever have the balls to help me. She's your goddamn mother! You won't even give her the chance to help you. You are the most selfish, petty, yellow piece of crap I ever had the misfortune to lay eyes on. I hope I drive you completely nuts. If you thought having me around was bad before, just wait. I'm going to make your life a living hell now.

"Newt, please. I just didn't think telling Gail and working her into a frenzy over my 'hallucinations' was going to help you or me. I'm just being pragmatic."

Don't try to talk your way out of it. There's only one reason you didn't tell Gail. You were too fucking scared. You're only interested in saving your own skin. Don't deny it; it just makes you look like a bigger loser than you already are.

"Fine, then. I'm a loser, and you're dead. We make a fine pair, don't we? And you can just get fucked with all the 'poor dead me' act, too. Maybe you could, just once in your afterlife, consider how hard this is for me, what the risks are to me. It won't make a damn bit of difference to you if Gail doesn't believe me. You won't be the one she's carting off to be dissected by every Tom, Dick, and Harry psychotherapist in the city. You won't have to find logical explanations to convince a bunch of pill pushing sadists that you're not crazy and don't need to be tied down to your bed. You'll just carry on, driving me to an early grave with your endless flow of self-serving chatter about how hard done by you are; about how I'm not doing a good enough job getting you out of limbo or wherever the hell you are. Well, I've heard the speech one too many times, and I'm done listening to it."

I turned on the radio, found a country station, Newt's least favorite type of music, and cranked it up as loud as it would go. It was one of my few defenses. He couldn't really hear the radio that well, but I'd built up a repertoire of country hits so I could sing along, delivering to my brother a hateful serenade that usually sent him running far from where I was. Me and Hank Williams were crooning out "Cold Cold Heart" when I pulled into the snow covered parking lot behind my building.

It felt good to have some quiet, some peaceful moments where I might be able to collect my thoughts and decide just what I hell I should do next. What that was, I didn't really know. I knew I had to find Rachel, but I didn't have any idea where to start looking.

I wasn't in the habit of spending so many waking hours thinking about another human being. I will agree with Newt on that point: I am a selfish bastard. It comes from spending so much time trying to protect my secrets from the rest of the world. The last person who occupied any amount of my waking mind was Audrey, and eight years had passed since I felt compelled to spend my spare pennies on thoughts of her or anyone else. I wasn't used to all the feelings riding the waves of my emotional sea. Every time I felt like I was ready to go under, abandon ship, and just forget everything, Rachel would appear at the helm trying wildly to control the course of my future. What did she have in store for me next? And why was this woman I barely knew exerting so much control over me? Okay, I knew the answer to that. I'd practically sent out a gilded invitation to her. My own stupidity was revolting. All the opportunities I had to become just a moment of oddity in her life—a strange phone call and nothing more—and I launched myself square into her worst nightmare instead. I was disgusted with what I was putting myself through and guilty for what I'd done to Rachel.

I didn't even get out of my car. I started it again and pulled out into the street. I wasn't sure where I was going, and it didn't really matter. All I knew was that I needed to be mobile, and I needed a drink. I didn't want to think about Rachel. I didn't want to hear Gail's voice in my head, delivering her cautionary tale about my inevitable future as a homeless rummy on the street. And most of all, I didn't want to hear

Newt whining and crying over the years of spilled milk and stolen cookies. After all, it wasn't my fault he was dead. I didn't kill him. The fact remained though that I needed a plan, some idea how to get on with things. I was seriously considering becoming a shut-in and applying for meals on wheels when I felt a hand grab my shoulder.

I screamed and swerved, my shock nearly landing me in a cluster of trees at the side of the road. The car bucked as it came up onto the curb and then stopped. I convinced my fingers to let go of the steering wheel only so I could ready my fists before I looked in the rearview mirror. Rachel Strong's face loomed before me, covered in dirt. Her hair was vaguely reminiscent of Medusa's, in the yellow orange of the streetlight I could almost see snakes writhing through the tangled mess of chestnut brown. Her teeth were chattering, but I couldn't tell if it was from hysteria or cold. She looked not just disheveled but deranged, a strange look of disorientation and terror on her face. I wondered briefly if that had been how I looked that day at the gas station. Not so dirty, but wearing that same expression of unhinged mania. If I had, who could blame them for wanting me out of society's way? I was certainly considering driving directly to the nearest psych ward and depositing Rachel on the steps, a note pinned to her jacket reading, "I'm Rachel and I'm very confused. Please help me."

But then I'd be just like my mother.

I turned around in the front seat so that I could see her completely. I gave her a quick once over in case she was hiding anything. I didn't know if I should look for weapons or physical injuries, but she didn't seem to be holding on to, either. Her jeans were torn where it appeared they'd snagged on some kind of wire. She wore only a thin sweater and no jacket, so I chalked the shivering up to temperature. I'd never seen another person look so absolutely harrowed and humiliated. She seemed to have shrunk to a child like size, but I resisted the urge to climb into the back seat and hold her.

Jesus Christ! This girl is crazy. She could have killed you. How long do you think she's been hiding back there? Christ, it's lucky you weren't on a bridge or something. What's she doing hiding in your car? What's the matter with her? What's the matter with you? Why don't you say something?

I was having a hard time hearing him over the loud thumping of my heart. I felt like it had moved out of its familiar spacious pad right next door to my lungs and taken up residence in the cramped notch just below my Adam's apple. I stared at this poor broken person, felt responsible for many of the shards of her I saw spread out on the back seat of my car, and wondered at the strange life I was living, all tangled and torn. Right then, in between heartbeats, I made my decision. Out loud, with the intention of someone else hearing me for the first time, I answered Newt in front of another person. "Newt, will you please relax. And give the girl a break. She's having a pretty rough week." I looked at Rachel with what I hoped was a sympathetic smile. "She'll say something when she's ready, won't you, Rachel?"

She stared blankly back at me, sure I wasn't speaking to her, but unclear who I was talking to. "Rachel," I continued, speaking softly to keep from spooking her, "do you want to go somewhere to warm up? You look like you're freezing cold."

Her eyes darted to me and then to the seat beside me, as if she expected to see someone there. She gave what I determined to be a nod, and I turned around to face the road ahead of me again. Thinking that the police station would be as warm as anywhere else, I put the car in gear and pulled off the curb I'd jumped when Rachel appeared so suddenly. I drove slowly, almost as though I didn't know where I was going. No sudden movements, no surprises. I didn't want to lose her like I had this afternoon. God, had that only been this afternoon? It felt like months had passed over the course of this unbearably long day. But then, I often felt like I'd been living one long arduous nightmare since Newt had started whispering to me from the other side.

Chapter 21

"Rachel," I tried to make my voice sound soothing, but it sounded to me like a symphony of violins imitating two cats caught in the throes of violent mating, "You really scared me. Have you been hiding back there all night?"

She didn't answer. I checked the mirror to see if she was still with me. She looked catatonic, but I saw her nodding.

"You must be freezing." I was trying to pretend that this was a common occurrence for me, that I regularly had people hiding in my back seat waiting to scare me half to death while I was driving. "I have a blanket in the trunk. Do you want me to get it for you?" I was stopped at a red light and turned to look directly at her again. She didn't answer. I was almost grateful as I feared that if I stopped and got out of the car, she might do the same, disappearing into the night just as she had vanished this afternoon. I turned the heater up as high as it would go and carried on when the light turned green.

"You know, Rachel, I wanted to apologize to you about the other night and the next morning." I swallowed hard, feeling like a jackass for ever walking out on her. "I shouldn't have left like that, I know. But if you want to know the truth, I was scared." I snuck another peek at her in the mirror. She was staring straight ahead. Her face held no expression. It was like staring at a stone wall and trying to find meaning in its cracks. I just kept talking, keeping my voice low. I told her that I hadn't been very honest with her, right from the start. I told her that she had every right to be angry at me, that I was a jerk, and I deserved everything I got. I even told her that I was grateful to her for giving me a taste of my own medicine.

That's it, Mac, now you're starting to win her over. She's got to understand now. You never meant to hurt her, tell her you never meant to hurt her.

I felt an energy I wasn't familiar with. It was liberating and terrifying all at the same time, freely answering Newt in front of Rachel. Of course, I had no idea whether she could comprehend any of what I was saying, but assuming she did, I was out on a limb that seemed to be holding strong. "Newt, I don't want to rush things here. Why don't you settle down? I think patience is what's called for here. Don't you agree, Rachel?"

I drove on, peering at her through my mirror every few seconds just to make sure she was still there. She hadn't made a sound until I addressed Newt again. Now, she looked right at me; met my eyes in the rearview mirror for the first time since she'd made her presence known. "Isn't Newt your brother's name?"

I laughed. Out loud in the car, I let out a big belly laugh that felt like it had been seeking an escape since the dawn of time. "Well, his name is actually Newton. He was named for Isaac Newton, but we called him Newt ever since I can remember."

"Why are you talking to him? Isn't he dead? Or is that just one more of the lies you told me?" Her voice was rich with anger. I would have preferred relief or understanding, but I was happy that she was at least talking.

"No, that wasn't a lie. He's been dead for ten years." I hesitated. It was a moment for and of truth. I felt like I was balancing on a high wire, but the net under me was only half complete. I was sure I would fall, but I didn't know if I'd land in the net or on the hard concrete below. I took one more look at Rachel in the mirror. It was time to let fate have another go at me. "I'm talking to him because he's talking to me." I almost whispered the words, letting them fall heavily on the vinyl seat and cracked dash.

The words were so much easier to say than I expected. I felt so light with relief and anticipation that I wouldn't have been the least bit surprised to find that I was levitating inches above the driver's seat of my car. I peeked in the rearview mirror to see if Rachel was getting as much solace from my confession as I was. She was staring at me, open-mouthed, with shock or disbelief or some other staggering emotion brought on by my startling revelation. She looked as though I'd told her that the moon had just exploded, and we were all going to have to live underground for the next 150 years. It wasn't the reaction I'd hoped for, but at least she wasn't screaming and attempting to jump from the moving vehicle.

"What do you mean he's talking to you?" She eyed me with practiced skepticism. "He's dead."

"Well, yes, that is true. But death isn't enough to shut some people up. Look, Rachel, I know this seems impossible. Believe me, I wish it was impossible, but the truth is that my brother died when I was 14 and started talking to me when I was 16. I can't really explain it, but it's some kind of afterlife duty he's got." And I carried on for a few more minutes, trying to lay out the scenario in a way that didn't make me sound like a complete lunatic, glancing in the mirror every few seconds trying to determine whether Rachel was getting my drift or whether she was getting ready to jump for safety. She was shaking her head, her eyes cast downward as though she was ashamed beyond belief that she even knew someone like me let alone invited him into her bed.

I wasn't sure if I really cared, though. I'd started now and really felt like I wouldn't be able to stop even if I'd wanted to. I guided the car onto a side road just around the corner from the cop shop and stopped. Turning to face her, I plunged in even deeper.

"Rachel, I know you know what I'm talking about. I read your letter to Milton Pasker. I know you can hear Melanie's voice. I know you can hear her suffering."

I was ready to continue baring my soul until the cows came home in order to get all this off my chest, but I was interrupted by the unmistakable sound of grief emerging from Rachel. She'd opened her mouth wide and was wailing, crying, and rocking back and forth in the back seat, her mane of hair shaking as she shook her head in horror or disbelief or something I couldn't identify. Her distress was so consuming, I got out of the front seat intending to join her in the back and provide some kind of comfort to her. When I opened the back door, her head shot up, and I saw the look of terror in her face. I hadn't even gotten in the back seat before she slid across to the other door and flung it open throwing herself out into the street in a dash for safety from me and my delusional stories. It didn't take a degree in psychiatry to figure out that she thought I was off my rocker.

And maybe she was right; maybe I was as loony as they come. Maybe I'd read too much into her letter, so desperate was I to have someone who might just understand a little of what I've gone through in the last ten years. I longed to relieve myself of this burden, so much so that I'd dragged this poor heartbroken girl into a special kind of hell—one where you can't know what is true and what is illusion—one where the simple obvious expectations of death became so warped and obscured by the tricks of fate that they were barely recognizable.

So how could I blame her for running away from me with all the speed that her world weary body had left in it? She ran with the practiced moves of someone being chased, looking back every so often to make sure I wasn't gaining on her. I watched her adrenaline carry her across the street and into an alley. Before long, she would be out of sight, and I would be back where I started from before she reappeared. I considered following her but to what end? She wouldn't even let me sit beside her in the back seat of a car. It was clear she wasn't going to accompany me to the police station in order to clear my name. Not that I had that as my prime motivation for keeping her near, but it certainly was to my advantage for her to show her face as a decidedly unmissing person. If she stayed gone much longer, I was sure to have another run in with the suspicious mind of Officer Danning.

Despite all this, or maybe because of it, I was more and more convinced of one thing. Something about this girl was important to my life. She had a significance of some kind that wouldn't allow me to let her go entirely. And even though I suffered chronically from constant doubt, second guessing my own judgment at every turn, I was still positive that Rachel did hear her sister's voice. After tonight's little tête-à-tête, I wasn't at all sure that Rachel believed such a thing was possible, but maybe I'd planted a seed in her mind. Left to germinate, I might get lucky enough to find acceptance sprouting where there was only disbelief before. She just might find that there was some truth to what I'd told her about my own experience with the whispers of the dead. And that truth might just help us both.

As it stood though, I was left sitting in my back seat, the engine of my car humming a plaintive tune accented only by Newt. Oddly enough, he was more concerned than indignant.

Wow, Mac that was intense. She really took off after you dropped the big one, didn't she? Do you think she's going to be okay?

"I don't know, brother. She's strung pretty tight right now. Do you think she believed me?" I didn't hold much stock in Newt's opinion but standing united with him was vaguely satisfying, a welcome change from the usual petty bickering we did.

I don't know. It doesn't look too good, does it?

"Nope, sure doesn't." I heaved myself over the front seat and put the car in drive. I pulled away from the curb and headed back toward home. "I wonder what she's going to do now. Do you think she'll come find me again? When she's calmed down a little?"

I don't know, man. It doesn't really look like she's ever going to calm down, does it? I mean, she's really freaked out. I don't know if telling her about me was the right thing to do. But thanks for doing it anyway.

"Well, I had to tell someone eventually, didn't I? At least I picked someone almost as crazy as me." I tried to make light of the confession, but Newt wouldn't have it.

Don't say that, Mac. Maybe this is going to change things somehow. I don't know any better than you do what the right way to solve this problem is. I know I've been hard on you, and you're right, I have been selfish. I'm just ready to get on with things you know. I don't want to stay here forever. I don't want you to be stuck in this, either. We have to try to stick together, but you've got bigger worries than I do. You're in danger out there. You could really land in some trouble if Rachel doesn't come clean with the police. And you took a big risk tonight telling her everything. She could be with the cops right now, telling them she just escaped from your car. She could tell them everything, and you and I both know they're not the kind of people who'll believe this cockamamie story.

If I could have, I would have stared at him, dumbfounded. It was the first time, maybe ever, that Newt seemed to see things from my perspective. If the circumstances hadn't been so awful, I would have jumped for joy. "Well, you're right about one thing, Newt. No one in their right mind is going to believe her story, and maybe that's a good thing for us. As confused as Rachel probably is right now, she's got a lot to think about. I don't know why, but I suspect she'll come back to me before she goes to the police. Maybe she just needs some time to let it all sink in. I hope she'll realize that she's not just imagining Melanie's voice, that I'm not crazy and neither is she." I let out a long sigh. The day was catching up to me. I felt tired beyond all human stamina. "I'm exhausted. All I want to do is go home and forget about everything that's happened today."

Newt agreed and then fell silent. Both of us were consumed by our own thoughts. My brother's rare show of solidarity left me feeling good but guilty about all the years we'd spent squabbling, wasting precious time and energy on the bitterness of our lot. We'd both been so preoccupied with our personal agendas of misery that we'd failed to address the reality of the situation. I had done little other than drink and wallow. Newt had done nothing but nag and prod me with ridiculous suggestions. How alike we were, after all. We'd done everything except search for a way to reach our common goal. It had taken the random appearance of a total stranger suffering in her own way to remove us from our own skins to feel the others' pain.

My car seemed to drive itself into its parking spot behind my building; I barely recollected the trip and yet there I was staring ahead, scanning the area in case Rachel had come back for another dose of the Mac Williams version of truth. The lot was empty but for the few cars inhabiting their regular spots. I knew Rachel was wily, but I also knew I'd given her a shock that would take more than a few minutes to get over. It was only wishful thinking that had me peeking in back seats all the way to the back door of the building.

A burst of gas heated air struck my face as I opened the security door. I ducked inside, welcoming the warmth as an old friend too long absent. Our troubles had grown exponentially in the last week, but I felt more optimistic than I had since I met Audrey. The storm before the calm. My slate being wiped clean. I didn't know what to expect in the days ahead, but one way or another, I sensed I was drawing close to an ending of some kind. I wasn't even sure that I cared much anymore how it all came out. I hoped for a happy ending, but any sort of resolution was looking like a golden dream right then.

Chapter 28

The buzzing of my alarm clock persisted until I'd forced myself onto my elbows to look across the room at the time. Seven fifteen. I got out of bed and switched off the drone. I'd made the decision the previous night that I would have to show my face at Eastglen today. It would be the last time I set foot on the prison grounds, at least as a free man. Who knew whether or not my late night antics with Rachel Strong were going to land me in there in a more punitive capacity. That being the case, I knew I had little left to lose. I certainly wasn't going to spend one more moment of my freedom sorting mail for degenerates. I planned to go in, make my apologies to the warden and turn in my magic marker.

I was surprised to wake up still in possession of that strange sense of optimism and liberty that I'd found last night. My resolve was stiff, and Newt agreed that Eastglen had served its purpose.

You've done what you had to do there, man. Now that you've found Rachel, there's nothing more there for you to gain. You know the more I think about it, the more I'm convinced that you ended up in this job so you'd be in a position to meet her. It all fits, Mac; I'm sure of it. Somehow, Rachel is the key to whatever is locking me in limbo. Besides, you know you won't miss telling people you're a mail censor.

"You got that right. Actually, I don't think there's anything I'm going to miss about the job. Except maybe Joe; I'll miss him a little."

Are you kidding? I thought you said Joe was a nut case. Morbidly obsessed.

"Yeah, he's kind of a freak, but I can sympathize. I'm not exactly the poster boy for regular guy, am I?"

Newt laughed. *I guess not.* For the first time in what seemed like years, he actually laughed. I heard it clearly and joined him in a good hearty brotherly chuckle that lifted me high above the sputtering of my car's engine and sent me to a place that felt like home.

"It's good to hear you laugh, Newt. It's been a while, hasn't it?"

Well, there hasn't been that much to laugh at, has there. I'm dead, after all. And the dead don't laugh. We say "boo" and other scary things designed to frighten the wits out of the living.

"God, Newt, I forgot you even had a sense of humor. It's nice to see it hasn't completely rotted along with the rest of you." He continued to chuckle as I drove out of the lot and on to face my last appearance at the prison. I couldn't explain what had happened to the two of us in the last day. It was like we'd achieved some kind of relationship, finally, after all these years, that wasn't based on mutual resentment and anger. It was like having a family again. And while it made me smile and feel relieved of so much of my burden, it also made me feel sad beyond words. I only then realized how much I missed having a brother. I once thought that I hadn't really lost him because he was lingering in between this world and the next, harping on me daily about his predicament, but the sound of his laughter seemed to physically pull at my heart, striking a melancholy note that made it all too clear that we'd both missed so much, lost so much.

I wasted no time in getting to the prison. Along the way, Newt and I discussed various plans of action. How was I going to deal with Warden Trippet if he brought up the letter I'd liberated from the prison? Honest mistake, maybe. Or, I could deny the whole thing. It would be a lot easier if I knew just what Rachel had said to him. I decided, much to Newt's displeasure, that I would just have to roll with that one as it came.

Don't be a moron, Mac. You've got to be prepared with some kind of story.

"Why? Look, Newt, I just don't know how he's going to come at me. What if he wants to know why I took the letter? What if Rachel told him I'm stalking her?"

Well, she wouldn't be far off from the truth, would she?

"Ha ha. You're hilarious. Maybe I'll just go in and resign first thing. I'll try not to even let him get a word in, okay? How's that for a plan?"

Well, it's not like I can stop you if I disagree. I just hope you can get in and out without getting arrested for mail tampering.

"That's it, Newt. Keep up with the positive thinking." I sounded testier than I felt, mostly because I was afraid that Newt was right. Trippet had more than enough power to have me brought up on charges. I was just hoping that my good record would stand up in the face of the accusations Rachel had made. After all, who was he more likely to believe, a respected employee who had worked hard and without complaint, or some crackpot girl who called up raving about some evil plot being hatched against her in the mail room of his prison? It seemed likely, when put in those terms that I might get away with nothing more than my outstanding vacation pay. I'd gladly take that alternative.

When I pulled into the staff lot behind Eastglen, I sat for a minute, steeling my nerves, practicing my "Who, me?" look and basically doing my best to stifle the sense of panic that was rumbling my stomach.

It's okay, Mac. You're going to be fine. Just go in there and quit. You've done it dozens of times before. You're a pro at quitting. Just walk into his office and say "I quit. No hard feelings.'" Then you can say your goodbyes to Joe and be on your way home. You should be in and out inside a half hour. Go on.

"Thanks, Newt. It's nice to know you think I'm such a good quitter. A real vote of confidence from my biggest fan." My sarcasm was evident, but I was relieved to have his voice in my ear assuring me that everything was going to be fine, that I would be back in my car and on my way home by nine.

Chapter 29

Warden Harold Trippet's office was an anonymous bureaucratic haven. He had a large wooden desk that spanned nearly the width of the room. On it sat a few manila file folders stacked neatly in the right hand corner. I was sure one of those files was mine, but I tried to avoid staring at them as Trippet's secretary ushered me into the office. Trippet himself only nodded at me and motioned for me to sit. I stared at the top of his head while he returned his attention to the file open in front of him. His hair was thinning on top, leaving a small patch of white shiny scalp that embarrassed me for some reason, like I'd caught him reading *Hustler* or walked in on him using the toilet. Averting my eyes from the source of my discomfort, I focused instead on the trappings of success in the department of corrections. A flag hung limp and ignored in the corner of the office closest to the room's prize possession, the window. Unlike the one in the mail room, Trippet's window showed an attractive row of blue spruce trees that lined the front of the prison. His rank spared him the privilege of a view out into the yard. He did not have to watch his charges as they roamed around the concrete, shooting baskets and trading cigarettes for drugs. He was exempt from the occasional fights and manly displays of prisoners stabbing one another with homemade weapons. Eastglen was only a medium security prison, but that didn't stop the inmates from exercising their God-given rights as society's miscreants to demonstrate the natures that landed them behind all that barbed wire. That pretty sight was for underlings and guards. The warden rated better than that.

I never really thought of Warden Trippet as my boss. I knew he was the supreme authority figure in the building, but he had so little to do with my day to day work in the prison that I felt like I should resign to Joe in the mail room. After all, it was Joe who would feel my departure with the increase in his reading load. Harold Trippet certainly wasn't going to trade in those spruce trees for a black felt marker and a letter opener. Nonetheless, I had no choice but to take a seat in the uncomfortable wooden chair in front of his desk. Usually reserved for inmates, the chair sat just a hair lower than normal, leaving its occupant in a position of undeniable inferiority. I tried to imagine what I could possibly say to this man who lived in a world filled with black and white guilt and innocence. How could I come up with an explanation that wouldn't make me come off as a complete lunatic? I sat in the chair waiting for the man to look up from what I could only imagine was the most recent complaint about my behavior.

Finally, after the passage of thirty or forty years, the warden closed the file and let out a long slow breath. It was almost as if he was stalling for time, dreading the moment when he would have to call me to task for my misdeeds. He looked up at me from the comforting oak of his desk with an expression like a high school football coach who just found out is star quarterback is quitting to learn the finer arts of long jump—disbelief, disappointment, and disgust all fought for supremacy on the field of his quietly lined face. I'd never noticed how deep set his eyes were before today. They dug into his face deep wells of vision that appeared to be more myopic than even my own defective pair. I hoped that his short sightedness wouldn't extend to my future as a free man.

Just as I was thinking that he really could make things far worse for me, I realized that he'd been speaking to me. I was holding my breath, listening to the thumping of my blood stream grow stronger and louder with each second I denied my brain fresh oxygen. It was only when I noticed the warden's lips moving that I realized he was talking.

"I'm sorry, Warden Trippet. Could you say that again? I didn't quite catch that."

Good one, Mac. Paying attention might just be a little important here, don't you think? See if you can get through this without getting arrested, would you?

I resisted with all my will power the temptation to tell my brother to keep his mouth shut while I focused my attention on the recap of the warden's opening words.

"I was saying that we seem to have a bit of a sticky situation here." The warden paused and looked at me as though expecting me to whip out an oil can and lubricate said situation to his satisfaction. He was going to be disappointed. After a few silent minutes in which I tried my hardest to look back at him in mute confusion about what he might possibly mean, he carried on, "Mac, I'll be completely honest with you here. I hope you can do me the same courtesy. I have been very pleased with your work in our mail room. You've been a conscientious employee. You do your work efficiently, and I feel that the Special Services department has benefitted from your presence. That's why I'm so shocked by the complaint before me. Normally in these circumstances, termination would be immediate, but because you've been such a model employee, I wanted to give you the opportunity to explain yourself before I made any kind of decision."

Another long pause, during which, I think Warden Trippet expected me to come clean, confess all my sins, perform an act of contrition and report directly to the mail room in time for today's delivery. I was the kind of problem Harold Trippet liked: quick, easy, and nonviolent. It was a far cry from the inmates threatening to riot over a loss of their TV privileges. Unfortunately, I wasn't about to give this off the rack suit a glimpse into what had been going on. I might be crazy, but I wasn't stupid. I sat there, biding my time, waiting for some inspiration to come to me that might explain away all the Warden's concerns. Nothing happened. I silently called to Newt for suggestions.

Beats me, little brother. You're going to have to tell him something pretty soon though.

Always so helpful when I need him. I cursed Newt under my breath and launched into some delay tactics in the hope that I might come up with a reasonable series of lies to extract myself from this office and from this prison permanently.

"Warden, what is it exactly that I'm supposed to have done here?" I hoped my voice didn't sound as shaky as it felt.

Mac, calm down. You sound guilty as hell.

Easy for him to say. He wasn't on the verge of losing everything.

"Well, Mac, I left a message for you indicating that I'd had a complaint from a young lady. Well, as it turns out this young lady is the sister of a victim of a horrible crime. An inmate here is responsible for her sister's death. She claims that you..."

I decided to cut him off before he could dig the hole too deeply. "Oh, is this about Rachel Strong? I can explain all that." I was talking fast now, trying to get out some kind of story before the warden had too much time to think about it. "Now that I look back at it, it was probably bad judgment on my part, but I really felt sorry for her. Sometimes people just affect you like that, don't they? Anyway, when I read her letter to the prisoner here who killed her sister, I felt awful for her. I know what it's like to lose a sibling. My brother died when I was only 14, you know." I risked a quick look at him. He was listening attentively, his eyebrows coming together in what I hoped was sympathy for my confessed loss. "Anyway, I just felt like I wanted to help her. She seemed like she was in so much pain, and I know what that's like, so, well, I called her. I know I shouldn't have done that. I know I'm not supposed to use any of the information I get through the prisoner's mail, but I just couldn't get this poor girl's suffering out of my head. It felt like I should offer her some condolences or something. I guess she was pretty mad about it. She didn't give me a very warm welcome, and I regretted it as soon as I'd done it, but I didn't mean any harm." I stopped, surprised at myself. I'd managed to work in several grains of truth, and when I sneaked a look at the warden I thought I saw just the faintest glimmer of pity in his face. I hoped I'd given him enough reason to chalk this up to good intentions executed badly.

The warden opened my file and made few notes while I felt my breathing return to normal. He put down his pen and looked directly at me, a shy sort of smile betraying his relief at not having to fire me on the spot. "Of course, Mac. I understand that it's difficult not to become emotionally involved sometimes. We're only human, after all. It's obvious that you didn't have any real mischief at heart. I think I can probably let this go without too much fuss. I'll have to put a disciplinary note in your file, and I don't think I can get away without indicating a suspension of some kind. Now, your co-worker Joe tells me you've been out sick for three days this week. How about if we count those days as time served as we say in the business, and you return to work as normal this morning?"

I was stunned. Not only was I getting away with my lie, I still had a job. I was tempted to just shake Trippet's hand and make my way to the mail room, but Newt's voice in my head wouldn't let me take that road.

Man, you are home free! All you have to do now is say "thanks, but I quit" and we're out of here. Then, we can get back to the real work here. I think I might have come up with some kind of plan to find Rachel. Come on, what are you waiting for? Christmas? A personal invitation from the queen? Get busy, and we'll get gone.

I knew he was right. As easy as it would be to go back to work, and forget about Rachel, I could never forget Newt. He wouldn't have that. If I stayed in this dead end job now, I really would be ready for the nuthouse. Newt would see to it personally. I met the warden's small eyes for a moment and then gave him my farewell speech.

"I really appreciate everything you're doing for me here, sir. I know that I could easily have been fired over this, and you've been more than understanding about the situation. I have to say that it's more than I expected and probably a lot more than I deserve. Especially now." I gulped some air trying to find words that would smooth over my exit. I stared at the flag, the Maple Leaf warped by the folds that no wind would ever blow out. I felt warped like that, compromised somehow. And then it came to me. I sat up straight in my chair and delivered the death blow to my employment at Eastglen. "Honestly, sir, I really feel like I've compromised my effectiveness here. I don't know when I'm going to be affected like that again by a letter or picture that passes over my desk. I just don't think that I can stay here in good conscience. I'm sorry to go, but I think it will be better for everyone if I just clean out my desk and turn in my Special Services badge."

It was Trippet's turn to look stunned. I think the last thing he expected was this. "Mac, are you sure this is what you want to do? I really think that we can move past this."

"I'm sure, sir. I wouldn't feel right staying now."

"Well, if you're sure, there's not much I can do to stop you. It is a shame to lose you, though, Mac. You've been a great addition to the staff here. The department will sorely miss you." He stood up and held out his hand in a standard good bye form and I took it without hesitation.

"I'm sure Joe will do fine. He practically runs the department as it is. And you'll be able to find a replacement for me in no time." I was getting antsy standing there. I wanted to be gone. I wanted to be far from the reminder of how I got into this mess in the first place. While I was planning my escape route back to my car, I noticed the warden's lips moving again.

"...guess we can have your final check ready for you tomorrow. Do you want to pick it up or shall we mail it?

"Mail it." I didn't hesitate. Wild elephants were not going to drag me back here if I could help it. "Well, Mr. Trippet, it's been a pleasure to know you and to work for you. I'd better be going."

"I might say the same to you, Mac. And if you need a reference for your next position, don't hesitate to give the office a call. I'd be happy to write a letter of recommendation for you."

Gail would be pleased to hear that. I didn't really care myself. All I was interested in was leaving. After a few more words of thanks, I backed toward the door, exiting with as much speed as was decent. One stop to say good bye to Joe, and it was adios to the big house.

Chapter 30

I moved through the administration wing of Eastglen with all the speed and purposefulness I could summon. I kept a look of stern determination on my face designed to keep away those of my former coworkers who reveled in idle chatter. I gave a terse nod to the group I passed in the coffee room, only pausing to note one of the guards supporting the long tired cliché of hanging around the water cooler, sharing gossip from the cell block with a secretary in an obviously successful attempt to impress her. I wanted to grab them by the hair and slam their heads together. Wasn't there enough misery in the place without them trotting it out to be used as pick up lines? I couldn't get out of the building fast enough. I almost changed my mind about returning to my desk at all, but I just couldn't leave the place without saying something to Joe. He reminded me so forcefully of a lost puppy that it would have been cruel to kick him like that.

I walked through the door of the mail room and let it bang noisily behind me, announcing my arrival to the only other member of this department's staff. Joe looked up from the work he was absorbed in and smiled broadly at the sight of me. I couldn't help but grin sheepishly back at him. Making friends hasn't been a strong point in my life. In fact, I've actively worked to avoid it, but I found myself looking at Joe with the realization that I would actually miss him.

"Hey, Mac. I thought you were never coming back. It's been so boring here without you. I've had to have lunch three times with that creepy guy from the library. He only ever has cheese sandwiches and chocolate milk." Joe gave me a warm smile before he continued. "Are you feeling better, Mac? What was wrong with you, anyway? I'm really glad to see you."

I could see him warming up to give me the full run down on everything I'd missed in the days that I'd been absent, and I almost let him launch into it. It felt safe to sit in this office and listen to Joe go on about whatever happened to be on his mind at that moment. Much safer than heading out into the world to find a crazy woman and get her off my conscience. The prospect of that made me want to call up the warden and tell him I changed my mind. I found myself looking at Joe with envy. He had it so easy. His world was simple and straightforward. Mine was not, a fact which was brought into sharp relief by the sound of my dear departed brother's voice cutting through the hum of the air conditioning system.

What are you waiting for? We're home free, brother. Get your shit, and let's get out of here. You want to stay for lunch with Joe the Morbid Loser or you want to get the hell away from here and on with our lives. Come on! Didn't I tell you I had a plan to find Rachel? Hurry up. Don't you want to get rid of me for good?

My loyalty to Joe was dwarfed at the image of me sitting serenely on a park bench listening to birds chirp without the nagging sound of Newt's voice attempting a two part harmony with them. I willed myself not to get riled up at the unkind words he'd spoken about Joe, at least until we were out of earshot. Instead, I summoned all my courage to deliver the blow that I knew was going to hurt Joe's feelings beyond measure. He was still staring at me, his wide grin a more authentic welcome than any I'd felt maybe ever.

I smiled back at him before I motioned for him to sit down. "Thanks for all your messages, Joe. It's nice to know that someone out there was worried about me."

His face lit up like I'd just given him the key to the city. He was beaming with loyal pride. He started to renew his line of questioning about my health, but I had to stop him mid-sentence. I wanted to get this over with and get out of cinder block hell. "Listen, Joe, I do really appreciate your calls, and everything you've done for me, but I, well, I just quit." I hurried through the rest of the explanations without meeting his eyes. "The truth is that I just don't want to read other people's mail anymore. It makes me feel, I don't know, weird. And I can't take any more of the degenerate stuff that comes through here.

If I see one more fat chick in latex I'm going to have to give up women for good. So, I told Trippet I was out of here. I'm just here to pick up my stuff, and then, that's it for me and the wonderful world of criminal rehabilitation. It's been really great working with you, though, man. You made this job a lot more bearable, if you know what I mean."

I looked straight at Joe and held my hand out to him. I could see the disbelief and hurt in his eyes. I don't think he ever conceived of the idea that I might not want to read all the sick crap that passed through our office. He took my hand and gave it a feeble shake. I felt like dirt, like I'd betrayed my best friend and sold him out to the Romans. I walked over to my desk and started opening drawers. It was only a few books I wanted. I didn't keep any other personal effects, and I just didn't see myself as the type of guy who needed to clean my employer out of staples and paper clips. I took a look out the window, my prized possession, down at the yard and into the hills beyond. "But just think Joe, you're in charge here, now. You run this department. You can even move your stuff into my desk. You've got the seniority. The window's all yours."

This brought a faint smile to Joe's lips, and he made his way across the room to where I stood. "Hey, I never realized you had such a great view of the yard. You can see everything the inmates are doing. Wow, can I really have your desk, Mac?" And the bright side materialized before Joe's eyes. I wouldn't miss the view but it was golden to Joe.

"Sure, I'll even help you move your stuff over if you want."

"Wow. Thanks, Mac." He and I busied ourselves moving his belongings over to his new work space, and he sat down in the only chair on wheels in the office and surveyed his surroundings like a newly crowned monarch staring out at his courtiers. I couldn't help smiling at his enthusiasm. I stopped suddenly though when the door opened and the mail bag entered the room. Joe rushed to take the huge sack out of Freddy's hands and drop it onto the big work table in the center of the office. When I heard the metallic clang of the rivets against the metal of the table, a chill rushed through me. Like I'd been dipped in icy water, I shivered spontaneously and remembered how desperate I was to get away from this place. Holding my few belongings under one arm, I repeated the gesture of shaking hands with Joe.

"Well, it's all yours now, Joe. I hope you enjoy it."

His eyes were shining now; he was excited about diving into the day's work. "Okay, Mac. Well I better get busy now that it's only me here." He was walking toward the bag, opening it and dragging out envelope after envelope as I made my way to the door. I took one last look around the room and counted myself lucky that the morning's events had gone so smoothly. Not wanting to push my luck, I backed out of the office, gave Joe a final farewell wave that he barely acknowledged, and headed toward the exit. I heard Joe give a low whistle, and I knew he must have found something depraved enough to make my departure nothing more than a small hiccup in his day.

I walked out of the prison without looking back, feeling in a strange way like I'd just been released early for good behavior. The chill air of September hit my face hard as I went through the double doors. It gave me a sense of renewal and hope. Liberating myself was having a profound effect on me. I felt calm and clear and excited. After all, didn't Newt say he had a plan? A plan to find Rachel and set us both free. Free. I said the word over and over in my mind. Feeling it more than hearing it. I couldn't wait to find out what Newt had come up with.

Chapter 31

Little brother, I have a confession to make. I don't really have a plan. I just said that to get you moving.

"What did you say?" I was sitting in the driver's seat of the car, waiting for it to warm up enough to get out of there. "You can't be serious." I was sure I'd misunderstood Newt. He couldn't possibly be that stupidly cruel. It wasn't human. Neither was my brother, apparently; I heard him laughing at my confusion.

No really, I have no plan. You were dawdling in there. I thought you were going to chicken out. I couldn't let you stay there. I had to say something to get you moving. It's not my fault you were getting all sentimental and mushy about Joe Blow back there. Now, come on, little brother, let's get going.

I thought my head was going to explode. I began to take deep breaths, trying to remember how well the morning had gone. My instincts were to fly into a rage of catastrophic proportions, but I struggled to master the urge to beat my head against the steering wheel until it was a bloody mess of matted hair and brain. Instead, I sat there, listening to the regular hum of the combustion engine and tried to feel numb.

Of the many disadvantages to losing an older brother at the age of 14, and, believe me, they are many, the worst is that I never had the opportunity for my shot at the title. For 14 years, he held me at his mercy. I was the victim of teasing, of open laughter at my expense, of strange science experiments in which I would be pinned to the ground while my loving older brother held a magnifying glass over the mole on my left arm in an attempt to remove it using the suns rays. I don't know how long I would have been trapped there, watching smoke rise up from the wispy hairs that covered my forearm if Gail hadn't appeared in the yard, complaining of a smell like burning flesh. Newt quickly hid the magnifying glass in his pocket, and I swore an oath of revenge against my brother that I never got the chance to exact.

Newt was bestowed with all the best of the physical qualities our dear departed Dan had to pass down. He inherited all the tall genes, the coordinated genes and, let's not forget the athletic genes that Dan had to offer our genetic make up. I didn't lose out on all of them, but I didn't get the same strong One A types that Newt got. I was always going to be a little bit shorter; I was never going to try out for the football team, except as the water boy; and the only fight I'd ever been in, I won by default because the other guy was so much drunker than I was. I'm not complaining about my genetic heritage. There's no point anyway, considering I can't pull up to Dr. John's genetic transplant clinic and reshape my DNA strand into something a bit more masterful. What I am complaining about is the fact that my stupid, selfish brother died before I had the chance to hit my growth spurt and even the score a little. I don't know that I would have been able to do much damage, but I'm pretty sure I wouldn't have ended up on the ground simpering like I did when I was ten. At the very least, I would have had 16 or so years to build up a good head of steam. The momentum alone probably would have allowed me to do a little damage. I wasn't talking broken bones or wired jaws, but a black eye sure would have been nice.

Instead of evening the score though, I had the painful denial of satisfaction that his untimely death brought. It wasn't enough that he had to completely ruin my life by dying and then coming back to haunt me like this, he had to cut off any chance at vindication I might ever have had. My advice to all those younger brothers out there is this—don't wait, hit your older brother now. You never know what's coming around the corner that might prevent you from getting even for all those taunts and tricks you suffered while you were helpless under his thumb. You wouldn't want to end up sitting in a car, being tormented by a dead sibling who hadn't grown any more compassionate with the passage of time.

Look, I don't understand you at all, Mac. You say you want to sort this out. You admit you've been dragging your heels, and now, when I try to get you moving in some direction, any direction, you get all pissed off at me. What's the problem? You're angry because you never got the chance to beat me up? Is that what's going on here? Well, I'm sorry. I'm sorry I got electrocuted and denied you the all important opportunity to get even. I'm sorry you were such a weakling runt when we were kids. I'm sorry you didn't have the guts to stand up to me then. Is that what you want to hear? Fine, well, I've said it. Now put the goddamn car in gear, and let's get out of here.

There were no words for the anger I felt right then. I seriously considered, at that moment, a warm bath with a razor blade for the first time since I'd been released from Lynnwood. At least dead, I might have a chance at being on the same fucked up metaphysical plane as Newt. Maybe there I could show him a thing or two about sibling rivalry. Even as I was thinking about it though, I knew it was no good. I wasn't through with living yet. In fact, I felt like I'd just started with the business of life. I'd felt more interested in life, my own and Rachel's, in the last week than I had in ten years, and I was getting comfortable with it. I couldn't just sink like that despite the pleasure it would give me to see Newt trapped like the rat he was for the rest of eternity.

Breathing deeply, I regained a small amount of calm. I put the car in gear and backed out of the lot. I heard Newt's voice; the drone of it making me feel nauseous. I couldn't concentrate on the words; I just kept my mind on the road ahead of me. One more turn to the freeway access and I was on the road home. Newt's voice was becoming clearer, as though it was being amplified by a giant PA system in my head.

"Newt, I think the best thing you could do for both of us is just keep your mouth shut for a while. I don't want to hear you or think about you for the rest of the drive home. I don't even want to acknowledge that you're my brother right now. Pretend you belong to someone else. Pretend you've moved on to the hell you so rightly deserve." I was seething with anger at him, but my voice was filled with calm exacting tones and nothing more. He must have known I wasn't kidding and for the first time actually paid attention to my pleas for silence.

I let my mind roam through the silence, appreciating it so much more because I knew it was killing Newt to keep quiet. Now, when we were on the verge of some kind of breakthrough, I knew he wanted to be talking more than anything except maybe resurrection. He could feel it as well as I could. Both of us could sense that something big was about to happen. But what?

That was the real question that scared me. I knew whatever was ahead was coming whether I was ready or not. And I knew that there was nothing I could do to stop the chain of events that I'd set into motion by making that first call to Rachel. I'd stopped wondering why I'd let myself be talked into making that call. There wasn't any point in questioning the mischievous machinations of fate. She was a meddling bitch with her own agenda.

It struck me that maybe that was the secret here. Not to be fooled by fate's buttinski ways. Not to be suckered into taking the bait and winding up without any control over your own destiny. The trick did not lie in what curve balls life threw at you but rather with how you attempted to catch those balls. I shook these thoughts from my head as I made my way through the waves of traffic washing over the roads. I couldn't stand the thought of being behind home plate, no mask, no pads, not even a glove to soften the sting of the wild pitches being hurled from only 30 yards away. I was alone, unprotected and couldn't read the hand signals from my pitcher.

My desperation must have shown through my anger because when Newt started talking again, he did it with what I'm sure I'd have to call sensitivity.

Mac? Little brother?

I cut him off, feeling like a viper just waiting for a target to inject with foul smelling venom. "Stop calling me little brother. You gave up that privilege when I got to be older than you."

Don't be ridiculous, Mac, his voice was quiet and positively gentle, *you'll always be my little brother. Don't you see that yet? Nothing we can do on this earth or beyond will ever change the fact that I'm your big brother. It's a fact of life.*

He said it simply and without the irony I thought the statement deserved, considering he hadn't had any taste of life since he let himself get the shock of all time on that fence.

*And please don't remind me that I have no business commenting on life.
I am more aware than you can possibly imagine that I am dead. But the facts
are the facts, Mac, and you and I can't change them. Gail had two sons, and
they weren't twins. You will always be my little brother. If you can't live with
that, then we're probably never going to get anywhere, and I should just get
comfortable here inside your head because unless you're ready to start facing
the truths out there, I'll be stuck here for fucking ever.*

He shut up then, and in the quiet his silence left, a scene from our
childhood leapt into my mind's eye. I saw him sulking in the corner
of our shared playroom when he was only nine. He faced the corner
of the room sitting on one of the low kiddy stools Gail had bought for
us. His elbow rested on his knee, his chin in his hand propping up his
head in a stance so much older than his few accumulated years. He
resembled a miniature version of Rodin's *Thinker*, and although I
wouldn't have been able to articulate it then, he seemed to reek of all
the angst he would feel later after his death. Angst caused by me
when I ratted him out to Gail for not sharing his Hot Wheels with me,
his only brother. She told him that if he wasn't willing to share with
his own flesh and blood, he could just learn to live without the toys
entirely. And she didn't mean just him, either. I didn't even have the
sublime pleasure of playing with the cars myself, torturing my selfish
brother with the image of me crashing them into each other, chipping
the paint.

"If you are going to squeal on your own brother, you don't deserve
to enjoy the benefits he's been denied." I wasn't even sure what she
meant at the time. All I knew was that she was punishing me for
Newt's crime. But was she? Maybe she was trying to tell me, tell us
both, that we would have to stick together—no matter what. She'd
always been a sneaky parent, devising clever lessons and then
slipping them in almost unnoticed so that we'd get the point without
ever realizing she'd masterminded the whole thing.

While I was certain my current situation was not some grandiose
plan of Gail's to teach me a lesson, the truth of this memory hit me in
the face hard. Newt and I had to stick together, and stick together we
had done. Through life and death we'd been stuck together

Chapter 32

By the time I pulled into the lot of my apartment building, I'd built up a staggering four alarm headache. I sat in the car for a moment after I'd killed the engine, listening to the ping of the mechanics cooling down in the morning air. I put my cheek against the still chilly window and felt the booming of blood squeezing through the tiny passages of my brain. As much as I felt like I was drawing to a conclusion of some kind, I seriously doubted that I had enough strength to even get out of the car, let alone find a way for my brother's spirit to move on. With each pulse of pain through my skull, I felt weaker and more alone than ever before. I was certain that I needed a drink; certain that something clear and strong would put everything back into perspective for me, but I knew there would be no end to Newt's whining if I put the car back into gear and drove to the nearest 24-hour wet-your-whistle stop.

I didn't know if I cared about his disappointment so much as I did about the griping I'd have to endure. I didn't have the strength to block it out. I rubbed my eyes, trying to wipe away some of the cloudiness that blurred my vision. I reached in the glove box and found a plastic bottle of pills shaking merrily beneath the label that promised relief without the stomach upset. I squeezed and pulled at the safety cap, finally beating it open on the steering wheel. Tossing two into my mouth, I chewed them into a dense paste that lined the surfaces of my mouth with their sour medicinal flavor. Washing them down with meager drops of saliva, I left the rest of the pills to fend for themselves, scattering them over the passenger seat of the car when

I let the bottle slip from my hand like a suicide would with all the pills that didn't make it into the system before the drowsiness set in.

I realized that I didn't have any idea what I was going to do now. I had no job and no money; I hadn't paid my rent and didn't know if I was going to be able to; the police were lining up to find me guilty of anything; and most importantly, I had a girl on the edge of a magnificent breakdown trying to gain vindication for my misuse of her. Things hadn't looked this bad when I'd left only a couple of hours before. Then, I had the idea that this mess could be sorted out, that I would be able to give up my life of secrets, exchanging it for something a little less isolated and a little more regular.

But that was the trick, wasn't it? Getting away from that place where all I knew were secrets, all I kept close to my heart were the lies I'd told over the years to protect myself from the know-it-alls who didn't know anything. It was going to be the biggest trick I'd performed yet because secrets are difficult things. They breed alienation and estrangement. They encourage you to make yourself unknown, a stranger to everybody, whispering in your ear that no one will understand, no one will be able to help. And soon, if your secret is big enough, it becomes your only friend—the only one to be trusted. I was tired of living like this, but I just didn't know how to do it any differently any more. It felt like there were only strangers and enemies out there. Just who was I going to trust with my secrets? I'd tried Gail once, but she'd thrown my confidence to the dogs when she had me committed. I'd tried Rachel, but she was too caught up in her own pain to help me. I couldn't really blame her for being preoccupied with whatever anguish she was feeling right now. If Newt and I were right about her sister communing with her like my brother did with me, she was rightfully confused and distraught. She hadn't had a decade to adjust to the fact that she was hearing voices from beyond the grave.

Even as I had that thought, I cringed at the B movie cliché of anything coming from beyond the grave. It was just my luck that the turmoil of my life could be summed up by something from a Wes Craven film. I could have sat in my car comparing my life to *Night of the Living Dead* all morning, but Newt was prodding me to at least go inside for a cup of coffee.

Mac! Mac! I'm talking to you. Come on, you'll freeze to death out here. Let's go inside where we can talk about this. Stop worrying so much. We'll figure out what to do. There's no point in hiding in your car. I can still find you. And it's not a very good hiding spot from the cops in case your man is looking for some answers again.

"Just a right little ray of sunshine, aren't you, Newt? You know I didn't really think I could feel worse, but you've somehow managed to find something to bring me just a peg lower. Thanks a lot. No, I mean it. You've given me a whole new outlook on things. Now, I can start worrying about getting arrested again."

Look, you are not going to be arrested. You haven't done anything. We're going to sort all this out before it ever comes to that. We'll find Rachel and get her to go to the cops. We'll make sure they know that she's just a confused, hurt girl who didn't mean any harm. We'll get through this, Mac.

The world started closing down on me. My vision was growing narrower by the second, and soon, all I could see was the outline of one word dancing before my eyes. I felt my mouth opening and hoped it wouldn't be a long wail of frustrated agony that emerged. Trying to master myself, I heard my voice crack as I uttered the only question that mattered to me anymore, "How?"

How were we going to do all those things? How would Newt make everything all right again? How would I ever feel any of the regular things people were supposed to feel, like love and trust and happiness? I felt the burn of emotion in my throat, wanted to vomit it up and expel it from my system like so many troublesome students in a parochial school. The how of it all is where I found myself paralyzed. I knew I had to do all these things. Somehow I needed to find Rachel, convince her to get the cops off my back, tell her that it was okay if her sister was whispering secrets to her from another dimension. And this was going to make it all better. This was going to make Newt's voice magically disappear from my mind. I suddenly found it difficult to believe that securing Rachel's sanity had anything at all to do with the enigmatic task that Newt was meant to help me perform. After all, who knew that Rachel would be thrown into my life so many years after Newt had died. There was no way to know when Newt died and entered limbo that one day some psychotic was going to rape and kill some girl whose sister would suffer from my

209

same plight. I'd read enough to know that you couldn't escape your destiny, but this wasn't the Delphic Oracle predicting that a king would be overthrown by his son. Too many factors were present here. Too many twists and turns in the story line had passed under my nose to believe that it was predestined that I'd go to work at Eastglen prison and eventually uncover Rachel and her own version of a troubled life.

This didn't change the fact that I was highly motivated to find Rachel and help her out. I was feeling more than a little responsible for pushing her into her current state, and I was ready for atonement. Despite this though and despite Newt's avid assurances that we were on the right track, I just didn't get the connection. I felt like I had to go through these motions, and I would, but I didn't have any real hope that it was going to solve my problem. Hope was over rated anyway. It was better to go on without any expectation of success. At least that way I wouldn't have to suffer so much the pain of disappointment. It wouldn't be such a surprise when I woke of the morning after and still heard the dead whisper of my brother.

I'd been sitting in the car, parked and getting colder by the second, for 40 minutes, completely unaware of the comings and goings of my neighbors as they made their way into the world. I was brought back to the reality of the present by a tap on the passenger side window. I jumped and looked up to see the face of my landlord, Edward, peering in the window, a tentative smile on his lips. I didn't want to meet with him in the front seat of my car, so I returned the smile and got out after I carefully locked all the doors making sure Rachel wouldn't have an opportunity to surprise me like she had the night before.

I came around to the passenger side of the car where Edward was waiting, that same questioning smile glued to his face. He was a dull man charged with managing the building I lived in. He knew how to fix a dryer and had a nifty set of wrenches he used to tighten pipes and change faucets. I hadn't really had much to do with him in the years I'd lived there, other than my monthly hand over the rent meeting, but he was a decent enough guy who expected everyone to fit into one of the neat compartments society had shown him over the years. I suspected he was going to give me grief about how late my rent was, so I opened with my apologies.

"Hi, Edward, how are you? Listen, I've been meaning to drop by my rent check, but things have been a little haywire this week. Do you want to come and get it right now? I have it all written out and everything." I thought I sounded pretty casual. I didn't think I was coming off like the panicked freak I felt myself to have become.

Edward looked at me, his smile faded a bit into a look of concern, and I thought I must have been mistaken. I must have looked and sounded every bit of the insane jerk I seemed to be. I couldn't even fumble my way through any more small talk, I just stood there, looking back at Edward looking at me.

He opened his mouth twice before he actually spoke, as if he wasn't sure how to begin. Crazy thoughts invaded my mind during the silence of his hesitation—the cops had been to see him and now he, too, was convinced I was a mass murderer; I was being evicted bodily for not paying my rent on time, and he was just here to give me the name of the warehouse where all my belongings had been taken; he'd heard me talking to no one and had made arrangements for the paddy wagon to pick me up. I wanted him to speak so badly I saw myself grabbing his arm and twisting it behind his back until he spilled everything he ever knew or thought about. Of course, Edward was about a foot taller than me and had the shoulders of a linebacker, so there was no way I was about to force him into anything, and it was only my imagination that put all those words into his mouth anyway. Newt was nestled in one corner of my brain telling me to keep calm.

Don't do anything stupid, Mac. Let him say whatever he has to say. It's no big deal. He just wants the rent. He is not your enemy. He's nothing to you or me except a landlord. Just breathe easy.

"Mac, did you know you've been sitting in your car for over half an hour. I saw you pull in from my kitchen window. When you didn't get out for so long, I got kind of worried. Is everything all right?"

The genuine interest in his voice touched me. I wanted to tell him that everything was definitely not all right, that I didn't know if anything would ever be all right. Instead, I heard myself dealing out another lie that was bathed in just enough truth that I might recognize it some time in the future.

"Yeah, Edward, everything's okay. I was just thinking. I quit my job this morning, and I've been thinking about what I'm going to do now. I just got sort of lost, daydreaming about what I might do next.

You know, should I be an astronaut or a fireman now. That sort of thing. Nothing earth shattering. Anyway, do you want to come get the rent now, or should I drop it off later today?"

I shut him and his concern down by telling him I was, as of this morning, unemployed again. He forgot all about me sitting in the car on a freezing morning in September and started worrying about me turning into a deadbeat right before his eyes. Edward had seen me change jobs four or five times, and even though I'd always managed to pay my way, my lifestyle clearly made him uncomfortable. He squirmed in his jacket and rubbed his hands together. His voice took on a significantly colder tone, "I'll get the check right now, if it's convenient."

"Yeah, it's convenient," I sighed. "It'll be one more thing to cross off the to do list, you know, quit job, pay rent, have breakfast." I tried to sound nonchalant, but it came out more like sadly desperate. My weak smile was lost on Edward's now stern face. He was back to being all business, and I was all alone again.

With the rent check in his hand, I shut the door behind Edward and turned to look at my home, although why I called it a home was a mystery to me. It was strewn with newspapers all open to the crossword page. Books lay, open and closed, on just about every surface that wasn't otherwise cluttered with laundry or dirty dishes. I couldn't even remember the last time I'd bothered to straighten up the place. I had an impulse to torch everything and start over somewhere else, but like most of the impulses I'd had in the last while, I figured it needed to be suppressed. I hadn't exactly been batting a thousand with my choices in the last three months, so why add arson to the list of errors I had on my stat sheet?

I sat down heavily in the one armchair I owned. It was an ancient, brown overstuffed piece of the seventies. I hated it, but it served its purpose, and no one could deny its comfort. I grabbed at one book after another, looking for something that might distract me for a few minutes. I wasn't ready to face the questions that my morning had left me with. I read the first paragraph of *The Three Musketeers* four times before I decided that this was maybe the first time in my life when I'd found no solace in the pages of a book. My whole life, I had escaped my troubles by immersing myself in the lives of fictional characters. It was so much easier to be the clerk on the graveyard shift in an all night convenience store when you had the company of Percival Keene or Athos and company or even Yossarian and his troop of desperate warriors trying to survive.

I could not remember a time when I did not read for pleasure. In fact, I could not remember a time when I did not read. On the first day of school, after I'd recovered from the terror of having my name announced in front of a room full of strangers, my teacher, Miss Briggs, instructed the class to open our reading primers and started talking about how the first thing we would learn to do in the first grade was read. I looked around the room at my fellow victims of state-sponsored education and saw the looks of fear and concern springing up on nearly every face. All I could think as I paged through the dull, predictable stories about Dick, Jane and their dog Spot, was *What do you mean, learn to read?* I was honestly shocked at the fact that none of the other kids knew that all those letters they'd been learning to draw actually came together to make words and stories. Apparently, they thought the alphabet was a really fun little song to sing, but that was the extent of it. I, on the other hand, had been reading my own bedtime stories since I could remember having bed time stories. Gail would sit with me and turn the pages as I read the complete works of Dr. Seuss, *The Story of Ferdinand*, and my personal favorite, Maurice Sendak's *Where The Wild Things Are*. As I got older and more precocious, so did my reading. By the time I was twelve, I'd read *The Martian Chronicles* and *Fantastic Voyage*. I was also the only person I knew who had read all of the *Tales of Narnia*, letting myself be swept into worlds so different from my own that I developed a love of fantasy writing that warmed me up for the biggies like Carl Sagan and JRR Tolkien. It certainly didn't make me fit in any better with the kids in my class, but I didn't need them so much because I had all those ready pals within the words on the page. Isolationism starts early, I guess, but I was glad for the means of protection and escape. Indeed, it's the main thing I'm grateful to my father for. Maybe the only thing.

The gift I got from my father was not his physique or his timing but, rather, his love of books and reading. Gail often reminded me, back in the days when we still spoke like mother and son, how much of Dan she could see in me when I held a book. "You wrinkle up your forehead just like your father did when he read. I've never seen anyone but the two of you do that. You really are your father's son, Mac." She would ruffle my hair and go back to whatever it was that she was doing, but I always caught her sneaking looks at me, a furtive and bittersweet smile playing along her mouth as she remembered her husband through her child. It always made me happy that I could remind Gail of Dan in some way. And happy, too, that I was like him even if it was a similarity that stopped when I closed the book. Now, of course, Gail was the closed book. I wouldn't imagine that seeing me read would bring memories of Dan rushing back to her anymore. She didn't seem to have a memory for anything but my long list of shortcomings. I wondered if a day would ever come when she would tell me one more time that I looked like Dan. I wasn't hopeful.

The pages I held limply in my hand felt dry, like they would crumble into ashes like so much burnt paper. There was no reprieve in fiction today. I had too much reality to overcome. There was only one way for me to find a little peace. I got up and headed for the door, pausing only to respond to Newt's nervous questions.

What's up, Mac? Where are you going? We've got some thinking to do here. What are we going to do about Rachel? What are we going to do about the police? We've got to come up with some kind of plan to get you out of this mess, don't you think?

"Oh, it's just me now. is it? I thought we were interested in getting you out of this mess. Well, I tell you what. I have a little plan of my own for this afternoon. Why don't you put your thinking cap on and see what you can come up with. We'll talk about it later and compare ideas. Right now, I have to get out of this box for a while." And I cut him off from my thoughts. I walked out of the apartment, ignoring his monotonous drone, thinking solely about my destination.

Chapter 33

I pulled into the parking lot at Dodger's and shut the car off. I was plunged into silence as the radio cut off with the engine. George Straight had been crooning on the country station I employed to shut out my dead brother. A part of me hated to do it, but I just couldn't bear to hear his voice anymore for a while. He'd had me on an emotional rollercoaster all day—well, through most of the last ten years actually—and I just wasn't equipped to deal with it anymore at that moment.

In the soundless vacuum that was my car, I could hear Newt begin his cautionary tale about the evils of drink. I knew he was scared that I would just drink myself into a stupor by five and be completely useless until tomorrow. It was with good reason that he harbored this fear because that was exactly what I intended to do. I locked the car and made my way to Steve's door. He'd only been open for about ten minutes, so I had the place to myself. I walked up to the bar and slid my keys across it to Steve. He took them wordlessly and stowed them in his cash drawer. On his way over to me, he filled a glass with ice and picked up a bottle of vodka. He put both in front of me and went back to wiping the grime of the previous night off the bar.

I stared at the bottle. It was a cheap well vodka that would do the job for which it was distilled but wouldn't make any promises it couldn't keep about smooth, clean flavor. I was fine with that. I wasn't interested in anything but its utility. I knew that I'd promised myself I wouldn't use the ease of inebriation to iron out the hardships in my life anymore, and I wanted to keep that promise. But I kept seeing poor Rachel, dirty and scared. And I heard Gail over and over telling me that I was certainly going to become a drunk, living in the gutter. And I heard Newt big brothering me, trying to bully me from the grave. I hesitated only a second before I poured the first of many drinks I would have that day. I picked up the glass, held it to the light in a silent toast, admiring the clarity of it, wishing for that transparency in my own life. If only I had the kind of life I wouldn't mind having people see through. Not me, though. I had too many secrets. I had to build a solid wall designed to misdirect and mislead those approaching me. And I'd gone and let that wall get a huge dent in it when I started up my antics with Rachel. I felt stupid and sorry for myself, but the first big swallow tempered that. The second made everything seem a little less pressing. By the third glass, my predicament was almost funny—not funny, ha ha, but funny, peculiar. It took until the fifth glass for me to find it funny, ha ha.

By that time, of course, pretty much everything was funny, ha ha. As the afternoon wore on, I was joined by Estelle and Reggie and the few other loyal afternoon barflies who could always be found in their usual places at Dodger's. Steve hardly spoke to me, but I couldn't tell if it was because he was still pissed at me about bringing the cops here, or if he just knew I was on some kind of a mission. He'd seen me on binges before. After the third one, we made a deal that he would let me get as pie-eyed as I wanted, providing I turned my keys in when I arrived. As long as I didn't get into any trouble with any of his other patrons, I could stay and drink as much as my tortured little soul demanded. I'd never gotten into more mischief than he could stand, and he made sure I got home without killing myself or anyone else. The system had worked to everyone's satisfaction so far. Sometimes, Steve would have to utter a few words of caution if I was getting too out of hand, but I was such a passive drunk most of the time that those occasions came very rarely. The one time he cut me off, I'd tried to pick a fight with a guy who reminded me unbearably of Newt.

It was the guy's tone of voice more than anything else. He was so smug and condescending that I felt myself becoming unglued as I listened to him tell me how much better I'd look if I just hit the gym a couple times a week. In my liquor addled state, I was sure I could give him the beating of a lifetime, despite the obvious physical advantage he had over me. Fortunately for me, Steve caught my arm as I was winding up to deliver one hell of a right cross. Also fortunately for me, Steve thought the guy was as much of a punk as I did. So, while I didn't get the boot from Dodger's, my opponent did. I got a lot of threats from Steve to stop running me a tab, and he cut me off, but I got to stay and listen to him play his favorites on the old Wurlitzer he had in the back of the bar while I sobered up enough for any taxi driver to let me in their cab.

Today, there would be no fights though. I was much too tired for that. After liberating half of the contents of the bottle on the bar, I got up and staggered over to the juke box, fumbling in my jeans for change. I was sure it was the only machine of its kind left on the planet that charged only a dime a song, three for a quarter. I weaved in front of the flashing lights while I tried to focus on the unending list of ditties it offered. Most were golden oldies that had no redeeming qualities other than being light hearted. I got my quarter into its slot on the third try after I'd made my choices and then I went about the business of trying to get my fingers to press all those buttons on the machine. I knew I'd managed to get at least one of the songs right when, after much complicated action on the part of my digits and the record arm, I heard Bob Dylan's cat scratchy voice start the mournful dirge of one who has lived his life as a rolling stone.

I only remember bits and pieces after that. I had a couple of meaningless conversations with Estelle, telling her how much like my grandmother she was. I'd never met either of my grandmothers, but she didn't know that, and it seemed to make her happy that I was drawing such an unlikely comparison. She smiled shyly at me and admitted that she'd always wanted grandchildren. I asked her why she didn't have any, and Steve appeared at the table, ushering me away from her. I was reluctant to give up. "Wait a minute. What's the big idea? I'm having a conversation here. I just wanted to know why Estelle doesn't have any grandkids. Is that some kind of a crime?"

Steve hushed me as he guided me back to my stool. "You jackass, Estelle never could have kids. It's a bad memory for her, what kept her from having a family, so don't go pestering her and churning all that up again."

My curiosity was palatable, but a warning look frcm Steve kept me far from Estelle and her mysterious past. That would have been just the excuse he needed to kick me out, and I wasn't done anesthetizing myself yet. I wandered from table to table bumping into chairs as I wove my way around the bar, always ready in case anyone had an answer to my questions about the purpose of our existence. "No, really, doesn't anyone have the any idea why we're all on this stupid planet?"

My question was met with silence. The kind of silence comes at 3:45 in the morning when you've awoken from troubling dreams only to discover that you are, in all ways, alone. I poured another couple of ounces of vodka and slammed it back. I noticed that Steve had gone into the back room to change one of the draft kegs and grabbed my opportunity while I could. I staggered over to Estelle's table and sat down.

"Now that we can have some privacy," I said nodding toward the store room, "we can carry on our conversation. You were about to tell me why you didn't have grandchildren." I gazed at this woman who must surely be in her sixties with a look that I hope reminded her of all the apple cheeked children she had longed for all those years.

Estelle put down her cards and picked up her wine glass with both hands. She appraised me for a moment or two before she clucked her tongue against her teeth and began talking. Her eyes glazed as she moved from the present and this dirty bar into the past where things must once have seemed quite rosy. "Well, if you really want to know, I'll tell you. Life doesn't always work out the way we imagine it will you know." Boy, did I know.

"I was about 16 years old and the big war had just ended. We were all celebrating. For days on end, we would rush to the train station to welcome home the next batch of braves who'd risked everything. They were so handsome and dangerous. You just knew by looking at them that they had seen more than any living being should. They'd been a party to evil like the world had never known before. That's what war does to a young man. It changes him, makes him capable of things he wouldn't have ever thought he could do. And sometimes when a man is changed like that, he can't ever get right again. It was my bad luck to run into that kind of man.

"It was Saturday night. I can remember it just like it was yesterday. The church in my neighborhood was throwing a social for all the soldiers come home from war. We, my girlfriends and I, we weren't supposed to go because we were too young to be mingling with men like that, but I was determined to go and have myself a dance with one of those fine uniforms. I had to sneak out, wearing pedal pushers and a tee shirt so my father wouldn't be suspicious. I hid my dress and shoes in a bag outside my bedroom window and doubled back to pick them up. It meant I was going to have to change behind the church, but I was willing if it meant I could get inside. There was a little alley way between the church and the minister's house that wasn't very well lit, so I figured I'd slip in there, put on my dress, and be ready to dance the night away in no time. I hadn't counted on there being anyone else in that alley."

Suddenly I wanted her to stop. I knew I didn't want to hear the rest of Estelle's story. I turned my eyes to my glass and took another drink. Estelle did the same and then reached out for my chin and lifted it so our eyes had to meet. "You wanted to hear my story, didn't you? Well, you'll have to listen to all of it. Now where was I?" And she kept on, smiling while she finished her tale.

"I had just got my pedal pushers around my feet. My shoes were off and all I had to do was pull my dress down over my hips. It was then that I heard voices beside me, two of them, talking low about the girl with no pants on. I knew they were talking about me, knew I was in trouble, but before I could get out a scream, one of them was behind me holding his sweaty hand over my mouth. I squirmed and fought, but I was too small to fight back against two strong men who had the memory of all that blood and death right in the front of their minds. I imagine they'd forgotten what it was like to feel human. At least they were quick about it, and they didn't beat me up too bad. I was bruised up and pretty sore, but there were no marks to explain to my father when I came home later that night. I was lucky I guess. It could have been a lot worse. I didn't end up pregnant with a bastard, but it ended any chance I might have had to have anybody's child at all. That's why I don't have grandchildren, Mac. Satisfied?"

She didn't say it meanly. I don't think she meant it meanly. I'd been seeing this woman in this bar for years, and she'd seen me get on my soap box plenty of times. She knew I didn't mean any harm by asking about her life, but she wasn't going to make it easy for me, either. Her recount of the event was factual and almost cold, like she was talking about someone else, but when I looked into her eyes again, I could see the pain she hid in there. All I could do was mumble my apologies. She patted my hand and picked up her deck of cards. She began shuffling them as I stood and tottered my way back to the bar.

The world was a shitty place to be. I said as much to Steve before I put my head on the bar and passed out.

Chapter 34

I woke up only a few minutes later, but I felt as groggy as if I'd been sleeping for days in a drug induced coma. Steve was shaking me.

"Mac, come on. Wake up. Wake up, Goddamnit!" He shook me hard again, and I lifted my head slowly off the bar. I looked at Steve, willing my eyes to focus on the middle version of the three Steves I saw when I looked in his direction. He put a cup of coffee down in front of me and watched as my quivering hands picked it up and guided it toward my mouth. My stomach contracted painfully as the hot liquid made its way through my system. I could feel the bile rising up. It took me a minute to right myself enough to stagger to the bathroom where I could vomit enthusiastically in privacy. That was the only other condition of my binges—I was not allowed to puke anywhere but in the men's room.

The tile floor rushed up to meet me as I tried to lower my head enough to hit my target. I managed not to bash my head against the porcelain of the toilet, but found myself staring at the filth around it as I lay welcoming the cool that only the floor could bring to someone in my state. After a few minutes of heavy sweating, I righted myself and expelled at least the last three of the drinks I'd swilled back in my effort to shut out all that was real. It had worked about as well as everything else I'd done in the last week. And now, because I was too curious for my own good I had the image of a teenage Estelle being raped in an alley behind a church to add to all the other images I had stored in my head. It fit nicely between Audrey's bleeding wrists and the tangle haired Gorgon that Rachel had become.

I sat on the floor of the stall for a while determined to hang on to some of the buoyancy that I'd felt four or five drinks in. It did little good. I was past the point of alcohol elation. Now, I just felt hollow and vaguely nauseous. And just in case I didn't feel bad enough, I had Newt to rub salt in my wounds.

What a pretty picture you make lying on the floor of the bathroom with your face pressed up against the base of a toilet. So impressive. Did you get enough to drink? Maybe you'd like to go a round or two with another bottle. I'm sure you could puke a little more. Wouldn't that be fun? Come on, Mac, let's go get you another drink. You probably need it.

"You better shut fucking up before I do go get another drink." It was a hollow threat. There was no way Steve was going to serve me another drop of liquor now. His last rule about my binging—I was cut off at the first sign of retching.

I was splashing my face with cold water when Steve joined me in the men's room. He handed me several paper towels and evaluated the damage I'd done to myself since he'd seen me last. Apparently, I didn't rate too high on the yardstick. "Jesus, Mac, when's the last time you took a shower?"

I did my best to smile nonchalantly at him. "Don't kid yourself, Steve. I got this dirty lying on your men's room floor." I rinsed my mouth with water from the sink and spat it out before I looked at him again. Steve was shaking his head, looking generally disgusted with me.

"Look, kid, I think you've done enough damage in here today. It's time to hit the road." He was standing behind me, looking at me through the reflection in the mirror. I saw the concern in his eyes, and I knew that he, of all people, really did have my best interests at heart. I was touched, and I started to tell him so. "You know, Steve, I want to say thanks for worrying. It really is nice that you care about what happens to me."

Steve glowered at me in the mirror. "Don't be a jackass, kid. I don't care how drunk you get, but you're starting to piss off some of my other customers. Now, get yourself together, and I'll get you a taxi." I wasn't exactly surprised at his response. Steve wasn't the kind of guy who wanted anyone to know he had a genuine positive feeling about another human being. Still, I felt as though I'd just taken a boot to the gut. He kept up his gruff act all the way back to the bar where my jacket hung from the back of my chair. I got it on and Steve walked me outside.

The shock of cold air outside was sobering. I still had more alcohol than blood streaming through my veins, but my head felt a little clearer, and I didn't think I was still the slurring mess I'd been an hour ago. I lit the last of my cigarettes and tossed the empty pack into the gutter. "Well, Steve, as always, a great time at Dodger's." I swayed dangerously as I inhaled long and deeply, holding the smoke in my lungs until I felt even dizzier. I exhaled audibly as the taxi pulled up to the curb. I fumbled with the door handle, failing to get my fingers to do my mind's bidding. Finally, Steve reached over and opened the back door for me. I slid into the taxi, trying hard not to look at Steve again.

He reached in and slid a fresh pack of cigarettes into my jacket pocket. "I'll hang on to your keys, Mac. You come get them when you're ready." I nodded, grateful for everything Steve had ever done for me. "And, Mac—take a shower. You reek." And he turned on his heel before I could say anything. That was the thing with Steve. He was a big softie at heart, but he had to play the role of the hard ass just to live with himself. I patted the bulge in my pocket and smiled at the small kindness that made me feel a little more human than I had five minutes ago. I turned in my seat and watched Dodger's recede in the back window as the taxi drove off.

I was anxious to get home. I didn't know why really because there was nothing waiting for me there. I just felt like being out in the world was making me more vulnerable than I had any desire to be. I was still buzzing from all the vodka I'd drunk, and my mind was clouded by the effects. I couldn't think straight enough to make any decisions, but my thoughts raced from one imaginary scenario to the next. All I really wanted to do was shut down for a while, sleep like the dead and wake up to some other reality. I should have been more careful about what I wished for.

When the taxi pulled up to my apartment building I stuffed ten dollars through the opening in the sliding Plexiglas barrier that separated the driver from his fare, protecting him from the threat of assault and robbery so frequent in this greed stricken and dangerous world. I got out quickly and headed for the front entrance wanting more than anything to lie down. It wasn't until I'd stepped in through the first of the security doors that I wished I'd stayed in the taxi. Waiting for me in that glass cubicle was Officer Danning wearing a smug look that only read trouble for me. I had a fleeting hope that he was just there to tell me that they'd found Rachel and that he was sorry for the misunderstanding. But I could tell by the look on his face that John Danning wasn't sorry for anything other than the fact that he hadn't taken me downtown after our first encounter.

He didn't waste any time getting down to business. "Mr. Williams. I've been waiting for you."

My brain said "Run!" My mouth, on the other hand, led with a vodka induced remark loaded for bear with sarcasm, "Officer Danning, how nice of you to come calling. Care to come inside for a drink?" I fumbled with my keys thinking I might be able to slip past him and hide out in my apartment.

Danning smiled a wider smirk than before and said in cool tones, "I think maybe we should have that drink at my place, Mr. Williams." I looked at him with a contrived look of confusion, but I could tell he wasn't buying it. Ever the polite officer though, he laid out in terms a three year old could understand exactly what he had in mind. "Mr. Williams, I'm going to have to ask you to come down to the station with me. Some new information has come to my attention, and there are a few things we need to talk about."

He stood there between me and my door, watching me struggle internally with the situation. I had no idea what to do. Newt was advising a quick getaway, but there was no way I was going to turn my back and make a break for it with an armed cop standing only two feet away from me. I might have been reckless with drink, but I hadn't ever been able to cultivate a death wish that would allow me to get shot fleeing from a uniform cop. I knew I didn't want to go anywhere with this guy, but I didn't see how I could avoid it. No excuse was going to placate Danning. No fantastic story was going to make him disappear into the late afternoon cloud. I didn't see how I could do anything but get into his cruiser and let myself be taken in.

I felt so much like a criminal already that it wasn't even humiliating to be stowed in the back seat of the police car. Actually, it was a relief to be able to sit down again. I still felt pretty shaky, not to mention the sensation of balancing on a teeter totter somewhere between half drunk and half hung over. Danning was talking to me, but I couldn't follow the line of his conversation. I remember asking him if I needed a lawyer, but the question seemed so clichéd that I didn't even wait for him to answer before I started giggling. And then I couldn't help myself. I couldn't stop giggling even though I knew I was making the wrong kind of impression. I tried to will myself to stop, but everything just seemed so funny by then that even Newt's cautioning words struck me as hilarious beyond belief.

Danning stopped talking, and in the rearview mirror, I could see his lips pursed so tightly that his mouth nearly disappeared. I thought he looked like an angry school marm, the thought of which made me laugh even harder. Eventually, my energy ran out, and long before we'd reached the station, I'd slumped down in the back seat and passed out. Just before I drifted off, I remember thinking, *Serves him right. He'll have to carry me into the station. That'll teach him.* What lesson I thought it was going to teach him was not clear, but I was happy to make the whole process as difficult for him as I could. I probably should have tried harder to stay awake.

Chapter 35

I woke up to the smell of stale urine and the sound of metal clanging angrily against metal. I was disoriented enough for the first moments of consciousness to think that I was still in the men's room at Dodger's. When I finally opened my eyes, I was greeted by the sight of a urinal attached to the wall. This supported the illusion I possessed that I was still under Steve's protection. It wasn't until I noticed that the walls were grey cinder block instead of yellowing dry wall that I felt a growing urge to panic well up inside my chest. I sat up rapidly and banged my head on the bunk above me. Looking around, I realized the bars in front of me meant I had been napping in a jail cell. It came rushing back to me then—the cop at my door, the ride in the cruiser. But I didn't have any memory of why I was here. That meant either that no one told me, or, more likely, that my subconscious mind stored the information out of reckoning to protect me from a terrific bout of self-induced hysteria. I decided to go with the unbelievable but comforting thought that I was brought in because I was too drunk to converse with at my apartment. Until I knew otherwise, I was going to do my best to deny that this was anything other than a drunk tank stopover.

My resolve to play dumb was quickly dismantled by the whispers of my brother. As though afraid he might be heard, he kept his voice low, but I could still hear him clear as day. His whisper was tremulous and tinny as though fear was choking his voice at the point of origin, wherever that might have been.

Mac…Mac…are you awake? What the hell happened? You're in jail.

"Yes, Newt, I am in jail. I see that being dead hasn't really dulled your sense of the obvious much." I couldn't bear the prospect of a lecture from Newt at this point. I really hoped I wasn't going to have to listen to a series of increasingly annoying versions of the I-told-you-so speech he'd gotten so proficient at in the last years. Now really wasn't the time to add guilt onto the already overwhelming heap of regret I felt. I thought moving right into a plea for his help would put him on the right track.

"You don't have any idea what I'm doing here do you, Newt?"

He whispered fiercely, *No, I don't have any idea why you're in a jail cell. I can only hear and see the stuff that you hear and say, asshole. And you passed out. It makes it a little hard to talk to someone when they're sleeping off an alcoholic stupor. I can't believe you got drunk. I hope you're happy now, Mac. You've really gotten yourself into a load here. I hope it was worth it. How do you ever expect me to get out of here when you can't keep your face out of the bottle for longer than a day at a time? And now look at you, locked up under their thumb. You'll be able to do a lot of good from behind bars.*

It was my turn to whisper with some ferocity. "You self-centered, arrogant, dead fuck! I can't believe you. I'm on a cot in a cell in a police station, and all you can do is gripe about your sad little story." I put on an affected voice, a whining imitation of my brother. "Poor Newt who has it so bad. Poor Newt who can't find his way to heaven because he's too stupid."

It was taking all the control I had not to start screaming curses at him. "You know what I think. I think you couldn't find your way out of a paper bag because you'd be too busy looking for someone else to do it for you. You're pathetic." I was breathing heavily now, my pulse racing with disgust. "Now, I need to think, and as you obviously can't be bothered to help me, you can either shut the hell up, or you can shut the hell up."

I knew he was fuming, but at least, he kept quiet. He probably wished more than anything that he could come back from the dead to deliver the beating he was so sure I deserved. I would have given good odds that he was fantasizing about pounding my face to a bloody pulp, but I was holding all the cards, for whatever they were worth from behind bars. I took another look around while I tried to keep myself from retching after working my heart rate up enough to spread the poison through my veins all over again.

I couldn't see anyone from my vantage point on the lower bunk of the tiny cage I was locked in. I could only guess that the cops had tossed me in here to sleep off my vodka consumption. Presumably, they would check on me eventually, looking for some sign that I still lived. I imagined that after that I'd get my first experience with the inquisition. It promised to be about as fun as the one in the thirteenth century, but I was hoping for something a little better than a stake, a bunch of kindling and a cassock wearing religious zealot carrying a pack of matches at the end of it all.

I let my aching head rest back on the paper thin pillow to contemplate the enormity of my budding hangover. I probably would have confessed to any and all unsolved crimes if the cops would only deliver to my bedside a large glass of water and a toothbrush. The realist in me knew that they would likely be more interested in keeping me as uncomfortable as humanly possible. Break the spirit through deprivation and reap the benefits of confession. It was sounding more and more like the Medieval Inquisition all the time.

It has been an interesting practice throughout our collective history to regularly beat down the naysayers and challengers of truths generally accepted by western civilization—although what civil has to do with it escapes me. I understand fully that there can be no holding onto power if you are regularly going to be faced with those who express doubt and contradict your particular party line. After all, what tyranny would be complete without a repression of opposing opinions? And if it can be a violent squashing of ideas, well, so much the better for the power mongers. That way fear will help keep the temptation of discord from blossoming in the hearts of the rest of the population. Our modern lifestyle doesn't subscribe to the belief that this kind of repression is still going on in our society, but I'm here to tell you that it's alive and well, just laying in wait with the patience of Job for an opportunity to spring on some unsuspecting challenger like myself. Well, not like myself, actually. I already went to bat against the establishment and got struck out in three easy pitches.

I thought of all the people before me who stood up to be counted as one who would not just challenge the truth, but provide perfectly reasonable proofs to support their dispute. There were few who could be considered successes. Fewer still who achieved any kind of positive result in their own lifetime. My favorite example of outcast rebel was Galileo. What disappointment he must have felt in his church, in his fellow scientists as they all crumbled one after another like a house of cards, even in humanity in general, I imagine. There he is, on the verge of some of the most significant and important conclusions of all time, and he has to live with the fact that, proof or not, his Pope simply would not accept that the earth wasn't the center of the universe. How sad it must have been for him to spend his life looking through his telescope at the broad images of the universe only to be told that if he wanted to keep sucking down spaghetti and red wine, he was going to have to keep his ideas to himself. I'm sure there were others, but he was the only example I could come up with who didn't actually feel the flames as punishment for his heresy. Of course, he was forced to live under house arrest by order of the peace loving Jesuits and the Cardinals of the Inquisition, but at least he got to live. I guess that's something.

My musing on the workings of our paranoid society did little to improve my state of mind. I was entertaining a growing hysteria at the prospect of being locked behind bars for another five minutes let alone the rest of my life. Welling up inside, right next to the profound drinker's remorse that I felt, was an unbearable urge to break down and cry. I felt more like a lost child than ever before. My efforts to dislodge my brother from his suspended state had done nothing but land me in more trouble than I really deserved. I wasn't a bad person. I hadn't committed any crime. Hell, I'd even been civic minded enough to stay away from the wheel of my car when I got trashed. And here I was, head pounding, a need for the privacy of my own bathroom quickly growing in my bowels, staring ahead at parallel iron bars imprisoning me before I was ever judged. Full-fledged panic was close at hand. I didn't know what shape my freak out was going to take, but I was certain that it probably wouldn't do much to help my cause.

I tried to get up and make my way over to the porcelain bowl attached to the wall, but I felt like I was stuck to the cot with cement. Fear was paralyzing me. The only thing that seemed capable of moving still was my mind, and it was racing at dangerous speeds through all the ugly scenarios I was sure my future held. I hadn't felt this afraid of anything since the first time I came out of shock therapy. It was a sick fear accompanied by a heart pounding panic that I wanted to attribute to alcohol poisoning, but that I knew had little to do with how much vodka I'd had to drink earlier in the day. At least, I thought it had been earlier in the day.

I realized then that I had no idea what time it was. I made to look at my watch only to discover that it wasn't on my wrist. I supposed that the cops had it now, along with the conspicuously absent pack of cigarettes that Steve had slipped into my jacket pocket before sending me off to my doom in that taxi. Taking stock of the situation, I tried to imagine how long I'd been in this cell. It couldn't have been more than a few hours. I generally don't pass out for longer than a couple hours at a time, at most maybe four. The sun had just been starting to fall into the west, so I guessed that I left Dodger's around 5:30. That meant I'd been picked up by the cops around six. My best guess was that it was somewhere near nine or ten on Friday night. I hoped at the very least I was screwing up Danning's plans for the night. It was a puerile thought, but I found a small measure of comfort in it anyway. Just the thought of him having to tell his girlfriend that he was going to have to cancel their date because he had to work late gave me some satisfaction. I really hoped she was the kind of girl who would be peevish about it. At least then, I could imagine that he was going to be denied sex until he'd made amends with flowers or some other costly trinket.

The thought of Danning having to beg forgiveness from his girlfriend brought a smile to my face. I reveled in the iota of happiness I felt until I saw, in the dim light provided by the single bare bulb hanging from the ceiling, a figure standing on the other side of the bars. The way the light caught him, I couldn't make out his face. He stood there, an anonymous juggernaut representing all the authority figures I'd worked so hard to dodge and protect myself from all these years. He didn't even need a face as far as I was concerned. He was just one more drone.

I wondered if I just pretended I was still passed out, I could buy myself a little more time to think. After all it seemed the day of reckoning was here, and I had no clue what I would do or say to protect myself from the obvious peril this cop represented. Just as I decided to give the ruse a shot, the uniform at the door began banging on the bars of my cell with his knight stick or his cuffs or some other object hard enough to create a substantial din. The noise was like hot needles piercing my eyes and driving into my brain. Even in a state of perfect health, no one could have feigned sleep in the echo chamber that my prison suddenly became.

I opened my eyes and sat up a little, resting my weight on my elbows. I still couldn't really see who was waiting for me at the door, but I didn't need to know his name. It was enough to know the uniform. I didn't speak, preferring to let him make the first move. When he finally took a step to the right, the light caught his face, and I saw Officer John Danning on the other side of the door, a small smirk on his face.

"I see you're awake." He rapped the offending object, his Billy club, against the bars a few more times. At least it was obvious he was going to be an asshole. "I hope you liked your wake up call. I wanted to let you have your beauty sleep, but I didn't think it was going to help much." He guffawed at his little joke. He honestly guffawed. It was a little hiccup of a laugh that made his shoulders hunch forward and his chin bob out and down. He reminded me so much of a village idiot that I had a hard time keeping a straight face. I bit my lip until I tasted blood to keep from showing any kind of emotion.

When I didn't answer, he smacked the bars one more time and said with a lot more force, "Get up, Williams. We've got some talking to do." I sat upright and got my equilibrium as he unlocked the cage door and swung it open. I could visualize myself charging through it, knocking Danning to the floor as I made my daring escape running right into the arms of the ten or more cops that were probably on the other side of the door marked EXIT. Maybe Danning saw the image in my eyes because he stood up a little straighter, coming up to his full intimidating height and glowered down at me. "Come on. Let's go."

He watched me carefully as I walked by him, and I feared for a minute that he might turn his club on me as I passed through the narrow space provided by the open door. Instead, as soon I was through, he swung the door shut with enough force to send a tremor through my system as it clanged ominously shut. It had a sound of permanence to it that made me feel, if it was possible, even more nauseous.

He guided me out and into another room that was hardly different from the first except that it had no cage and in place of the cot and urinal, there were three chairs and a table. There was no clock on the wall and no windows, even ones with bars, to look out of. I was as much a prisoner there as I had been in the cell. Only now, I'd have to ask to use the bathroom, which I did immediately.

Once I'd had my first police-supervised crap, and I sincerely hoped it would be my last one, Danning escorted me back to what he called the interrogation room. I went in first to discover another pawn of government sitting at the table waiting for us. Even sitting down, he looked big. I would have guessed that he was about six foot four, and he had enough weight behind him to find a position as middle back on just about any football team. He looked away from the papers on the table and directed his attention to me. He stared through coke bottle glasses that magnified his eyes to an unnatural size, disproportionate with everything else about his face. The huge blackness of his eyes created a sharp contrast to the almost white hair that squirted out of his head with the unruliness of a clown's fright wig. For the second time in just a few minutes, I had to stifle the laughter I felt growing in my throat. Fortunately, Newt began anew at that moment, and it became immeasurably easier to keep a straight face.

Okay, whatever you do, Mac, stay calm. No hysterical fits, no shouting, just stay cool, little brother.

I wanted to wind up and deliver a roundhouse to his chin, but it was pretty good advice. Instead, I took a chair across from the mysterious Officer Whitehair and tried to look innocent as a lamb.

That's right, no posturing. Let them lead the way. Just answer their questions, and we'll be out of here.

I really hoped he wasn't going to keep up the coaching all the way through this long night. Before he could continue with his tutoring in Cops 101, I decided to break the ice. In the least terrified voice I could get my larynx to produce, I started asking the question that was eating holes in my mind.

"I came in with a full pack of cigarettes, but they seemed to have fallen out of my pocket. Would either of you gentlemen have one you could spot me?" I was polite and made certain not to let the accusation I wanted to make slip out. I thought I'd done pretty well at firing off the most important question I was able to form at the time. I looked at one, then the other, only to find four eyes with the same confused look in them. The two stared at me. I suppose they were surprised that my first question was nicotine related instead of survival minded, but the two were one and the same as far as I was concerned. If I didn't start raising the level of nicotine in my blood immediately, staying rational was not going to be something I could attempt under these conditions.

Danning just shrugged his shoulders when the mystery inquisitor looked at him. Instead of getting a cigarette, I got an introduction. Danning gestured to the man seated next to him, "Mr. Williams, this is Detective Howe. Detective Howe, this is Mac Williams." I felt like I should pump his hand in a jocular bonding moment, but somehow I couldn't bring myself to shake hands at this meeting. I just looked at him and nodded, keeping my hands folded in front of me.

Detective Howe trained his magnifiers on my face and gave it close examination before he spoke. His voice was low and smooth. I half expected him to try to sell me some Dr. Jurd's Snake Oil Tonic, good for all that ails me, but that wasn't the line he was towing with his calm velvety voice. "So, Mr. Williams, it kind of surprises me that you're not more curious about why we've brought you here tonight. If it were me, I'd be torn up wondering what a good citizen like yourself could possibly have done to land him at the police station, but you don't seem to care at all. That's pretty interesting, wouldn't you say, John?"

Officer Danning remained mute, but nodded his assent, that same small smirk on his lips. Howe continued, "Well, just in case you are curious, and you're just trying to play it cool, I won't keep you in suspense any longer." He continued to look straight at me. I met his stare just to show him I wasn't afraid, but I couldn't hold his eyes for long. I had the feeling he was boring into my thoughts with those glasses of his. I looked away, stared instead at the bulge in his shirt pocket that looked so much like a package of cigarettes my mouth started to water. Detective Howe was unaware or more likely totally unconcerned with the withdrawal I was suffering. He carried on, doing me the favor of telling me why they'd brought me in. "It seems, Mr. Williams, that you and I have some of the same interests."

What, does he think you both like to go bowling or something? I wish he'd just get on with it.

I tried to remain focused on the Detective across from me. Now was not the right time to start with Newt. The black beetles behind the glasses continued to stare incessantly at me. I could only imagine that he was waiting for some kind of answer, but I wasn't about to oblige him.

Right at that moment, silence seemed to be the safest route. The pause grew uncomfortable and Howe shifted in his seat. He leaned forward pushing a file folder toward me. "Right in that folder you can see some of our same interests if you like." He waited for me to pull it closer. When I didn't move, he slid it back with the other folders on the table.

"Still not interested in playing? Well, let me just lay my hand on the table for you, then we'll see what you have to say. Now, I know you've met my friend John here." Howe flipped through the papers in front of him until he found what he was looking for. "It seems he paid you a visit at your apartment on Thursday. He was asking you all about a nice young girl called…" he paused while he checked the file again, "Rachel Strong. Isn't that right?"

I nodded.

"Now, on Thursday Rachel was missing, and we were quite anxious to find her. It seems that you claimed to have had a little fun with her on Monday night, is that right?"

Another nod.

"Okay, well, now we're getting somewhere. So tell me, Mac. It is okay if I call you Mac, isn't it?" I shrugged my indifference. "So tell me, how is it that a nice girl like that let an ugly spud like you get in her pants?"

He's just trying to rile you up, Mac. Don't let him. Don't react.

As if I couldn't have figured that out on my own. I shrugged and maintained my silence.

"It also seems that you called Officer Danning to report that you'd seen Miss Strong on, let me see, it was…" He did some more paper shuffling, but I got the distinct impression that he wasn't the kind of man who needed to check his facts every few seconds. In fact, I was pretty sure he was employing the practice as a technique to shake me up. It was working pretty well, but I did my best to keep an impassive expression locked on my face anyway.

Howe resumed his revelations. "Yes, here it is, you said you saw her on Thursday afternoon, not long after the officer spoke to you, is that right?"

More nodding which, I was gratified to note, seemed to be getting on Howe's nerves.

He sighed. "Well, that certainly is convenient, isn't it? And have you seen her since that afternoon?"

Now came the hard part. Did I answer them truthfully? Should I tell them I saw her again on Thursday night, or should I just keep my mouth shut? Newt was advising more silence, but I was a little tired of that game. Instead of answering his question, I decided to plunge in head first with my own offensive strategy. "Look, what's going on here? You bring me in, take my watch and whatever else you want; you throw me in a cell; and now, you want to insult me and make me regurgitate information you already have. You know what? I'm not interested. How about this instead? You tell me why you felt you had to interrupt a perfectly good afternoon drunk, and I'll see if I can't help you out. And, I'd like my cigarettes back now." My words sounded a lot more confident and brave than I felt.

Oh, you've pissed them off now. Why couldn't you just keep your mouth shut for once?

"I haven't pissed anyone off." The words were out of my mouth before I knew what I was doing. I wished for a rewind button and a whip for my internal censor's punishment of 50 lashes. Fortunately, Howe was looking at me perfectly calmly. Apparently, he thought my statement to Newt was a question put to him after my abrupt outburst.

"No, you haven't pissed anyone off, Mac. We're probably all a little tense here." He was soft now, like a pitying Samaritan. He reached into his pocket and pulled a cigarette out of the package. Tossing it across the table to me, he leaned forward to strike a match. I inhaled the first of the smoke like a starving man over Sunday dinner, greedily taking as much of the tar and nicotine into my lungs as I could. I exhaled and felt a greater sense of relief than I thought I'd ever known. While I took drag after drag, normalizing my mental state, Howe slid the file folder over to me again. This time he opened it.

I started coughing immediately. Choking on the smoke, and on the bitter fluid that was creeping up my esophagus, threatening to force itself up my throat, through my mouth and out onto the photograph exposed in front of me. I'd seen a lot of photos as a censor at Eastglen, some I thought I'd never get out of my head, but they all paled in comparison to the one in front of me. It was a picture of a girl, I guessed she must have been in her twenties, but it was hard to tell accurately because her face was covered in bruises, black and blue like the sky before a thunderstorm. She had cuts all over her arms and neck like she'd been wrestling in razor wire. Her brown hair was matted over the left side, and the true color of Kodak showed the bright red blood that had oozed out of her skull and onto the white tile beneath her. She was so undeniably dead; I didn't know what to say. My hands shook slightly as I pushed the photo away from me and took another long drag off my cigarette. Then the obvious conclusion struck me. They thought this poor dead girl was Rachel, and they thought I was responsible for getting her that way.

Jesus, Mac. They think you killed Rachel.

"You think I did this?" I stared at them disbelievingly, mouth fully agape. It wasn't possible. They couldn't think I was capable of this, could they?

Chapter 36

"Now we're getting somewhere, Mac." Danning looked positively delighted at my revelation. Apparently, he thought a confession from me was imminent. I was happy to disappoint him.

"You guys are out of your minds. I didn't kill anyone. I told you before, and it's still true. I left Rachel Strong's apartment on Tuesday morning, and she was alive then. I saw her at my apartment Thursday afternoon. Come on, she even talked to my bartender. Ask him," I said motioning to Danning, "Steve told him that he talked to her on Wednesday."

"Well, that may be true, Mac, but that was Wednesday, and now it's Friday, isn't it? A lot can happen in a couple of days. And I think a lot did happen in the last few days. You work at Eastglen Prison, isn't that right? Is it true you weren't at work all week?"

Don't answer, Mac. Keep your mouth shut. They're trying to trap you

"I don't care. I'm telling the truth." And I'd done it again. If I didn't get myself together, not only were they going to get me for murder, I'd spend the sentence locked up in a nut house. My answer wasn't what they expected, but they seemed to be going with it anyway. In my mind, I was commanding Newt to keep his own mouth shut.

"I'm glad to hear you're telling the truth." Howe's voice was silky. "We'll get along so much better if you keep that up. Now, is it true you haven't been at work?"

"Yes, but that has nothing to do with Rachel. I just hated my job. In fact, I hated it so much, I quit it this morning."

The two cops exchanged significant looks, and Howe made a notation on his pad. "Is that right? Seems like a kind of sudden decision. What made you choose today?"

"I just got sick of it, that's all. I couldn't do it anymore. I just couldn't look at all those..." I stopped short feeling suddenly like I was playing right into their hands.

"All those what Mr. Williams?"

"All those pictures." I finished quietly.

"Oh, I thought you were going to say all those bars all over the place. Or all those prisoners paying their debt to society. I thought you might have quit because you didn't want to spend any more time there than you had to in case you ended up back there in a different sort of capacity, you might say." Howe's tone had turned icy now. He meant business with this accusation, and I was at a loss how to make him see otherwise without convincing him I was completely insane. "Isn't that what you were thinking when you left the prison today? Weren't you thinking how you'd better make tracks before everyone gets on to you?"

It scared me more than a little that I had been thinking that very thought as I was leaving Eastglen. Building on the fear that must have been showing on my face, Howe now turned to another file on the table. Opening it he said, "Now, that reminds me of something else. I was wondering how you managed to even get that job, considering your history."

I narrowed my eyes, suspicious of everything now. "What do you mean by my 'history'?"

"Well, since you're so determined to be honest with me, I'll be as plain as I can with you. Maybe you could enlighten us as to how someone who spent the better part of a year locked up in a psych hospital ever landed a job working in the prison system. It seems to me they'd want to weed out the undesirables from that kind of job, especially the ones who are, how should I put it, unbalanced. Wouldn't you think so, John?"

John just nodded again, his hyena like smirk growing wider. I was outraged, and my temper started to boil up and over onto the two sneering faces before me. "How did you get that information? That record was supposed to be sealed after I was released. They told me no one would be able to get into it. You bastards! What gives you the right to go prying into my past?"

Howe's face had slid into a malicious grin. "I think you've been watching too much TV, Mac, and not paying very close attention by the sounds of things." He tapped his pencil on the file in front of him. "You were over the ripe old age of 16, sweetheart, and that makes you and your visit to the crazy house open season for us. So now, maybe you'd like to tell us all about it. Or would you prefer that I just read the notes in your file?"

First chance I got I was going to burn that fucking file and feed the ashes to these two gorillas. "You better start reading, if you even know how. I'm not telling you anything."

"Now, that's not the spirit of cooperation we're looking for, Mac. I was hoping you'd want to clear everything up so that you can be on your way. But if you want to make things more difficult, well, that's your right." Howe's easy tone couldn't hide the threat that hid just under the surface of his words. He shuffled through the file lingering on different pages as though he was reading them for the first time. I'd already seen enough to know that this guy had probably committed the details to memory while I'd been sleeping off my vodka in that cell.

Mac, Mac, this is really serious. They're going to lock you up for murder and throw away the key.

"I know this is serious." I would have bashed my head against the table if it wouldn't have made me look even less credible. *Newt*, I said in my mind as calmly as was possible given the circumstances, *I can't convince them that I'm not a nutcase if I keep answering you, and I can't keep much straight in my own mind right now, so can you please, pretty please with sugar on top, shut the fuck up!*

Okay, okay, sorry. I'm really freaking out here.

He said it as though I was meandering along like this was a regular occurrence for me. I eyed the two cops. They were looking expectantly at me, as though waiting for me to say something. Finally, when I didn't give them any more to work with, Danning stepped toward me and spoke, "Get that, he knows this is serious. Well, it's nice to find out you're not some kind of retard on top of being a killer. Tell me, Macbeth, do you kill all the women you sleep with? You could probably make a case for it being mercy killing. I'm sure after giving it up to the likes of you they wouldn't want to live anyway."

He let his nasty grin slide back to reveal his sharp pointy canines. He reminded me of a rabid dog. I half expected to see him begin to foam at the mouth in his demented excitement. Seeing the saliva on his lips I was sickened, had to turn away from the sight before I vomited all over him. Although it was a tempting idea to soil those perfectly polished shoes with whatever putrid acid lurked in my stomach. I looked instead at the man still seated across from me. He stared back at me, an indecent leer on his face. He would have liked nothing better than for me to go off the deep end right in front of him.

I kept my mouth shut and waited for them to make the next move. I didn't have to wait long. "Your doctor said that you used to hear voices. Well, that's an interesting defense right there, isn't it? Maybe you were hearing voices again the other night. Did those voices tell you anything interesting? Did they tell you that Rachel was evil? Did you kill her because they said she was a slut and a whore? I'd understand that you know. If you had some special circumstances like a psychotic condition that compelled you to do these things, I think you could probably make a good insanity plea." He slid the photo of the dead girl in front of me again. "What are the voices saying right now, Mac? What do they say when you look at your handiwork?"

I looked at Howe while I closed the folder. I couldn't bear to see, even in the periphery, the vision of that girl pulverized beyond recognition. I was angry now, but it burned in a cold way that masked all the fear I'd felt only moments before. "You don't read so well, do you, Detective? Did you have to do remedial work in school so you could get your diploma? It's a wonder you managed to pass the exam to get on the police force at all. Although it can't be a very hard test if this guy made it." I jerked my thumb at Danning who moved toward me menacingly.

Howe held up his hand, stopping Danning in his tracks. Maybe he thought this new strategy of his was working, that I was going to give up and tell him everything in my high and mighty desire to show these two dunderheads just how much smarter than them I really was. I was smarter than them though, and I wasn't telling them anything I didn't have to.

His voice resumed its silky good cop quality. "Maybe you'd like to tell me what you meant by that uncomplimentary remark, Mac."

"Well," I said as condescendingly as I could, "if you could read, you would know that I didn't ever hear voices. I heard *a* voice." Saying it out loud, I felt foolish. Did I really think I was getting the upper hand by confessing that I heard only one voice instead of a bunch of them? If that was going to be my high card, I was definitely losing my ante. The only thing to do was plunge ahead. "Yes, and if you could understand what it is that you were reading, you'd also know that at the time I was suffering from the trauma of losing my only brother in a violent and sudden accident. And if you could manage to get through all the big words without crying, you would also know that I was fully recovered when I left Lynwood. If you like, you can even ask my attending shrink, and he'll tell you the same thing. I can dial the numbers if the phone is too much for you to handle." I sat back in my chair and waited.

Detective Howe was scowling. I could almost see the little wisps of angry steam coming out of his ears as he reached his boiling point. I was sure the only thing keeping him from slapping the little punk across from him, namely me, was the camera mounted in the corner of the room. I didn't think I'd ever say it, but thank God for Big Brother and his tell tale little red light.

Instead of backhanding me, he took a deep breath while he pulled the photo of the dead girl out of the file and put it on the table in front of me. "So, did your brother tell you to do this? Did he tell you to smash her head in after you broke her nose and blackened both her eyes? You know you shattered her cheekbone and her jaw. You must have been pretty angry to do all that. What happened? Did she turn you down for a second roll in the hay?"

They really think you killed that girl, Mac

"I know," My voice was low, awestruck at the truth of the situation. I wasn't even sure I cared that I'd answered Newt out loud again. These two cops were convinced I beat this girl they supposed was Rachel to death. I had to get more information before they made a real case against me. I was about to start digging when Howe came back at me.

"What do you mean you know, Mac? You know about all the injuries. Well, I guess you would, since you're the one who gave her that beating. Come on, Mac, you can tell me. It's true isn't it? Your brother made you do it, didn't he? He's the one responsible for all this. He's the one who drove you to it."

My head was spinning. I almost answered yes in the confusion of the moment. Newt *had* gotten me into all this. This *was* all his fault. I closed my eyes. I was dizzy and tired and starting to feel the full effects of the hangover that had been toying with me for the last few hours. I realized I still didn't know what time it was or how long I'd been there. I was going to ask, but I didn't know if it mattered enough for me to bother. The two cops were still there when I opened my eyes again. They both wore eager expressions, kids about to set off on their first two wheeler bike ride.

My head felt heavy, and I bowed to the urge to rest it somewhere, laying it on the table in front of me. I closed my eyes again, but now all I could see was the face of a battered dead girl that I desperately hoped wasn't Rachel. The image made me snap my eyes open again. Howe and Danning were still staring at me. I opened my mouth twice to speak, but I wasn't sure what it was I wanted to say or ask. Finally, I opened my mouth a third time, "Could I have another cigarette?"

"Sure, Mac, take the whole pack." Howe took my cigarettes from his shirt pocket and tossed them across the table to me. My lighter followed, and I seized them both, quickly pairing smoke with fire to satisfy my need. Howe was standing now, motioning Danning to the door. "Why don't we leave Mac alone to do a little thinking?"

The two of them left the room, shutting the door firmly behind them. I waited for the click of a lock, but it never came. I wondered what would happen if I just stood up and walked out of here. Would they try to stop me? Could they even be holding me here like this against my will? Was I going to be arrested? I put my head down on the table again trying to find some logical answers to all the questions teeming in my head.

Chapter 31

I woke up suddenly, my heart pounding in my chest, breathing hard enough to have just finished a marathon. Looking around, I realized that I was still sitting in the same room, and I felt the bitter disappointment of reality. I had no idea how long I'd been sleeping, but I was willing to guess that I'd only dozed off for a few minutes. The red light on the mounted camera winked at me, reminding me that someone was always watching. I didn't know what they would make of me falling asleep. I was groggy with sleepiness and discomfort. It was hard to make what had been happening come into focus in any sensible way. I knew I was here because the cops thought Rachel was dead, and they thought I did it. It didn't make sense, though. I couldn't have done it.

I had been in my apartment since Tuesday. Except for that painful dinner with Gail, I'd been home the whole time. Wasn't that right? No, that wasn't right. I'd been to see Steve. What day was that? Was that yesterday or the day before? And he'd seen Rachel. He told me he'd seen her. When was that? I was trying to remember if the cops had told me when Rachel had been killed. I couldn't keep the facts I had from jumping around with the ones the cops had given me. But hadn't I seen Rachel just last night; she was fine then. Well, not fine exactly, but definitely alive. Of course, both times I'd seen her, she vanished pretty quickly. The more thinking I did, the more difficult I was finding it to really explain how she had disappeared into thin air.

And then a thought struck me. An evil, vile, terrible thought that I wished I'd never had. What if I hadn't seen Rachel? What if in addition to hearing the voice of my dead brother I was now seeing figments of a hopeful imagination? Maybe the cops were right. Maybe I was crazy. Maybe I had killed Rachel. That would certainly explain a lot. I did have a huge unaccounted for black out on Monday night. And I seemed to be having some trouble sorting out the days since then. I saw the girl's face again, her hair all matted with blood, and I gagged violently. What if I *had* done that to her?

Fear and doubt like I'd never known before crept into my heart. I'd never wished so much that I was the dead one in my family. I was sitting in a police station, very likely about to be charged with murder, and I wasn't sure I could say I hadn't done it with any certainty. I felt tears welling up in my eyes, hysteria in my chest. My breathing grew ragged and fierce with the prospect that I *was* the monster they were looking for. The only person in my life who knew everything and still believed I was sane had been Audrey, and she was so unbalanced that she slashed her wrists. It wasn't a stirring testament to my stability. Maybe I was every bit of the crackpot these cops though I was.

Mac, get a hold of yourself. You're letting these assholes get to you. You did not kill Rachel on Monday night. You said it yourself. Steve talked to her on Wednesday. Remember, he told you all about their conversation when you went to pick up your car. You can't have forgotten the bitch slap he doled out to you.

I touched my cheek where Steve had slapped me only the day before. It was tender and bruised, and I had never felt so pleased about an injury in my life. "Okay, but what does that really prove except that I didn't kill her until Thursday?"

Are you serious? You're talking about this as though you think you might really have done it. You did not kill Rachel. Let's face it, Mac, you don't have the stomach for it. You couldn't beat Rachel to a pulp. You wouldn't anyway, even if you could. Not when she's the only chance you have to sort your life out.

"How do I know that? How do I know that she's the key to all this? How do I know I'm not completely insane? I'd like, just once, to believe what everyone else believes. I'd like to not be a freak for just five minutes."

What the hell is that supposed to mean? You'd rather confess to a murder you didn't commit than believe that you're not crazy. Well, I've heard it all now. You want to spend the next 25 years in prison as some armed robber's bitch because you think it'll mean you're not a freak. Does the phrase "hopeless case" mean anything to you? Take a look at that picture again. Do you really think that you have the guts to stand over a girl like Rachel and beat her with your bare hands until she's dead? I know you pretty well, little brother. Take it from me, you don't have it in you.

"Well, maybe that's the problem. Maybe you don't know me so well because you don't even exist. Maybe I've just been coping these last ten years, keeping my mouth shut at the right time, so that no one suspects that I'm off my rocker."

Newt was still talking, pleading with me to see reason, but I couldn't think anymore, couldn't even listen to him. I put my head back down on the table. I was sick, stomach sick, heart sick, soul sick. I didn't know when I'd ever been this tired before. I just wanted the whole mess to go away, so that I could lie down and find some peace. When I closed my eyes the crushed, bruised face of the victim jumped back into my mind. Behind my eyelids, all I could see was red congealed blood, blackened flesh. I started to gag at the thought that it had been my fists that did that. I couldn't hold the sick back any longer. It was consuming me from the inside. I assumed the crash position and felt my stomach begin to contract; my whole body began to heave as I purged the remainder of my alcohol consumption. The contents of my stomach splattered the floor around me. The heaves continued violent and raw, pushing me off the chair to the floor where I crouched on all fours like a dog. I could feel the saliva dripping out of my mouth in a steady stream while sweat poured down my neck and back. I tried to calm myself, but each spasm brought more pain and panic to my whole body.

I'd created quite a pool of muck by the time Danning and Howe returned to the scene. I didn't know if they stumbled in by accident, or if they'd been watching me the whole time on the closed circuit monitor they had set up somewhere on the other side of the door. The two of them stood over me, disgusted and yet quite pleased with themselves, as though my retching was some kind of testimony to my guilt. Once the bulk of the puking was done, I lay my cheek on the floor, resting and trying to get my breath back. I felt wholly and completely beaten.

"Now, we're getting somewhere." Danning chuckled as he spoke. "The guilt getting to you, is it?" I looked up at him. He was showing his canines again, licking his lips in anticipation of the conclusion he sought. The sight made me gag again, and I rolled over so I wouldn't have to look at his cherry red cheeks, so excited by my misery. I wanted with all my heart to see him pushed into traffic by a bum he was rousting at a bus stop. I gave him the finger in the only gesture of rebellion and protest I had strength for. His smile vanished, replaced by an ugly sneer. I felt the steel toe of his shiny boot make contact with my lower back, and I nearly blacked out as the pain shot through my body, leaving each of my nerves jangling with agony.

Howe was talking, but I could only make out a distant buzzing. I coughed and tried to right myself on the floor, but my dizziness kept me from getting past a kneeling position. I slumped sideways leaning on the chair for support. Finally, Howe extended a hand to help me up. I brushed it away. "Fuck you!" I muttered. It felt so good to say that I started yelling it at the two of them. My exhaustion and fear and the panic I'd barely been able to suppress finally boiled over, and I pounded the chair I leaned against, flinging nonsensical curses at the top of my lungs first at Danning, then at Howe.

They started to approach me, but I'd had much more than I could take. I took the legs of the chair and threw it toward them, scattering them like bowling pins. I saw Danning push a button next to the door, and before I knew it several hands were on me, pushing my face into the floor, my nose and mouth finding the acrid bile I'd deposited there. A knee rested painfully on my back digging into my spine between my shoulder blades. And then I felt myself being lifted upright onto my feet. I wanted to struggle, but all the fight abandoned me as quickly as it had set in. I let the two uniforms drag me through the door and back into the cage where I'd awoken about a million years before. They tossed me unceremoniously onto the floor of the cell, slamming the door shut once I lay sprawled there, facing the toilet on the back wall. I didn't move, didn't even turn my head to look at Howe when he spoke to me.

"Well, that wasn't very smart, was it, Mac? You're not being very cooperative, and that's only going to make things worse for you in the end. I think you should just sit in here and have yourself a little think about your circumstances, Mac." I heard him toss something at me, but I didn't look up to see what it was until I heard his footfalls recede and the door close behind him. Once I was sure I was alone, I sat up feeling completely miserable. I looked around to see that Howe had been human enough to leave me with my nicotine, if not my dignity.

Gathering all the strength I had left, I got up and went to the sink. It was stained yellow and brown and smelled so strongly of mildew that I had to work to keep from gagging again. I splashed my face with the icy water that sprayed out of the taps and stared into the mirror as the water dripped off my nose and chin. Its mottled finish reflected a wretch of a human being with empty eyes and hollowed cheeks. I was surprised that it was me staring out of the mirror. I looked into my own eyes for some hint of truth. I didn't want to believe it. I couldn't have done it. Newt had to be right. I wasn't a murderer. I lay down on the cot, the mantra ringing in my ears. *I'm not a murderer. I'm not a murderer. I'm not a murderer.*

I lay there, willing myself to become numb to everything around me. Time became meaningless. I let the events of the last week filter through the camera of my mind's eye watching them like I would the much too late movie in the long nights when I waited for sleep to find me. The sound of Newt's voice soon faded into a quiet drone and then stopped altogether leaving me to feel only the silence of the tomb pressing down on me. I could have been dead already except for the jagged emotions that poured over me every time I opened my eyes and realized where I was.

My head pounded with the ache of dehydration. Each beat of my heart, each drip of water from the rusty tap beside me set my teeth on edge and reverberated through the blood vessels of my brain. I had no idea how much time passed while I calmed down and waited for the next scene in this horror. I suddenly knew what Newt must have been feeling all these years. I was trapped like a rat, no means of escape and no measure of control. It was a large vat of pity that I felt myself sinking into, drowning in the words and pictures that filled my mind instead of my lungs, suffocating my belief that things would all work out, that everything would be okay. Nothing would ever be okay. How did I ever think that I was anything but crazy? I'd deluded myself into thinking that the rest of the world was just limited in their comprehension, that the masses didn't have the imagination capable to accept that there might really be more to death than meets the eye.

Mac, don't do this. Don't let this shake you. You're not crazy. I'm really here.

His voice was desperate, just as my own would be if I was trying to save my neck. "Newt, how do I know that? How do I know anything anymore?"

Mac, you know because I'm telling you. Look, if you really were crazy and I was just a figment of your imagination that drove you to kill someone, then why did I wait until now? What's so special about now that I would tell you to beat Rachel to death? Admit it, if what the cops said was true, why haven't you been picking off girls every chance you get? Besides, how often do you listen to me?

I stayed quiet, considering. When I really thought about it, I wondered at the same thing. Why hadn't I been violent before now?

You don't have an answer for that one, do you? The truth is hard to accept, Mac, but the truth is that I'm real enough. It's the cops who are living in fairy tale land. They want to solve this case fast and they probably don't even care that much whether they've got the right guy or not. Look at them, civil servants, carrying guns and feeling superior to everybody. They only know what they can guess and what they're told.

Newt was quiet again for a long time. I stewed on what he'd said. I'd believed it before. Why was I having such a hard time believing it now? Ever since I'd gotten out of Lynwood, I'd felt like I knew something the rest of the world didn't. I hid my knowledge, just like so many purveyors of truth had hidden theirs in a play for safe passage through the maze that society set up for the masses. And now, when faced with something so horrifying, I was ready to let my beliefs crumble. I was ready to lay down for whatever punishment might be deemed suitable for my crime. But my crime wasn't killing Rachel. I could feel that in my heart now, and I'd be damned before I took the blame for it.

With each moment that passed, I became more and more convinced that my first instincts were right. My only crime was allowing myself to be bullied and brow beaten by two cops who probably didn't even have their facts straight. I could smell the sweat that seeped out of Rachel's pores as she sat in the back seat of my car only the night before. I could see her, wild eyed and troubled by the things going on around her that she couldn't explain and couldn't accept. In the absolute quiet of my mind, I felt my certainty grow that the girl in the picture, that poor beaten and bloodied girl was definitely dead, but equally definitely, not Rachel.

Chapter 38

I sat up on the bunk pressing my fingertips together while I cleared my head. It was time to get some things straight. The cops had been running this show up until now, but I was growing more and more indignant at my treatment. This was no banana republic where I might have my passport confiscated while I enjoyed the special pleasures of dysentery in a third world jail, only to have the document ransomed back to me in exchange for my gold watch and all the money in my wallet after they'd made rudimentary copies of it to sell on the black market for more money than I'd make in my lifetime. The more I thought about it, the more their control over me dwindled from the position of owning my psyche and playing around with it like a Rubik's cube to possessing only the key to my physical captivity. I was wondering if I could make a good civil case for wrongful imprisonment when Danning returned to release me for what I could only assume was to be another go in the ring with him and Howe. They'd held me down in my weakness before. I'd had no strength to fend off their attacks. The weakness of my spirit caused by so many spirits had tapered off, and while I was still aching, I felt my nerves finally settle. A cold, sharp edge of reason took my mind, clearing it for an offensive match that I was determined not to lose.

You're going to need help, Mac. You're going to need someone from the outside to help get you out of this.

I ignored Newt for now. I was thinking about my next move with the cops. There was only so much truth I was going to be able to tell them. Danning waited for me at the door, holding it open, not

249

speaking but still smiling in his delighted sadistic way. I let him stand there while I got up and washed my face again. The cold water seemed less jarring now. I felt like it was bracing me for the things to come. I slowly dried my hands and then went about the business of cleaning my glasses, happy to make the asshole behind me wait as long as possible. Finally, I patted my pocket to make sure my cigarettes were where I left them.

When I turned to the door, Danning had lost his smile and was scowling at me. I would have been happy to throw another barb at him, but I didn't trust him not to react with his boot again. Instead, I smiled sweetly at him which seemed to infuriate him even more than I could have hoped. He grabbed my collar roughly and pushed me ahead of him. I could hear him muttering, "Little punk. Who does he think he is? He'll get what's coming to him. We'll see how tough he is once he gets some company in that cell."

I smiled even more broadly as I led the way back into the now too familiar surroundings of the interrogation room I'd occupied before. It was rank with the vomit I'd left. The floor had been mopped, but the residue of the bile left its mark mingling with the odor of stale cigarette smoke and old sweat. I breathed deeply despite myself, gagging internally at all the human misery that this room had witnessed.

Neither Howe nor Danning seemed to notice how the walls pulsed with loss and confusion, guilt and despair. It was like manna to me, strengthening me in my resolve to not add my own scent of desperation to the ugly mix I felt seeping into my pores as I stood just inside the door. My smile gone now, I saw that Howe was at the table waiting for us. He looked up at me, scowling even more deeply than Danning. He gave a curt nod motioning for me to sit. I took the chair across from him and waited for his next move. He didn't make me wait long.

"So, you've had a few hours to think, Mac. I bet you're ready to get things off your chest now."

"You're right about that. I've been wondering, while I've been locked in that cell, just why it is that you're keeping me here. Did you arrest me when I wasn't paying attention?" I let my question echo around the hard surfaces of the room. I'd spoken loudly with an authority I didn't really feel, steeping myself in courage I didn't really have.

Howe looked surprised, but quickly covered his expression with a renewed anger toward me. Instead of answering, he pushed the photo of the girl in front of me again. After a long pause, he finally spoke. "What do you think?"

I didn't wait to tell him what I thought. "I think that you two bumbling idiots are trying to bully me into confessing to something I didn't do. I also think that you don't have a clue what happened to this girl, and your own incompetence is scaring the hell out of you. Now, do you want to tell me whether or not you're arresting me, or should I just start adding up the bill for my civil suit?" I leaned back in my chair, lit a cigarette, and blew the smoke in Howe's general direction.

A bit too cocky for my own good, the smoke seemed to push Howe right over the bounds of good judgment. He wound up and slapped me hard, so hard that the cigarette flew out of my mouth and onto the floor. I winced and felt tears spring to my eyes. It was the second blow that side of my face had felt this week, and I promised myself that next time I was in this situation, I'd try to find assailants who had opposing dominant hands. My left cheek was stinging, but I just shook my head. "I guess I can add police brutality to wrongful imprisonment when I lodge my complaint with your boss."

It wasn't a hollow threat, but it didn't seem to faze either Howe or Danning much. I hadn't really expected them to lay down their weapons and roll out the red carpet for me as I left, but I thought it might stir up some doubt in their minds at the very least. They were either too stupid to be scared or too sure they had the right man to care what idle threats I made. I went back on the offensive.

"I'll take it by your silence that you're not arresting me. If that's the case, then maybe you'll tell me what's to stop me from just getting up out of this chair and walking right out that door?"

Howe was ready for me this time. "Only the charge of public drunkenness that Officer Danning here filed when he brought you in. It's a good thing you were so difficult when he picked you up, otherwise, he might not have bothered. We decided that we should keep you here until you could face the judge in the morning. That way, at least you'd be sober by the time you had to answer the charge. Don't worry though, it's only a hundred dollar fine if you're found guilty, but it does have the advantage of allowing us to," he smiled again, oily and snakelike, "have a little time alone with you."

"You charged me with public drunkenness, for taking a cab home from the bar, and walking from it to my building. Well, I must have been in public for about thirty seconds. No judge is ever going to buy that." I was bristling with anger.

"Won't really matter if the judge buys it or not, four eyes, at least not once we've got you for killing this girl."

I was really beginning to hate John Danning from the core of my being. I didn't look at him, but kept my eyes trained on Detective Howe's fright wig of hair. He looked like an aging clown trying to keep his outdated act going even though most of his make-up had worn off. So, they were keeping me here on a charged stretched so thin through their embellishment that even blind justice herself would see through it. Until I hit the courtroom though, there was little I could do about getting out. It was clear that I couldn't stand up and walk out of there right then, but I promised myself that I would walk out.

That's the spirit, Mac. We're not going to let these assholes get the better of us.

I ignored Newt's camaraderie. I couldn't afford to start answering him again. "I guess I owe you an apology Officer Danning." He met my eye, startled at my remark. "I guess you're not quite as stupid as you look." I smiled and Danning moved toward me wearing an expression of deep dislike. He looked as though he would have been happy to reach into my mouth and rip my tongue out from its roots to keep me from speaking again.

"Sit down, John." Howe spoke quietly, but his voice carried enough authority to stop Danning in his tracks. He reluctantly took a seat next to his boss, and Howe redirected his attention to me. "You appear to have recovered your sense of humor, Mac. Not that you're expressing it very wisely. I think you'd better stop being such a smart ass and start answering some questions."

Before he could start asking, I fired a few of my own questions into the room. "Oh yeah, well how about this. I'd like to know when this girl was found. And where? I pay taxes for a reason, right? Surely, there are some people working in this building who actually know what they're doing. Someone must have figured out something like a time of death." I was building up a good head of steam now. "I'd like to know who planted in your pea brain the idea that I, of all the people

252

out there, am responsible for this? Or did you two rocket scientists come up with it all on your own?"

I was breathing with the quickness of adrenaline surging in my bloodstream, giving me invincible courage. I thought there was a pretty good chance I was going to get slapped again, but while the threat hung heavy over me, it never materialized. Maybe neither of them wanted to take the chance that I might not be bluffing about the law suit, and I was sure that neither one anticipated my aggression. After all, only a couple of hours before, I'd been laying on the floor of this very room, puking and shaking like a sick child. Neither of them reacted in any obvious way to my accusations. I saw Danning sneak a questioning look at Howe, but they both remained silent.

"Maybe if you could muster up a thought between the two of you, you might think to ask me what I was doing when you think that I might have been beating this girl's brains in. Don't they teach cops the word 'alibi' anymore? Or maybe you two were just out sick that day."

And, Mac, how do you know that girl is Rachel? Are you sure it's even her? They haven't given you any reason to believe it is. Go on. Ask them for proof that it's Rachel. Did they get her parents in to ID her? What are you waiting for?

"You think you're so smart! You don't have a fucking clue what's going on here. This asshole," I motioned to Danning, "he can't even figure out how to dial Rachel's parent's number. I bet you two monkeys aren't even sure this *is* Rachel Strong." It was a bold statement, but Newt was right, I certainly couldn't tell if the bloody pulpy mess in the photo was her or some other poor girl. All they really had right for sure was the hair color. It could have been any brunette in her twenties, and I felt the seeds of conviction grow in my stomach right next to the hollow feeling left by the absence of any kind of nutritional stimulus. I felt a wave of dizziness that made the room tilt awkwardly for a moment. I maintained my stony glare with difficulty, adjusting my next move to suit the growing discomfort I felt. "And on top of keeping me here on a, what do the shysters call it, a trumped up charge, you haven't fed me. I'm not saying another word until I get some food."

"Who do you think you are, ordering us around like bell hops?" Danning was on his feet again.

"Actually, Einstein, I'm ordering you around like you're a waiter. Try not to mix up your metaphors like that. It just makes you look even more foolish, if that's possible." I was pushing the limits of my own bravery far past any reasonable boundary. I was really just waiting for the other shoe to drop while I blustered on making demands and hurling insults. I think they called it shooting from the hip at one time, and that's certainly what it felt like, pulling the trigger, shooting out whatever ammunition I could muster without the luxury of time to take aim. All I had for sure was a target. I sputtered on, like a firecracker with a damp fuse, but once I got going the show was formidable.

"I'd also like to know whose bright idea it was to deny me any kind of phone call. And I'm fairly confident that a lawyer is meant to be at least an option for someone who has been charged with a crime—even something as petty as public drunkenness. Or did you forget about that part? It wouldn't surprise me if you had, judging by the way you've run your investigation so far. Maybe if you're really lucky, you'll be able to take some remedial police work classes while you're out there writing traffic tickets for the next twenty years."

Danning stood suddenly and stalked out of the room; I hoped in search of some kind of food product to quell the insistent pangs of hunger in my restless stomach. That left me alone with a very irritated Detective Howe. He leaned across the table stopping only when he was just inches from me. When he finally spoke, it was barely more than a whisper, but it was controlled in a way that chilled me with its coldness. "You certainly got your dander up, son. Maybe we left you alone a little too long. You seem to have built up quite a dislike for Officer Danning and myself. I can't say I really blame you. I think I might behave in just the same rude way as you have. I would probably be grasping at all the same straws myself if I was wearing your shoes. The thing is that for all your big talk, I can see that you aren't anything but a little punk chicken shit. You're trying hard to throw us off you, but I'll tell you this, I'm stuck like glue to you, Mac. I've got your number here, and I'm going to make sure it ends up on a pretty orange jumpsuit over your heart." He stabbed at my chest hard, repeatedly as he spoke. More than anything I wanted to grab it and twist it until it came off in my hands, but I sat there unflinching, silence incarnate.

It was only a few minutes until Danning returned with a box of store bought doughnuts. I couldn't resist the opportunity or suppress my laughter. "You couldn't have come up with something a little less clichéd? Not real big in the imagination department are you, Officer?" It made it very difficult for me to take the whole process seriously when the cops were only inches from being characters in a cheap detective novel. You know the kind, bumbling cop jumping to all the wrong conclusions while the clever private dick is doing all the really hard deducing. I half expected to see Sam Spade saunter through the door to pick up the pieces of the ruined case that lay on the table underneath the three glazed donuts Danning had brought to serve as my meal.

Clichéd or not, I greedily grabbed at the donuts, plunging one after another into my mouth. Through a shower of crumbs, I managed to spit out my next outrageous demand. "Coffee." I went on chewing while Danning exited again, returning in seconds with a steaming cup. He slid it roughly toward me, slopping some over the edges. It was ancient, thick and murky with age, but I brought the cup to my lips with an ardent desire that would have been indecent if it hadn't been so close to pathetic. Soon the frenzy ended and I was left, not really satisfied, but at least sustained for the moment. I reached into my pocket and withdrew my cigarettes. I surveyed the two cops as I brought one to my lips and lit it carefully. I immediately resolved to write a thank you letter to every tobacco company out there. Cancer and heart disease might be bad, but they paled in comparison to being held down by The Man without benefit of the calming effects of my habit.

For the first time since I'd left Dodger's, I felt almost comfortable. My head was still thudding with the lasting effects of dehydration, but I had at least managed to squelch the hunger that had been driving me to distraction. It was time to go back on the offensive. "Well, now that that's out of the way," I blew smoke rings up to the ceiling knowing it would further infuriate Danning because it was an act filled with glib insubordination. "I believe you were about to answer my questions."

Before either of them could answer there was a knock on the door. Involuntarily, I jumped in my chair, a little surprised at the fact that we three were not alone in the universe. The door opened and I saw another generic uniform wave Howe over to the door. He rose and the two exchanged a few words in undertones that I couldn't make out. When Howe returned to the table, he was wearing a leer, shameless and joyful. "That's right, Mac, you were asking about phone calls, weren't you? Well, I wouldn't want you to think we didn't have your best interests at heart, so the last time we put you down for a nap, I took the liberty of making a phone call on your behalf. It seems to have brought you a visitor." He was still smiling, the malice barely contained behind his lips stretched thin across his mouth. I was scared to ask, but I didn't have to. Danning opened the door again, and there, following the uniform who had knocked at the door, was my mother.

Chapter 39

Wow! They called Gail.

"You called my mother?" It was as much a question as a statement of total disbelief. I gaped at Howe, inspiration dissolving into desperation one rushing moment later.

"Don't be asinine, Macbeth. Of course they didn't call me. Why would they? Why would you?" Gail always opened well. I went from being a towering pillar of civil indignation to an eight year old caught feinting the measles in only four sentences.

I was stunned. I couldn't make my mouth work right. All the bluster I'd felt through the last hour and a half, melted into the puddle of coffee left on the table. I slumped in my chair, beaten with a hit well below the belt. Gail was boring deep holes into my skin with her eyes. I looked at her briefly and immediately regretted it. She was pale with rage, clenching and unclenching her fists in an effort to keep from exploding in front of the police.

With a tremor in her voice that only my practiced ear could detect, Gail addressed herself to Detective Howe in even, measured tones designed to smooth over her son's undoubtedly lamentable first impression. "Detective Howe, is it?" She smiled shyly at him, an apology hidden between the lines of her lips. He nodded dumbly and she continued. "I wonder if my son and I might have a few moments alone, if it wouldn't be too much trouble."

Detective Howe exchanged a look with Officer Danning and then smiled indulgently at Gail. "Of course, ma'am, you take as much time as you need." He rose and made for the door, motioning to Danning to follow him. "We'll just be right outside this door. If you need anything at all, you just let me know."

Gail smiled and thanked both the cops in turn. For a minute, I thought she might actually have been flirting with Howe the way she let her gaze linger on his face for a second longer than I thought was appropriate. She followed them with her eyes all the way out the door, turning to me once the door had clicked shut behind them. Her gaze immediately turned grey with repressed anger.

I wanted to throw up again. How could she be so polite to the men who had been holding her son for no good reason? How could she stand there and smile at them? How could she be staring daggers at me, as though she already knew I was guilty of whatever crime they were accusing me of? I didn't want to believe it, but this was exactly the kind of reaction I would have expected from her, and exactly the reason I never would have called her. Before I could tell her so, Newt piped up.

Wow, she looks some kind of mad, Mac. I'd have asked the cops to stay if I were you. They might have provided you with a little protection. Do you remember that time when I locked you in the basement with my glow in the dark monster models? She had that same expression on her face when she found me. At least you're too big to get the wooden spoon. My ass hurt for a week after that.

I had clearly slipped into that alternate dimension again. There could be no other explanation for my brother comparing my mother's anger at discovering me in jail suspected of murder to him getting a spanking for an act of childish mischief that took place eighteen years ago. I physically shook my head to try to discern what was really happening here. Gail's patience wore out right in front of me. Apparently, my mute head shake pushed the limits of what I could get away with at that moment.

"Don't you dare shake your head at me, Macbeth Williams! I cannot believe that I am sitting in a police station at eleven o'clock on a Friday night with a son 'in custody'. That's what they told me at the information desk, that you are 'in custody'. Can you even imagine how that makes me feel?"

She's not wasting any time playing the guilt card is she? It always was her favorite.

I felt deflated even though this was the reaction I would have anticipated if I'd known she was going to show up in the middle of this. Even as the air was leaking out of me, I could feel the hard steel of my isolation rising up in an effort to protect myself from her traitorous brand of mothering. "How you feel? No, *Mom*, I can't imagine how you feel? Frankly, I can't imagine much of anything right now, not how you got here or even why you bothered to come." I said it quietly with acid on my tongue.

"I am just appalled." She carried on as though she hadn't even heard me. "When that bartender friend of yours called me, I was sure he'd gotten the wrong number, but how many Macbeth Williams could there be in this city?"

I wanted to be encouraged at the mention of Steve's name, but it seemed he was against me too. "Steve called you? Why?"

"Well, after the police called him, I imagine he thought I might like to know my son was in trouble." She was almost breezy about the way she said it, like she was talking about the arrival of the carpeting she'd ordered last week for an office building she was renovating. In a flash her anger was renewed, white hot. "He told me that the police had called him to—I cannot believe I am about to say this about a child of mine—'check your alibi'! What do you have to say for yourself?"

I can't see clearly. Are her hands shaking? I don't think she was ever so mad at me that her hands shook. You might be safer in that cell, Mac.

At least Newt was enjoying himself. He hadn't ever grown out of the 16-year-old mentality that let him enjoy the wrath of parent toward sibling. If I was getting the wooden spoon, that meant he probably wasn't. The distinction between the spanking and the long prison sentence was a little more than he was able to comprehend. He had clearly lost touch with the reality of the situation.

She was still standing hovering over me, judging me just as she had been my whole life. I guessed that she was waiting for me to apologize or something. When I remained silent, she exhaled, exasperated beyond recognition. "I just don't understand you. You have all this potential, and you just sit there and do nothing worthwhile."

Oh, I always hated it when she started talking about how much I could be doing if I only applied myself.

"You know, I don't want to say it, but I've almost been expecting something like this. I told you yesterday that your drinking was going to get you into trouble. I don't know why I bother. It's not like you ever listen anyway. Now look where you are."

I bet she's going to bring up all her sacrifices next?

"Do you have any idea how hard it is to raise a child? I've worked hard to give you a good life. I've made sacrifices, so that you wouldn't have to. I tried hard to teach you right from wrong, and look where it's gotten me. Sitting in a filthy police station wondering how I'm going to bail you out of this one."

Told you. I knew it. Remember that time she caught us shoplifting from the Chinese grocery down the street. Remember how she made us apologize to every member of Old Man Chang's family for taking a pack of gum and a chocolate bar. "I apologize for taking food out of your family's mouth. It was disrespectful and wrong. I promise I will never do it again." And then we went home for the real lecture. I didn't think I'd ever see her that mad again.

"So tell me, Mac, what have you done to have the police checking on your alibi?" She spat the words out at me, as furious as she was suspicious.

Are you going to tell her the truth, Mac? I think you should. I know she's angry, but I think she can help. Maybe she can get you out of here, and then you can find Rachel. Providing, of course, that Rachel's not really dead.

"Shut up!" I was panting, breathing hard with frustration and confusion. Gail and Newt were bearing down on me so hard and fast I was having trouble keeping up. I couldn't tell who was talking, who was angry, who was living, who was dead. "Just shut up!" I needed some quiet to figure out what to say and do next. I took off my glasses and started cleaning them on my shirt. The spots smeared together giving Gail and even more contorted expression of fury. Shocked that I would speak to her like that, her face had closed in on itself; all but her eyes which bulged unattractively in an expression of outrage.

"I can't believe that you would talk to me like that." Her voice shook noticeably. "I've come all the way down here to help you. Imagine what it felt like for me to tell Chuck that I had to go to the police station because you were being held there. And this is the thanks I get for my concern—you shout at me for asking what's happened."

I really lost it then. "Listen to yourself. Oh, don't think you can fool me with your insulted tone. You didn't come down here to help me. You came down here so you could witness first hand the disappointment your son has become. Well, take a good look because I'm about two seconds from asking the cops to lock me back up. I'd rather sit in a cell forever than have you lift a finger for me." The words hung in the air long after they'd left my mouth. Hanging between us, they hovered over the rift that had widened over the years until I couldn't see any of the Gail I knew. I just wanted her gone, but if I thought she was going to go quietly, I was much mistaken.

"Now you listen to me, you little shit." I knew she must have been seething with anger; Gail never swore but in the direst of circumstances. "I didn't ask for you to drink yourself into an alcoholic stupor. I didn't ask for you to be unable to hold down a decent job for longer than six months at a time. I wasn't the one who decided to quit school in favor of life in the gutter. Now, we are going to sit down and discuss this like adults."

"Do you hear yourself? Do you hear how you sound? I'm in jail, okay. For all intents and purposes, the cops have me, and they aren't letting go. Those two apes you were flirting with are drooling over the prospect of finding a way to keep me in here for good. And all you can do is stand there whining about poor you and how hard this is for you, and how you didn't ask for this. Well, guess what Gail, I didn't ask for this, either. You want to talk about it. Fine we'll talk about it." I grabbed Howe's file folder off the table and found the photo of the girl they'd been waving under my nose. "Here," I threw the photo across the table to her. "That's why the cops brought me in. Satisfied?"

The picture floated down face up onto the table just inches from Gail's hand. She looked at it briefly, and then more carefully as she determined just what she was looking at. She pulled her hand away like it had been burned, recoiling with horror. She sank down into one of the chairs beside her. *Now,* I thought, *now she would get her dander up on my side. Now she would see how wrongly I was being treated and judged.*

"Oh, Mac." I could hear tears welling up in her throat. "What have you done? What did you do to this poor girl?" She was choking on her disgust when she looked at me.

I couldn't believe my ears. How faithless could she possibly be that she would think I was capable of something as vicious as she saw in that photograph? I started to laugh at the absurdity of it all.

Whoa buddy, you all right. This doesn't really seem to be a good time to be laughing. I know you're disappointed in Gail, but you've got to give her a chance. She's going to get it. You've got to make her believe you.

"Believe me? She's not ever going to believe me. She thinks I did it. She believes I'm guilty. How's that for some good motherly support?"

"Mac, you're not making sense. Why are you talking about me like I'm not here? Oh God, you're having a relapse aren't you? It's another Mental Health Crisis, isn't it? I was always afraid that this might happen one day. Dr. Maaken told me it was a possibility. I just didn't want to believe it. Is that why you did this? Are you hearing voices again? Did that have anything to do with what happened to this girl?" She was staring at me with fearfulness, afraid maybe I'd turn my fists on her next.

I just looked at her. I'm sure she could read the discouraged sadness in my eyes. I just didn't know what to say. How would I ever convince her of anything when she didn't even offer me the benefit of the doubt long enough to ask me if I was responsible? I sat there, feeling the angry frustration I'd felt for so long rise until I couldn't bury it any longer. It exploded out of me in a sobbing plaintive wail that made Gail jump with surprise.

I banged my fists on the table, crying openly, tears rolling down my face in a steady stream that dripped endlessly into my open mouth and down onto the sleeves of my jacket. Slumping with a desperate desire to shrivel into micro particles, I slid off the chair and onto the floor. My mouth was open, but no more sound would come out. It was locked open in a silent moan of unhappiness and loss that seemed to split my whole being into sharp edges cutting away any attachment I had to the world. I'd never felt so alone or so abandoned in my life. I hoped Gail would just leave. I hoped she would get up and walk out and never come back. I couldn't live with the empty hope that she was going to see, really see all that had happened to me since Newt died. I heard her rise from her chair, its legs scraping across the gritty tile floor. Footsteps followed, and I prayed that her shoes were the last part of her I'd ever see. I closed my eyes and waited for the door to close behind her. I didn't care what happened to me now. I didn't care if Danning and Howe formed a lynch mob and strung me up. I didn't care what happened to Rachel, if she was dead or not. I didn't care if Newt ever got out of limbo. None of it mattered anymore. I laid down, ready for whatever evil was going to take me next.

"Mac," I heard her voice, soft now, scared still, but in control. "Honey, I think we should call a lawyer. And I think I should call Dr. Makken, too. He might be able to help." She'd come over to my side of the table, leaned down to touch my back. I flinched and pulled myself away from her touch. She was kneeling on the floor next to me. I edged myself as far away as the small room would allow. "Mac, did you hear me?"

"Why don't you just leave? It's what you want anyway. You can go on home to Chuck and forget about me. I don't need you or your help." I couldn't stop crying. There were so many more angry words I wanted to say to her, but I couldn't stop sobbing long enough to do it. She moved toward me again, but I held my hand out, trying to keep her at bay. "Don't you get it, Gail? I don't want you here."

What are you saying, Mac. You don't mean that. You want her here. You need her help to get out of here.

"I don't need her help. I don't need anything she has to give, Newt."

"I knew it. I knew it was happening again. I don't understand why you won't just be honest with me, Mac. I want to help you. I really do." She was keeping her tone as even as she could, but she wasn't able to hide the note of triumph in her voice when she spoke. "I'm going to get to a phone and call Dr. Maaken right away. Everything is going to be okay, sweetheart. Just relax."

My tears stopped. I was overwrought at the thought of even one five minute conversation with Maaken. I knew he'd have me committed again regardless of whether or not I was the one who laid hands on the girl. "Don't you get it, Gail? I was honest with you. That day in the hospital when I told you what was happening; that was the truth. You just didn't believe me. You haven't believed me since

Newt died. Don't cringe when I say his name. He wouldn't like to know you do that whenever I mention him. He wouldn't like to know that you never talk about him. Imagine how it's been for me all these years, trying to hide from him the fact that you took down all his photos and hid them."

She took down all my pictures?

"Yes, Newt, and all your trophies and awards, too. They all disappeared into a box that ended up who knows where. Maybe in the basement. I don't know; I was never able to find them." I shot an accusing look at Gail. "She pretends you never existed, my brother. I guess it's easier for her that way. But that's pretty much been her style since you died, taking the easy way out."

Why didn't you tell me before?

"I don't know. I didn't want to hurt your feelings, I guess. I mean it was bad enough that you've had to hang around so long after you'd died. I didn't think knowing that Gail made all her memories of you disappear would make you feel much better." I kept my eyes trained on Gail. She looked torn somewhere between grief and terror with a little confusion thrown in for good measure.

I can't believe she got rid of my trophies. Even my one for Most Valuable Player that year in hockey?

"Yep, even the hockey trophy. She doesn't seem like such a great mom now, does she?" I felt startlingly calm suddenly, as though speaking freely to Newt in front of Gail had liberated me. I felt an urge to laugh at Newt's irritation, but nothing about the rest of the situation seemed very funny.

Looking at Gail, who was growing more agitated and unsure about everything with each passing moment, I felt a twinge of pity. "Don't you remember, Gail? Don't you remember what it was like before Newt died? Can't you try to remember what it was like? What you were like?" I wanted so much for her to understand, to believe that this otherworldly metaphysical thing with Newt was really happening. I felt like my life depended on it. Without it, I would sink into whatever bog was available and wait there until I drowned. For as surely as I was trapped in this room, she would do everything she could to see me locked up again if I couldn't convince her.

She stared at me vacantly, reminding me forcibly of how Rachel had looked after I'd confessed to her about Newt. It must have been a standard issue look for this situation. Her hands twitched uncomfortably, and I thought that she might get up and walk out in search of a phone and a quarter to call Dr. Maaken. Desperate wasn't the right word to describe how frantic I was to remind her of how things used to be. She had once been invincible in my eyes, and while I was ready to grant that she was human, I begged to whatever power it was that held Newt hostage to grant her just one more moment as that Gail gone so long from my life.

"Please Gail, try to remember all those things you taught us as kids about souls going on and never really leaving us. How could you teach us that if you didn't really believe it yourself? Was it all a lie for you? Was that how you kept Dan alive all those years? Was that what your desperation drove you to? Lying to your children so death wouldn't seem as scary and finite? It's okay, Gail; it wasn't a lie. It was true. It is true. Newt does talk to me. He has a purpose here that won't let him leave until he's done what he has to do." I was sure I sounded hysterical, rambling on about trapped souls and predestined tasks, but I didn't know how else to make her see the truth. It was only her teaching that brought me any understanding of this whole crazy situation, and the irony of it was that the teacher refused to believe her own lessons.

She didn't respond but just continued to stare. If anything like comprehension or revelation slipped into her eyes even for just a second, I must have missed it. I called on Newt looking for anything that might convince her that her only living son wasn't a complete whack job. "Come on, Newt. There's got to be a way we can prove it to her. Isn't there something only you would know? Something I can tell her to prove that you're real?"

He was quiet for a while. A first for him. "Think, Newt. There's got to be something. Newt? Are you even listening?" I kept badgering him until he broke.

Of course I'm listening, you idiot. You don't think I'm interested in what happens here? There's only one thing I can think of, but I don't want to tell you.

My head spun in frustration. Was my brother really this selfish? "I'm sorry. I must have misunderstood what you just said. You don't want to tell me the one thing that might convince our dear mother that you're real. Are you out of your maggot ridden mind? Just tell me!"

I promised her when I was 15 that I'd never tell you. She said it would hurt your feelings too much.

"Are you serious?" I was in some kind of absurd play, obviously. "I think that whatever hurt feelings I might have will probably pale next to Gail actually believing that I'm not insane, don't you. God, you are so stupid sometimes."

Okay fine, just remember you wanted to hear it. She told me you were a mistake. He paused a second, and then continued again so quietly I had to strain to hear what he was saying. *She told me that Dan really didn't want another child. He wanted her to get an abortion. There, are you happy now?*

I felt like I'd been kicked in the stomach. My father hadn't wanted me. I could feel the tears welling up in my eyes again. They seemed to snap Gail out of her reverie. "What? What did he say?"

"He said that Dan didn't want me. He said that he wanted you to get rid of me." I was cold, shivering at this news. Somehow, it didn't seem fair that to prove myself sane I would have to lose my father all over again in this new and supremely painful way while I cowered on the floor of an interrogation room.

It was as though the words flicked a switch in her mind. She seemed to snap out of the trance that had held her captive in her grief for years. Her mouth dropped open, and she started to speak a few times, struggling for words that might fit the moment. "Oh my god, it is true. Newt, honey, can you hear me? Oh God, baby." She looked at me, huddled in the corner and came over, her face now streaming with salty rivers. "Oh my God, what have I done? My Mac, my poor child." On her knees now, she took me in her arms and held me close to her breast like she had when I was six. She rocked me in her arms while I cried deep sobs of anguish and relief. And I poured out 12 long years of pain and anger and fear onto her like Ahab on his whale only I found instead of the emptiness of revenge, the endless bounty of my mother's belief. I told her all about Rachel and the dead girl and all I'd gone through since Danning had picked me up. And she listened and believed while she stroked my hair; and so many years melted away while she whispered over and over again, "I'm sorry. I'm so sorry."

Chapter 40

It was an eternity that we sat there on that floor. All the time we needed to realize that we really were mother and son, united always by blood and circumstance and, finally, after all these years, love. Gail cried hard for the sins she'd committed when she gave up herself in favor of the persona she thought would save her from more pain. All the happy good mother smiles she adopted; all the pretty dresses and home cooked meals; all the would be dads that came and went; all of them were just hollow attempts at a life she never really believed in anyway. And none of them ever came close to giving either one of us any amount of happiness. It's a devious trick on the parts of pain and loss that forces us to feel it no matter how long we push it aside and bury it in dark corners that we rarely let our minds travel to. For 12 years, Gail had refused to have memories of Newt, and for eight years before that, she wiped nearly clean the slate that held all her memories of Dan. But for all her efforts, the mourning never went away, her sadness lingered just under the surface out of sight, but not by any means, out of mind. She bought herself some smiles on credit and forged ahead, delaying the inevitable day when it would all break out of her, that day on the floor of the station house.

Our reunion as mother and son, as poignant as it was, was short-lived. All the tears stopped when the door opened, and Detective Howe strode in. He looked like he'd had about enough foolishness from me, and he meant to get down to business this time. I was sure I was in for another haranguing session with him over the dead girl in the picture. I felt just as scared as I had before, but there was a new sense of urgency about my terror. It seemed more important than ever that I find a way out of this mess. I stood and smoothed out my clothing in an attempt to gather myself. Helping Gail up, she did the same, reaching for a Kleenex out of her purse, she began wiping away the tearstains on her face.

Gail was applying some fresh lipstick, looking into a small pocket mirror, an act I thought seemed irrelevant at best, when Howe opened his mouth to speak. Before he managed to get a word out, Gail was addressing him, not meeting her eye, but rather concentrating on filling her lips with a pale pink color, "Detective, I really do think it's time to let my son go, don't you?" The lid of her mirror clicked shut with a decisive sound. She met Howe's eye with her steady gaze. It was hard to believe that only minutes before, she had been a puddle of human misery on the floor.

After his initial surprise at Gail's statement—so sure was he that he would be able to count her as an ally in all this—he recovered himself and fixed her with a grin I imagine he mistakenly thought was good natured and placating. He seemed to be searching for the right words to make it clear to Gail that I wasn't going anywhere. "Mrs. Williams, I'd be happy to let Mac go right now, but we have a little outstanding matter than needs to be dealt with first. Perhaps your boy didn't fully explain what he's doing here." His voice was smooth, but held a cold excitement, betraying the enjoyment he felt in his role as master of ceremonies at my own private inquisition. "It seems that Mac here got himself into a bit of trouble with one of his girlfriends. I don't want to shock you, Mrs. Williams, but…"

Gail cut him off with a razor sharp look. Then she began her tirade. "What shocks me, *Detective*, is how someone as careless and sloppy as you could ever have made the rank of detective in the first place. I believe that at a very minimum, you are required to provide my son with legal counsel if he requests it." She turned to me. "You did request it, didn't you, Mac?" I nodded mutely, happy to let someone else go to bat for me for a change. "I'd like to know just how long you were planning to hold my son before you got him that legal counsel. Were you just banking on driving him into making a desperate confession by denying him food and water? Or maybe you thought you'd trick him into a confession by deluding him into believing that he was crazy. Do you have any idea of proper police procedure, or did your lackey just have such a hard on for my son that he had to find him guilty of something? I'm sure if that is the story you want to go with, your superiors will be happy to stand behind you right up until the time I file my law suit against you two personally and the department, too, just to make sure there are lots of hard feelings."

I'd never heard Gail be crude like that before. I smiled in spite of myself. *Hey Newt*, I thought, *Gail just said "hard on,"* and I felt like I was 13 again, suppressing a giggle with my brother at our mother's risqué language. Howe's bushy white eyebrows came together in a deep scowl. Obviously, he didn't find the situation quite as humorous. Nor did Gail, as she pointedly frowned at me and told me to sit down. She did the same and gestured Howe into the chair I had occupied for most of the evening. It seemed a strange reversal of fortunes to see Howe now sitting in the hot seat trying to fend of Gail's attacks now coming from every angle.

She had risen to the occasion like I had only imagined in my wildest dreams she would. I had relinquished the hope that she would ever come to my defense again, and here she was brow beating a cop with all the weapons in her arsenal. Howe, for his part, was growing more and more uncomfortable, but he was too good an actor for me to know whether it arose from any truth he might have seen in Gail's threats or from his patience wearing thin. We never got to find out. Gail was looking through her address book and talking about lawyers again when we were interrupted by Danning bursting through the door.

His face was a mottled red that spread from his neck to his scalp, the hue clearly visible through the thin hair that barely covered the top of his forehead. He was breathing heavily, not from exertion so much as, it seemed, panic. Sweat had beaded on his upper lip and he wiped it away before speaking, trying to master himself, "Detective, could I talk to you for a minute?"

It was hard to tell if Howe was relieved or disappointed by the interruption as the expression on his face changed little as he rose up and strode over to where Danning stood by the open door. They exchanged a series of heated whispers that I strained to hear, but that Gail seemed to ignore as though they couldn't possibly concern us. I continued to focus my stare on the pair of them, saw Howe look toward us once, and Danning repeatedly as his whispering grew more rapid and strained. Finally, Howe spoke loudly, dismissively to him, "I said I would handle it. Now, start the paperwork."

Danning quickly retreated closing the door behind him. Howe paused at the door for a minute, not speaking, clearly deciding his next move. I expected to be hauled off for fingerprinting any second, and I was making a list of books I hoped the prison library carried when he made his way back to the table. He started collecting the papers that lay strewn all across the table, gathering them into the file folders; last of all, the photograph of the dead girl disappeared in between the stiff manila and we were left staring at Howe waiting for an explanation.

"You were right, Mrs. Williams. It is time we let your son go." He went to the door, files in hand, opened it and stood there waiting for us to pass through it.

Newt shrieked with triumph. *I knew Gail would get you out of this. I knew it was all going to be okay.*

He wasn't so interested in the finer points of the investigation, but I was a little more attached to the experience I'd had at the hands of this cop and his flunky. I needed some explanations. Did this mean I was no longer a suspect or did it just mean they didn't have enough evidence to pursue me right then? I felt more than a little excited at the prospect of walking out the door and into some long overdue freedom, but I wasn't about to sail off blindly hoping that my ordeal was over. I looked at Gail. She raised her eyebrow, as skeptical as I was. She and I both knew that it never paid to be too sanguine about anything before all the facts were in.

"Detective, I'm not sure I heard you correctly. Did you say that I was free to go? Just like that, I can waltz right out of here when only minutes ago you were convinced I was a violent, voice-hearing menace, a danger to myself and my community, isn't that what you said?" I tried to control it, but it was hard to keep the sarcasm out of my voice. "I think that you're going to have to explain to me why it is that you are so eager to release me now, after all the special moments we've had together in this room."

Howe hated me with his whole being, I was sure. He exhaled his disgust and closed the door again leaving his hand on the knob ready to make a break for it. I could see that whatever it was, the last thing he wanted to do was give me an explanation. Finally, when he could put it off no longer, he spit out the truth in short order. "It seems that Rachel Strong was picked up about an hour ago just outside your building. Apparently, she was wandering around, waiting for you. She's very confused, but she claims that she filed her own missing person report. She's quite adamant about it. It seems that Officer Danning was a little enthusiastic about your involvement with her. He, uh, he didn't exactly follow proper procedures." He stopped as suddenly as he'd started. Apparently, he thought that was enough, but I wasn't near satisfied.

"So, you have Rachel here in this building, and she's telling you the same thing I told Danning yesterday. And that's all you have to say? That, and you're free to go. No apologies or anything, just here's your hat, what's your hurry."

"Well, the department does extend its apologies for the inconvenience, and I assure you Officer Danning will receive an appropriate reprimand..."

"The department extends its apologies. Well, that's nice, isn't it, Gail? The department apologizes. Well, I tell you what, right after you go get my watch and my wallet, I'll expect a big fucking apology from you, too. And you can line up Danning behind you. And after that, I'm going to find the best litigation lawyer I can and send him crawling down your throat because I..."

"Mac, that's enough." Gail put her hand on my arm. Out of habit, I started to pull away from her, but when I met her eye, I remembered that she was no longer on all sides but mine. She gave me a conspiratorial wink that said we'd discuss the particulars of suing the police once we were out of the station. She turned her steely look back on Howe. "But I do think you owe my son some sort of apology." We both waited expectantly.

"Fine." Howe looked as though this was a bigger crime than the one he'd believed me to have committed. "I apologize for any unnecessary hardship you may have felt while we held you under suspicion of murder." He drew his lips together in a tight line, and I knew that was the best I would get from him. His knuckles were white from gripping the door handle so tightly. He released it and returned to the table, sitting down heavily, the physical drain of his confession besting him. "You're free to go. You can collect your possessions from the clerk at the property desk on your way out."

271

Gail and I wasted no time getting out of that room. I was signing for my things when Danning joined us, a sheepish grin on his lupine face. He clapped me on the back with a jocular boldness. I strapped on my watch and pocketed my wallet before turning to face him. "So, well, I guess I kind of screwed up." He said it as though he'd dialed a wrong number. "I mean we all make mistakes, don't we?" I just stared at him. "I mean, it's not like I meant to screw you over. I was just trying to do my job. So, no hard feelings right?" He extended his hand to me expectantly, but I let it hang there empty. I couldn't believe this guy was sucking up to me, hoping to ward off whatever departmental discipline was around the corner for him. I couldn't believe he was looking for a handshake after all that had transpired between us. At least Howe had shown a little integrity. I gazed at him with contempt and turned away. He lingered behind me for a minute, as though trying to decide whether or not to go for another attempt at reconciliation. Finally, when he realized he was going to get nothing from either Gail or myself, he slunk away in the direction we'd come from off to find, I hoped, a suspension without pay waiting for him. I shook my head in disbelief.

"Can you believe that jerk?" Gail looked like she was doing a mental tally of all the things that had gone wrong for the police tonight, and just how much it was going to cost them. Personally, I didn't care much about any lawsuit, I'd already won more tonight than any judge could award me for the pain and suffering of my experience. I only had one thing left to do. Turning back to the property clerk, I asked the only question I still cared about the answer to. "The officers told me that you had a girl called Rachel Strong here. Would I be able to see her for, just for five minutes or so?"

The clerk nodded. "Hey, Ernie, the kid here wants to see the crazy we just brought in. Can you take him in?" A short desk jockey stood up and motioned for me to follow him. Gail nodded at me, taking a seat. I walked behind Ernie through the maze of the station house until we arrived outside a cage that looked very much like the one I'd spent so many hours in that night. Ernie left me looking at her. Rachel was lying on the lower bunk in the fetal position. I called her name, softly at first, then, when she didn't move, a little louder. She jumped at the sound of my voice, sat up and stared at me, recognition setting in as an embarrassed smile rested at the corners of her mouth. Her hair had been smoothed out, and she'd changed her clothes since I'd seen her last, but she looked like she was badly in need of several days rest and a decent meal. She looked, if not happy, at least relieved to see me.

"Mac. You're okay, then." Her shy smile appeared and was then replaced quickly by a look of remorse so profound I thought she might begin crying. "I'm so sorry, Mac. I don't know what I thought I was doing. I've been a little confused the last few days, but I guess you know that." She paused and I waited for her to continue. When she did, the emotion cracked through her voice and tears began to well up and escape the borders of her eyelids. "I thought you were crazy. I thought I was going crazy. All that stuff you told me on Monday night and then again last night, and then," she dropped her voice to a whisper, "Melanie's voice in my head like that, I, I just thought it couldn't be true." She trailed off running out of steam.

"Rachel, listen to me." I said the words earnestly as if our lives depended on them. "It is true. Believe it. I don't advocate telling the police your story, but you can stop thinking that you're crazy. You're not."

She grinned at me. Her face lit up, and I felt like I'd do just about anything to help this girl. I remembered Audrey and her campaign to set me free. I didn't know if helping Rachel would set my mind at ease about Audrey, finally, after all these years, but at least Rachel would have one ally to help her. "I'm so sorry about all this. I'm sorry that you have this burden to bear, but I think I can help you if you want."

She rose and walked toward me. Reaching through the bars, she grabbed both my hands and squeezed them tightly. We looked at each other for a long time. I could see the hope flare up in her eyes, and I promised myself to not abandon her to a life of fearful alienation and angst. "Thank you, Mac." She whispered it breathing the words hot onto my neck, and in spite of myself, I felt a jump in my lower abdomen and a spasm of excitement.

We continued to hold hands, not speaking until Ernie returned to check on us. At the sound of the door opening, Rachel released my hands. I felt an unexpected sensation of emptiness, the cool air on my palms reinforcing the absence of her touch. She recovered quickly, picking up on a conversation we hadn't even started yet. "No, my parents are on the way here. They're going to be pretty upset, but I think they'll understand once I explain what happened." She winked at me. "I'll have to start sessions with my shrink again, but I don't think much else will happen. Of course, they threatened to charge me with making a false police report, but if they do, they do. I'm not worried. My dad's not short of lawyers. We'll work it out. I should be home by some time tomorrow." She was so calm and practical. "I'll call you when I get out, and we can talk." My admiration was growing at an exponential rate. This girl floored me. Just as Audrey had so long ago, and just as Gail had only hours before. It seemed, I thought as I walked out the doors of the station and into the frosty September night, that all the women I let into my life would be my best source of amazement and strength.

It was God from the Machine if I'd ever seen it. A few hours ago, I'd been sure that I was bound for prison, guilty or not. It seemed so unlikely that I could be outside the station, waiting to go home with my mother of all people, that I pinched myself to make sure it wasn't all some dream cooked up by my subconscious to protect me from the truth. I looked at the welt forming on my arm where I'd twisted the skin and smiled at fate's absurd sense of humor. I pulled my collar up around my neck to shut out the wind while I waited for Gail to pull her car up to the curb. I lit a cigarette and watched the smoke mingle together with my breath.

"Well, Newt, you were right about one thing. There really is something about Rachel. Don't you think?"

My voice rang out clear in the cold air. I waited for an answer, gloating and smug, from my brother. "Newt? You there?"

Silence.

"Come on, Newt, quit playing around." Gail pulled up at the curb and honked. I looked around as though expecting to see him if not hear him.

Nothing.

I got into Gail's sedan and felt the warm air of the heater on my face. She turned to look at me, and I realized it then. It was over. After all these years of wasting time and arguing and hiding, in an instant, faster than I could snap my fingers, Newt was finally gone.

"Are you all right, Mac?" Gail peered closely in the dim light at me.

Was I okay? I wasn't sure. I felt free and alone, but in a way that didn't scare me. Had I finally gotten what I'd been searching for all those years? Had I achieved my Tabula Rasa? No, I hadn't, but as it turned out, I was wrong about that too. I didn't really want it afterall. We never get a clean slate again. All the marks we make on it are indelible, permanent accounts of who we are; a record of the building blocks that define us. I didn't want to give that away. Not now. Not ever.

I rolled down the window and flicked my cigarette out into the night. "Yeah, I'm all right. I'm just fine."

Printed in the United States
40119LVS00003B/50

9 781413 756067